Cynthia Harrod-Eagles is the author of the hugely popular Morland Dynasty novels, which have captivated and enthralled readers for decades. She is also the author of the contemporary Bill Slider mystery series, as well as her new series, War at Home, which is an epic family drama set against the backdrop of World War I. Cynthia's passions are music, wine, horses, architecture and the English countryside.

D0255955

By Cynthia Harrod-Eagles

War at Home series

Goodbye Piccadilly:
War at Home, 1914
Keep the Home Fires
Burning: War at Home, 1915
The Land of My Dreams:
War at Home, 1916
The Long, Long Trail:
War at Home, 1917
Till the Boys Come Home:
War at Home, 1918

The Bill Slider series

Orchestrated Death
Death Watch
Necrochip
Dead End
Blood Lines
Killing Time
Shallow Grave
Blood Sinister
Gone Tomorrow
Dear Departed

The Morland Dynasty series

The Founding
The Dark Rose
The Princeling
The Oak Apple

The Black Pearl
The Long Shadow
The Chevalier
The Maiden
The Flood-Tide
The Tangled Thread
The Emperor
The Victory
The Regency
The Campaigners
The Reckoning
The Devil's Horse
The Poison Tree
The Abyss
The Hidden Shore
The Winter Journey
The Outcast
The Mirage
The Cause
The Homecoming
The Question
The Dream Kingdom
The Restless Sea
The White Road
The Burning Roses
The Measure of Days
The Foreign Field
The Fallen Kings
The Dancing Years
The Winding Road
The Phoenix

Pack Up Your Troubles

War at Home, 1919

Cynthia Harrod-Eagles

SPHERE

First published in Great Britain in 2019 by Sphere
This paperback edition published by Sphere in 2019

1 3 5 7 9 10 8 6 4 2

A CIP catalogue record for this book
is available from the British Library.

ISBN 978-0-7515-7427-2

Typeset in Plantin by Palimpsest Book Production Ltd,
Falkirk, Stirlingshire
Printed and bound in Great Britain by Clays Ltd, Elcograf S.p.A.

Papers used by Sphere are from well-managed forests
and other responsible sources.

MIX
Paper from
responsible sources
FSC
www.fsc.org   FSC® C104740

Sphere
An imprint of
Little, Brown Book Group
Carmelite House
50 Victoria Embankment
London EC4Y 0DZ

An Hachette UK Company
www.hachette.co.uk

www.littlebrown.co.uk

For Tony

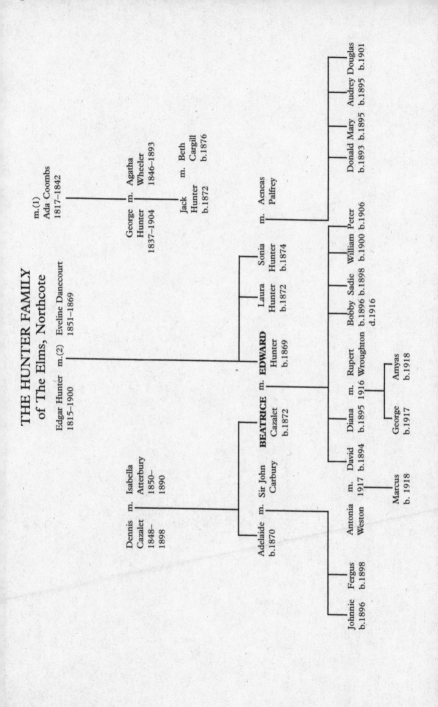

THE HUNTER FAMILY
of The Elms, Northcote

Edgar Hunter
1815–1900

m.(2) Eveline Danecourt
1851–1869

m.(1) Ada Coombs
1817–1842

George Hunter
1837–1904

m. Agatha Wheeler
1846–1893

Jack Hunter
b.1872

m. Beth Cargill
b.1876

m. Aeneas Palfrey

Donald
b.1893

Mary
b.1895

Audrey
b.1895

Douglas
b.1901

Laura Hunter
b.1872

Sonia Hunter
b.1874

EDWARD Hunter
b.1869

BEATRICE Cazalet
b.1872

Bobby
b.1896

Sadie
b.1898

William
b.1900

Peter
b.1906

d.1916

Diana
b.1895

m. Rupert Wroughton
1916

George
b.1917

Amyas
b.1918

David
b.1894

Dennis Cazalet
1848–1898

m. Isabella Arterbury
1850–1890

Adelaide
b.1870

m. Sir John Carbury

Antonia Weston

m. 1917

Marcus
b.1918

Fergus
b.1898

Johnnie
b.1896

CHAPTER ONE

December 1918

A truck with the Red Cross symbol painted on its sides and roof pulled up in front of the Gare de l'Est in Paris, and two men and two women got out. The women were middle-aged, with cropped hair under sensible hats, wearing long boots under army-style greatcoats. The two men were younger and, as goodbyes were said, seemed half reluctant and almost tearful.

One of them, Morgan, went for another round of handshakes. 'I feel so guilty,' he moaned.

'Nonsense,' said Laura Hunter, briskly. 'You've done your duty. The war's over. Of course you must go home.'

'Your mothers will be longing to see you,' said Lady Agnes Daubeney – always called Annie.

'Anyway, we sent the telegram yesterday, so you have to go,' Laura added. Privately she wondered how easily they would get a train to Bar-Le-Duc. The railways were still heavily occupied with moving the military, and the Gare de l'Est in particular was the starting point for Strasbourg for the Army of Occupation. But longing for home would find a way.

At the last moment, Jean-Marie rushed back to bestow a caress on the ambulance's battered bonnet and cried, *'Au'voir, Mathilde!'* in a choked voice, and then they were gone.

1

Laura laughed. 'You'd think she was a family pet being put to sleep.'

'Don't mock. I feel attached to her too,' said Annie.

'She's served us well, the good old girl,' Laura agreed. 'Now we'd better go and get her stripped out.'

Matilda was one of Lady Overton's X-ray ambulances, paid for by public donations. Each ambulance had been given a woman's name, and women of the same name all over the country had been invited to donate whatever they could. The lure of the namesake had proved irresistible: there was a Margaret, an Alice, a Helen, a Gladys, a Bertha . . .

Annie and the boys – young Frenchmen excused military service because of disability – had learned to operate the X-ray machinery at the military Radiological Institute in Paris; Laura had joined them as their driver.

'What an adventure it has been,' Laura said, as she drove towards the Hôpital de la Pitié. The purpose of the Overton ambulances was to X-ray wounded soldiers as close to the Front as possible. In the latter stages, the conflict had changed from the static war of trenches to a war of movement, in which the enemy could be anywhere, and danger could strike from any direction. For six months Laura had been driving through twisting and largely unsignposted lanes, finding the Front by following the noise of artillery, picking a way through shell holes and the rubble of ruined villages, dodging German aeroplanes, which, at that stage of the war, would strafe anything.

It had been exhilarating, perhaps the most exciting thing she had done. But come the Armistice, trade, as she put it, had fallen off. Then Lady Overton had received an urgent plea from a Paris hospital for X-ray equipment, and had decided that since Matilda was out there, and not really needed any more, she should donate hers. So the mission was over.

'What will you do now?' Annie asked, watching the

battered streets of Paris reel past. There were shuttered shops, shell-damage, boarded-up buildings, rubbish blowing along gutters and weeds sprouting from cracks in façades. But life was beginning to return.

'I don't know,' said Laura. 'What about you?'

'I'd really like to go home,' Annie confessed. 'See my family. Rest. We've hardly stopped all year. And I don't feel awfully well.'

'You don't look quite the thing,' Laura said, with a sideways glance. 'Have you still got that rash?'

'Yes. It doesn't bother me much. It's the constant tiredness that pulls me down.'

'You should go,' Laura said firmly. 'And you don't need to sound apologetic.'

'But don't you want to go home?'

'Not yet,' said Laura. 'It doesn't feel finished to me. And what is there at home for me in any case? I'm horribly afraid women are going to be forced back into the box now the war's over. I can't see them letting us have any more fun.'

Annie smiled. 'I'm sure you'll find something,' she said. She knew of Laura's colourful past. This war had been a liberation to restless spirits like hers. 'I don't exactly long to go back to dusting the drawing-room and arranging flowers myself. I'd like a rest – but after that, perhaps you and I can start on a new adventure.'

'Come and find me when you're ready,' Laura said. 'Ah, this is it. I wonder where they want us. Round the back somewhere, if I'm any judge.'

With the X-ray equipment carefully stripped out, Matilda felt much lighter, and jounced and leaped over the uneven cobbles with renewed vigour and increased rattling. Laura headed back to the lodgings they had secured the night before, rooms in a cheap hotel in the Montmartre area, chosen because there was a garage and workshop at the end

3

of the road, where the vehicle could be sheltered. She dared not leave it out in the street for fear it would be damaged.

They travelled in thoughtful silence, until Laura said, 'You know, the day is still young. Or young-ish. If you pack up quickly when we get back, I can drive you to the station, and I bet you could get on a train today. You could pick up a night crossing at Calais and be home by tomorrow morning.'

'What a restless creature you are!' Annie laughed.

'No sense in kicking your heels in Paris when you could be hugging your mother and sleeping in a proper bed.'

'Are you so anxious to be rid of me?

'Immeasurably. I can't bear to see a fellow-creature suffering.' She inched the accelerator closer to the floor, and Matilda flew off an irregularity in the road and came down with a thump. 'And when you get home, show that rash to a doctor.'

'I hate our doctor. He's an old fool.'

'Go to Endell Street and see one of the lady doctors. Or find a dashing RAMC chap on leave and corner him. But see someone. I don't like the look of it.'

'I will. But are you sure you'll be all right on your own?'

Laura laughed. 'I'm forty-six years old, and I have a rifle. No harm can come to me.'

She spent a couple of days cleaning out Matilda and thoroughly overhauling her engine, while she waited for a reply to her query to Lady Overton as to what to do with the empty ambulance. A telegram came, saying, 'No further use for it. Do with it as you please.' And on the same day came a message from Major Ransley, saying he had a few days' leave and proposing they met in Paris. 'There's a wonderful little restaurant I used to frequent in my salad days. I'd love to take you to it.'

If it's still there, Laura thought. And if it's still open. And if it's still wonderful. But it would be good to see him again. In the latter stages of the war they had both moved about so much it had taken great concentration to keep track of each other, let alone to meet. Laura wondered what difference the Armistice would make to them; whether and when he would go home, and what she would do with her life in either case.

So now, two days later, here they were in a café in a side street off the boulevard Saint-Germain, facing each other across a small table. Laura said, 'It's wondrous to think that four weeks ago we were all jigging about in the street, kissing complete strangers with excitement . . .'

'Speak for yourself,' said the major, genially. 'As I remember, I was in the middle of an amputation when the Armistice was announced. Poor devil,' he added. 'I don't know why it seems worse that he was wounded at the last minute like that. A limb lost is a limb lost. His name was Strickland, and he was only nineteen.'

'Please tell me you don't remember the name of every "poor devil" you operated on.'

'I should hope not,' he said. 'There were so many. Leaves of Vallombrosa come to mind. You were saying?' She looked blank. 'You were telling me about your promiscuous kissing of strangers.'

'Oh! Yes. I was going to say we were all so excited then, but now I feel flat, and vaguely uneasy. What happened to the euphoria?'

'You have to remember,' Ransley said, pouring more wine, 'that it was not peace, only a cease-fire.'

She considered the implications of the statement. 'Do you really think the Germans might start up again?'

'A lot of the top brass fear just that. Some believe it was a mistake to let them march back by battalions, in uniform, with guns. We should have made it clear to them that they'd been beaten. Sent them back under guard on trains and lorries.'

5

'Why does that matter so much?' Laura asked. 'Or is this just one of those differences between men and women that we shall never understand?'

'Partly – but it's also a matter of what the politicians and newspapers will make of it back home in Germany. *We* know they couldn't have lasted much longer, that they were thoroughly trumped, but the top chaps of the new German republic won't want it to be seen in that way. Their pride and their jobs will depend on painting a rosier picture. I'm afraid they may just use the armistice as a breathing space to regroup.'

She nodded slowly, thinking, *All the more reason, then, for me not to go home.* But she said, 'I'm astonished you found this place again.'

'I have a very good sense of direction,' he said, in wounded tones.

'And even more astonished it has the same proprietor.' He had greeted Ransley like a long-lost son, with tearful embraces and a flood of French. 'You must have come here a lot to have made such an impression on him.'

'I was quite a regular at one time. It was a literary haunt in those days. I saw Bazin here, and Daudin – and Zola himself on one occasion.'

'And did you understand what mine host was saying to you?'

'Didn't you?'

'I got my French in the schoolroom. His was altogether too authentic. And his accent was nothing like Miss Yorke's.'

Ransley laughed. 'He promised us a meal fit for a king. And then spoiled it by lamenting that there was nothing in Paris to make a meal out of. I suspect it may turn out to be horse – I hope you aren't squeamish?'

'The week before the Armistice, I ate donkey. Or attempted to. You know how old a donkey has to be before it dies, and I'm sure it was too valuable for its owners to kill it before it dropped dead naturally. So horse is a step up for me.'

The meal in fact turned out to be tastier than anything either had had recently in war-ravaged France: a stew that Laura guessed was rabbit, made delicious with lots of onions and herbs, and a sweet omelette filled with quince jam, which seemed like a miracle. They all craved eggs, which had been in such short supply for four years. How mine host had got hold of them they did not enquire, after he delivered the dish with an enormous flourish and what was almost a wink. He had obviously pulled more than a rabbit from his hat, in honour of his old and honoured customer.

'And the really good thing,' Ransley had commented, as he studied the wine list, 'is that a lot of fine pre-war wines have been lying maturing in deep cellars, safe from German shells, and with no one to drink them.'

And so they came, after coffee – vile, eked out in the usual way with chicory and who knew what else? – to the lighting of cigarettes and undisturbed conversation.

'I ducked, this morning,' Laura said, 'when an aeroplane came over. It was only one of ours – on a joy-ride, I suppose.'

'They're still going out on reconnaissance flights,' Ransley told her. 'Seeing what the Germans are up to.'

'Over Paris?'

'Well, that could have been a joy-ride. But I've heard they're sending several squadrons to Strasbourg to be the eyes of the occupying army on the Rhine.'

'Very well. But my point was, how long will it be before we stop ducking? Or flinging ourselves to the ground when a car backfires?'

He grinned. 'Did you do that?'

'Yesterday,' she admitted. 'Don't make me blush. I tore one of my stockings, and if you knew how difficult it is to get replacements . . .'

'As soon as things are back to normal, I shall buy you a dozen pairs.'

'And I shall keep them in a drawer unused for ever and

gloat over them. But when will that be – normality? Have you heard when you're going home?'

'My latest contract doesn't end until April. And there's still plenty to keep us busy over here. Accidents and illness keep on happening, cease-fire or no cease-fire. And there are the wounded who haven't been evacuated yet to take care of, not to mention the prisoners of war starting to trickle back, with multiple sicknesses and untreated injuries.'

'But you've been out here so long, you could get transferred to England if you made a point of it,' she suggested.

He looked apologetic. 'Perhaps.'

'You don't want to go back,' she said.

'Do you?'

'The FANY aren't going,' she mentioned.

'They have an organisation behind them.'

'Ah, but I have an ambulance. Lady Overton gave it to me. All it needs is a couple of benches and stretcher frames to be fitted. My present landlady has a son who could do that for me. The poor fellow's a *mutilé de guerre*, but perfectly capable of a job like that, and he'd be glad to earn a bit of money.'

'And then what?' asked Ransley.

'Back to Hazebrouck or Pop or somewhere like that. You know there's never enough transport. I can ferry the wounded, and be a taxi for nurses and officers going back and forth. If you aren't going home for six months,' she concluded, 'I may as well stay.'

He laid his hand over hers. 'That's very flattering. You're staying for me?'

'Don't be vain,' she said impishly. 'It's just that it would be poor-spirited not to see it through. And if the Germans should start up again—'

'Let's not think about that,' said Ransley, hastily. 'Too frightful. Let's think instead about us.'

'Us?' she said warily.

'Getting married. We can do it over here, you know – it's

quite legal. You said you wouldn't marry me until the war was over—'

'*You* said it wasn't over – it's just a cease-fire.'

'My dear,' he said, 'why so defensive? If you've changed your mind about me . . .'

She saw she had hurt him, and hastened to reassure. 'I still feel exactly the same about you,' she said. 'But . . . Well, it may seem odd, given my unconventional behaviour, but I'd like to get married in the traditional way, back home. My family would be so pleased – they gave up on me years ago. It needn't be a big affair – that would be ridiculous at our age – but I would like them all to be there. And you have sisters, wouldn't you like them to be present?'

'It shall be just as you please,' he promised. 'Even if it does mean another five or six months without you.'

'You'll be so busy, the time will fly past.'

'You could be right. The Royal Engineers will be starting to clear unexploded shells next month, and no doubt that will create plenty of new customers.'

She winced. 'I hope you're properly appreciated.'

'Well, strange you should say that. Modesty almost prevents me mentioning it, but if we *are* to be married –'

'There's not a shred of doubt about it.'

'– then I ought to tell you. I've been awarded the DSO.'

Her face lit. 'My dear! For anything in particular?'

'Those last few months, running a field hospital close to the line. I've been lucky,' he said abruptly. 'Four hundred and seventy RAMC officers killed, God knows how many wounded, and I come out of it unscathed, with a gong and a beautiful woman into the bargain.'

'That,' she said, her eyes bright, 'is worth a celebration. What's your landlady like?'

'Sour.' He caught her drift. 'No bon, I'm afraid.'

'I think mine will turn a blind eye. The bed's small and the mattress isn't up to much, but . . .'

'Wanton woman!' he said softly. 'It's a good job you've agreed to marry me. The world isn't ready for a wild spirit like you.'

At The Elms, it was the day for Mrs Chaplin, the charwoman. She could usually be relied upon for a bit of tasty gossip, so everybody appeared on time for their lunch, as they called the mid-morning snack. There had been no bacon for breakfast, the delivery girl having fallen off her bicycle again and not arriving until too late, so Cook had put out a bit of cheese to go with the bread, which went down well. Thank the Lord, she thought, that wasn't short. She was making a big maccheroni cheese dish for their dinner, which dealt with the meat shortage – though Munt the gardener would no doubt complain. But he complained about everything.

Having chewed her way through a first slice of bread, Mrs Chaplin piped up with the magical words, 'Have you heard?' and they all leaned forward slightly.

'Go on, Mrs Chaplin, dear,' Cook said, topping up her tea.

'That girl Lillian, as used to work here—'

'She was a housemaid,' Cook translated for the scullery-maid, Eileen. 'Before your time. She left to work in a munitions factory.'

'Well,' said Mrs Chaplin, gathering the story back, 'turns out she's dead.' The gasps around the table were gratifying. 'I had it from my Ben, who had it from Don Spignail when he come in to have a new kidney link put on a collar, and *he* heard it from his Rosemary that's a ward-maid up the District Hospital.'

'Whatever happened to her?' Cook asked, reserving sympathy until she learned if it was warranted. She had warned Lillian against the munitions factory – but would she listen?

'Well, they reckoned in the end it was liver disease. And

10

her only sixteen, seventeen next March. They didn't spot it at once, on account of liver makes you go yellow, and she was all yellow anyway, from the TNT. And then she got all swelled up – in her belly, like – and her dad thought she'd got herself in the fambly way and give her a thrashing, but she swore Bible-oath she weren't, and in the end she was that sick she had to go to the hospital and they said it was her liver. Swelled up something chronic, she was, and her face all puffy, and they reckoned they couldn't do nothing for her. She died Friday night, and Rosie Spignail said her liver was that big when they looked at it after, it weighed near-on ten pounds. No wonder they thought she was having a baby.'

'Good job she didn't,' Cook said absently. 'When those munitionettes have babies they come out yellow as well.'

Ada, the head house-parlourmaid, looked at her reproach-fully. 'You might show a bit of pity. Poor Lillian! What a terrible way to go – and her so young.'

Cook was embarrassed and, like many an embarrassed person, covered it with defiance. 'Well, I warned her! I told her how it would be. And she wouldn't listen. Oh no, she had to go and work in a shell factory! It's not just accidents and explosions kill you in them places, there's all sorts of sickness. Of course I'm ever so sorry for her. And her parents. Such a pretty girl, she was. But you let it be a lesson to you,' she added, rounding on Eileen. 'There's many a girl thinks herself too good for service and ends up in more trouble than she bargained for. You've got a good place here, and don't you forget it.'

'Yes, Cook. I know,' Eileen said meekly. 'I'd never go off like that. Me mam'd kill me if I went and worked in a fact'ry.'

'Don't be a fool,' Ethel snapped. 'That's only munitions factories. Ordinary factories are all right.'

'Don't see you movin' out,' Munt growled. 'For all your flighty talk, you keep on stoppin' here, don'tcha?'

Ethel wouldn't argue with Munt. She knew the futility of it. She stood up. 'I got to go. Got to get my baby up from his nap.'

'It's not your baby!' Munt called after her, as she went out.

Ada looked thoughtful. 'She's right, though, isn't she? Some factories are all right to work in. And not all the girls in the shell factories got sick.'

'I'm just trying to look out for young Eileen here,' Cook said, cross that her campaign was being undermined.

'Wish I could see a great big liver, all diseased,' said the boy, Timmy.

'You do not,' Cook snapped automatically.

'I do too! I ain't squeamish. I know a boy 'at works at the morgue, down the 'orsepittle. That's what I want to do when I grows up, with all corpses and legs come off and bodies cut up and stuff.'

Munt leaned over and clouted him round the back of the head. 'That's enough o' that. We've had enough of bodies cut up through four years o' war.'

'He was such a nice boy when he first come here,' Cook said, giving Munt a malevolent look. 'I don't know what you do to boys, I really don't. You're a bad influence.'

'It's the war,' Ada said. 'Everything goes to the bad. Armistice don't seem to have made much difference. I wonder sometimes if there'll ever be an end to it all.' Her husband had been killed in France: they had only had two days together as man and wife.

Cook agreed. 'Nobody where they should be or acting the way they should, everything broken down or missing, and we've still got all these shortages. And that Spanish flu coming back again, they say. And now this dreadful news about Lillian.'

'And Emily,' Ada said. 'I wonder whatever became of her.'

'Don't you worry about her,' Cook said. 'That little

12

madam! Goes off home to Ireland on holiday and never comes back. And not a word to me that was like a mother to her. Leaving me to worry about her week after week.'

'Nothing'll ever be the same again,' Ada said mournfully.

Beryl, the under-house-parlourmaid, whose contribution had been to get outside as much bread and cheese as she could before she was stopped, spoke up through a mouthful. 'What I don't understand is, if the war's over, why aren't the sojers coming back?'

'Use your sense, girl,' Munt said. 'There's more'n three million men in the army. Can't bring 'em all back in five minutes.'

'Could bring back some, though,' Beryl said.

'Ah,' said Munt. 'That's where the trouble lies. Which ones?'

'What d'you mean?' Ada asked, but he wouldn't elaborate.

He finished his tea and stood up. 'Come on, you young limb,' he said to Timmy. 'I got digging for you to do.'

In a moment, they were all on the move, Eileen to clear the table, Beryl, sighing, to polish the front-door brass, Mrs Chaplin to carry on scrubbing the larder shelves. Ada lingered a moment to check the linens book and, finding herself alone with Cook, who was staring in a blank way at the calendar on the wall – a present from William last Christmas, it had a picture of an AirCo DH5 on it – said, 'Heard anything from your Fred yet about when he's coming home?'

Cook snapped out of her reverie. 'Not a word. Last thing he said, there was some rumour going round that they might have to go to the Rhine.'

'It's a crying shame,' Ada said. 'After all that time over there, and they can't tell them when they can come home. And your Fred's been out there from the beginning.'

'Near enough,' Cook admitted.

'And there's the master stuck out there somewhere with his company, and Master William with his squadron . . .'

'At least they *will* come home, sooner or later,' Cook said, laying a hand on her arm. 'Not like your poor Len.'

'Or Master Bobby,' Ada said. 'I feel so sorry for the missus. This family's given so much.'

'You've given most of all, Ada dear,' said Cook. 'There should be a medal for the likes of you.'

'Oh, I'm all right,' Ada said. 'I must get on – I've still got the drawing-room to do.'

And she went quickly away. Too much sympathy wasn't good for you – and it was a funny thing, but somehow it made the sadness harder to bear.

14

CHAPTER TWO

Summoned by his commanding officer, Captain Sir Edward Hunter presented himself at battalion headquarters, which for the time being was an abandoned house in the centre of the village. It was a square, substantial villa, which had once housed a prosperous merchant, his family and servants. The British Expeditionary Force had retreated through here in August 1914, fighting all the way, and many of the locals had fled the advancing Germans. Where were they now? Would they ever return? Nobody knew. France was a land of such ghosts.

The adjutant showed him into what had probably been the morning room, where Colonel Prewitt Dancer was using a small breakfast table as a desk. The room had that knocked-about look one grew used to in places armies had passed through. A great chunk had been broken out of the marble mantelpiece, the wallpaper was torn, there were pale oblongs where the pictures had been removed – for safety, or looted, who knew? – and here and there a drawing-pin flew a tiny flag of paper where some notice had been hastily torn down.

Prewitt Dancer looked up. 'Ah, Hunter,' he said cordially. 'Sit down, make yourself comfortable.'

There was no fire, and it was hardly warmer in here than outside. Edward removed his cap, and unbuttoned but did not remove his greatcoat. He took the spindly dining chair opposite the colonel, who read on for a moment, then tapped the document in front of him.

'The government's scared stiff of Bolshevism,' he said. 'Germany's riddled with it, and the French have had their problems, as we know.'

Edward nodded. The previous spring, large parts of the French Army had mutinied, leaving the British holding the war alone. It was believed that red revolutionaries had infiltrated the trenches.

'But in my experience,' the colonel went on, 'the average British soldier is as much interested in politics as he is in Virgil's *Georgics*. What does Tommy want, Hunter?'

'In general, beer and fried potatoes,' Edward said. 'At the moment, specifically? To go home.' It was hard to blame them, he thought. While the war went on, they had complained remarkably little about having to be over here, away from their families: there was a job to do, and they were determined to do it, however long it took. But as soon as the Armistice was declared, they'd expected to go home straight away. Most of them thought they would be on a boat to Dover the next day. They couldn't understand – and why should they? – the logistics of dismantling the vast war machine.

When the Armistice was declared, Edward's battalion had been near Mons: right back where the war had begun four long, weary years ago. After a few days of 'make and mend', the order to move had come through, and the men had been tremendously excited, assuming they were marching towards the coast, a ship, and Blighty. In fact, they had marched south-westwards to their present position at Landrecies, on the edge of the Forest of Mormal. Why they had been moved, no one, not even the colonel, knew; and no one knew what was to happen to them next. There were rumours, of course, that they might be sent to the Rhine; less credible tales had them bound for Egypt, Mesopotamia, India, even Russia.

Edward's problem was keeping them occupied, so that

16

the troublemakers – there were always some – could not get a fast hold. That meant maintaining spit-and-polish, inspections and parades; marches and exercises to keep the men fit; foraging and reconnaissance expeditions to tire them out; and football, rugby and concert parties to keep them amused. The barrack-room lawyers among them might try to foment rebellion by saying the war was over and they were entitled to take it easy, that they should refuse to march with full packs, or clean rifles they would never fire; but Edward knew that if they weren't kept busy and under discipline, they would be even more bored and miserable.

'To go home, yes,' Prewitt Dancer agreed, and drew another piece of paper in front of him. 'I'm afraid we may have trouble about that. I have the first demobilisation orders, and they include two of your men, Higgins and Freeling. Looking at their records, it seems they were coal miners, caught up in the latest comb-out. Which means they have only two months' active service.'

'Yes, sir. I know them.' They were Yorkshire lads, big, slow-talking and friendly.

The colonel went on: 'The government's priority is to get the country's economy running again as quickly as possible, so they're prioritising what they call "pivotal men" – coal miners, engineers and so on.'

'One can see the sense of that,' Edward said warily.

'Indeed. And clearly those who've only recently left civilian employment can be slotted back into place more easily than those who've been out here several years. So it will be a case of last in, first out.'

'Oh,' said Edward. Of course, now he saw it. The men would naturally feel it wasn't fair, and that those who had been in longest should be discharged first – especially those who had volunteered before conscription. It would be a poor show if patriotism were punished.

'The men won't like it,' said the colonel. 'So I'm giving

you advance warning to keep an eye on the known trouble-makers, and do everything in your power to keep the men occupied. There'll be some leave warrants coming through, which might help. And I want you to submit to me a list of your longest-serving men, especially any who have been in since 'fourteen or 'fifteen, and I'll see about getting them discharged as soon as possible. I shall claim some flexibility for the health of the unit.'

'Yes, sir.'

'Meanwhile, those who won't be going home for Christmas, which will be the majority, need something to look forward to. Concerts, theatricals – you know the sort of thing. I'm badgering the quartermasters to get some decent grub for their Christmas dinner. Decorate the mess – paper chains and so on. Organise some carol singing. And we might look into a small present for each of them. It needn't be much, cigarettes, chocolate. If those of us with funds chip in, I'm sure we can manage something.'

'Yes, sir,' said Edward, and added, 'We might ask our families at home to organise some packages, as well.'

'Good idea.'

'I had thought of running a Christmas-card competition – get the men to design one, with a prize for the best.'

'Excellent. Any other little competitions you can come up with – quizzes, races and so on – to keep their minds off their troubles . . .'

'Of course, sir,' said Edward. 'Any further news about what's happening to us in the longer term?'

Prewitt Dancer shook his head. 'There's still talk that we might be going to the Rhine, but nobody seems to know for sure. We'll just have to sit it out and do the best we can.' He looked apologetic. 'You must want to go home as much as anyone. I know I do. I haven't seen my wife for three years. But I'm afraid none of us officers will be getting leave for Christmas.'

18

Edward was stoical. 'It's best to know, at any rate,' he said.

He walked back to the company HQ, through a chilly drizzle so dense it was almost a fog. The sky was low, grey, weeping; it caught like rags in the bare branches of the trees. The cobbles under his boots were slippery. And he thought, not for the first time, that war was – or should be – a young man's game. But the unprecedented demands of this war had dragged more and more civilians into its maw, and with the conscription age eventually raised to fifty-two, it had taken those who would never have dreamed they would have to serve. In the last six months he had marched and fought and slept on the hard ground and eaten poor rations; he was certainly fitter than he had ever been in his life before, but he was tired. He was almost fifty, and this was no life for one who had been a soft, desk-bound banker. He missed the comforts of life, his home, his club, his office and its known, controllable, absorbing work. He missed his wife and children. He wanted to go home.

Arriving at his own office, he was greeted by Lieutenant Anderson, who rolled his eyes in warning towards a very young subaltern in a very new uniform who was standing awkwardly in the background. 'Sir,' he said, 'this is Second Lieutenant Graves. Just been sent out to us from England.'

Edward welcomed the bewildered young man with a hand-shake and a few bracing words. Inside, he seethed. It really was beyond common sense to be sending out new officers when the war was over and there was nothing for them to do.

When an orderly had taken Graves away to settle him in, Anderson burst out, 'What on earth are they thinking of, still sending us people? We were short of officers two months ago when we were fighting, and *now*, when we're supposed to be winding down, we've—'

Edward stopped him wearily. 'It's the army machine,' he said. 'Hard to stop and harder still to turn round. No point

19

in griping about it.' He moved to his desk. 'Let me have the personnel list right away, will you? And see if you can't rustle up some tea.'

Of the Hunters overseas, only Jack, Edward's cousin, got home in time for Christmas. He arrived on the 23rd, preceded by a telegram that had Beth, his wife, veering wildly between happiness and anxiety. It seemed almost too momentous an occasion to be enjoyed.

She met his train at Waterloo station, but though she was there in plenty of time, she almost missed him. He had to stand in front of her before her eyes stopped scanning the crowds.

His mouth twisted. 'Am I that changed?'

'Oh, Jack!' she cried, hugging him fiercely.

But he had seen it in her face. He pushed her gently away. 'Don't choke the life out of me. I've not been feeling quite the thing these last few days, anyway.'

She thought she had never seen a man so thin, his cheeks hollow, his skin pallid and dull. And his hair was completely grey now. But mostly it was his eyes that had deceived her: there seemed nothing of her Jack in them.

'It's so wonderful that you're back,' she said, making an effort to sound normal. 'We'll get a taxi outside – it'll be easier than the rank here. Is that all your luggage?'

'I had the rest sent on,' he said. His voice was flat and dull, too. 'This will do overnight.'

'I didn't have much notice,' she said, walking beside him to the entrance, 'but I got in a little supper – things I know you like. Though, being December, there's not much in the shops. Thank Heaven for Fortnum & Mason, that's all I can say. I expect you'll want a bath first – you always do. I've given Mrs Beales the rest of the day off, so we can be private. I can manage supper all right, and we can eat by the fire in our dressing-gowns if you like . . .'

She knew she was chattering to cover her shock. Her voice trailed away, and then she said again the thing she could say with all sincerity, 'It's so wonderful that you're back.'

'You know, don't you,' he said, 'that I'm still in the reserve.'

'Dear, I've been married to you for eighteen years. I do know that much,' she said.

He continued doggedly, 'It means If Fritz starts up again I shall be straight back in.'

'Oh, surely not! You've done your bit. You were one of the first in. And anyway, he won't – will he? Fritz?'

'I don't know. No one does. I'm just saying, it's not peace yet.'

He sounded exhausted. She hailed a taxi and it swerved over to the kerb. 'Here we are,' she said cheerfully. 'Ten minutes and we're home. Ebury Street, please, driver. I left the fire banked, so the house will be nice and warm,' she went on, as they started off. 'Though it's been really mild this last week. Wet, though. Rain nearly every day.' Please stop me talking, she prayed to some higher power. I hear myself, and I can't stop. 'And you're back in time for Christmas, that's the best bit. Everyone will be so excited. Edward's not getting leave, nor William, and Laura's not coming back until some time next year.' Jack didn't respond, staring blankly ahead at nothing. The real question crowded up into Beth's throat. 'Are you sick?'

He started to answer, and went into a paroxysm of coughing. It sounded so horrible – hollow and rattling – that she went cold all down her spine. She fished out her hand-kerchief to give to him. She saw the driver glancing anxiously at them over his shoulder. Everyone thought about the Spanish flu, these days, when anyone showed any symptoms.

'Darling,' she said quietly, so the driver wouldn't hear, 'please tell me. Is it the flu?'

'Of course not,' he said, with faint irritation under the

weariness. 'They wouldn't have let me come home if it was. You know we have to let the company doctor run the rule over us before they let us out. Just a bout of bronchitis, he said. Tiresome, but nothing more. Don't fuss.'

'I never fuss,' she said, with dignity. 'But I'm allowed to be concerned when you cough. I *am* your wife.'

She thought he would make a joking remark in reply, but he just turned his head away, and, almost too low to hear, he said, 'God, I'm tired.'

He'll feel better after a bath and something to eat, she thought, to comfort herself. He's so thin, they haven't been feeding him properly, that's all. He's always been as strong as a horse. Rest and good food, and he'll be my Jack again. Four years and four months she had been waiting for the day on which he would come back for good; and now the day had come, and it didn't feel as if he was here at all.

It turned colder on Christmas Day. For once the rain stopped and the sun came out, so it was a pleasant walk to church. Sadie carried in her pocket, like a talisman, a letter from John Courcy, who was in charge of the horse hospital in Le Touquet. He'd had leave in November, so was not due any more for a long time, and he had no idea when he would be demobilised. There was still, he said, a great deal to do, for though there were no more battle injuries, there were still accidents, sickness and overwork to deal with. 'And as units disband, a decision will have to be made on what to do with the horses and mules. We have a lot of paddock grazing, and I suspect we may become a staging-post.'

A staging-post for what, though, he didn't say. Sadie wondered a lot about the horses. There were millions of them out there. Bringing them home would involve an awful lot of ships, and wouldn't they be needing those for months to come, to bring back the men? She didn't want to think – she *really* didn't want to think – what the alternative might be.

Courcy's letter ended with the words she treasured.

Things are pretty bad here, in so many ways, and I survive by thinking of you, and our lives together when I finally do get home. Dearest Sadie, you are the bright spot in my life. I wish I could tell you when I shall be back, but at any rate, don't worry about me. I am as well as can be expected. Write soon and tell me all you are doing. I love you more than words can say. Ever yours, John.

He had asked her to marry him when the war was over. But she hadn't told anyone about his proposal: she was afraid that speaking about it might make something terrible happen.

The church was unusually full – there had been a definite falling-off in attendance after the first year of the war – and after the service, everyone lingered outside to talk. It was something that had not happened for years: there had been too many topics to avoid. People blinked in the watery sunshine as though just waking up from a long dream. The overall tone was not one of jubilation, as it had been in November when the Armistice had surprised elation out of them, but of quiet relief.

The exception was Mrs Fitzgerald, the rector's wife, who hurried over to where the Hunters were talking to Mr and Mrs Oliver of Manor Grange, bringing with her a young man in uniform and an air of triumph. 'My nephew Adolphus, on demobilisation leave!' she exclaimed. She and the rector were childless, and her nephews and nieces were all she had to boast about. She did so now with such determination that after a few moments he turned away from the group towards the one person who seemed to be on the outside of it – Sadie.

She had met him in 1915, a slender young man with a pink-and-white complexion that showed his frequent blushes, shy blue eyes and a sensitive mouth. The complexion was weathered brown now; the mouth was firm – almost grim – and the slender shape had filled out with muscle. As for the shyness, there was instead in the eyes a sort of steely reserve. She read in it a suffering he would not be able to express to other people: it reminded her a little of her brother David's withdrawal when he first came home. But David had been grievously wounded. What this young man's wounds were she couldn't tell.

'Miss Hunter, isn't it?' he said.

She recognised a desperate attempt to start a conversation in competition with his aunt's, and was ready to help him along. 'That's right. Sadie Hunter.' She waited for more, but he seemed to have no words. She sought for a subject to get him going. 'Have you still got your violin?' she asked, to show that she remembered.

'Yes,' he said.

'You were going to take it with you to the Front,' she mentioned.

'An officer at training school said it would be too risky, that it would be sure to be damaged. So I brought it home when I came on embarkation leave.' He stopped abruptly.

'That must have been hard for you,' she persevered. 'Being without it.' Music had never played a large part in her life, but she knew what it meant to have a ruling passion. Her life without horses would have been barren.

'Yes,' he said.

She understood that the terseness was not disinclination to talk, only an inability to break past a barrier that had been put in place to save his life. Even robust men had found the war almost unendurable. How much worse for a boy who had not even been able to bear his aunt's bullishness?

So she kept trying. 'Are you still hoping to join an orchestra? You said you wanted to be a professional musician.' His mouth tensed. 'You weren't sure your parents

24

would allow it. But you're of age now – you can do as you please, I suppose.'

'My aunt—' he began, and stopped.

'Has a lot of influence?' He nodded. 'I used to be quite afraid of her,' Sadie said musingly. 'And she does have a very forceful way of talking. But, after all, what can she actually *do*?'

He was looking at her with interest now, and she thought he was on the brink of something more than polite exchanges. But he only nodded again.

'Are you staying in Northcote for long?' Sadie tried next.

'I don't know,' he said. She waited. 'There's illness at home,' he continued, with an effort. 'They're keeping me out of the way.'

'I'm sorry.'

The focus of his eyes changed. 'Is that your dog?' he asked.

Sadie turned her head, and saw Nailer hovering a few feet behind her. He liked to call in on outdoor gatherings: people congregating together often meant food, and outdoor food often got dropped. He met Sadie's eyes from under his bristly eyebrows – like hedges rimed with frost – and wagged hopefully.

Sadie turned back, and saw a hint of warmth in the closed-off face. She had seen it before: animals could reach into places humans couldn't touch. 'I'm not sure about that,' she said, 'but I suspect *he* thinks I'm *his* human.'

He seemed about to answer, but his aunt had spotted him talking to someone unimportant. 'Dolly,' she said sharply, 'come. We must speak to Mr Worthington – he's our Justice of the Peace. And his wife – such a charming woman – she was a Russell-Drury, so she's a distant cousin of your father's.'

He had to obey. Sadie smiled sympathetically. 'It was nice talking to you, Mr Beamish,' she said. 'I hope we meet again while you're here.'

Instead of replying, he gave her a slight bow before turning away. Four years ago, she would have felt cheek-scaldingly snubbed; today's Sadie understood much more. She felt she had made a connection.

On Boxing Day the whole family went over to Dene Park. Diana had asked them to come and help make Christmas pleasant for the wounded who couldn't go home. They were all, except the very ill, extremely cheerful, and it seemed to Sadie at times that they were cheering up the visitors, rather than vice versa.

She was used to visiting the wounded, and Antonia was natural with everybody, but her youngest brother Peter was awkward and shy at first, then became too boisterous. But he was a good-hearted boy, and soon corrected his manner. Sadie was disappointed that David did not seem inclined to get talking to any of the officers. Instead, he helped carry round food and drink, making rather brittle jokes about spillages and his limp. She would have thought he'd be moved by fellow-feeling, but his experience and his wound seemed, on the contrary, to shut him off from them.

And her mother was kindly, attentive, but remote, and she saw that the wounded officers were accepting her ministrations in the impersonal way they accepted medical treatment. Diana, however, was a revelation: she was warm and almost informal with the wounded officers, and it was clear they adored her. It helped that her mother-in-law was not in residence – she always spent Christmas at Sandringham. One of the officers, a sandy-haired young man called Farraday, who'd had both legs amputated, told Sadie that they called the elder Lady Wroughton the Dragon.

'When the Dragon's away,' he said, 'our Lady Wroughton smiles much more and laughs at our silliness and— Well, we'd all die for her, you know. She's so beautiful. Is she really your sister? You don't look much alike.'

'You are a clot, Farraday!' said a voice behind Sadie's

shoulder, before she could form an answer. 'Don't you know better than to praise one woman to another woman's face?'

She turned and saw a tall, fair infantry officer looking down at her with interest. 'Even if they're sisters?' she said.

'Especially if they're sisters,' he said. He stuck out his hand. 'I know you're Miss Hunter. I'm Ivo Rainton, Guy Teesborough's brother.'

'I've heard you spoken of,' Sadie said. Lord Teesborough had been a close friend of Diana's late husband Rupert, best man at his wedding, and was joint trustee to his children. He had been sent to Dene after a serious wound, and he had featured a great deal in Diana's conversations of late. 'How is your brother?'

'Coming along,' Rainton said. 'They get him out of bed for a while each day now. He could be walking by spring. And, of course,' he added, with an arch look, 'the scenery here does him so much good.'

Sadie followed his glance to where Diana had just delivered a mince pie to Guy Teesborough and was leaning over him adjusting his pillows. It made a pretty vignette.

'Your mother's still in Malta, isn't she?' Sadie asked. Lady Teesborough had been running a hospital there.

'Yes. She'd have liked to come home for Christmas, but there are still so many sick coming back from the east, she felt she couldn't leave.'

'It's a difficult time, really, for everyone, isn't it?' Sadie said. Christmas inevitably made you think of those who would never share it with you again. 'So what brought you here? Are you on leave?'

'Demobilisation leave. I came to cheer up poor old Guy, but since I find he's as cheerful as can be, for some reason, I shall dedicate myself to the rest of the chaps, who don't have their own personal ministering angel.'

Sadie smiled. 'You're very different from your brother,' she said. Guy, whom she'd met once or twice when visiting

27

Diana, was very nice, but rather serious, as older brothers who inherited titles tended to be.

'I hope that's not a disparaging comment on my looks,' he said, pretending offence.

Sadie laughed and was about to reply when Diana came over and said, 'We're going to have a sing-song. Sadie, come and play – I'm busy with the mince pies.'

She was off again before Sadie could answer. 'That's a sentence I would never have expected to hear from my sister's lips,' she said to her retreating back.

'Do you play?' Ivo asked.

'Very badly,' said Sadie.

'I play rather well,' he said, 'so I'll rescue you from the task, if you'll come and turn for me.'

When it came to it, he seemed to know the carols and songs by heart and didn't need the music, let alone anyone to turn. But she stood by dutifully and made pretence. She suspected he had been flirting with her, which was surprisingly agreeable. She did feel rather guilty, however, about poor Lieutenant Farraday, and vowed to go back and sit with him for a good long chat when the singing was over.

William's squadron moved just before Christmas to an airfield near Le Cateau, where they took over from a squadron that was off to the Rhine.

The area was horribly quiet: from Amiens to St Quentin to Cambrai to Arras the land was ruined, desolate, deserted. It had been fought over, and fought over again, and no one lived there now. The civilians had not returned to try to resurrect their lives from the wreckage of abandoned equipment, burned-out buildings, shell holes, pools of yellow, poisoned water – and everywhere the crosses, scattered singly or gathered in pathetic groups, like huddled sheep. As dusk closed in at the end of the day, the silence would become too noticeable. It was like being buried alive, William thought.

28

So at night the young men gathered noisily in the mess, drinking too much and singing the most raucous of flyers' songs. And in the daytime, they spent as much time as possible in the air. That was quieter, too – no thud of shells, no heavy cough of Archie, no lethal rattle of machine-gun to interrupt the song of the wind past the rigging. But at least they could fly away from desolation, over places that were still green, and see movement and habitation again. William enjoyed swooping in low over previously forbidden places – German aerodromes and bases, French towns and villages that had been occupied for four years. He flew as far as the Rhine, waving cheerfully to troops below marching to join the Army of Occupation; over the Dutch border; over Strasbourg; over Brussels – places the Allies had strained every nerve to reach, whose conquest had meant more than life itself.

But even that pleasure palled. The young men felt trapped halfway between peace and war, and only in the mess, in each other's company, was there any comfort. They had a boisterous Christmas dinner, with plenty of roast goose – there wasn't a turkey to be had anywhere – and puddings sent from home by a committee of mothers headed by Chubby Partridge's mater, who always feared her boy was going hungry. There was an extra ration of rum for the ground crew, and a dozen of real claret produced by Captain Considine, who was mysterious about its origins but insisted that it was 'pukka'. And on Boxing Day there was a barrel of beer and a no-holds-barred rugby match on the field, officers against ground crew, which resulted in a large number of superficial injuries and a narrow victory for the latter, who had in their number an engine fitter who had played for a club at home.

After Christmas, after the fun and games, the silence seemed even more oppressive. William flew to Landrecies to visit his father, and was fêted at his mess, the dining-room of the Hôtel Mercure.

And at Le Cateau he received a visit from his cousin Fergie, a flyer with the American air service, who called to say he was going home.

'You mean, to Ireland?' William asked. His aunt Adelaide, his mother's sister, had married Sir John Carbury, with an estate in Kildare.

Fergie looked a little shame-faced. 'No, back to the States. Mother's pretty upset about it – she expected me to head back to Donadea as soon as I was out. I'll always love the old country, but once you've lived in the States you don't want to go back.'

'Does Johnny feel the same?' William asked.

Fergie shrugged. 'He's the eldest, he'll inherit the land from Pa, so I guess he'll have to go back and learn how to take care of it. But what would I do in Ireland?'

'What will you do in America?'

'Oh, a flying job. I don't know what yet, but there's bound to be something. America's so big, rail travel takes days. Imagine if you could fly from the east coast to the west. It would open up the whole country.'

Fergie was guest of honour in William's mess, where there was a lively discussion on the subject of civil aviation, and also considerable drinking and singing, before Fergie departed for his own base, and demobilisation.

A few days later, their CO announced that he was being invalided home. Captain Considine became CO in his place and was made up to major, and William was promoted to captain. There was general rejoicing in the mess: as Foley said, 'They wouldn't be handing out promotions if they were going to break us up.' The Rhine? The Middle East? Nobody seemed to know what was to happen to them, but they stayed optimistic.

CHAPTER THREE

Edward's other sister, Sonia, was married to Aeneas Palfrey, of Palfrey's Biscuits. During the war he had diversified into army-ration biscuit, as well as jams, cakes and bottled fruit; and, through lucrative government contracts, and the new custom of sending hampers to the Front, Palfrey's had done very well.

There was no outward change from the increased wealth. The big house in Kensington was just as chaotic, always full of people. With friends and neighbours dropping in unannounced, you never knew how many would eventually gather round the enormous dining-table. Constant traffic meant a certain comfortable shabbiness: refurbishment went on at hap-hazard and couldn't keep up. Sonia was an ineffective chatelaine, by nature nervous, indecisive, and self-absorbed. Her orders were incoherent and frequently contradictory, but the servants were fond of her and only exploited the situation a reasonable amount. The children tried now and then to establish greater order, but nothing much ever really changed.

While some women had blossomed because of the war, it hadn't suited Sonia. The air raids had terrified her, her son Donald being conscripted had convinced her he would die, the social changes she saw all around unsettled her, and she was too bound up with herself to be of any use to charitable activities. But one thing she did know was how to give a party, and on Sunday, the 29th of December,

Beattie, David, Antonia, Sadie and Peter took the train into London to spend the day at the Palfreys' with every expectation of enjoyment. An added attraction was that Beth and Jack would be there, the first time they'd had a chance to see them since Jack came home, and in the evening various friends and neighbours would be joining them for a buffet supper and music.

The talk at first was, naturally, about the general election, which had been held on Saturday, the 14th of December – the first time an election had been held on a single day. Because of the difficulty of getting the votes back from those serving overseas, the result had not been announced until the 28th. It was a landslide victory for the Coalition.

'Well,' Sonia said vaguely, 'I suppose it's only right. They did get us through the war.'

It was also the first election in which women over thirty had been allowed to vote, and Beattie agreed with Beth that it had been a strange experience to go into the voting booth. 'Almost unreal,' Beth said. 'I half expected the policeman to notice me and say, "Come on out of there, you!"'

'But you must have felt proud,' Audrey urged. 'Aunty?'

'I'm not sure "proud" was what I felt,' Beattie answered. 'As Beth says, it seemed rather dreamlike. When one remembered all the strife and pain and ugliness over so many years, for it all to end in one pencil cross on a piece of paper was – odd.'

Aeneas talked of the 'coupon' element of the election. Certain candidates had been sent a letter, which became known as the Coalition coupon, saying that they had the support of the government for their candidacy, which meant certain election.

'Did Mr Beresford get a coupon?' Sadie asked. Edward's former work colleague, Christopher Beresford, had been elected to Parliament for a north London seat.

'I couldn't tell you,' Aeneas said. 'I'm glad he got in,

though. Your father thinks he's a good man, and we need the right sort in Westminster..'

Sadie said, 'I'm glad for him too, but I should think as a good man he might feel uneasy about being couponed in, rather than fighting fair.'

'Oh, Sadie, there's no such word as "couponed",' Audrey protested.

Sadie grinned. 'There is now!'

The one cloud on Sonia's horizon was the continued absence of Donald, who was still with his battalion in Mesopotamia.

'But he's come through the war all right, Mumsy,' Audrey pointed out, 'and he *will* come home. We should be glad about that.'

'At least he got to go,' said the youngest son, Douglas, always knows as Duck. The war was over just when, at seventeen, he could have looked forward to serving.

There was a small part of Audrey that didn't want the war to be over either. Since Donald had been called up, she had taken over his management job in the family factory. Nothing had been said, but she was pretty sure that as soon as he came home, she would be expected to stand aside for him. And then what would she do?

Her twin, Mary, had abandoned her WVR uniform on the day after the Armistice with no regret. She was glad to feel that she had done her bit for the war effort, but she and Audrey were very different in character. 'It's going to be wonderful, having everything back to normal,' she said.

'But what is normal?' Audrey said.

Sonia was quite clear. 'Normal is having you girls nicely at home.'

'Sitting with our hands in our laps, waiting for the right man to come along and marry us?' Audrey said.

Sonia didn't notice the sarcasm. 'I'm sure there'll be someone for you soon, dear,' she said. '*If* you learn not to frighten them off with all your free talk and boldness.'

'Oh, *Mumsy*!' Audrey cried despairingly.

'It's no use looking at me like that,' Sonia said. 'Men don't like girls to be too clever.'

Sadie caught Audrey's eye with sympathy, and said, 'I think men have changed since before the war. There are lots now who don't mind women being independent-minded.'

'Well,' said Mary, 'all I want is to be an old-fashioned wife and keep a nice home and entertain like you do, Mumsy. And when Clive comes home . . .'

She had an understanding with Clive Amberley, the son of a neighbour, who had proposed to her on his last leave, back in September.

'Isn't it possible to be a thinking woman *and* a wife?' said Antonia, part amused, part appalled. The war had seemed, in its later stages, to open a door for women. Yet the old idea that a woman with a mind was not really a proper woman hadn't died. She looked at David for support in her argument.

But he shook his head, not meeting her eyes. 'There's going to be merry hell when the men come home, if the women don't get out of their way. You may think men have changed, Sadie, but I can assure you they haven't. A man needs to work and support his family. What's he going to do, where's he going to fit in, if the women hang on to the jobs?'

Aeneas, puffing his pipe, said, 'There's truth in what you say, David. Our fellows have fought and suffered out there for four years to preserve a particular way of life. Their reward must be to come home and find that way of life waiting for them.'

'Poppa, that's so old-fashioned!' Audrey began.

He went on relentlessly: 'And I must say I don't like seeing girls striding about in trousers, smoking, with dirt under their fingernails and all their hair cut off.'

'I never have dirty fingernails!' Audrey exclaimed.

'I quite like short hair on some women,' Beth put in. 'When it suits their faces.'

'That's not the point,' said Aeneas, calmly. 'I was going to say that women have done the men's work admirably. Some of our female factory workers are better and quicker, and certainly less trouble than the men were. But there's got to be a compromise. I don't know where we'll find it, but we must. For men to be men, women have to be women.'

'He's got you there,' Jack murmured to Beth. She threw him a glance, hoping that she saw him looking better for his week of being fed and nurtured, but unsure that it was the case.

'Women should have long hair,' Sonia decreed. 'It's not natural to cut it off.'

'Then shouldn't all men have beards?' Beth argued. 'There's nothing natural about shaving, after all.'

'Fifteen all,' Jack murmured.

'I don't like all this disputation,' Sonia said, in a quavering voice. 'It upsets me. It's exactly the sort of thing that happens when women stop behaving like women.'

There was a slightly awkward silence, and Antonia broke it by saying, 'I don't have an answer to the philosophical dilemma, but in my own case, I can promise David that I shall be behaving *very* like a woman for the foreseeable future. I'm going to have another baby.'

With all the Hunters gone to Kensington, the servants had the day off. Eileen and Beryl went home to see their respective families. Munt didn't work on Sundays, but he had turned up anyway, to enjoy the peace of his shed, his paraffin stove and his seed catalogues.

Maybe when the master came home, he could plant some flowers again, instead of all these vegetables. 'Not that there's anything wrong with veg,' he conceded to Nailer, who had gravitated towards the stove's warmth. There were lots of opportunities for competitiveness in veg: his parsnips, for instance, were the longest, straightest and whitest in the neighbourhood. 'But you can't beat a nice chrysanth. Or a dahlia. And my roses—' He broke off for a moment's silence in memory of his roses. It had broken his heart to grub them up.

Nailer wagged his tail in sympathy.

Munt noticed. 'Ah, you got nothing to worry about. Give you a warm fire and a biscuit, s'all the same, ent it? War and yuman suffering don't mean nothing to you.'

Nailer knew the word 'biscuit', and wagged harder.

'I must be going sorft in me old age,' Munt rumbled. 'Talking to a blessed 'ound.' But in a changing world, where most change had been for the worse, Nailer represented continuity. Munt got up to reach for his pipe and matches from the shelf, then sat down again, his knees cracking like pistols. He rubbed them and said, 'Gettin' too old for all this. But don't you tell nobody. I'm not ready to get pensioned off yet.' Not working meant being at home with Mrs Munt, and he and Mrs Munt had stayed happily married for forty years by hardly ever seeing each other.

Nailer folded down with a sigh on the bit of old mat in front of the stove, crossed one front paw over the other, laid his nose neatly on top, and closed his eyes. His ears remained vigilant, listening to the rustle of turning pages and Munt's occasional cough and sniff, just in case he should open the biscuit tin.

The weather had stayed dry and frosty, and Ada decided to go for a walk. She went as far as to invite Ethel, always a martyr to boredom, to come with her. 'Cook can listen out for the baby. It'd do us good to get out in the fresh air.'

Ethel declined. 'Leave him to her? Not likely,' she said.

Cook said to Ada, 'I don't know where you get these queer ideas. Fresh air indeed!' She spent her life trying to keep the outside out. She hated an open window or door. In the winter it meant cold and damp and germs getting in, in the summer it was dust and flies. With no Sunday dinner to cook for upstairs, she was going to spend the day by the fire with her feet up. 'And if you got any sense, you'll do the same.'

'No, I think I'll just have a short walk,' Ada said. 'I feel a bit cooped up.' She went to get her coat and hat.

'Cooped up?' Cook remarked to Ethel, who was warming the baby's bottle at the stove. 'I don't know what's come over that girl. She's changed.'

'Everybody's changed,' Ethel said shortly.

'I've not,' Cook said indignantly

'Ha!' said Ethel. 'You been like a bear with a sore head for weeks.'

'I have not!'

'You nearly went crackers when you broke that mixing bowl.'

'Well, it was my favourite.'

'And when your egg whisk went in the bin with the eggshells – I thought you was going to kill Eileen.'

'She's got to learn, hasn't she?'

'You got it back all right.'

'That's not the point.'

'Oh, I know what the point is. You been making everyone's life a misery cos the war's over and your sweetie's not come back. Well, I wonder why that is.'

'He can't come till he's demobbed, stands to reason,' Cook said, reddening.

'Not written either, though, has he? Talk's cheap when you can't do nothing about it, but funny how it's all gone quiet now he might have to make good on his promises.'

'Don't you dare say things like that, you wicked girl!'

'Reckon you've heard the last of Sergeant Fred McAusland and his big talk about Australia. And you haven't got the wit to notice that Ada gets upset when you boast about him. You keep reminding her of what she's lost.'

'Ada and me is old friends. You're just a newcomer. Don't you tell me how to behave to my own friend.'

'Call that friendship? You called her a girl just now. She was a married woman, but you still think she's a little house-maid you can shove around and bully.'

'Ooh, I wouldn't have a wicked tongue like yours for all the world!' Cook cried.

'And I wouldn't have a hide like an elephant, like you do,' Ethel retorted, wrapped the bottle in a tea-towel and stalked away.

Left alone, Cook had to make herself a strong pot of tea to calm herself down. She hadn't realised the others had noticed she was a bit snappy, but now it seemed they had, and she supposed Ada had rather been tiptoeing about her recently. But, typical of that Ethel, she had got hold of the wrong end of the stick entirely.

She and Fred were only *un*officially engaged, because of the war, but she didn't have any doubts about him. He'd said that as soon as he was discharged they would get married and go to Australia, where he planned to open a butcher's shop in Adelaide, and live happily ever after. He'd promised her a nice little house with a jacaranda tree in the garden. She'd gone as far as to ask Peter what that was, and he'd brought down his encyclopaedia and shown her a picture. Very pretty, she'd thought, and an unusual colour. You didn't expect mauve blossom on a tree – though Peter had pointed out that wisteria was mauve. But that was different, she'd insisted, though she wasn't sure why.

No, she didn't have any doubts about Fred, even though he hadn't written for a while. It was herself she wasn't sure of. While the war went on, him and her and Australia was all a lovely dream. But now it was about to become reality, she'd got cold feet.

Any normal woman would prefer marriage over service, and Fred was kind, funny, capable. Altogether too much of a catch for a fat, forty-eight-year-old cook. But he seemed to want her, and since he'd never been married before, it looked as though he was choosy. So she didn't doubt him.

But service was all she had ever known, from the age of twelve when she'd gone as a kitchen-maid. And she'd been with the Hunters twenty-five years. To leave everything and everyone she knew and travel right across the world to a strange country, strange people, a strange life she had no experience of . . . never to see dear old England again . . .

She'd been on tenterhooks ever since the 11th of November, expecting Fred to burst in at any minute – or at least to write and tell her the date when he would. And then there'd be no more messing around. She'd have to go. She swallowed in panic even thinking about it. It was too much. It was too *real*.

She took the tea tray into the sitting room, put it down on the small table by the fire, and was about to make herself comfortable when there was a knock on the back door, which immediately opened with a cry of, "Ullo 'ullo! Anyone home?'

It was the voice of Pearl Hicks, daughter of their old postman Bill Hicks. She had worked in the sorting office for six years, and had taken over her dad's walk when he was called up with the raising of the conscription age. She wasn't the first lady postman in the area: Mabel Cobb had been doing the deliveries over the Church End side of Northcote since 1916. But Mabel Cobb was a tough old bird and well able to handle herself. Pearl was only twenty-two and there were those who thought she was just too young, and others who thought females should *never* be trusted with the Royal Mail at all.

Cook wasn't sure where she stood in the argument, but

though Mr Hicks had always come right in after knocking and said those very same words, she couldn't help feeling it was cheek on Pearl's part not to wait outside. She went through into the kitchen, where Pearl stood on the doormat, sorting through a sheaf of letters.

She grinned cheerfully, her tough, springy curls almost pushing her cap off. 'Morning, Mrs D! Quiet in here today. Family away?'

'Just for the day.' Cook had always offered Mr Hicks a cup of tea, and he had sometimes accepted, depending on his load, but she drew the line at offering tea to Pearl, whom she suspected of wearing rouge.

'Well, nice to have a day off,' Pearl said. 'Got one here for you.' Her eyes twinkled. 'From France.'

Cook's heart jumped, and she felt obscurely annoyed with Pearl and wanted to damp her everlasting chirpiness. 'You won't be delivering the post any more, once the men get back,' she said.

Pearl was undampened. 'You never know! Anyway, there'll always be a job for me in the sorting-office. Skilled work, that is. Well, I better get on. Byesie-bye.'

She thrust the letters into Cook's hand and tripped away like a blessed fairy, Cook thought – except for the boots. The rest of the post was for the family, and she took it out into the hall before coming back to her own, putting off the moment. She poured a cup of tea and took a restorative sip before opening it.

Well my Margaret you must a thought I was in Timbucktoo, with not writing all this time, but we been busy, Lord knows how with no Fritz shooting at us, but they keep us jumping. Anyway I wanted to find out what the Griff was before I wrote to you, when I was getting out and all that. Now hold on to your hat, they tell us we are going to Germany. I know youl be fed up, a lot of us were, but it wont be for long, not more than three months, then they swear weel be let go. So you can wait a bit longer for your Fred, cant you? I wish I was coming right home now, but Im quite looking forward to seeing Colone, they say its a fine city, and see what Fritz gets up to in his own back yard. Now don't you go thinking anything has changed because Im still your Fred and your still my girl and don't go forgetting it because when I come home were getting hitched right off, I cant wait to sample your rock cakes, dont you go baking them for anyone else! And when I get home Im going to give you such a big hug you might never recover. Your Fred.

The letter was so like him, he might have been standing next to her talking.

So now she knew. Three months! Nothing going to change for three months! The relief, just for a moment, was enormous. And then she felt guilty for feeling relieved. Poor Fred! Poor all of them, not coming home. She drank some tea and read the letter again. And after the second reading, perversely, what she felt was disappointment. Definite, wistful disappointment.

When Ada opened the front door, David stalked past her without a word, and went straight upstairs, leaving Antonia to answer the polite questions. We came home early because Mr David felt tired. No, everything's all right. Very nice, thank you. Nothing now, thanks – perhaps later. I'll ring.

And then she went upstairs too. David was in their sitting-room, limping about agitatedly, his stick thumping the carpet with each step as if he were killing ants. He hadn't said a word all the way home – Aeneas had insisted on ordering the car out for them – so she didn't know what mood he was in, but she knew it was a mood. Her heart was heavy, but she went in to face him with a smile.

He turned on her. 'What the devil were you thinking?'

41

'David—'

'You weren't going to tell me? You just explode a shell under me in front of everyone without warning?'

'I didn't plan to announce it like that,' she said. 'I was going to tell you first, of course—'

'Oh, of course!'

'But poor Audrey was in a corner, and she needed a diversion—'

'That's what this is to you? A diversion?'

'What's the matter, David? Why are you being like this?'

'How far along are you? When did this happen?'

'I don't know exactly,' she said defensively. 'I wasn't really sure until last week. I think it's three months, but—'

'Have you seen the doctor?'

'Not yet. I was going to tell you first.'

He limped over to the window, and stood staring at the blackness, his back to her. 'Instead of which you tell the whole world and make a fool of me.'

She began to feel angry. 'How is it making a fool of you? You should be happy.'

'Happy? Happy?' He turned again, and his face was a stranger's. 'In case you haven't noticed, I'm a cripple with no prospect of a career. I have a wife and child to support but I live in my father's house, on his charity. And you thought it would be a good idea to increase that burden with another child, did you?'

'David, don't!'

'It's bad enough being like this, without . . . You don't know what it's like, having people hold doors for you all the time and hover over you being helpful and looking at you with pity. *Poor chap! One of our heroes. Gave his all for his country.* Except that I didn't, did I? I was only over there a few months, I achieved nothing. I'm nobody's hero.'

'You're—'

'Bobby was the hero! I just got stupidly wounded, enough

to make me a useless burden, and now I've got a kid to support, and no job, and my wife goes ahead and gets pregnant – *again!*'

'It takes two to make a baby,' she protested.

'You lured me into it!' he cried, and it was so ludicrous she almost laughed, but managed not to, because if she had it might have done him irreparable damage. She knew he was in pain, not just from his leg, but from his soul, and it was the latter pain that was the worst, the one that could kill a man.

She tried to speak quietly, rationally. 'You're not useless, and you're not a cripple. You walk with a stick – well, so do lots of people. And you're not without prospects. You have a magnificent brain, and now things are getting back to normal, you will get a proper job, something worthy of you. Just now it makes sense to stay here, leaving aside the fact that your mother needs the support while—'

He put his hands to his head. 'Oh, stop!' he shouted. 'Do you hear yourself? You don't know what the hell you're talking about! Just for God's sake shut up!'

Instinctively she felt there was someone outside in the passage. 'Don't shout,' she hissed. 'The servants will hear.'

He closed his eyes and stood, half leaning against the windowsill, his face white and drawn, breathing shallowly, like a hurt animal.

'David,' she said softly, 'please. This is *good* news. You should be happy.'

'Go away,' he said, his eyes still closed. 'Leave me alone.'

She wouldn't plead. And she absolutely would *not* cry. She looked at him a moment longer, then turned and went out. Her head flicked right, spotting the figure at the end of the passage. It was Ethel. Their eyes met in a long look of understanding. Ethel had never particularly liked Antonia, and was jealous of her relationship with baby Marcus; but when men raged, women drew together.

43

'The baby woke up, madam,' Ethel said neutrally. 'I was going down to get him some warm milk.'

'Yes,' said Antonia, and her hand moved instinctively to cover her belly, to protect the place where the new child was growing. Ethel's eyes did not move, but Antonia knew she had seen the gesture.

Ethel said, 'You look as if you'd got a headache, madam. Would you like me to make you a cup of tea?'

The kindness – unexpected, because Ethel was never needlessly kind – almost made her cry. 'That would be lovely,' Antonia said. 'Thank you.'

Two days later, at breakfast, Antonia made an announcement. 'I've had a letter from my father,' she said. 'He and Mrs Turnberry have fixed the date of their wedding for the nineteenth of January. It's to be very quiet, but I'd like to be there.'

'Of course,' Beattie answered for them all. 'You should go.'

'There's no need for you to come, though, David,' Antonia went on. 'The journey, at this time of year . . .'

David cleared his throat. 'Quite,' he said. 'You go, dear.'

Sadie, watching under her eyebrows as she pretended to eat, noticed that their eyes did not quite meet. There was some trouble between them, she brooded. David should have been happy because of the new baby. What was wrong with him?

'I thought I'd go ahead of the wedding, because there are bound to be things to arrange. And the house has been a bachelor home for so long, it will need to be made comfortable.'

'When did you want to go?' Beattie asked, since no one else spoke.

'I thought tomorrow. And stay for a few weeks. If that's all right? I'd like to take Marcus with me,' Antonia went on. 'Daddy's always asking about him. He hasn't seen him in ages. And may I take Ethel to help with Marcus? Because Daddy's servants aren't used to babies.'

'Yes, of course you can have her,' Beattie said.

And Sadie, looking from face to face in a troubled way, said absently, 'She wouldn't want to be parted from him anyway.'

CHAPTER FOUR

The servants knew something was up. Ada had seen them come home early, seen Mr David's face as he stamped past. And though nothing had been said, there was no mistaking An Atmosphere.

Ethel remained tight-lipped, even when Cook asked her directly what was going on, why was Mrs David going away? 'Going to see her dad,' was all she would say.

'Why's Mr David not going as well?' Cook tried.

Ethel shrugged. 'Ask him yourself,' she said.

Cook switched her attack. 'Who's going to be doing your work while you're away? That's what I want to know.'

Ethel gave her a stony look. 'Taking the baby with me. What work you talking about?'

'Well – waiting on Mr David. Upstairs.'

'It won't be you. That's all you need to worry about. Where's Mrs David's peignoir that was in the drying-room?'

'Nula was mending it yesterday – the lace was coming off the sleeve. She must've put it in the linen room for ironing.'

'You don't iron chiffon,' Ethel said.

'You've not known that for long, so don't give yourself airs!' Cook called after her. 'You're not a lady's maid, you're just helping with the packing.'

Mr Weston met them at the station in his old Rover. Reading his daughter's face with the skill of long intimacy, he asked her nothing, kissed her cheerfully, exclaimed over his grandson and, when the porter had loaded the luggage, drove away at his customary 12 m.p.h., easing his way round the potholes and slowing cautiously for the blind corners.

Antonia appreciated his reticence. She knew she would tell him eventually. She looked around at the familiar landmarks. There was the Half Moon, low and cottagey, which in late spring was almost buried under its draping wisteria. Then the Spread Eagle, marking the edge of the village, bigger, with fake Tudor beams, looking a little shabby now, after four years of war. Then the village green, with the church hall on one side and the Four Corners teashop on the other, and the glimpse through the bare treetops of the square tower of St Mary's. Then rows of neat thatched cottages and, finally, there was the square red-brick house with the notice fixed to the gate: ST HUGH'S SOLDIERS' CLUB.

It was there that she had first met David, when he and his friend Jumbo had walked into the village from the nearby training camp for something to do, and stopped for a cup of tea.

'So the club's still going,' she said.

Her father, glad that she had broken the silence, said, 'I think we're needed more than ever. The camp is a demobilisation centre now, and there are a lot of confused and unhappy men who don't quite know what to do with themselves. I hope you'll feel like helping.'

'I'm here to arrange your wedding and make the house suitable for a bride,' Antonia said, with mock sternness.

'Oh, Yvonne isn't fussy,' he said lightly.

'She may be too polite to say anything,' Antonia said, 'but that doesn't mean she doesn't notice. You should be ashamed, Daddy, not to want her to be comfortable.'

'You shall arrange things however you please,' he said genially. 'We've put you in your old room, as David wasn't coming – thought it would amuse you to have your old things around you. He is well, is he?'

'Yes, quite well. Improving slowly.'

'Mrs Bates has been baking all morning, so I'm sure there'll be a lavish tea waiting for us. Don't bother to unpack. Just take off your hat and come straight down.'

'Haven't seen you for a while,' Cook said, as Frank Hussey came in through the back door.

'I've had a bad cold,' he said. 'Didn't want to spread it around. Not with this flu about.'

'Any news of your new master coming home?'

Sir George Pettingell had died in November, with his son and heir Martin at the Front.

'Nothing yet,' said Frank. 'With him being on the staff, he might have to go to Paris for this peace conference. *I* hope he comes home, though.'

'Why's that, Frank?' Cook asked. 'Here, just hold the oven door open for me, will you? It *will* swing back on me. Use the tea-towel – it's hot.'

Frank held back the door while she moved the potatoes from the bottom to the top, letting out a heavenly smell of roasting beef. 'I could fix that door,' he said. 'Only wants the hinge tightening.'

'Lovely, you can do it after, then. What was you saying?'

'About wishing Sir Martin would come back,' Frank said, turning as Ada and Beryl came into the room behind him. 'Mr Orwell's put off his retirement again. He doesn't want to go while there's no master in residence – for all that I do most of the work now anyway. And I can't get his job until he does go. Where's Ethel?'

He addressed the question to Ada. She blushed and looked at Cook, who busied herself over the stove to avoid answering.

'What's going on?' Frank demanded. 'Is she ill?'

'Oh no, nothing like that,' Ada said. She went past him

48

to the table to start loading cutlery onto a tray. 'I got to get on and lay upstairs for luncheon.'

Frank's big hand curled softly but implacably over hers, halting it. 'Ada, you're looking shifty. What's she gone and done now?'

'Nothing,' Ada protested. 'All it is, Mrs David's gone for a visit to her father and taken Marcus with her, so she's taken Ethel as well, because his servants couldn't cope with a baby. Not that he's any trouble, but they've not had children in the house for years. O' course, now Mrs David's father's getting married—'

'I don't give a fig for Mrs David's father,' Frank interrupted. 'How long is Ethel going to be away?'

Ada avoided his eyes. 'I don't know. The wedding's on the nineteenth, I b'lieve, so at least until then. Let me go, Frank, I got work to do.'

He released her. 'That's another two weeks. She went away and left no word for me. That's why you look so guilty, isn't it?'

'*I* don't look guilty,' Beryl said stoutly. 'I ain't done nothing.'

Frank ignored her and turned to Cook. 'No message. Not a word.'

It wasn't a question, but Cook answered it. 'No, Frank dear. But you have to remember—'

'It's all right.' He stopped her. 'You don't need to try and spare my feelings. I always knew I proceeded at my own risk.' He stared down at his hands, and he looked so sad that for a moment every female in the kitchen – including Eileen, who'd just come in from the scullery with the tureens – wanted to pet and comfort him.

'It'll only be a few weeks,' Ada said at last.

He looked up, straightening his shoulders. 'Will it? I'm not so sure. She's been telling me these two years and more she doesn't want me. Maybe I should have listened.'

'Oh, Frank, don't give up on her,' Ada pleaded.

'Looks like she's given up on me,' Frank said. 'Think I'd better be off, Mrs D.'

'Not staying for your dinner?' Cook said, shocked.

'No, thanks all the same.' And he walked quickly and lightly across the kitchen and was gone.

'Well!' Cook said, breaking the silence his departure had left.

'She's done it now,' said Ada.

Edward came to attention and saluted as the King approached. The King, very grey now, his nose and cheeks reddened by the cold, was followed at a short distance by the Prince of Wales, slight and boyish, looking like a child dressed up in army uniform; and Prince Albert, so gaunt in the face that, oddly, he looked older than his brother.

Edward expected them all to pass by – this was just a general inspection, something to cheer up the men still waiting for their discharge, and to celebrate regaining the territory lost for most of the war. But the general walking beside the King murmured something to him; the pale blue eyes came round, fixed on Edward, and the party stopped.

'Ah, yes, Sir Edward,' the King said, returning the salute so that Edward could lower his hand. It was just less than a year since the King had knighted him at Buckingham Palace, but he was sure His Majesty couldn't remember one among so many. He waited, his breath clouding on the air, feeling the numbness of his cold feet and the slight chafe of his khaki collar against his neck. He had one of those moments of intense awareness, of standing outside himself. He wondered how on earth he had come to be there, standing on a churned-up, muddy road in rural France, dressed in British Army uniform and masquerading as an officer, looking into the face of the King of England.

The King spoke. 'Jolly well done,' he said. 'We need chaps

like you to make sure everything runs smoothly. Perhaps the most important chapter in our history. Much depends on it. I'm sure we shall be hearing more of you, Major.'

'Thank you, sir,' Edward said, since something seemed to be required. He had no idea what his sovereign was talking about, but the last word suggested it was a case of mistaken identity, which would explain much.

The royal party moved on, Prince Albert throwing him a glance and a slight, shy smile as he passed. The Prince of Wales was talking volubly, with hand gestures, to the officer on his other side and had no attention to spare for him.

'I saw you were a little bewildered,' Prewitt Dancer said, when Edward presented himself at HQ in response to a summons, after the parade was dismissed. He fiddled with a piece of paper in front of him. 'Fact of the matter is, Hunter, you've volunteered for a special duty.'

'I have, sir?'

'Actually, you were recommended to the prime minister as just the man for the job, and it was assumed that you would accept it. Dash it,' he added, with a stern look, 'you're still in uniform. They could have made it an order, y'know.'

'I appreciate the indulgence, sir,' Edward said. 'Perhaps you'd let me know what I volunteered for.'

'The Peace Conference,' the colonel said. 'It's to open in Paris on the eighteenth, and the politicos will need experts to guide them through the technical details. Lots of experts in different fields. They'll be discussing everything from prisoners of war to international aviation laws, but one of the most contentious subjects is bound to be money – not least, war reparation.'

'How much Germany will have to pay?' said Edward. 'That will be . . . difficult.'

'Quite. So they need some damned good financial brains to put 'em straight, and Forbesson at the War Office recommended you. Of course, you're not exactly unknown in government circles, so the PM jumped at the suggestion. A chap would always sooner deal with a chap he knows.'

Edward didn't quite know what to think about it. It was an honour, of course – a tremendous honour. And it would be fascinating to be a part of what were bound to be historic deliberations. On the other hand, it would be difficult, complex, with plenty of opportunities for setting backs up and getting oneself into trouble. And it would mean a delay to his demobilisation—

'How long will the conference last, sir?' he asked.

'God knows,' said Prewitt Dancer. 'Months, certainly. A year perhaps. Every aggrieved nation will want to have its say, everyone will disagree with everyone else. Matters so complicated God couldn't straighten them out will be on the table.' He fixed Edward with a gimlet eye. 'Have you got something more important to do?'

'No, sir,' Edward said. 'I volunteered, you remember.'

The colonel's expression softened. 'Good man. Knew you'd do it. And, damme, if they'd asked me I'd have jumped at it, even though it means not going home. You'll see history being made. Can't turn down a chance like that.'

'No, sir. What happens next?'

'You'll have today and tomorrow to wind things up with your company. Then you'll get orders for Paris, leaving tomorrow night. Get settled in – get some decent lodgings before the hordes descend – find out the lie of the land.'

'Will I have time to go home before—'

'Sorry, no. There'll be discussions before the discussions start, if you follow me, and not long to sort out some kind of agenda. And once the bigwigs arrive . . .'

'I understand,' Edward said. His ingrained tiredness abated a little before a wave of excitement. 'Anything else, sir? I'd like to get a letter off to my family.'

Prewitt Dancer smiled. 'Just one more thing, and I suspect

you'll want to include it in your letter. The job comes with a promotion. You've been gazetted major, with the appropriate increase in pay, of course.'

Edward allowed himself a smile, too. 'I thought the King had made a mistake when he called me "Major".'

'Not at all. Just a matter of timing. You know the army – the bod in question is always the last to know.'

'Is that from Dad?' Peter asked over a slice of toast and jam. 'Is he coming home?'

'No,' Beattie said absently. 'He's not.'

'What, not at *all*?' Peter demanded, in disappointed tones.

Beattie looked up. Her youngest, twelve now, had put on a sudden spurt of growth recently. He would be tall, like his brothers, though not as tall as David. He was a runner, too: at his school, Lorrimers Guild, he had already been picked as a back for the junior rugby fifteen. 'He's going to Paris instead, for the Peace Conference,' she answered. 'To advise on finance.'

'Advise who?' Peter wanted to know. 'The generals and such?'

'The politicians, I think. Prime ministers and presidents. And he's been made a major,' she added.

Peter hooted with joy. 'About time, too! Wait till I tell them at school! Willy Andrews's father's a captain in the navy, and he's always going on about a navy captain being higher than an army captain.'

'How long will he be away?' Sadie asked.

'He doesn't know,' said Beattie. 'Months, anyway.'

'It's a great honour, isn't it, Mother? To be advising the world on behalf of the whole country. I still wish he could come home, though. I know it's selfish, but the war won't seem over until he does.'

Beattie made an assenting sound and went back to her letters, hearing Sadie's and Peter's voices in the background without knowing what they were saying. No, the war wasn't over yet, wouldn't be until the boys came home, but for her and millions like her it would never be over. She saw it in women's eyes every day, women who outwardly were functioning normally but were concealing a black emptiness inside. Women who had lost husbands, fathers, sons, lovers.

When someone died in normal times, there was shock and grief, then a funeral, with weeping, loving arms to comfort you, and then a slow healing. But with war, they went away and just – *never came back*. No funeral to mark an ending. No comfort from others because they were in the same boat; and it wasn't patriotic to make a fuss. If you wept, you wept alone and in secret. And the gaping wound did not heal. Peace might be declared, but the war didn't end. In some ghostly realm, the lost men still marched and fought, and you waited, your mind knowing they were not coming home, your heart like a dog at the door never really understanding.

In a way, it was a relief that Edward's return was to be delayed. There would have to be, she thought, some sort of reckoning between them. Was any kind of married life possible? The thought of their living estranged for the next twenty or thirty years chilled her to the bones, but how could they get over the rift? She had betrayed Edward in the worst possible way, and Louis's death had made it impossible to rewrite the story. Had he lived, she would have had to choose: either to leave Edward, who could then, after a period, have started a new life without her, or choose Edward over Louis, allowing him to salvage his pride. But she had not had to choose, and Edward would never be able to be sure that she'd have chosen him.

And in other ways the war did not seem over. Her war work continued. The canteen was still much in demand; there was still poverty and need among soldiers' families; and when the boys did come home, she guessed there would be difficulty in slotting them back into their lives. Those who could not find work would only add to their families' poverty. And there would be the wounded and disabled, who would need help, whose families would need help, for a long time to come.

She came back from her thoughts to notice that the voices had stopped, and realised both children were looking at her.

'Are you all right, Mother?' Peter asked. 'You looked awfully queer just then. Have you got a headache?'

She recognised the anxiety in his voice. Bobby had died, David was wounded, Dad and William were absent. Only Mother remained to secure his world, to represent some kind of continuity.

'No, of course not,' she said briskly. 'I was just thinking. Is that David coming down at last?'

'It takes him longer to get ready without Antonia,' Sadie excused him

'Ring the bell, dear,' Beattie said to Peter, 'for fresh coffee for him.'

Sadie was schooling one of the horses, a bay, up at Highclere, weaving him in and out down a line of bottles. It was good for making them supple, and teaching them to answer light aids. Mrs Cuthbert came up to the gate and watched for a bit. Sadie reached the end of the row and, turning, saw her. She rode over.

'He's getting very good at it,' she said. 'I think he'd make a good polo pony.'

'I suppose that's something we'll have to start thinking about,' said Mrs Cuthbert, allowing her fingers to be investigated by the soft, curious muzzle. 'There has to be some sort of future for these fellows.'

'Yes, and I don't suppose being able to ignore shell fire will be very useful,' said Sadie. 'We shan't have to do our firecracker training any more.'

'I'm wondering how long the army's going to be happy

55

to go on feeding them,' said Mrs Cuthbert. 'We've heard nothing from the Remount Service since the Armistice.'

'We've probably slipped through the cracks,' Sadie said. 'You know the army.'

The only difference was that no new horses had arrived. Most of the volunteer girls had left as well, some reluctantly, obeying urgent summonses from their parents; others gladly, looking forward to a different sort of life, with perhaps a fiancé coming home. That left just Mary Russell, who was worth at least two women, and Winifred, who had been silent and shy when she arrived in 1915, but had blossomed through contact with the horses and was now very confident with them, though she still said very little unless spoken to.

'I thought they'd disband us as soon as the war was over,' Sadie said, slipping down from the saddle. 'I was dreading it.'

'I know,' said Mrs Cuthbert. 'But I shall always have a few horses, just for fun, and you'll always be welcome to come and ride them, you know that.'

'Thank you,' said Sadie. She didn't add, and didn't need to, *but it won't be the same*. Working on the remounts for the army had been a proper job. She needed to feel useful. A movement in the distance seen over Mrs Cuthbert's shoulder prompted her to say, 'There's someone in the yard. Are you expecting visitors?'

'No,' said Mrs Cuthbert. She turned to look. 'He's in uniform. I wonder if it's someone from the Remount Service.'

'It's not Captain Casimir,' said Sadie. 'Oh dear, I hope this isn't bad news.'

Mrs Cuthbert waved, and the stranger waved back and approached. Sadie laughed. 'Reprieve!' she said. 'It's Mrs Fitzgerald's nephew, Captain Beamish. We were invited to the rectory for supper on Thursday and he asked me what we did up here at Highclere. I said he could visit, but I didn't think he would. He must be keener on horses than I thought.'

Mrs Cuthbert gave Sadie an affectionate look. She had

no idea of her own attractiveness: with a glamorous and beautiful older sister, she was used to thinking of herself as the ugly duckling. The approaching young man was fair and good-looking, and there weren't as many of *those* around as there once were. A girl of Sadie's age ought to have an eye for opportunity. 'It's your birthday soon, isn't it?' she asked, on the back of that thought.

'Next Saturday,' Sadie said, surprised by the sudden question.

'And you'll be twenty-one?'

Sadie waited to understand the direction of thought. With no clues, she added helpfully, 'We don't make much fuss about birthdays in our house.'

'So I remember,' said Mrs Cuthbert. The young man was within earshot now, and she greeted him. 'Captain Beamish, how nice to see you. What brings you to Highclere?'

He shook hands with Mrs Cuthbert, but his eyes kept slipping sideways to Sadie. After some polite exchanges, Sadie said, 'We don't allow idle hands up here, you know. You're welcome as long as you've come to help.'

'In any way I can,' he said.

'Then you can help me exercise. The horses need to be taken out every day.'

'I'd be glad to,' he said.

'You can ride one, and I'll ride one and lead one. That'll be three down,' Sadie said, unlatching the gate and leading the bay through. 'Are you coming too?' she asked Mrs Cuthbert.

'No, I'll take a couple later. I've things to do up at the house. Take a good long ride, dear, get them thoroughly tired out. Why not go up to the Beacons, show Captain Beamish the view?'

'When did you learn to ride?' Sadie asked, as they walked the horses along the dry path over the crown of the hill.

'When I was a child. You ride wonderfully well,' he said. 'I shouldn't care to be leading that chestnut from the saddle – he looks a handful.'

'Oh, there's no harm in him,' Sadie said. 'He's just young. Would you like to canter along here? He'll settle better if he's had a run.'

When they reached the Beacons – a high place with a fine view over the hills and the Rust valley – they stopped and dismounted. 'This is one of my favourite places,' Sadie said.

There was an outcrop of rock, and they sat while the horses grazed. 'The view's better in the summer, when the leaves are on the trees,' she apologised.

'Oh, but winter has its own beauty,' he said. 'It allows you to see the bones of the landscape, the underlying structure. And the colours are more subtle – the browns and ochres, and the indigo of the shadows.'

'You have an artist's eye, Captain Beamish.'

'Does it have to be "Captain Beamish"?'

She looked doubtful. 'Your aunt calls you—'

'Yes, I know. "Dolly". Adolphus is the most monstrous name to be cursed with. Can you imagine how I was tormented at school?'

'It must have been difficult.'

'I was afraid "Dolly" would carry over into the army, so I got my word in early. My second name's Sambourne, so I told everyone I was always called Sam. I've got used to it now – anything else sounds strange.'

'All right,' she nodded. 'I'll call you Sam.' They were silent a moment. Then she said, 'Have you thought any more about the future? About music?'

'I've thought about little else. I want to play – it's the only thing I want to do. I know my father won't approve, but what you said – about my being of age – has stuck in my mind. The thing is, my mother's awfully ill at the moment, which is why I'm staying with Aunt Honoria, and I don't want to start up any rows until she's better.'

'I understand. But when she is, you'll stand your ground, won't you?'

'I don't know why you care so much about my silly problem,' he said wistfully.

'Because of the war,' she said. 'People have had four years taken out of their lives. Some, like my brother, have had the whole of their future taken away. It's made me realise how important it is to do what you really want. If music matters that much to you –'

'It does,' he assured her.

'– then you can't let your parents stop you, however much you respect them. You've done your duty. Now you must live your own life.'

'Aunt Honoria says she only has my good at heart when she opposes me. She says musicians aren't respectable, and they never earn much money.'

'Do you want to be respectable, the way your aunt means it?'

'Not really.'

'That world was blown away by the war. But some old people can't change their thinking, and there's nothing you can do about it. You must simply stand up to them.'

'You sound so determined. I wish I had your spirit.'

'Oh, you have it, if only you're prepared to use it. Don't be so mushy!'

Now he smiled. 'Mushy! You're right. I won't be mushy any more. What an inspiration you are! I didn't know many girls before the war, but the ones I knew weren't a bit like you.'

'The war's changed everybody,' she said, a little absently.

He cleared his throat, and she turned her head and realised how close his face was to hers. She felt his warm breath on her cold cheek.

'Sadie, I know we haven't known each other long, but I feel as if it's much longer. I do like you awfully. Could we—? Would you—? I mean, could I take you out somewhere one evening? There's going to be a concert at St Peter's Church in Westleigh next week – Bach and Mozart. I could get tickets for it. Would your parents allow it?'

She felt a pang. Gently she said, 'You should know, I have someone. He's in France, but we have . . . an understanding. When he comes back . . .'

He blushed with mortification. 'I'm sorry. I should have realised. Forgive me.'

'Please don't apologise. It was awfully nice of you to ask me.' She scrambled to her feet. 'We ought to move on, before the horses get cold.'

He stopped her. 'I hope I haven't made things awkward,' he said. 'You're so jolly nice to talk to. And you've given me such good advice. I hope we can still be friends.'

'Of course,' she said, eyes averted. 'And I'd like to know how you get on – with the music and everything. Really. I'm interested.'

He smiled, as if her embarrassment had given him strength. 'Friends, then. And I *will* let you know.'

CHAPTER FIVE

Antonia had found plenty to do. The maids, Iris and Maud, had done nothing, beyond a thorough cleaning, to make her father's house ready for a lady. It was comfortable in a masculine way – like a gentlemen's club or a university don's set.

She consulted with Mrs Turnberry about the wedding, and found that while she had modest ideas they were nowhere near as modest as Mr Weston's. Because of their age and widowed status, it was seemly for it to be a quiet affair, but she had invited a number of friends, and there was to be a lavish wedding breakfast, and a cake. She was grateful to have Antonia to consult about suitable apparel; and to know that Antonia would make sure her father dressed properly too.

Mrs Bates was thrilled with the opportunity to make a wedding cake. 'What a pity it's winter,' she said. 'There's nothing nicer than fresh white roses to put round a wedding cake. I might see if I can manage with Christmas roses. They grow them in the vicarage garden.'

In addition to the wedding preparations, there was the soldiers' club to keep going. Some of the men needed practical advice, but often they only wanted someone to talk to, and Antonia had always been a good listener. It was a relief to be too busy to think about herself. Nobody had yet noticed her condition. Ethel, who was in a position to have given her away, had obviously said nothing in the servants' hall, for which Antonia was grateful. Besides, the wedding was filling up everyone's spare thoughts. When it was over – ah, then, she knew, things would have to be faced.

She'd had a bread-and-butter letter from Beattie, to which David had added a footnote hoping she and Marcus were well and asking politely after her father. She tried to read some warmth into it, but it was difficult. He did not mention her pregnancy or say he missed her – did not even enquire if her visit had an end date yet. On the whole, she wished he had not written anything. In ignorance there might have been hope.

In the second week of January, William's squadron was informed officially that it would not be going to the Rhine.

'It says here,' said Considine, who was reading the official notice in the mess at breakfast, 'that demobilisation will commence immediately.'

'But there's still hope, isn't there?' said Partridge. 'Dash it, there must be something that'll keep us together.'

'I heard that they're sending several squadrons to Russia to help the Whites,' said Pearson.

'They could change their minds about the Rhine,' William put in. It seemed intolerable that they should be split up.

'We'll keep working,' Considine decreed, 'so that if anything does come up, we're ready. Formation flying this morning – we could all be better at that. And tomorrow we'll practise firing at ground targets.'

But the following morning an order arrived from Wing for the release of the four American pilots, so practice was postponed in favour of a farewell flight over the old familiar terrain. The Yanks packed their kit, and there was a beano in the mess that night.

'What'll you do back home?' William asked Wilkinson, who was long and gangling, almost too tall for a pilot.

'Got to find a flying job of some sort,' Wilkinson said, drinking from his pewter mug of beer as though the answer might lie in the bottom. 'You've applied to the RAF, haven't you?'

'Yes,' said William. 'But they're reducing the numbers so much, there's not much chance of getting taken on. And even if they take me, it won't be much to write home about after all this.'

'It was a rotten war,' Considine said, 'but the queer thing is how we're going to miss it. Where were you this afternoon, Yank? I was looking for you.'

'Took one of the motor-bicycles, had a ride around. Saying goodbye.' He cleared his throat. 'Couldn't go without paying my respects to Dobbs.'

Dobbs, his close friend, had been buried in the little military ground outside the village. The cross over his plot had been made with the propeller of his own aircraft.

Gossett, another American, joined them. 'When I get home, I'm going to lobby the government about parachutes. My pa wrote me they're thinking about a programme to develop them. Only *thinking*!'

Wilkinson grinned. 'If there's a programme, someone'll have to volunteer to test 'em. Whaddaya think about that, Gossie?'

'I'll do it,' said Gossett. 'As long as I can jump out over a good big haystack.'

On the day before the wedding, Antonia went over to Mrs Turnberry's house to oversee her last preparations. When she got home, her father met her at the door.

'I thought we'd have a cosy supper in front of the fire in my study, the way we used to,' he said, helping her off with her hat and coat. His room, dark and infinitely masculine, booklined and smelling of leather and woodsmoke, was just like his study at St Hugh's, where he had been headmaster for most of her childhood. It gave her a jolt, that familiarity: Daddy's study, where she had always found sanctuary. There he had taught her Latin and Greek, told her stories, occasionally disciplined her, often praised her, always listened to her, solved her problems as far as it had been in him to do so. He was a man for sons, and Antonia ought to have been a boy, and while he had loved her without stint, he had probably imparted a slightly masculine cast to her thinking. She had only occasionally regretted it.

He sat her down and gave her sherry, took the chair opposite, and said, 'Supper's all ready, we can have it when we want. Nothing will spoil: it's soup and cold beef and baked potatoes, in the slow oven. I wanted Mrs Bates to have the evening off, since she'll have a heavy day tomorrow. How was Yvonne?'

'Nervous,' Antonia said, and chatted to him lightly about Mrs Turnberry and the wedding. 'I suddenly realise,' she concluded, 'that I haven't asked you about a honeymoon. Are you planning to go away, or is that too frivolous?'

'Whether it's frivolous or not I couldn't say, but we both feel we've been cooped up for four years. We did talk about going away.'

'Abroad?'

'I don't think Europe is quite ready for the Baedeker tour.'

'And it's not good travelling weather,' Antonia agreed. 'Where, then?'

'Just into the west country. Yvonne's people are from there originally. She'd have liked to see some of the places again.'

'But what's to stop you?'

'I don't want to close the club,' said Mr Weston. 'We have a number of lady volunteers but there's no one I'd like to leave in charge. It wouldn't be fair on them.'

Antonia spoke before she thought. 'Well, *I'm* here. I can run things while you're away.'

64

'Ah,' he said, with a lightness that suggested he had been working up to the question. 'So how long *will* you be here?'

She opened her mouth and shut it again, reddening slightly.

'You *were* intending to tell me, weren't you?' he went on gently. 'You always brought your troubles to me. What's wrong, my love? I know something is. What's happened?'

'Oh, Daddy,' she said helplessly. The fire crackled, the light glinting on the gold tooling of leather books, glowing on her father's dear comfortable face. So she told him. It all came tumbling out, and in her anguish, she did not notice his lips whiten or his fingers clench as she told him everything.

She ended in tears, and it was a relief to cry. 'He doesn't love me,' she concluded. 'You warned me right at the beginning.'

'And as I remember,' he said slowly, offering his hand-kerchief, 'you knew that yourself. But you married him anyway.'

She blew her nose and wiped her eyes, comforted by the smell of his bay rum. 'I thought he would come to love me over time. Not as I loved him, perhaps, but enough.'

Mr Weston looked at her sadly. She had married a gravely wounded man who'd needed a nurse. His lovely, clever, good daughter, who should have been the adored consort of some educated, energetic man who could really appreciate her, had been wasted on a needy, selfish boy.

She raised her head defiantly. 'I know what you're thinking – but, Daddy, remember I was already an old maid. You always thought I was a great prize, but no one else ever asked me.'

'It doesn't follow that no one would have,' he said calmly. 'But there's no point in talking about might-have-beens. We have to deal with the world as it is. What are you going to do?'

'Stay here for a while,' she said.

'Dearest,' he said gravely, 'you are a married woman. You're having a baby. You have to go back.'

She gave him a bitter look that hurt him. 'I thought you'd be on my side.'

'I am. But you can't abandon your marriage. You took a sacred vow. We don't do things like that.'

She sighed. 'I suppose you're right. And I didn't mean to stay here for ever. Just – for a little. He hurt me so much, Daddy. I need to be away from him for a while. Just for a few weeks.'

He studied her face. 'Are you thinking he'll start missing you, and send for you?' She looked away from him, into the fire. 'Or even come and fetch you? Oh, my dear.'

She didn't answer. Tears began again. Yes, he knew her very well, her darling father. Wordlessly, deep inside, she hoped David would find his life empty and cold without the comfort she provided; even deeper, and more wordlessly, she feared—

'What if he doesn't?' asked Mr Weston, very gently. She wiped her eyes again, but the tears kept seeping. 'This is your home,' he said. 'There will always be sanctuary for you here. But you have to think of the children. They don't deserve to be tarnished by disgrace. Yes, I'm sorry, but it has to be faced. Whatever the rights or wrongs of the case, it will always be a disgrace for a wife to abandon her husband. You have to go back. You have to go back before the baby comes.'

Antonia wiped her eyes again, straightened her shoulders, and said, 'I know. I will, Daddy. I won't shame you. Just let me have a few weeks to – to think. I'll do the right thing, I promise.'

'Very well. I trust you.'

'And you and Mrs Turnberry must have your honeymoon tour.'

66

He smiled suddenly. 'What will you call her, after the wedding? You really can't call her Mrs Weston.'

'I don't know. I'll have to see what comes naturally.'

Laura found St Omer *en fête*, for a wedding between a FANY and an RAMC officer. The couple and their colleagues were so exuberant with joy, their celebration had engulfed everyone they met, and almost the whole town had crammed into the abandoned aircraft hangar where the wedding breakfast was being held. FANY ambulances, decorated with ribbons, provided transport, and Laura was swept up too, and cheerfully carried some medical orderlies – who seemed to have been celebrating for quite some time already, and sang loudly and beerily over her shoulder as she drove.

'What are their names?' she yelled back. 'The bride and groom?'

'Couldn't say, miss!' He sang: '*When this lousy war is over* . . .' And the others joined in, in different keys.

The hangar was decorated with bunting, trestle tables were laid out, and there was a band consisting of a squeeze-box, three fiddles, a mouth organ, a fife and a home-made double-bass that had started life as a packing case. There were barrels of beer and local cider, and a feast as uneven as the band, featuring every sort of food that could be begged, foraged, poached, or had been donated by well-wishers. And when the eating slowed down, they danced. At one point Laura found herself whirling in the arms of the bridegroom, who shouted over the noise, 'Have we met? Never mind, doesn't matter. Everyone's welcome today. I'm Leonard.'

'I'm Laura. Do you know Major Ransley?'

'RAMC? Yes, we've met a few times. Wait a minute – you're *his* Laura? Lord, you're a legend!' he bellowed, as the band rose to new heights of discord. 'What are you doing here?'

'Looking for him. Have you—?'

Another madly whirling couple bumped into them, and he cried, 'There's my bride! Must have a dance with my bride!' There was a confusion of arms and feet, and Laura found herself danced away by a young RAF officer, who sang loudly in her ear – unfortunately not the same song as the band was playing.

She excused herself when they reached the end of the hall, and went to lean against one of the doors, left open for air, though it was freezing outside. She lit a cigarette, thinking wistfully of Ransley. It was hard to stay in touch when they kept moving him about. She had gone to Hazebrouck, only to find he had left there; St Omer had apparently been his destination, but it didn't seem he was here either.

A person in FANY uniform came up to her and asked her for a light. She was an older woman, with steel-grey hair in short curls and a firm, healthy face, who said, 'My husband would be shocked if he saw me smoking, but you can't get through a day in the ambulances without. I suppose we'll have to mend our ways when we go home.'

'When will that be?' Laura asked.

'Oh, not for weeks, with any luck. I'm dreading a return to normality. Though we've all agreed we're determined to keep the FANY together when we get home, peacetime or no peacetime. You're not FANY, are you?'

'No, I'm an independent. I was driving an X-ray ambulance, but the equipment got donated to the French. I kept the bus, though, so now I'm just transport for anyone who needs it.'

The woman offered her hand. 'I'm Beryl de Fontenay, by the way.'

'Laura Hunter.'

The woman's eyes widened. 'But you're my niece's friend! You opened that wonderful women's club in Pop together. I'm Ronnie Mildmay's aunt.'

'Aunt Beryl – of course. She talked about you a lot. Where

is she now? The last I heard she was going to help run a canteen somewhere near Pop.'

'That's where she is,' said the other. 'You should go and look her up. Frankly, she's wasted making tea. I'm sure our boys appreciate it, but Ronnie's such an energetic person . . .'

'I remember,' Laura said, laughing.

'It's such a shame you lost your club. You should—'

At that moment they were interrupted by two infantry officers, who seized them and whirled them away, saying, 'No slacking, ladies! Dancing is the order of the evening!'

She hadn't been back to Poperinghe since they were bombed out. The damage was obvious and extensive; but the place that had been abandoned before the advancing Germans when she had last seen it was thronging now. Pop was a primary route for discharged soldiers going home to Blighty, and for wounded coming back from the northern section of what had been the line; and there were still officers and men going on leave and coming back.

She knew that Ronnie's canteen was somewhere on the road to Ypres, and when she found it, between Brandhoek and Vlamertinge, she almost missed it: it was less a canteen than a coffee stall. She still wasn't sure she had the right place when she pulled Matilda into the side of the road and got down. It was a cold day, not the dazzling frosty cold that exhilarates, but the creeping, miserable cold of a damp, swampy place in the middle of winter. Everything was grey, and instead of a sky there was a drizzling fog, to which one's breath merely added a little more cloud.

But there was Ronnie, bundled up in some kind of hairy fur jacket – pony, perhaps, or even goat – with her hair concealed under a khaki Sister Dora cap, her hands in fingerless gloves, handing over thick mugs of tea and bully-beef sandwiches to a couple of Tommies, who looked pinched by the weather, watery-eyed and red-nosed. She looked enquiringly across at

Laura, and then her eyes widened, her face split in a grin of delight, and she abandoned her post, hopped out of the van and rushed to grab Laura's hand and wring it.

'Laura! Dear old Laura! What a sight for sore eyes! What are you doing here?'

'I met your aunt Beryl in St Omer. She told me you were still here.'

'How is she?'

'Not going home unless they make her.'

'She's an inspiration! How are *you*? You're looking well! Have you married your lovely surgeon yet?'

'Not yet – his contract doesn't finish until April. And I seem to have mislaid him.'

'Careless of you!'

'I went to St Omer looking for him, but he wasn't there. Trouble is, he can't write to me until I'm settled somewhere, but I can't settle while I'm looking for him.'

'I see your problem. And you thought he'd be in Pop or Ypres?'

'No, I came to find you. I have a serviceable ambulance, and there's still lots of demand.'

'I should say there jolly well is! There are still accidents – bags of 'em! And they're still evacuating some of the more remote hospitals. To say nothing of the flu.'

'Is that bad here?'

'My dear! The weather is perfect for it. And gathering the men together in these demob camps does wonders for spreading it. They say the whole of Étaples is sneezing.' An idea struck her. 'You know, I wonder if that's not where your major is. Might be worth going to look.'

'Yes, good idea – but what I really came here for was to fetch you. I'm all right on my own as a taxi service, but stretcher work requires two. And . . .' She hesitated an instant, then plunged in. 'I'm lonely. Annie was supposed to come back, but she's ill – some kind of lung thing.'

'How awful!'

'Yes. And whatever I do, it'd be much more fun with two. You're wasted on a coffee stall. Even if you don't have to cook.'

'Sandwiches, buns and pies, but I don't make the pies. They come from a bakery in Steenvoorde. And my sandwiches defy geometry. Or perhaps I should say redefine it! Do you really want me to come with you?'

'Lord, yes! Will you?'

'Any danger of a cuppa tea here, miss?' came a peevish voice.

Ronnie looked over her shoulder, distracted. 'Yes, coming right now!' she cried, then turned back to Laura. 'I've got to mind the shop until I'm relieved – Amy comes on duty at about five o'clock.'

'I'll come and fetch you then.'

'Have you got anywhere to stay tonight? Right, you'd better share my room. I've got digs at the Charles Hotel – you remember it?' Laura did. 'We'll go out for supper, have a night's sleep and start out tomorrow. How's that?'

'Perfect.'

'And if we don't find your major together . . . *Yes, I'm coming!* Dear Laura!' Ronnie bestowed one last squeeze of the hand and dashed back to her stall. Laura went back to Matilda, and decided to drive on into Ypres to see if anyone there wanted transport. She could easily keep busy until five o'clock.

The meeting of the Soldiers' Comforts Fund committee had finished, and Beattie and Mrs Oliver walked out together, to find that it was snowing, an unpleasant, sleety sort of snow, turning the world into disagreeable shades of grey and brown.

Mrs Oliver paused in the porch in dismay. 'What a nuisance,' she said.

71

'I have an umbrella,' Beattie said. 'If you walk home with me, you can telephone for a taxi from my house.'

'That seems like a good idea. Thank you. May I take your arm? It's easier to walk close together that way.' They set off, stepping carefully on the slippery pavement. Under the clouds it was as dark as dusk, though just after midday. 'What on earth are we going to do about Mrs Wilkes?' Mrs Oliver mused after a moment.

'There's little we can do,' Beattie said. 'One can't interfere between husband and wife. And the baby clearly isn't his. Even Mrs Wilkes doesn't pretend it is.'

'I'm afraid we may see more of that sort of thing as the men come back,' said Mrs Oliver. 'Wives have had to cope alone, and in some cases—'

'Yes.' Beattie stopped her. She didn't want to discuss the infidelity of women. 'He's within his rights to refuse to support it, I suppose.'

'But he's not within his rights to hit her.'

'Of course not. But I think the poor man is deranged by the war.'

'I'm afraid,' said Mrs Oliver went on, 'that even in cases where the man is not – er – unbalanced, he may find it difficult to fit in again. Especially if there's no work for him.'

'They get unemployment insurance,' Beattie said absently.

'For twenty-six weeks. It's a useful buffer. But work is more than wages to a man. It's what defines him. He has served his country: it will be hard for him to come back and find himself superfluous.'

Beattie looked out from under the umbrella, through the falling snow, grey-white against darker grey, muffling the world. 'Isn't it strange,' she said, 'how when the Armistice came, we thought the gates would fly open and we'd walk out into a sunlit world of peace? But nothing seems to have changed.'

'Yes. It's all still with us – war work, shortages, hardship.

The men aren't home. And everything seems so drab. And so difficult.'

'Regarding Mrs Wilkes,' Beattie said, after a moment. 'She mentioned something about her mother?'

'Yes – she's a widow. Lives in Harrow, I believe.'

'It might be best if we encouraged Mrs Wilkes to go and stay with her. And take the baby. We can provide her with the fare out of the Fund. And perhaps a few shillings to help with the budget until she finds work.'

'I suppose it's best,' Mrs Oliver sighed. 'Wilkes might soften his attitude, given time. And she can't stay where she is, that's for sure. The room in old Miss Plastow's cottage is too damp for a baby. And Wilkes knows where she is. If he were to go round there, poor little Miss Plastow might be frightened to death.'

CHAPTER SIX

As the motor pulled into the yard, Sadie's heart fell: realising that the long-expected visit of Captain Casimir of the Army Remount Service had arrived. She slipped the bridle off the chestnut, rubbed his forehead in farewell, and stepped out of the stable as Casimir climbed out of the car. He stood for a moment lighting a cigarette, looking comfortable in his heavy regulation greatcoat. Nailer, who had been ratting in the feed store, came to the door and gave one sharp bark of warning, which brought Mrs Cuthbert out of the tack room. She caught Sadie's eye across the yard and gave a curious little shrug that said, *Well, we shall find out now, at any rate.*

'You must have thought I'd forgotten about you,' he called cheerfully.

'We have ten horses ready for you,' said Mrs Cuthbert. 'More than ready, in fact. They're so highly schooled now, we're thinking of teaching them to read and write.'

'I'm sure they're a tribute to your methods. Could I see them? Perhaps you'd indulge me in a little display.'

Mary, Winifred and Sadie tacked up three of the horses and led them to the inner paddock, where straw had been laid round the perimeter against the mud. They mounted, and rode round at the walk, trot and canter. Sadie led them over the small brush jump in the centre a couple of times, and then down a row of poles she had got Podrick to erect, to replace the line of bottles, which tended to get broken. At the trot and then the canter, they wove in and out in a sinuous dance.

Casimir called out, 'Very good! That's enough, thanks – I've seen all I need.' When they rode over to him, he added, 'Let's get out of the cold and have a chat. Tack room? A cup of tea wouldn't come amiss.'

In the tack room, Casimir pulled off his fleece-lined leather gloves, doffed his cap and unbuttoned his greatcoat. The kettle was kept always simmering on the stove, and Sadie quickly made tea and poured five mugs, while Casimir lit another cigarette and chatted mildly to Mrs Cuthbert about the weather. When Mary and Winifred came in, having handed the horses to Podrick and the boys, he began.

'You must have been wondering what was happening. I'm sorry you've been left in the dark so long. There's been a lot to organise. It's something of a nightmare for the army, dealing with over a million horses and mules, most of them now surplus to requirement.' He frowned and said in a lower voice, almost as if to himself, 'I don't think sufficient thought was put into what the situation would be when the war ended.'

'I've been thinking,' Sadie said anxiously, 'that finding the transport to bring them back would be difficult, when you must need the ships to transport the men.'

Casimir looked as though he'd have preferred her not to think so clearly. 'Only those horses actually owned by officers are guaranteed to be brought back,' he said. 'By this stage of the war, there aren't many of those.'

The girls exchanged a look. Mary braved the question. 'What's going to happen to the rest?'

'Oh, it isn't as bad as you might fear. The heavy horses and most of the mules will be sold to the farmers. There will be a big demand once people return to their land. And carters and traders will want vanners once things return to normal. We've held one or two sales already. We don't get much of a price, with the country so impoverished by war, but it's better than nothing. And at least we don't have to go on feeding them.'

'John – Major Courcy thought the Horse Hospital at Le Touquet might be a centre for dispersing the horses,' Sadie ventured.

'Yes, he was right. They have extensive paddocks. We collect them all together in depots as the units demobilise, and sort them out. The army will need to retain about twenty-five thousand horses, so they'll be shipped home as transport becomes available. And the Indian Army will want remounts – several thousand. Obviously, we'll pick out the best, the youngest and healthiest. And we plan to sell a large number here. There'll be auctions held in different parts of the country. That's where you come in.' He turned his gaze to Mrs Cuthbert.

'Explain,' she said.

'When we bring the horses home, we'll have to house them immediately in depots, where they'll be rested, fed and assessed. We'd like you to be one of the depots. Get them back into condition, sort out any little faults they may have picked up, get them ready to be sold.'

'How long would we have, to work on them?' Mrs Cuthbert asked.

'It would vary, depending on the dates of the sales that are set up, but three or four weeks, probably. I don't need you to school them up to the standard I've seen this morning,' he added, with a smile. 'Just make sure they're steady, and quiet to handle, tack and ride.'

'And what will happen to the ones we have here now?'

'If they're all like the three I saw, they're too good to go into auction. I will recommend they go to the Indian Army. The commissioners set very high standards, even for troopers' horses, and the officers are all mad keen on polo. I shall make arrangements for them to be picked up in the next day or two, and then you can expect a batch of horses from France within the week – if you decide you want to stay with us.'

Mrs Cuthbert hardly needed to consult the young women. A glance around was sufficient to gather their eager looks and nods. Sadie spoke for them all when she said, 'I'm so relieved. I was afraid you'd come to disband us.'

'On the contrary. There's still a lot to do. The service is talking about selling sixty thousand or so here in England, and it will take months to process them. We can probably keep you busy until the end of the year, if that's what you want.'

Casimir and Mrs Cuthbert talked about practicalities, such as payment of overheads, delivery of fodder, shoeing, veterinary visits and so on, and Sadie lapsed into thought. John Courcy's last letter reported that he had caught the Spanish flu. He had written from hospital, having been there a week, saying that the worst was over but that he would be another week recovering. He told her not to worry, and she tried not to. It was good to know that her job was safe for the time being, and she didn't have that to worry about as well. When John came back, she supposed it would take time before they could marry – he would have to get work and find somewhere for them to live – so she was glad she would have something worthwhile to occupy her.

At last Casimir crushed out his latest cigarette and prepared to leave. 'Are there any more questions, while I'm here?'

It was Mrs Cuthbert he asked, but it was Sadie who spoke, having been assailed at the last moment by an unwelcome thought.

'What happens to the others?' she said.

'The other what?' Casimir asked, busy with his buttons.

'Horses. You said you'd pick out the youngest and healthiest to bring back. What will happen to the rest?'

He looked at her for a long moment before answering. 'Those that are too old or weak to sell will have to be destroyed, I'm afraid.'

'But – you're talking about thousands and thousands!'

'Most will go for horsemeat. There's a desperate food shortage over there. Manes and tails – horsehair fetches a good price in furniture making. Hides, too. Bones and hoofs for fertiliser. So they won't be wasted.'

Sadie knew that beside her, Winifred was holding back tears. Mary showed nothing in her face, and Sadie hoped she was the same.

Animals were slaughtered every day for food and skins: you couldn't be sentimental. But horses were different. She didn't know why, but they were. There was a special spiritual bond between man and horse. And she knew, because John had spoken of it, how deeply the Tommies became attached to the horses and mules that shared their dangers and hardships during the war, that served and trusted them. There would be grief and anger that no better reward came to their equine friends than oblivion.

'I understand,' she said, and was proud that there was no wobble in her voice.

Casimir gave her a kindly look. 'It seems harsh, I know, but there's no other way.'

Sadie nodded. She did know. It was not possible to give tens of thousands of worn-out horses a happy retirement.

She gathered Mary and Winifred with a look and said, 'We'd better get on. We still have six to exercise, and it looks as though it's going to snow again.'

The snow that came down on Le Cateau had nothing sleety about it. Each flake was perfect, soft, and cold, and fell with deadly intent, blanketing the land, silently filling the dykes and drains, piling on roofs, obliterating landmarks, as though intending to leave nothing to know the world by – nothing but unbroken whiteness.

There was no more flying, and fewer airmen to do it. The squadron had diminished daily, like a village struck by plague. The skilled mechanics, who had kept the machines airborne and had been there from the start, had departed for Blighty, wanted for important work. Men and NCOs had left in trucks for demobilisation camps. Officers had gone off in ones and twos, despondent, philosophical and eager by turns. Equipment and tools had been recalled into Stores, and now, finally, in mid-February, the aeroplanes were taken away. Their beloved SEs were to go to the depot to be broken up; the four Camels were to be dismantled and shipped in crates back to the manufacturer. What he would do with them was unknown.

The mess was reduced to three – Major Considine, Captain Hunter, and Lieutenant Foley, cared for by one orderly and one cook. The mess dining tent where twenty-six had made noise and fun round the big table was too empty, too cold, too draughty, so they dined at a small table in the mess hut, knocking elbows and knees, but at least not haunted by the missing faces – those who had departed for Blighty and those who had departed this life, whose portion was now a rectangle of cold French clay.

One of the three despatch motor-bicycles had been left to them and Foley went out on it, braving the elements, on trips to revisit places he had seen and strafed from the sky, or just for something to do. The other two went in fear of saying a premature goodbye to him. They imagined him skidding on the icy roads and diving head first into a tree.

William sat on the edge of Considine's desk one afternoon, while Considine lounged in his chair, tipping it back onto two legs, waiting for Foley to come back, 'Dead or alive,' as he said laconically.

'What are you going to do when you get home?' William asked, staring out at the blank landscape.

'Oh, nothing just at first. Lie around, enjoy the luxury, let my family pet me. Not for myself, you understand,' he added, 'but because they've been longing to do it for three years, and it's only fair now to let them have their turn. What about you?'

'Same I suppose. Though I'm not sure my mother's really the petting sort. You'll be getting married, I suppose?'

'I don't know. I may do, if I meet the right girl.'

'But what about your fiancée?' William said, puzzled, indicating the framed photograph that lived on Considine's desk, of a handsome, dark-haired young woman.

Considine laughed. 'Oh, Lord, no! I haven't got a fiancée. That's my sister, Eva. She's a topping girl. There's just the two of us.'

'There's six of us,' William said, without thinking. 'I have two sisters and three brothers.'

'That must be nice. Especially the sisters.'

'I suppose so. I always got on with Sadie – she's next to me in age. My older sister Diana was always . . . Well, she's a Beauty, so it was different. But I can't imagine either of them giving me their picture to take with me to the war.'

'Eva and I have always been close. I'm looking forward to seeing her again.'

'But what will you do when you've finished with the petting?' William asked.

'Hang around at Brooklands, I expect,' said Considine. 'My family's place is at Weybridge, so Brooklands is practically in our back garden. That's what got me interested in aeroplanes in the first place. Anyway, that's the place to be. There are bound to be all sorts of flying types coming and going, and if there's any chance of picking up a job, it's there. What will you do?'

'Well, of course I'd like a flying job, if it's at all possible,' William began.

'I say, look here,' Considine said, straightening up so that the front legs of his chair came down with a crash, 'why don't you come and stay at our place? Then we could go and lurk together – join forces, make 'em notice us!'

'I'd love to,' William said, 'but what would your people think?'

'Oh, they'd love to have you,' Considine said airily. 'Don't worry about that. Also, I've got a 1910 Maxwell E at home. She's garaged and up on blocks at the moment, but she's a wonderful beast. An American brought her over, used to race her at Brooklands, and when he went back, he didn't want the trouble of shipping her home, so my father bought her for me as a birthday present. Of course, the race track's been closed to motors since the government requisitioned the site, but we'll find somewhere to have some fun with her. Do say you'll come! You could meet Eva,' he added, as though it were the greatest treat.

'Of course I'll come,' William said. 'Thanks awfully.'

'That's settled, then,' said Considine. He looked at his watch. 'I hope Foley's not going to be much longer. I want my pre-dinner drink. Do you think we ought to start without him?'

William was not a great drinker, but he was willing to go along with his CO. 'Why not?'

'Press the tit, then,' said Considine; and when the orderly appeared, he said, 'Two pink gins, Bentley. Large ones.'

'Oh, just a beer for me,' William demurred.

Considine grinned. 'You heard the man, Bentley. Two large pink gins for me, and a glass of beer for Captain Hunter.'

David was angry. It was bad enough that Antonia had gone off to her father's wedding, making it clear she didn't want him to accompany her, taking Ethel and leaving him to the clumsy ministrations of the housemaids. No one but Ethel knew how to lay out his things properly in the morning. No one but Antonia could massage his leg. And who was there to keep him company, to talk to him, amuse him, ask him how his day had gone? His mother and Sadie were too preoccupied with their own selfish concerns, and Peter was just a child. He had enough of children anyway, with the succession of little boys who came to him for tutoring and cramming.

And that was another thing: it was Antonia who kept his diary, reminded him each morning of what he had to be doing that day. It was she who chose his neckties. She made sure his fresh shirts were ironed the way he liked them. She made sure his breakfast eggs were not too runny or too hard. She had abandoned all these duties to go off on a pleasure jaunt, and then had had the gall to write and say she was staying on in Hampshire while her father went on a honeymoon tour with his new wife. At his age! It was unseemly. Antonia should not have encouraged them.

Eventually anger gave way to self-pity. Who cared for him? No one! His life was ruined, he was useless and forgotten. He had fought for his country – it wasn't his fault he had been wounded before he could kill a single German. He had suffered, no one knew how much! Now he had a game leg, and had to earn his living as a pedagogue, a damned dominie. And it wasn't even a living. He was a charity case. A beggar.

From there it was a short step to remembering that awful evening when she had blurted out in front of everyone that she was pregnant, and he had . . . He had . . .

Yes, why had he reacted like that? He went cold all over, remembering his words, his rage, Antonia's white face as she bore the tirade. What had come over him? The announcement of a pregnancy ought to be a joyful thing. Why had he minded that she had not told him first? Everyone was delighted. He should have been delighted. Instead, he had lashed out at her so cruelly that she had felt forced to run away from him and hide at her father's house.

The horrible, shameful thing was that at the time, he had enjoyed it. He had been filled with a sort of ecstasy of anger, a joy in having power over another human being when he had so little over his own life. He remembered the surge of elation through his body as he beat her down verbally. Oh, God! What had he become? He so often felt angry these days. What might he do next? He regarded himself with loathing, and with fear. Was he losing control? Was he losing his mind?

Antonia. She had gone. It felt as though she had moved out. Places in their bedroom where her little things had always lain unnoticed by him were bare. The scent of her had faded from their rooms. Perhaps . . . perhaps she would never come back. Well, why would she? He couldn't support her. He was useless as a husband. If she had to live as a dependant, it might as well be in her father's house. If she didn't come back, it might be better all round, a solution. He should never have married her.

He thought then of Sophie, his first love, who had jilted him for another man when it was clear he would never be whole again. He thought of her with the wistfulness of unattainability. Beautiful Sophie: another man's wife now. Sophie, sister of his best friend Jumbo.

He wished Jumbo were here, but Jumbo had fallen at Cambrai in 1917. Of course, he and Jumbo had never talked about matters of the heart. But Jumbo would have listened. He tried to imagine the conversation, to project what Jumbo would say in reply. He saw Jumbo's rather round brown eyes open in faint surprise, heard his gruff, rumbling voice: 'You must get her back. Dear chap, you must write to her.' Yes, that was what Jumbo would say. He was a simple soul: it would appear simple to him.

Perhaps it was simple. Did he think about things too much? When you were tied by the leg, there wasn't much to do but think. Nula would have said, *It does no good to brood.* Yes, and Nula would tell him to write to Antonia, too. *Apologise like a man,* she would say, *and she'll forgive you.* Other people's problems were simple. It was when you lived inside them you saw the complexities.

What if he wrote to Antonia and she didn't forgive him? What if she really had gone, and never came back?

He got up, with the restless, jerky movement of a man trying to escape his own thoughts, and limped downstairs.

His mother was in the morning-room, reading a letter. She didn't look up as he came in, and his irritation rose again. His own mother didn't care enough to acknowledge his presence!

'Really, Mother,' he said, 'you must get some more staff. My sitting-room fire's only just been lit, and the room won't warm up properly before my first pupil arrives.' Now his mother looked up, but with a vague expression, as though she hadn't properly listened. 'Ethel always does it first thing, but now she's away it gets forgotten.'

'I'll speak to Ada,' Beattie said absently. 'The girls have a lot to do.'

He noticed at last that she was not her usual self. 'Is something wrong?' he asked belatedly. He looked at the letter. 'Not bad news?' He quailed. 'It's not Father?'

'It's from your aunt Addie,' Beattie said. 'Your uncle John has died.'

Beattie's sister in Ireland had written that her husband had never really been the same since the Easter uprising in 1916.

It's been hard on all of us [she wrote], *wondering all the time who you can trust. Every time there's a knock on the door you wonder if armed men are going to burst in and*

84

shoot you. Or if a bomb's going to be thrown through the window. Every little sound at night makes you jump. But it was hardest of all on my poor man, because he worked so hard for our people, and always tried to be fair, and took their side if they were treated unjustly. And then to have them turn against us! It broke his heart. He'd been unwell for some time, and that evening he collapsed over dinner, and the next day he was gone. Heart, the doctor said. He said at least it was quick, but he didn't know that Jock's been dying these two years. Beattie, I don't know what to do with myself. I thought the boys would come back as soon as the war was over, but of course they were enlisted so they had to go back to the States in the first place. I've cabled them the news, and written to ask them when they're coming. I've had to have the funeral without them. It was a sad affair, but quite a lot of the villagers came and stood outside the church, which I suppose was their way of saying they knew he was a good man, because of course they couldn't come into the church, being Catholics.

There was a silence, after Beattie had told him what she knew. She was thinking of her sister, and how they had been girls together in Dublin, going to dances, poring together over dance cards, pressing flowers from posies left by admirers, dreaming of love and marriage and their future lives. They could never have imagined how things would turn out.

'I suppose,' she said aloud, 'we'll always divide our lives from now on into "before the war "and "after the war". They're like two different countries.'

It didn't matter that David did not know the thought process that had led to that statement. It would make enough sense to him. He brooded over his own problems. She glanced at him, coming out of her thoughts to see him clearly for the first time that morning. It hurt her heart that he looked so unhappy.

'David, what's happening with Antonia. When is she coming back?'

He didn't want to answer. 'You know she was staying while they had the honeymoon.'

'But that was only supposed to be three weeks. They were coming back on the ninth of February, weren't they? How long is she going to stay there?'

'I don't know. Does it matter?' he said harshly.

Did it? Beattie wondered. Antonia's new stepmother would make sure she was looked after, wouldn't she? Except that the former Mrs Turnberry had never had children. And Mr Weston, though he loved his daughter, would not know what to do for her.

'You must miss her,' she said. 'And Marcus. He should be here, with you. With us.'

David looked up, seeing a way out. 'You must miss him too, your grandson.'

'Of course I do. Little children change almost day by day. The things you miss will never come again.'

'Perhaps I should write to her, tell her we want her to come home,' he said neutrally.

Beattie considered him carefully. She guessed there had been a quarrel, though what it could have been about she had no idea. He had hardly spoken about Antonia since she had gone away. But there was something in the way he would not meet her eye that suggested he wanted her back now but was too ashamed to say so. He needed to be helped along; and she was his mother. Who better to help him?

'Perhaps you should go down to Hampshire. It would be polite to pay a wedding visit to her father and his new wife. I'm sure they'd take it kindly. Then you could accompany her on the journey home. She ought not to travel alone in her condition.'

'You're right,' David said. 'Not that I'd be much use in an emergency—'

86

'David, you're to stop talking like that,' Beattie said sharply. 'You walk with a stick, that's all. You're still a man. And you're her husband.'

'I suppose if there were robbers, I could hit them with my stick,' he said. It was supposed to be a joke, but neither of them found it funny.

'I must write to your aunt,' Beattie said, turning away.

CHAPTER SEVEN

Mr Weston had been shut in his study for over an hour with a particularly disturbed soldier. He saw the lad off, went looking for female comfort, and found his daughter in the drawing-room, writing at the table in the window. She looked up, anticipated his enquiry, and said, 'Yvonne took over in the club. She said I should rest.'

'Quite right,' he said, crossing the room to her, noting that she had settled down to calling his new wife by her first name. 'What's that you're writing?' He looked over her shoulder. '*The Adventures of Ben, the Circus Pony?*'

'I was tidying drawers in my old room and came across the manuscript. Don't you remember? I was writing it before I was married.'

'I remember,' he said.

'And your publisher said that, after the war, he might be able to publish it?'

'He said there was a growing demand for children's literature.'

'I'm not sure about literature,' Antonia said, 'but I think I can tell a story. If Marcus were a little older, I could try it out on him.'

'Well, it's a nice, restful occupation for someone with swollen ankles.'

She laughed. 'You noticed.'

'I don't pretend to know much about *enceinte* ladies, but

I remember your mother having to put her feet up on a footstall. Though, of course, in those days the condition was never mentioned. Men were supposed to pretend ignorance of the process.'

'I remember my mother telling me the stork left me under a gooseberry bush.'

'That would have been your nanny, not your mother. Eleanor would never have been so vulgar.' His eyes lit on an envelope on the table, and he recognised the hand. The situation, he felt, was too serious for diffidence. 'You've had a letter?' he asked.

'It came while you were in your study,' Antonia said. 'You can read it if you like. It's good, I think.'

The letter, Mr Weston thought, seemed to have been very carefully constructed: he sensed the ghostly presence of many drafts, torn up. David was proposing a visit of congratulation, in compliment to the new Mrs Weston, and hoped it would be acceptable. Unless Antonia sent a telegram to the contrary, he would arrive the next day, and propose himself for an overnight stay. 'And then, if you feel your visit there has been long enough, I can escort you home the next day.'

He hadn't, Mr Weston noted, left much time for deliberation. Neither did he actually say he wanted her to come home. But it was a step in the right direction. 'Yes, it's good,' he said. 'And it's behaving as he should, to call on Yvonne. Do you want him to come?'

'Oh, yes!' Antonia said, before she could stop herself, then added, in a lower voice, 'I miss him so much, Daddy.'

'Then I think you should send him a telegram to say his visit would be most welcome, to all of us. So that he should be in no doubt.'

'Yes, I'll do that,' she said. 'Thank you. You're so kind to me.'

He put his hand on her shoulder. 'Who has more right?

How are the ankles? Shall we go and find my grandson and see if he wants to play?'

The telegram left David no way of changing his mind, and he wondered if that had been its purpose. He suspected Antonia's father was behind it – but he didn't want to change his mind anyway. He had braced himself for the confrontation.

At least Long Marcham was well served with trains, because of the nearby army camp, so he had only one change, in London. There was no one waiting for him at the station, but he hadn't told them what time to expect him. There was only one taxi. Two other passengers hurrying to claim it saw his stick, and stood aside for him. He thanked them, but with a wry mouth. That was what he had become – someone strangers pitied.

It was the furthest he'd been in a long time, and even sitting still wore him out when it was in a poorly heated railway carriage. The grey afternoon was subsiding into dusk by the time the taxi pulled up outside the square red house. Mr Weston's man Baxter came out at once to carry his bag. David manipulated his stiff limbs with stiffer pride, concentrating on his feet in case the path should be frost-slippery, so he did not see, until he reached the lighted rectangle of the doorway, that Antonia was there, waiting for him, with an uncertain smile. He stepped straight up to her, put his arms around her, and kissed her, never mind that Baxter was watching.

The hard swelling of the baby inside her pressed between them, startling him. How much it had grown in the time she had been away! Into her ear, he whispered, 'I'm sorry,' and he felt her melt against him. He was surprised at how easy reconciliation was. He had expected huge barriers to overcome, but it seemed they had been in his mind.

She released him and stepped back to let him come in.

'You must be longing for some tea. Come into the drawing-room. There's a good fire.'

Baxter relieved him of coat, hat and gloves, and he followed the slim back of his wife (*that* view hadn't changed) into the drawing-room, trying not to hobble as his cold limbs rebelled against a day's inaction. Mr Weston and the new Mrs Weston, seated either side of the leaping fire, rose as he entered.

'Come and take this chair,' Mr Weston said. 'You must be chilled right through. Yvonne, my dear, ring for the tea.'

And moments later, when Mrs Bates and Iris came in with the laden trays of a lavish tea, they were followed by the trim, familiar shape of Ethel, in her ribboned cap, leading by the hand the unfamiliar shape of his son *walking*. It was a bow-legged and unsteady walk, and lasted only halfway across the room before he descended with a bump onto his well-padded rear. David remembered what his mother had said, that babies changed every day and that what you missed never came again.

'He's walking,' he said aloud. He had missed his son's first step.

'Yes, sir,' said Ethel. 'Not very well yet, but he's that proud of himself, all-fours is not good enough now for Master Marcus.'

He held out his arms, and Ethel scooped the baby up and brought him to his father. Marcus stood on his lap, bending and flexing his remarkably muscular young legs, and studying his father's features with the forensic attention of an explorer presented with unusual fauna. And then his face bloomed into a welcoming grin, he grabbed at David's nose and said, 'Da!'

'Little man!' David said, as the baby bounced cheerfully. He had a great surge of feeling that was half sorrow. But it was so much better than anger.

Sadie had retired to the hayloft for privacy to read John's letter. It had arrived that morning, but she hadn't had a

91

chance to open it yet. It was short, one page, but she was used to that. Just to hold the paper he had held and written on was like reattaching herself to life. He apologised for the delay in replying to her last: they were overwhelmed with work. He was back at his post after his illness, but the dreadful weather was making things more difficult, and the Spanish flu was now laying his assistants low.

I am very glad you have had good news about your own work [he went on]. *I know how important it is to you. And it pleases me to know that some of the animals we send over might end up with you. We have sad doings here every day, when the Tommies leave their horses to go home. One fellow being parted from a pair of mules, Nancy and Nellie, wept into their manes like a baby, and I swear the mules were ready to cry too. They had been together three years, since the beginning of the Somme campaign. We heard of one Australian officer who shot his horse, fearing it would be sold to a French farmer who would overwork it. I have no word yet when I shall be discharged. The work seems never ending and the process here seems likely to go on for many months yet, but I assume I shall be due for leave at some point. Then be sure I shall hurry with all possible speed to your side, my dearest Sadie.*

There were two xs at the bottom of the page below his scrawl of a signature, and she put her lips to them, hoping he might have done the same, then felt like an idiot. A veterinary surgeon would not be so foolishly sentimental.

She heard voices below, Mrs Cuthbert's and another woman's, and crawled through the hay to look out of the hatch. The visitor was Dame Barbara Woodville, head of the local Red Cross, a handsome, grey-haired woman with a military uprightness of carriage. Sadie didn't want to be disturbed yet, and pulled her head back in; but as the women

92

stopped just below to talk, she couldn't help overhearing them.

'. . . rather sad news,' Dame Barbara was saying. 'Evadne Beamish has died. Did you know her?'

'Only by name, but of course I know her sister, Honoria Fitzgerald. And her son paid us a visit here recently. Such a nice young man,' said Mrs Cuthbert.

'Oh, yes, Adolphus,' said Dame Barbara.

Sam, Sadie corrected in her head. *He likes to be known as Sam.* So his mother had died. How sad! He had called at The Elms before he left to go home, telling Sadie he had been summoned as his mother had taken a turn for the worse. Evidently, he had got back just in time to say goodbye. She felt very sorry for him.

'I went to school with both of the Sambourne girls,' Dame Barbara was saying, 'though it was Evadne I knew better. She was the beauty, and the Sambournes expected her to make a good marriage. We thought at one time she might marry my brother – Dick actually offered for her – but in the end it was a love match. Her parents weren't pleased, because Arthur Beamish was in trade. Some kind of engineering company.'

'I've heard of Beamish bicycles,' said Mrs Cuthbert. 'Would that be it?'

'Yes, I think so. Bicycles and sewing-machines – and during the war he branched out into aeroplane parts, so he's done very well. They have a fine house at Aylesbury. But the Sambournes were old-fashioned: to them, trade was trade. They were more pleased, I think, when Honoria married that wretched Dr Fitzgerald, with nothing but his stipend, and quite a lot older than her. *They* had no children, and Evadne had only the one. And now she's dead, so young. Liver disease, I believe. It's tragic.'

'At least Adolphus survived the war.'

'Yes, and he can take over his father's business. I dare say

93

Arthur will want to retire soon. He adored poor Evadne. Her death will knock him for six, I'm afraid. Yes, Dolly will take over the business – it's just a shame he can't carry on the Sambourne name. It's an ancient one, you know. The old Sambournes were very unhappy that they only had daughters.'

'Yes, it's— Oh, don't step backwards! There's a rather nasty puddle just behind you.'

'Thank you. I see it. Well, I mustn't keep you talking. You must be busy – I know I am.'

'Yes, what did you come for, Barbara dear? If it's a donation . . .'

'No, actually I came to see Miss Hunter. Is she here?'

'She's somewhere about. Why don't you come into the tack room where it's warm, and I'll get one of the girls to find her?'

Sadie wriggled backwards and slithered down the ladder quickly, so as not to be found eavesdropping. She was picking hay off her clothes and out of her hair to tidy herself when Winifred found her. 'Mrs Cuthbert wants you in the tack room,' she said. 'There's a lady with her, in a proper army greatcoat, except there's a red cross sewn on the sleeves. I wish I had one – it's so cold.' She observed Sadie's efforts at her toilette dispassionately. 'You've got a bit of manure on your nose,' she warned.

Dame Barbara was standing by the stove when Sadie went in, a tin mug of tea in her hand. She looked very aristocratic. Sadie wondered who her brother was, that Sam Beamish's mother had rejected for a factory owner she loved.

'Miss Hunter,' said Dame Barbara, and gave her a very raking inspection. Her eyes were blue and frosty, but she had a mouth made for smiling – an interesting contradiction.

'You wanted to see me, ma'am?'

'Yes, I have a favour to ask – and that includes you, Annabel, because you'll have to manage without her for a couple of days.'

'If it's in a good cause . . .' said Mrs Cuthbert.

'Oh, very. You see, Miss Hunter, there's a lot of this dreadful Spanish flu on the Continent, and the men are spreading it among themselves in the demobilisation camps. Then they bring it home to England. What we *don't* want, if we can help it, is to have it spread to the wounded, just when they're below par and vulnerable. So we want to create isolation hospitals and keep all the flu and fever cases together. Now, Mount Olive hospital—'

'Used to be a fever hospital,' Sadie anticipated.

'Just so. It's set apart, and on good high ground with lots of fresh air all round it. It's just what's needed, but it means moving out the present occupants.'

'I see, ma'am. Where to?'

'Mostly to Dene Park. So many of *their* bed cases have recovered and gone home that they have spare capacity. Lady Wroughton has kindly said she'll make more space available if needed, though I'm hopeful we can manage without any more disruption. So what I need you for, Miss Hunter, if you're willing, is to drive an ambulance and help ferry the men over. It will probably take a couple of days.'

'Of course I'll do it,' Sadie said.

'You don't need my permission,' said Mrs Cuthbert. 'We're not busy here, until the new batch of horses comes in.'

'Thank you. We're so short of drivers. Such a lot of girls in the VAD and the WVR threw off their uniforms the moment peace was declared. I don't suppose I could tempt you, Annabel . . .?'

'I don't mind volunteering my car, if there are walking cases. I couldn't drive an ambulance.'

Antonia's old room, where she had been sleeping, had only a narrow single bed, so a guest room had been prepared for David. The evening had been conducted politely and pleasantly, and after dinner, David and Mr Weston had even got into a conversation reminiscent of their old, lively discussions. David had forgotten how much he missed the intellectual stimulation. As he talked more freely, Mr Weston seemed to warm to him; Mrs Weston and Antonia exchanged looks of approval across the room.

But now the awkwardness was back. As Antonia checked that he had everything he needed, David stood halfway between the door and the bed, not knowing what to say.

At last she could fiddle about no longer, and turned to him to say, 'Well, then, I'll leave you to sleep. You must be tired.'

'No, not really. Well, yes, a little. You must be, too. Being . . .' He made a round gesture to indicate her pregnancy.

He looked so young in his uncertainty. 'Do you need help with buttons, or anything?' she asked kindly.

'Oh – yes, you might do my collar stud for me.'

She stepped close, and he lifted his chin for her. She removed the stud, then without asking tackled his cuff links. He looked down at her curly hair, smelled the verbena soap she washed it with, felt the warmth coming off her body. His body stirred. It was a long time since—

She looked up, and he felt himself colour.

'David,' she said.

Just that; but it broke a dam. 'I'm so sorry,' he said. 'I don't know why I said those things. I didn't mean it. I hated it when you went away.'

'Did you?' She said it neutrally.

'I was so angry,' he said, bewildered. 'I don't know why. I'm angry such a lot of the time, and I don't know why.'

'It's the war,' she said. 'It changed people. It's changed everything.'

'Not you,' he said. 'You're just the same.'

'Is that a good thing?' He looked as if he didn't understand the question. 'I know—' she began, and stopped, on the brink of something that had never been said, perhaps never

96

should be said. 'When you married me –' she stopped again '– you didn't really love me,' she finished, and felt suddenly breathless, as though she had gasped icy air.

'What do you say?' He seemed genuinely surprised and, underneath, apprehensive, as though footsteps were moving towards his hiding place.

'Not the way you loved Sophie.'

And she waited. In her womb, the baby stirred, and she felt a small foot pressing against her flesh from the inside – surely the strangest thing any human being ever experienced. And a man could never know it. She felt huge pity for men, all men, locked in their masculinity and the demands it made on them, the need to strive, the need to fight, the need to overmaster. It must, she felt, be exhausting, compared with the slow and gentle gestation of a new life.

As David felt around blindly for words, thoughts rushed through his head with frightening lucidity. She was right, of course. He had loved Sophie with a romantic passion he had never felt for Antonia. He had married her on a whim, and out of need. There had been kindness and affection between them, though not so much of that from his side lately, in all honesty. He had failed her again and again, and had told himself in his arrogance and anger that it was *she* who had failed *him* – by not being Sophie.

And where did that leave them? What could he say to her that was true, and fair, and would sustain her? Because – he realised it in that split second – he did not want to lose her. He saw, like a landscape revealed for an instant by lightning, how bleak his life at home would be without her. He wanted her to come back, but he wanted her to be happy, too. He truly did. And with that realisation, relief came to him, and words.

'Sophie was just a boy's madness. A dream. Not real. You're my wife, and I want you to come home. I know I often make you unhappy. I don't mean to, and I'm sorry for it. I'll try harder in future – if only you'll come home.'

'Of course I will,' she said. 'I always meant to. It was just . . .' A long pause. 'I thought you didn't really want me to.'

He had used up all the good words. So he took her into his arms and held her close; and felt an extraordinary thud against his stomach. Startled he pushed her back a little and looked down, and said, 'What was that?'

She smiled up at him, and said, 'That was Hunter minimus. Here, give me your hand.' She took his reluctant large hand and laid it over her swollen belly, and held it in place when he tried to pull it away.

'It that him kicking you?' he asked in wonder.

'That's him kicking,' she said.

'Oh my God!' Another thud. 'Does it hurt?'

'No!' She laughed.

'He's strong,' David said. 'He's going to be a sportsman.'

'Of course he is,' she said. 'An athlete and a rugby player and a concert pianist and a great philosopher, and probably prime minister as well. But mostly he's your son.'

'My son,' he said. He pulled her close again.

She rested her face on his chest, and felt her great love for him. And relief.

During the day the snow turned to slush, and the slush froze overnight, which made driving conditions treacherous, especially as Mount Olive was situated at the top of a steep hill. The wounded had to be moved slowly and carefully, and with a limited number of ambulances, the whole process took the rest of the week.

On the 1st of March, Sadie was standing by the cab of the ambulance, stretching her arms and shoulders – the heavy steering was heavier still at low speeds – while the orderlies moved the latest of her wounded across the gravel towards the main door of Dene Park. Nailer, who had come with her for the ride, had jumped down as soon as she opened the door, and was busily marking bushes, patches of grass and the pedestals of urns.

There were no flowers in the latter. Everything in sight was grey, dirty-white and brown, and the house, which had been designed to overawe, looked grim in its early Georgian starkness, its many windows seeming to glare down forbiddingly at the ant-like activity it was forced to endure in these degenerate days.

Sadie glanced down at herself, and thought how well she fitted in. Her old brown coat was too short for her now, showing three inches of navy serge skirt above her scuffed, heavy boots. She had thick grey woollen gloves, a grey woollen scarf wound several times around her neck, and a dowdy brown felt hat, made shapeless by being pulled down hard over her ears against the wind. Just for a moment, her soul sickened; and as she longed for spring to bring flowers and sunshine, she also longed, just for once, to wear something pretty and go dancing, to be frivolous and act like a girl. She had never cared for those things before the war, when there had been the prospect of them. At sixteen, she could afford to despise them. Now, after almost five years of hard work and drabness, she realised she had probably missed her chance. The world had changed; and she was twenty-one – too old.

Someone came out from the great door and, though soberly dressed, seemed like a ray of sunshine. Diana's golden hair gleamed under a smart black hat with cock feathers on it. Her coat had a fur collar and cuffs, and nothing could dim her beauty. Sadie called to her, waving, and Diana came across. Nailer abandoned the latest plinth, from which a rather chipped Greek god wearing nothing but a large leaf smirked down at him, and raced to greet her. 'Nailer, no!' Sadie called: Diana had never liked him, and he had muddy paws, plainly destined for her nice black coat. For a wonder,

Diana only made a smart sidestep, and reached down to pat the wiry bullet head with her leather-gloved hand, pushing him backwards in the same movement.

'It's all right,' she said to Sadie. 'This is only an old thing.'

Sadie grabbed Nailer, urged him into the cab and slammed the door. 'It's good to see you,' she told her sister. 'How are you? How is everything?'

'It's rather a chore, fitting in all the new boys, but it's good to be busy.' Diana said. She looked Sadie over with a critical eye. 'I was hoping to see you. It's been such ages. Any word from Father?'

'Just the usual – that he's terribly busy and doesn't know when he'll be home. But we heard from William yesterday. He's been moved to a camp near Dover, and he'll be home next week on demob leave.'

'Oh, that's good,' Diana said vaguely. She had never been close to William as Sadie had. 'Are David and Antonia back?'

'Yes, and I'm glad. The house seemed awfully empty without them. But poor Antonia seems to be coming down with a cold.'

'That must be hard for her, in her condition,' Diana said.

'Yes, and Ethel is so fierce and protective, she's trying to keep her away from Marcus, in case he catches it,' Sadie said. 'Such a tussle of wills!'

'What about you? Are you going to go on playing with your horses?' Diana asked, recoiling slightly as Nailer shoved his head through the open cab window, as though he planned to jump out.

From the tone, Sadie decided her sister wasn't meaning to be hurtful or dismissive. 'Yes, for quite a while, as far as we can gather. I'm pleased. As you say, it's good to keep busy.'

'But now the war's over, you ought to start thinking of other things as well.'

100

'*Now the war is over, we're going to live in Dover,*' Sadie sang. 'What other things?' she asked.

Diana was giving her that inspecting look again. 'I've had you on my mind quite a bit recently. Once things get back to normal, I want to take you under my wing and make sure you have a proper start – parties and dances and so on. I always meant to. When I got engaged to Charles, we talked about it. But the war rather got in the way.'

'I'm too old for that now,' Sadie said in alarm.

'There's no reason you shouldn't have some days in London when the Season starts,' Diana said firmly. 'We'll stay in Park Place and I'll make sure you meet the right men.'

'I don't want to be paraded like a horse at Tattersalls.'

'Horses again!' Diana said. 'Is that all you think about?'

'Not *all* . . .'

'I want to see you well married. It's the least I can do for my family. I have all this . . .' she waved her hand around to indicate the estate '. . . and there will be lots of really nice young men coming back and ready to look for a suitable wife.'

'I'm hardly suitable,' Sadie objected. Diana didn't know about John Courcy – and, of course, if she had known, would not think *him* suitable. Sadie meant to keep him a secret until he was safely home and all was irreversibly settled.

'You're *my* sister,' Diana said superbly. 'And you're really quite pretty. With the right clothes – don't worry about them. I'll see to everything. And manners are much freer than before the war. You'll fit in quite well.'

Nailer, bored with all the talking, nudged the back of Sadie's head with his hard muzzle, then nibbled experimentally at the rim of her hat. Sadie swatted him away. 'I'm quite happy as I am. You needn't have me on your conscience.'

Diana looked away at the misty, weeping horizon. 'You may be happy, but you never think of me, all alone here in

101

this big house. You never think that *I* might want a bit of company.'

Sadie was affected. Diana's life, she thought, must be lonely, for all she had servants surrounding her. It hadn't occurred to her that she might miss her only sister. She said, in a softened tone, 'I was actually thinking just now about dancing. It would be nice to have a little fun in London with you. Thank you for asking.'

Diana was satisfied, having won the point. 'Next month, when the Season starts properly. I'll let you know when the invitations start to come in.'

'But please don't try to pair me off with suitable men,' Sadie added. 'I'm not interested.'

Diana only smiled serenely. She thought she wasn't interested. But she would be. Diana would see to it.

CHAPTER EIGHT

William's homecoming was not as he had expected. He'd thought of a returning hero's welcome: laughter, exclamations, hugs. He had seen himself standing before the fireplace, telling his adventures to a rapt circle. There would be fine dinners – perhaps with guests. Cook would prepare his favourite dishes. But instead there was limited attention for him for it was a house of sickness. Antonia was ill.

'We thought it was just a cold,' Sadie told him – she had hugged him, but briefly, preoccupied like everyone else. 'But she got much worse, and Mother called Dr Postgate in, and he says it's the Spanish flu.'

'Oh Lord!' William said. 'It's everywhere in France. Don't say it's come to Northcote as well?'

'We have had a few cases,' Sadie said, 'but Antonia's father wrote to say that their local camp had it badly, so she probably caught it from one of the soldiers because you know they run a club for them, and Antonia was helping with it.'

'How bad is it?' William asked.

Sadie looked grave. 'Pretty bad,' she said.

On the advice of the doctor, they had set up a system of quarantine, in the hope of preventing a spread. No visitors came into the house. A trained nurse had been hired, who slept in the room with the patient; Ada helped her, and kept the room tidy. The other servants stayed well away; Sadie took the meals up and handed them in at the door, and carried messages. But no one, apart from the nurse and Ada, went into the room; and when they took fresh air, they walked in the garden alone.

'I'm sorry,' Sadie concluded. 'It's not much of a homecoming for you.'

'I'm afraid I'm just an extra burden, in the circumstances,' he said.

'Oh no! I'm so glad to see you. We all are.'

He bit his lip. 'I really wish I could help.'

'There's nothing anyone can do,' said Sadie. 'It's just nursing and waiting.' She frowned. 'Except you could try to keep David company. He's awfully upset – especially not being able to go in and see her. You might distract him.'

William's face cleared. 'Yes, of course. I'll play cards with him or something.'

David was beside himself. Antonia had started to feel unwell the day after they had got home, just when he was planning his campaign of trying harder to make her happy. He'd had no time to put it into effect. She had said she thought she was getting a cold, and he had taken her word for it, but then had come the rapid deterioration and collapse. Postgate had seen her, and had shaken his head.

David knew what that shake meant. She was in danger. If she died, what would he do? Guilt rose up to choke him. He had never been a good husband to her. He had not treated her as he should have. He thought of her kindness, her patience, her devotion. He thought of life without her.

He tried to read, but the words shifted about meaninglessly on the page. He'd have liked to play his gramophone recordings, but the house had to be silent. He was not allowed to see Antonia, and he shunned everyone else's company, hating the pity he imagined in their eyes. So he stayed in his sitting-room, just across the passage from the bedroom, sitting motionless, staring into the fire. He was wrapped in a black cloud, as he had been in the first days of his home-coming after being wounded. The black cloud that had suffocated him until Antonia had come to bring him back into the light. *If she died . . .! If she died . . .!*

As David was frantic about Antonia, Ethel was frantic about her baby. He must be kept safe at all costs. She didn't even want the doctor near him – coming from examining Mrs David, bringing her germs to Ethel's precious child! She had no authority to forbid him, but she glared at him furiously when he touched the child or leaned over him. If he had coughed or sneezed, Ethel might well have attacked him with whatever object was nearest to hand.

The other servants she could certainly keep away, and she did. Miss Sadie, alone, seemed to understand, and volunteered to bring the nursery tray up as well as Mrs David's. 'I don't go into the room,' she had told Ethel soothingly. 'I just put it down on the little table outside the door.'

'All right, miss,' Ethel said grudgingly, thinking *Better you than that Beryl – who knows where she's been?*

'I promise if I have the slightest symptom, I'll let you know,' Sadie said.

'Yes, miss,' said Ethel. So far, Marcus was showing no signs of disease, and she meant to keep it that way. She could not forbid the family access, but Peter was not interested in babies, and Mr David was too wrapped up in worry about Mrs David to think about him, so it only left the missus. Beattie enquired twice a day about Marcus's health, and liked to hold and play with him, and Ethel could only watch, on tenterhooks. It was a worry when Mr William came home – being as he'd just been with other servicemen, and that was where the germs were coming from, wasn't it? – but, like Peter, he wasn't much interested in babies. Miss Sadie passed on his good wishes, but he stayed away, and she was glad.

Ethel brooded over her Marcus, and guarded him like a jealous dog.

William found David hard work – indifferent to his company and unwilling to be engaged in conversation. He seemed to prefer playing cards to talking. They played hand after hand of cribbage. William had an idea that David thought it the only way to shut him up.

One evening, William went down to dinner and found his mother alone in the drawing-room. The fire had not long been lit – coal was still short – and the room felt dank and clammy. Beattie was standing right by it, as though trying to warm herself, but she looked up as William came in and said, 'I was trying to remember what it was like before the war. When the house was always warm. Fires in every room. And we had sherry in here before dinner, your father and I. I wore gowns that left my arms bare, even in winter.'

'I remember,' William said. 'You had a lovely blue one. With a sort of rose thing on the front.' He made a vague circle over his breastbone. 'Silk, I think.'

'Yes. I always wore my pearls with it.'

'You always changed for the evening,' William remembered. Now she was in a tweed skirt and a blouse with a thick cardigan over it, and she hugged her arms around her as though the cardigan was not enough.

'Strange to think what store we set by those little ceremonies. But it was – civilised. I expect you used to have a drink before dinner in the mess?' she asked.

'Yes, we did.' He looked at his hands. 'There was quite a lot of drinking, I'm afraid. You know what it's like.'

It was a foolish thing to say to a woman – but, of course, she *did* know. 'Your grandfather despised sherry,' she said, with a faint smile. 'He always had a pink gin. Would you like something now?'

William was about to say no, feeling embarrassed, but then thought that perhaps she wanted something. So he said, 'I'll have a glass if sherry, if you're having one.' She nodded, and gestured towards the tray in the corner. When he gave her the glass, she was still standing in front of the fire, so he stood too. She looked at him as though she had just noticed him. 'I've hardly spoken to you since you got back,' she said. 'I'm sorry.'

'It's all right,' he said.

'You – you look very smart in your uniform.' She was still staring. 'I feel I hardly know you,' she said. 'You were just a boy when you went away. Then there was the flying. One heard the figures. One hardly expected you to survive. Especially—'

'After Bobby,' he finished for her.

'You were like Bobby's shadow,' she said.

He sipped sherry, not understanding.

'Were you afraid?' she asked abruptly.

He thought about it, feeling she ought to have a true answer. 'No,' he said at last. And, 'There wasn't really time.'

She was silent now, and he took his turn to examine her. As a child, you don't really think of your parents as separate people. Now he saw a middle-aged woman who had been very beautiful; who was beautiful still, in her own way – and he realised for the first time that a woman of such an age *could* have beauty. But what came from her, most of all, was a great sadness, such a well of it, he sensed, that it made him shiver. It was Bobby, he thought. It must be harder for her than for anyone else to lose Bobby.

He wanted to say something to her, but had no words. He was relieved when Sadie came in, and said, 'Where's David?'

'He said he didn't want any dinner,' William said.

'Is he all right?' Beattie said, in quick anxiety.

'Just worried, I think.'

107

Sadie frowned. 'We're all worried. We have to support each other. He *must* come down.'

'Leave him alone,' Beattie said. 'You don't understand what he's going through.'

'I understand he's being awfully selfish,' Sadie said. 'I'm going to fetch him.' And she went out.

William felt awkward. Beattie was staring at the fire again, lost in her own thoughts. 'My friend Considine was talking about inviting me to stay,' he said. 'He lives in Surrey. I thought it might take a strain from the household if I went there for a bit. Or would you prefer me to stay?' He didn't want to be called selfish too.

'She's become very hard,' Beattie said, as if she hadn't heard him. She sighed. 'Nothing seems right with your father away.'

There was silence in the room, until Sadie came back with David, and Peter following close behind. His natural young voice saying, 'What's for dinner? I'm starving!' was like a breath of fresh air.

And Beryl appeared at the door. 'Yer dinner's ready,' she said, forgetting again how Cook had told her to announce it.

'She's no substitute for Ada,' Sadie said to William, as they followed their mother out. 'Diana would have a fit.'

Visitors came to the door to enquire after Antonia. Sadie was usually the one who had to go and talk to them, and in that way she learned how many people loved her sister-in-law. In her quiet work about the parish, Antonia had made her mark. There were also, of course, the impertinent and the ghoulish, the latter gaining some perverse thrill from the fact that Antonia was pregnant. Two lives for the price of one, Sadie thought bitterly, as she employed her wits to shame them without sounding rude.

The rector came, and could not be kept out entirely. He

had to be received in the drawing-room while being told he could not see the invalid.

'I quite understand. I only wished to express my concern. This wretched disease – it sometimes seems as though it's a punishment on us.'

'Like the plagues of Egypt?' Sadie said, interested in his thought process. 'To punish us for what? Do you think it was wrong, then, to fight the war?'

He looked startled. 'Oh – no! Of course not. No, no. I'm sure . . .' He was not used to people asking him questions, especially when he hadn't meant anything in particular by his words. Long years in the job had given him a stock of phrases that came out more or less without his volition. And he had spent four years supporting the war, because he had to: otherwise his parishioners' losses were unendurable. He could not now talk about it as a mistake, a wrong-doing, a lightning rod for Divine Retribution.

'God's ways are mysterious,' he said at last. That at least was something no one could argue with.

Sadie looked at him with sympathy. It occurred to her that she had never really seen him close up before, and she saw now how old he was, and how worn. The war had suited Mrs Fitzgerald, who had sprouted like bindweed in its stony soil and climbed vigorously all over everything; but the rector looked diminished, thin and grey and somehow indistinct, like a chalk drawing being washed away by the rain. It must have been hard for him, she reasoned, trying to justify God's ways when the world was upside down and mad and horrible. How many grieving people had come to him for comfort, or even just explanation, when he could have none to offer of either?

'You'll pray for her?' she suggested kindly

He came back with a start from his thoughts. 'Oh – of course! Yes, naturally I will.'

'And for all of us,' Sadie added. They all needed it.

109

He rallied, laying a cold twig of a hand over hers. 'Trust in Him, my dear,' he said, in a rector's voice. 'He will answer your prayers.'

She showed him out.

Lights burned in the house. The doctor's car was parked outside. In the kitchen Cook, in her thick felt dressing-gown, her hair in its night-time pigtail, made relays of tea and cocoa for any who wanted it, and for those who didn't, too. Her eyes were red, and every now and then a sob escaped her, though she was trying to be strong. She didn't deserve it, was what she kept thinking. *That nice Mrs David, that did so much good.* What was God thinking? There were wicked people enough in the world that the world would be well rid of. Why take her? And the poor innocent little unborn baby . . . She couldn't bear, literally couldn't bear, to think about the awfulness of that. She missed Ada, out of reach in quarantine, wanted to talk to her so bad. Beryl was no use – and she'd gone to bed, in any case. Though how she could sleep at a time like this . . .

Someone rattled at the back door. Beryl must have remembered to bolt it before she went to bed – wonder of wonders! Cook went to open it, and when she saw Nula outside she almost fell into her arms.

Nula patted her absently, like a horse. 'How bad is it?'

'Doctor's here,' Cook said, her breath hitching like a child's. 'She may not – may not last the night.'

'Ah, mercy me!' Nula cried softly.

'How did you get here?' Cook asked.

'I knew yesterday it was bad. I had a feeling, so I didn't go to bed, and when I saw Dr Postgate's car go by, I guessed how it must be.'

'Well, it's a blessing to see you,' Cook said tremulously.

But Nula said impatiently, 'I'm not here for you. I must go to the mistress.'

Cook withdrew like a snail. 'She's in the morning-room,' she said, with dignity. 'I took her some cocoa.'

Nula nodded and started for the door. Cook said, 'She's ever so upset. I never realised she cared so much about Mrs David. I always thought, well, that she felt she wasn't good enough for him.'

Nula didn't reply as she went away. Guilt burned more than sorrow, she thought. That was what Cook hadn't learned yet. And the unborn baby – who *wouldn't* care about that?

'It can't do any harm now,' Dr Postgate said to David.

David stared, his face strained and white, his eyes red and desperate. 'What are you saying? You mean—?'

Postgate laid a steadying hand on his arm. 'You should prepare yourself,' he said. A groan broke from David – a sound like a hurt animal trying to speak. 'Don't upset her. Don't trouble her with your worries or fears. Speak calmly to her. Let her be happy.'

'Happy?' he said wildly.

'She may not know you,' Postgate said. 'Just – be there with her.'

In the dim light of one lamp in the corner, the scene was softened at the edges. The nurse's white cap was like a bird in the gloom, her blue uniform merging with the shadows, almost invisible. 'You needn't tiptoe,' she said. She gestured to David to come to the bedside.

'Is she – conscious?' he asked helplessly.

'It comes and goes. But I expect she'll know you're there. It's amazing what they do know. She has asked for you every day.'

He should have let me go to her before, David thought murderously as he sat, possessed himself of the limp hand, gazed at his wife's closed face. She had lost flesh, and the sidelong light emphasised the dips and hollows, so she seemed haggard, her eyes sunk in dark sockets. She looked as though

111

she would never wake again. He wanted to cry, but the wells were dry. He said quietly, 'Antonia.' And then, more urgently, calling her, 'Antonia!'

She did not stir. He was aware that Postgate had come into the room behind him. He and the nurse were having a sotto-voce discussion. Someone else was there, too, talking. He wanted to shout at them to go away, leave him alone with her.

There was a breath of a whisper from the bed, and he saw that her eyes had opened. She was looking at him. Her dry lips moved, but he could not make out words. He leaned closer, and the faint escape of air became *I'm sorry*.

'You've nothing to be sorry for,' he said urgently. It was important she understood that he had meant what he said in her father's house. 'I'm the one who should apologise. But it will all be better now. You'll get well, and we'll—' She had shaken her head slightly, wearily. He squeezed her hand. 'Yes! You must. Oh please, you must try. For me. I can't manage without you.'

'David,' she whispered. The eyes closed, then opened again. 'I'm sorry.'

He lifted her hand to his lips, then pressed it to his forehead, bending his head and closing his eyes, hoping the tears would come because the pain in his throat was dreadful.

The hand went limp in his. He opened his eyes. Hers were closed. Her breath dragged, and her face seemed to have sunk even more. She seemed to be sinking away from him, down into the pillows, down through the bed, down out of the world. He kept tight hold of her hand, as though it would stop her disappearing.

He must have fallen asleep, just for a moment, because suddenly his mother was there, shaking his shoulder. He jerked awake, looked wildly at Antonia. He was still holding her hand. 'Is she . . .?'

'No,' said Beattie. 'She's still with us. Come outside. I must talk to you.'

He had grown stiff, sitting, and staggered like a drunk out of the room. His mother steadied him at the door, her eyes searching his face in the way someone does when they're inviting you to be brave.

'It's Marcus, dear,' she said. 'Ethel called Dr Postgate to him. He's coughing and has a temperature.'

'What?' David said wildly. 'What are you telling me?'

'It might be the flu,' Beattie said, her voice calm, as it always was. Whatever happened to her, she never showed on the surface the turmoil within. 'Postgate isn't sure.'

'But— What—'

'There's nothing to be done but nurse him, and wait. Ethel's exhausted, but she won't leave him. I've persuaded her to sleep in the chair beside his cot, while I watch him. Postgate's coming back in the morning. You had to know. But you'll want to stay with Antonia while—' She bit the words off.

David knew she had been going to say, *while you can.* He stared at her, coming fully to his senses. 'All of them?' he said, his mouth twisting with bitterness. 'Antonia, now Marcus – and, oh, Mother, the baby! It can't survive, can it? Or can they . . .?'

'No, dear,' Beattie said. 'It's too young.'

'All of them? What is God doing to me?'

'Go back to Antonia, dear,' Beattie said, pushing him gently. She knew the thoughts going through her son's head. It wasn't God. This was man-made hell, all of it, and there was no one to rail against. It only made it harder, of course, to have no one to blame. Except yourself – ah, yes! *We should have appreciated her while we could.* But that was no help now. Guilt burned fiercer than sorrow. She knew about both.

CHAPTER NINE

Cook paused to rest her cramped wrist. Seeking inspiration, she re-read a bit of Fred's letter.

Colone is a nice city, lots of posh buildings and churches, not knocked about like London, well we didn't bomb it like they did us. Now the Union Jack flies over it, ha ha, sucks to you Kaiser Bill only you have to wonder what was it all about, we tried so hard to get here for four years and in the end we walked in singing Good-bye-ee. The local folk seem nice enough, not happy to see us, you couldn't expect it, but polite and trying to please. In the shops and caffs they are all smiles and very honest about changing money. German is quite a bit like English so we manage to get understood, better than in France. The grubs not bad, also better than France, no frogs legs or snails anyway, ha ha. Just a lot of sausiges but everyone likes a banger. No word yet when we are coming home, they say travel expands the mind, mine is getting bigger every minute. Some folk think my head is big enough already.

Cook flexed her fingers and picked up the pencil again. His words seemed so large and breezy to her, as if a window had been flung open – not just fresh air, but with different smells about it, like . . . like – exotic flowers and spices and such. He was in Germany, fancy that, and he'd been in

France and Belgium, and she'd never been further than Folkestone. She felt small and crabbed and shut in compared to him, like one of those things that lived in a shell on the sea-bed, creeping about in the dimness. What could he want with her? How could she ever live up to him? And he wanted to take her to Australia – *Australia*!

She carried on where she had left off. *She is still very weak and lays there so pale and feeble it breaks your heart, and the doctor says she's not out of danger yet, but we thought we'd lost her that night so we Thank God she's still with us anyway. It would touch you to see how devoted Mr David is, waiting on her hand and foot like as if he can't believe his eyes she's still there. Baby Marcus is up and down, but the doctor says it isn't the flu, Thank God, he thinks it's brownkiters (can't spell it!) and is treating him according. The Mistress makes Ethel take a rest now and then, she says she'll get ill otherwise and who would nurse her? But she doesn't like it, and if he coughs she's straight in.*

She stopped again, and racked her brain for something to say that was not about the Family. But that was her life, wasn't it? She had lived every day through them; the rest of the world seemed too big, too loud, too hard-edged. She would get hurt out there. In here, in her kitchen, it was warm and safe. But she'd never be able to explain that to anyone, not even Ada – though Ada would understand without explaining. But Fred!

She glanced at the clock and put the pencil down, not without relief. Time to make Mrs David's next meal. Little and often, the doctor had said. Consommé and gruel and beef tea and suchlike. Anything she could get down her, poor soul, because there was the unborn baby to think of.

Bobby's bicycle, which Sadie had taken over early in the war, had worked hard ever since, and was showing its age. Its most annoying trait was the shedding of its chain.

Replacing it was a fiddling job, to say nothing of a dirty one, and likely to end in nipped fingers.

It went again as she was cycling home up the hill in the dusk, and flung her unceremoniously onto the grass verge. Nailer, who had been travelling in the front basket, landed cat-like on his feet, gave her an affronted look, and stalked off to investigate the undergrowth. She thought he would probably take a short-cut through the wood and be home before her.

She had just passed the army camp on Paget's Piece, and reflected as she wrestled with the oily loops on how it had changed. In 1914 it had been filled with volunteers – and how the residents of Northcote had lined the roads and cheered when they finally marched off to war! Later, conscripted soldiers had received less of a fuss, but still you waved if you happened to be out when they were passing. You were proud of 'our boys', even if you were too busy to do more than look up from your work and throw a smile.

Now it was a 'demob camp', and not such a nice place. It was hard not to feel sorry for the soldiers, who had come back from France but were still not free to go home. They had nothing useful to do, and in their frustration were impatient with 'square bashing' and 'bull', so the camp already had a shabby air that would have made a war-time sergeant-major froth at the mouth.

The new secretary of state for war, Winston Churchill, had ordered that, while large numbers of soldiers had to be retained for the time being, there should be accelerated demobilisation for the oldest, those who had joined earliest and those who had suffered the most. That was well and good, and no one could argue with the fairness of it; but the Tommies were never given the details of the decisions, and those who did not get their orders naturally felt they had as much right to go home as those who did. They *ought* to be civilians by now; so why should army rules apply to them? Rumours went around, of riots and disobedience. In January, two thousand soldiers had demonstrated in Dover town centre. In February, a company in a camp on the Isle of Wight had refused orders on parade, and the officer had drawn his pistol, upon which thirty rifle bolts had been drawn back and someone had shouted, 'Go on, then, you bugger, shoot if you dare!'

Sadie got the chain on at last, and cautiously eased the pedal round to bed it in. She saw a movement out of the corner of her eye, and looked up to see a soldier in khaki coming out of the trees. He paused, looking around, then came towards her. She assumed he was coming to help. 'It's all right, thanks, I've done it,' she said.

Only as he came closer did she notice the state of him – unshaven, unkempt, his uniform awry and mud-streaked – and begin to feel alarmed. He did not speak, but stared at her, and a crooked, unpleasant grin came over his face. 'All alone? Where you off to, then, miss?' he said.

'I'm going home,' she said, pushing the bicycle down onto the road, so that the verge would give her a little height advantage to mount it. Not for the first time, she wished she had a ladies' bike. It was hard to get on, even in breeches and boots.

He reached her before she could manage it, and caught hold of the handlebars. 'Not so fast, missy,' he said. She could smell his breath, an unpleasant mixture of beer and bad teeth. She tried to pull the bike away from him, but he kept a tight hold with one hand, and with the other grabbed her arm. 'Got anything on you?' he demanded. 'Got any money? I could do with a drink. Got a few pennies for a pore soldier what served his country? I got a thirst on me like a parrot's cage.'

'I don't have any money,' she said, beginning to be frightened.

'Garn! Posh young lady like you? You gotta have some.'

117

'I'm just going home from work. I don't have any money,' she asserted. 'I'd give you something if I had it.'

'Just have to give me somethink else, then, won'tcher?'

He wrenched the bike away from her and flung it into the road, and grabbed her other arm. 'Come on,' he said. 'Be nice. I served King and Country.'

He started to drag her backwards towards the trees, and she understood at last. She struggled violently. 'Let me go!'

'You're a skinny bit, but you'll have to do,' he said, grinning. His foul breath hit her face, making her flinch. 'Don't know as I approve of girls in trousis. Have to get 'em off you, won't I? Come on, darlin'. Don't make me hurt you.' He let go of one arm, reached behind him and pulled out a clasp knife. It looked sharp. Sadie hung back to the length of her arm, and lashed out at his face, but he was quick and caught her wrist with the knife hand, then transferred it to the other. His hands were so big, he could hold both her wrists in one. 'Firebrand, ain'tcher?' he panted. He put the point of the knife under her chin and forced her head up. 'Reckon you want a smacking, teach you some manners.' He had reached the trees and was dragging her into the wood. No one would see her there. She heard herself make a whimpering noise. He grinned. 'Oh yeah! I'll give you a smacking. Yeah, and summink else an' all.'

He looked down with a horrible leer to draw her attention to the front of his trousers – and at that moment stepped on a stone or some other irregularity and staggered slightly. She saw her one chance and seized it, lashing out and upwards with her foot. Her heavy riding boot made contact with the parts she knew, from having brothers, had to be protected during cricket matches. The effect was immediate. He howled, and, already off balance, fell backwards, letting go of her to clutch himself, sitting down hard on the leaf litter. She whirled round and ran, hearing him moan and curse her in the ripest language she'd ever heard. Frantic

118

with fear, she knew if he caught her now, he would hurt her badly.

And then something small and white shot past her, and there was a cry of surprise and a rippling, snarling noise. She was nearly out of the trees, but had to look back. He was on his feet to pursue her, but Nailer was dodging about in front of him, snarling. Then she saw him kick the dog, like a football, so he went flying through the air with a yelp of pain.

She reached the road. Behind her she heard furious barking, and the soldier's coarse cries: 'You come back here, you bitch!' The bicycle was lying there, but to pick it up and get on it would slow her down, and he'd be on her. She jumped into the road and ran, her desperate breath tearing at her throat. The road remained stubbornly empty. Why did no one come? Her riding boots were heavy, never meant for running in.

The soldier shouted, 'I'm gonna kill you!' but whether to her or Nailer she didn't know. She dared not look back again, but she could hear his boots thumping the road behind her. He sounded frighteningly close. She expected to feel his hand grab her any moment. She gasped in terror, tried to run faster.

But, oh, thank God, she heard a motor-vehicle coming! She ran into the middle of the road, waving her arms. If it didn't stop, she was dead – either way. It was a small, open-backed truck, the sort farmers used to transport bales of straw. It stopped with a skid of elderly tyres on the worn road, and a tall man in work clothes jumped out and ran past her, shouting, 'Hoy, you! Stay where you are!'

Sadie leaned panting against the warm bonnet, her thoughts spinning. Had that really been Frank Hussey or was she dreaming? He must have had his wits about him to assess the situation so quickly – thank God for him! She had got her breath back, and had started shaking with reaction.

119

Frank came back out of the woods, without the soldier, but carrying Nailer in his arms. 'He got away. Did he hurt you, Miss Sadie? There's blood on your neck.'

'He had a knife.' The point must have pierced the skin. 'He said he – he was going to – to—'

'The dirty swine,' Frank said, his face dark.

'He kicked Nailer. Is he all right?'

'Bruised, I think. He was limping, but I can't feel anything broken.'

'He saved me,' Sadie said, reaching out to stroke the rough head. Nailer licked her hand with an upward roll of the eyes, his most pathetic look. 'That soldier would have caught me if he hadn't gone for him.'

'What happened?' Frank asked. Sadie told him. 'Did you get a good look at his face? Would you know him again?'

Sadie shuddered. 'I think so.'

'What about his uniform? Did you see what regiment he was from?'

Sadie paused, going through her memory. 'I don't think there were any insignia,' she said. 'There was definitely no cap badge.'

'Deserter,' Frank said shortly. 'Most likely tore 'em off. But somebody will have missed him. We oughter go to the police.' Then he looked at her more closely, gauging her condition. 'Better get you home first, though. You're all shook up, and no wonder. Later's good enough for the police. He'll have made himself scarce by now, anyway.'

He helped her into the cab, and put Nailer on her lap, heaved her bicycle up into the back, got in and started the engine.

Sadie thought to ask, 'How did you come to be here?'

'Just passing. Thank God I was! Got to collect some stuff from Northcote station – engine parts, got offloaded there by mistake.' He glanced at her sidelong. 'You going to have hysterics, Miss Sadie?'

120

'No, of course not. I'm all right. I was so frightened. But it's all over now.' She considered. 'I kicked him,' she mentioned. 'In the cricket box.'

'Good for you, miss. He deserved it.'

She was running her hands over Nailer. He flinched, and looked at her uncertainly. 'I think you're right – he's got a bruised elbow. But nothing broken. He was a hero, Frank.'

'Yeah, he's a good old mutt,' said Frank, freeing one hand from the wheel, to ruffle the dog's head. Nailer sighed and settled down in Sadie's lap to enjoy the ride. She knew the dog was shaken because normally he would have been standing with his head out of the window.

They rode in silence up the steep hill, the engine labouring. Sadie felt very conscious of Frank beside her: his size, his maleness, a soapy clean smell and a trace of fresh male sweat; his big brown hands on the wheel. He had wavy light brown hair and blue eyes. She wondered why on earth Ethel didn't snap him up.

'I haven't seen you around much lately,' she said.

'Bin busy,' he said. 'I heard about Mrs David. Is she better now?'

'Very pulled down, but the doctor says she should be all right.'

'And Master Marcus?'

'He's up and down. He has a dreadful cough, poor little mite.'

Frank cleared his throat. 'I dessay he's well looked after.'

'Ethel hates to leave him even for a second.' Frank nodded, his eyes firmly fixed on the road. 'Frank, did you and Ethel quarrel?' Sadie asked daringly.

'Nothing to quarrel about,' he said, a spot of red appearing in his brown cheek at talking of personal things. 'She don't want *me*, Miss Sadie. I been fooling myself. I just wish – she must've bin upset with the baby being sick. I wished I could've been there and helped her. But she don't want me.

Blessed if I know what she do want,' he added, as if to himself.

'Women,' Sadie began, stopped, and then went ahead anyway. 'Women often don't know, not until the last minute. Sometimes they need helping along. I wouldn't give up, Frank, if you really care for her.'

'Never cared for another woman, not in that way,' he said bluntly. 'But I'm not a fool, and there's no sense knocking your head against a brick wall.' He stopped, and she didn't feel entitled to say any more.

The police came round later that evening. It was not Sergeant Whittle, who had his hands full. PC Andy Denton, who had been his second-in-command before the war, had been killed at Passchendaele. The new young PC, Robbie Arthur, who had been sent to take Andy's place, had been called up, and had been killed on the Lys in April 1918. So now it was Special Constable Albert Miles who attended Sadie – a retired PC and also Northcote's Scout master, too old for the army, and pretty nearly too old for this job, except that he was needed and there was no one else.

He was accompanied by a military policeman from Paget's Piece, who listened to Sadie's account, and said, 'It sounds as if it might be Private Sudden – Bert Sudden. He went AWOL a week ago. We thought he'd be far away by now. Usually they try to get home, but from what his mates say, he's got no one left. Comes from London, the East End, so he'd've probably drifted back there eventually. He's a bad lot, miss, a drinker and a fighter, and not to be trusted with women.'

'I must say, it's very alarming to think of him running loose about the area,' said Beattie.

'Don't you worry, ma'am – m'lady, I should say,' said Miles. 'We'll catch him all right. We've got everyone looking out for him. He can't get on a train or a bus but he'll be spotted.'

'He said he had no money,' said Sadie.

'And thanks to that very smart young man—' said the military policeman.

'Frank Hussey,' PC Miles interpolated.

'– we know where the incident took place, and we've got men in there with dogs searching for him as I speak. He won't get far.'

PC Miles cleared his throat. 'When we catch him, though, it'll be necessary for you to identify him, Miss Sadie,' he said apologetically. 'and then if it goes to court . . .'

'Miss Hunter will do her duty,' Beattie said, standing to indicate the interview was over. Sadie, she thought, was looking as though reaction had fully set in. She ought to go to bed.

Ada came in to see the men out, but at the drawing-room door, PC Miles turned back to say to Beattie in a low voice, 'Troubles like these, they make you wonder if the war's really over, don't they, m'lady?'

'They certainly do,' said Beattie.

Encouraged, he dropped his voice a notch lower. 'I don't know if you happen to recollect John Kitchen, m'lady, that was sales clerk at Rice's haberdasher's before the war? Dapper chap with glasses and a little moustache. Very good with ladies' – ahem – *things*.'

'Yes, I remember him,' Beattie said, frowning. She wanted to see to Sadie, not wander down memory's by-ways.

'Well, m'lady, he volunteered early 1915. Got wounded and taken prisoner in the Champagne in March last year. Repatriated in December, m'lady, come back here, and went to Rice's to see about getting his job back. Only now they've got two female clerks doing his job for the same money, so they didn't want him. Mr Rice, the way I heard it, told Kitchen he'd let him down by joining up when he didn't have to.'

'That's shocking,' Beattie said briskly, trying to urge him out of the door, 'but—'

'He did away with himself, m'lady,' PC Miles said, in a voice so low it was sepulchral. 'Couldn't find another job, couldn't face the future out of work. Hanged hisself in Chalkpit Woods. A coppicer found him this morning. That's why Sergeant Whittle couldn't come.' He shook his head miserably. 'So many troubles. Doesn't seem as if we'll ever get any proper peace.'

'It says here,' Ada said, poring over the paper, 'that they've dug up Edith Cavell. It says the body was in good condition and the face quite recognisable.'

'Coo!' said Beryl. 'Was she dead, then?'

'How could you dig someone up if they wasn't?' Cook said impatiently.

'Who's Edith Cavell?' Timmy asked through a mouthful of tea.

'She nursed soldiers in Belgium,' Ada told him. Well, he was only ten, probably too young to remember the fuss at the time. He ought to be at school, but nobody bothered much about it these days. 'She helped prisoners of war escape, and the Germans had her shot. Nurse and Martyr, they call her here.'

'All the more reason to be leaving her in peace,' Cook said. 'I don't hold with digging people up. Tampering with graves is a wassname – sacrilege. Her family'll have something to say about it, I shouldn't wonder. Her father was a clergyman, wasn't he?'

'It's her family that's behind it, according to this. They want her brought home.'

'I thought the gov'ment said no one was to be brought home, on account of only rich folk could afford it and it wasn't fair,' Cook objected.

'Well, I s'pose it's different if you're a hero –'

'All of them that fell in France was heroes,' Cook snapped.

124

'– and a martyr,' Ada concluded, but doubtfully. After all, Miss Cavell wasn't the only nurse to have been killed in the war. 'But she was the only one that was put up against a wall and shot,' she said aloud.

'Coo!' said Beryl, her eyes round.

'Anyway, it says here she's going to be given a state funeral in Westminster Abbey, and the King himself might go.'

'I wouldn't mind going to see that,' Cook acknowledged. 'It'd be a great sight. Remember when King Teddy died, Ada, and you and me stood out all night to get a good place to see the procession go past?'

'And they come past leading his little white dog,' said Ada. 'It made me cry, to see that little thing all on his own, looking round him, wondering what was going on.'

'Animals always did make you cry,' Cook said. 'I'd sooner cry for all those poor young men that never come home.'

'I cry for them, too,' Ada said quietly.

Cook was stricken. She'd forgotten for a moment about Len. 'Oh, Ada dear, I didn't mean . . .' she cried.

'Doesn't matter,' Ada said, getting up. 'I got to go and dust the dining-room. And, Beryl, the front-door brass needs doing.' And she went out, without meeting anyone's eyes.

Beryl, having just caught up with the *faux-pas*, turned slowly to stare at Cook, her mouth open. Timmy was staring too, though he didn't know why.

'Well, you heard what she said,' Cook snapped at Beryl. 'Get and do that brass. And *you* –' she turned so quickly on Timmy that he flinched and almost fell off his chair '– I don't know why you're still sitting there, when the boots haven't been touched, nor last night's knives!'

Timmy put down his mug and fled.

Sadie was nervous about cycling alone, but she told herself not to be foolish, that the horrible Private Sudden would be long gone, that most Tommies were good people, and that lightning didn't strike twice in the same place. Passing Paget's Piece, she always turned to look at the guards on the gate for reassurance, and quite often they would grin and acknowledge her. There were more soldiers around Northcote now, on demob leave, but they were often fellows she knew, and she wasn't worried in Northcote, anyway, with other people around. It was the long hill past woods and empty fields that worried her.

In Northcote one was also seeing men who had been discharged unfit: men without arms or legs, or with terrible facial injuries; and the others, less noticeable, with heart trouble or nerves shot to pieces. The sight of them wrenched her feelings and put backbone into her. She had no right to fear for her safety when they had put their own in the firing line.

And as nothing happened, time worked its healing magic, and she forgot to be nervous, actually forgot most of the time about the incident. Nailer limped for a couple of days, and enjoyed the rewards it brought so much that, even after his bruise was gone, he still sometimes put on a limp when he remembered, accompanying it with that pathetic upward eye-roll, and a heart-rending whimper. Sadie had long gone past the point of being moved by it when, at the end of March, she received an evening visit from Sergeant Whittle, in all his glory.

Sadie came out to him in the hall, where he had removed his helmet and was brushing snow from his shoulders. The weather had been cold and wet all month, but this last week, though there had been dry spells, it had turned much colder, barely above freezing.

'Is it snowing again?' she asked. 'Won't you come in by the fire?'

'No, Miss Sadie, thanks all the same, I don't want to drip on your carpet,' Whittle said. He glanced at Ada's retreating back. 'Bad enough to give your maid the trouble of mopping up after me out here. My business is soon told. It's about this soldier that attacked you, the deserter.'

'Bert Sudden,' Sadie said.

'Ah! I suppose you won't forget his name in a hurry. Well, I came to tell you you needn't worry about him any more. And the best of it is, you won't be needed to testify against him.'

'I'm glad about that. I was rather dreading it.'

'Right, miss, of course you were. Well, the way of it was, he turned up in Stepney, which was where he came from originally. They generally run home, deserters, though he didn't have any family left there. But it'd be the place he knew. The local police'd been warned to look out for him, and they nearly had him once, when he stole some things from a clothes-line – to disguise himself, like. They found his uniform later, dumped in an alley. Well, the householder gave chase and lost him, but he gave a good description to the police, and o' course now they knew what he was wearing. He was spotted in a pub, then hanging around the back door of a bakery, but he managed to slip away. Only everyone was looking for him, so his time was running out.'

'He must have been desperate,' Sadie said. 'How was he living?'

'Stealing food, from what we gather, from stalls and shops. And kitchens, when the door was left open. But he tried it once too often – snatched a pie off a park bench, right under the nose of the workman that was just going to eat it. Well, the workman gave chase, nearly had him a couple of times, till Sudden dodged under the barbed wire and down the embankment onto the railway line.'

'Oh no!' Sadie said softly, seeing where this was going.

Whittle nodded solemnly. 'Just as the down express was coming.'

'Was he killed?'

Whittle hesitated, then decided Sadie could take it.

127

'Knocked his head clean off. Found his body one side o' the track and his head the other. So that's that, Miss Sadie. You don't need to worry about it any more.'

'You're sure it was him? If his—'

'Luckily, the head got thrown clear onto the embankment, so they could identify him. It was him all right. Don't you worry.' He eyed her cautiously, and added, 'It'd've been a quick death – and more'n he deserved.'

Sadie reflected. 'What drove him to desert, does anyone know? I mean, he only needed to wait for demobilisation, didn't he?'

'He was up on a charge of mutiny – refusing orders and starting a riot in the camp – so he was looking at jail, not discharge. And he wouldn't have done any good in civvy life anyway. He had a rotten military record – fighting, stealing and worse. He was a waster, and a bad lot. You needn't feel sorry for him, Miss Sadie. He's better off dead, and the world's a better place without him.'

Sadie remembered the knife, his brutal grip, his foul breath, the way he had kicked Nailer. No, she needn't feel sorry for him – but, still, it seemed a terrible thing to say about anyone. She *was* sorry – if not for him, for the fact of him: that someone like him should have existed, a soul without hope of redemption.

128

CHAPTER TEN

So far, being home had been a holiday for William, and he hadn't minded it too much. He had enjoyed getting up late, pottering about, revisiting old haunts, seeing who else was back and renewing acquaintances. Though he was too young and eager to acknowledge it, the war had been a strain on him, and he needed to recuperate.

But a few weeks of the sybaritic life were enough. The absence of his father had prevented any serious discussion of his future, but as his energy returned, he asked himself the questions. He was nineteen, not too old to go back into education, but flying was the only thing he wanted to do.

His demob leave ended and he was out of uniform. On a rare dry day in that dismal month of March, he cycled down to Coney Warren, where he had been a trainee engineer in the aircraft factory. All he could do was to watch wistfully through the wire fence – but it was good just to see and hear aeroplanes again. He lingered at the gates into the evening, and was happy to see an old acquaintance, Percy Wakefield, coming out. They went for a glass of beer together and chatted.

Percy was not much comfort: he himself was being discharged at the end of the month. 'The RAF's shrinking all the time,' he said, 'and they've got plenty of machines already. Lord knows what will happen to the factory here. Nearly all the women fitters have gone, and a lot of the older men, too. I'm thinking of trying to find something in motor-racing. At least an engine is always an engine.'

William hadn't heard anything from Considine, and wondered whether to send a friendly letter enquiring after his health. But it might look like begging for an invitation. As April brought showers rather than constant rain, with more dry spells and more daylight, he grew restless, longing to be flying, fearing for his future. He didn't write again to Considine. But since David – at least, in his imagination – started to give him questioning looks, he went down to the motor-cycle shop on the Westfield Road and got himself a job demonstrating machines to potential customers. It was unpaid, except for a small commission on a sale, and few people were as yet buying, but it got him out of the house. The shop also did repairs, and the evenings would often find him in the workshop with oil on his hands, nose to nose with the mechanic, helping out. As Percy said, an engine was an engine.

Beryl gave her notice, to the consternation of the servants' hall.

'Lord knows she's not much of a housemaid,' Cook said to Ada, 'but she's another pair of hands.'

'I know,' Ada said gloomily. She was looking tired, Cook thought. She didn't have much to look forward to, poor thing, without her Len, and the worry of helping care for Mrs David had taken its toll. 'I don't see how I can do everything myself.'

'You can't,' Cook said stoutly. 'The missus has got to get someone else in.'

'Even if she does, I'll have to train them, which means doing half their work for however long it takes. And if they're anything like Beryl . . .'

Their eyes met. They both knew it might be someone worse than Beryl. There weren't so many wanting to go into domestic service, despite all its advantages. Girls'd sooner put up with nasty diggings and poor food, and be able to go out every evening. 'Dances, and rubbishing pictures – with *men*,' as Cook put it.

Beryl had fallen victim to the enchantment. A girl she met on her evening off had poured scorn on her servant status, and had painted a rosy picture of a freedom that fell nothing short of Nirvana.

'She thinks she'll be lyin' about on a wassname, a divan, eatin' peeled grapes, like one of them obelisks,' Cook said scornfully. 'She'll learn!'

Ada only looked worried. She had done her part in gently pointing out the difficulties of life outside, but felt it wasn't her business to dissuade the girl. Beryl had got herself a job in the big laundry on the Walford Road, at twenty-eight shillings a week. It seemed like a fortune to Beryl – her wages at The Elms were ten and six. Ada reminded her that she'd have to pay for lodgings, but she said triumphantly that her friend had mentioned a spare room going in the house where she lodged, for fifteen bob a week including breakfast and supper. She could get a midday meal at the canteen at work for a bob, and that left her seven shillings in hand.

But she would need money for the meters, for the light and the gas fire in her room, and for the geyser in the bathroom. Say, three shillings a week. Her fare to and from work – tuppence a day on the bus – took care of another shilling. Out of the remaining three shillings a week, Ada pointed out, she'd have to buy things like matches, soap, stockings, hairpins, to say nothing of shoe repairs and such new clothes as she might need, before she could splash out on sweets, cinemas, magazines and the other joys of freedom she anticipated. (Perhaps even *lipstick*? Ada saw it in her eyes.) And what if she got sick? There'd be no mistress to pay for the doctor.

But Beryl waved those concerns away. She was under a spell, and would run towards the glittering spires of that magical castle in the clouds, no matter what anyone said.

Her leaving made finding a new maid a matter of urgency. Beattie would always prefer to get one by recommendation, but with Ada looking so worn that it was impossible for her not to notice, she had to take the short-cut and go to the employment exchange in the High Street. The result was Aggie Mabbott, who said she was an experienced housemaid, though she'd done no parlourmaiding. Beattie decided that didn't matter as it didn't look as though they'd be entertaining for some time yet – not until Edward came home. Aggie was a fat girl with adenoids, which meant her mouth was permanently open in a depressing fish-like pout, but she seemed docile and clean.

Cook muttered to Ada that she looked as it she didn't know A from a bull's foot, and that she'd probably eat more than she was worth. But after a day or two, Ada said she was a hard enough worker, though you had to tell her everything. She thought she'd be all right. Having adenoids gave you that nasal voice and made you look and sound stupid, but it didn't necessarily mean you *were* stupid. She was willing to give her a chance.

'*We*'ve not got any choice but to give her a chance,' said Cook. 'Well, as long as she does what she's told, it don't matter if she *is* stupid. Better that than flighty, running after men and wanting to go and work in the factories. Look at the trouble we had with Ethel.'

'But Ethel's still here,' Ada pointed out.

Cook had forgotten which side she was arguing on, and so ended the discussion with a sniff. 'I got cakes to make,' she said, and went away.

Sadie wrote to John Courcy:

I'm back from my pleasure-jaunt to London with Diana, and I must say I enjoyed it more than I thought I would. It was nice putting on proper girls' clothes for a change.

132

Nula made over some of Diana's old things for me – which is a lot swisher than it sounds, because Diana's old things are beautiful. How many girls wear a countess's cast-offs?

It had all been done with no trouble to Sadie, because Nula knew her size and had a dress of hers as a pattern, so she didn't have to have a lot of fittings, which would have bored her to tears. Diana was taller than Sadie, but Sadie was more muscular, particularly around the waist, thanks to her work with horses, so it was a test of Nula's skill. Fortunately the new fashion that year was for loose, straight, rather Grecian dresses with a dropped waistline, often with a false half-belt at the front but nothing at the waist itself; hemlines were going back down after the wartime convenience of six-inches-above, and were just above the ankle-bone, sometimes layered and cut into points.

Nula adapted a cream lace over heavy cream silk afternoon dress, an orange-red and peach georgette evening dress, a navy silk dress and jacket, and a neat grey flannel skirt and jacket with emerald piping.

'The cream lace will do for an evening dress as well,' Diana decreed, watching Sadie try them on. 'And the navy silk will be good for afternoons or the theatre.'

'Gosh, they are so splendid!' Sadie said, looking over her shoulder at her back view. 'They *feel* so lovely, too. Who would have thought clothes could be so nice to the touch?'

'If you didn't mess about with horses all the time, you could have found that out long ago. Nula will have to cut your hair. Bobbed hair's acceptable these days, but it has to look as though it's intentional. You have lovely hair, and a nice bit of wave to it. And,' she added, as Sadie was helped into the georgette evening dress, 'your colouring means you can wear anything. Not many people could wear that shade.'

133

'You did,' Sadie pointed out. But Diana was exceptional, as they both knew.

'It wants a bit of jewellery,' Nula said critically.

'There's that silver filigree set of mine,' Diana said. 'It will pick up the silver embroidery on the bodice. Necklace, earrings and bracelet. I never wear it, because silver doesn't really suit me. You can have it, Sadie, to keep.'

'Gosh, no, that's too much,' Sadie protested.

'Please try not to say "gosh". And it isn't too much. I want you to do me credit. I'll lend you my short string of pearls, too, and the earrings that go with it. You ought to have had pearls for your twenty-first birthday,' she added with a frown. 'If Father had been at home, he would have seen to it. I'm surprised he forgot.'

'I'm not,' Sadie said, with a shrug.

'Let me see your hands. Oh my goodness! Sadie, how can you let them *get* like this? Padmore will have to give you a full treatment.' Her maid came forward to look at the horrors, and gave a feeling sigh. Diana took it up. 'And no complaining about sitting still for two hours—'

'Two hours!'

'—because it's your own fault. If Padmore weren't a genius with hands, this whole trip would be off . . .'

We stayed at Diana's house in Park Place, which is just behind the Ritz, so convenient for everything, Sadie wrote.

Park Place was the house Rupert had bought and decorated for Diana, and which was a monument to his genius. Everything about it was beautiful – colours, fabrics, textures, the furniture and ornaments – even the light and shade had been artfully wrought. And everything looked as though it had been chosen deliberately. It was a new idea to Sadie, that a house could be furbished all-of-a-piece, to a plan, or an overriding taste. Everyone she knew lived in a house in which things had been assembled over time and just as it happened: furniture inherited from parents and grandparents, carpets and curtains replaced as they wore out, articles given as presents; a gallimaufry of objects, tolerated because you were used to it – and if the things served a function, who cared if they didn't 'match'?

But as Sadie wandered from room to room, she thought that, though some people might think it an awful fuss and even rather vulgar, it was really a form of art. Rupert had breathed into this house his vision of how a dwelling-place should look, and every single thing belonged exactly where it was. Even Diana. Especially Diana. It was, Sadie thought, his tribute to her – the lovely frame in which to display her loveliness.

Diana seemed to take it for granted. She drifted like a sylph through Rupert's Arcadian landscape, without ever commenting on it, or pausing to gaze at some exquisite setting, or brush a lovely piece with a fond hand.

And when Sadie said, 'It would be rather fun, don't you think, to do up a house from the beginning, like this?' Diana had looked blank for a moment, and then said, 'Rupert did it all. I should have found it a bore.'

The highlight of the trip was an evening at the Hippodrome to see 'Joy Bells', a very jolly new revue, with George Robey, who made us laugh until we cried. Phyllis Bedelis danced most beautifully – she studied with Pavlova and Cecchetti, you know – but the most exciting thing of all was the band which played a new kind of music called Dixieland Jazz, which comes from New Orleans in America. They were called The Original Dixieland Jazz Band. The music jumps about and makes your feet fidget, and makes you want to leap up and twirl around – at least, it did me! When we went to a dance the next evening, the music seemed almost dull by comparison. Apart from the Hippodrome and the dance, we lunched at the Ritz with some of Diana's friends, went to a night-club, and tea'd at two different houses. I would tell you whose, but I can't remember the names, and I don't suppose you'd know them any more than I did. Our constant companion in our revels was Lord Teesborough, who was Rupert's best man, and who, I think, is rather sweet on Diana. He was very attentive, and has nice, gentle manners. I like him.

It was Guy Teesborough's release from Dene Park which had decided the date of the London spree. He was eager to enjoy his freedom after six months of hospital and, though still walking with a stick and unable to dance with Diana, he was the force behind the whole schedule, and seemed determined that Sadie, too, should have a good time.

'Diana's talked about you to me a lot recently,' he told her. 'She seems to think it's rather a miracle getting you to agree to come to London, and doubts she'll be able to do it again, so I must make sure you enjoy yourself so much you'll want to repeat it.'

They were accompanied by his brother Ivo Rainton, and Diana's friend Obby Marlowe, who had nursed in France and had just quit the VAD. Sadie liked her a lot – she seemed practical and straightforward, but declared herself ready for some fun, like Guy. 'They made believe we were nuns, you know, serving a vocation under strict convent rule,' Obby remarked at the Ritz luncheon, when war stories were being told. 'The slightest breach would have you sent back to England in disgrace. Well, I mean to be as bad as I can now, just to make up for it. And you must all help me.'

Diana had invited Bobby Pargeter to make the numbers even. He was a slender, fair young man who had served in the Sherwood Foresters and seen many ferocious 'scraps' as he and Ivo called them. He didn't talk very much, but he had a sly, sidelong sense of humour that amused Sadie.

She was glad to see Lord Teesborough so close to Diana: her sister was a person who needed a man at her side to worship her and smooth her path through life. Obby and Bobby Pargeter were obviously old friends and often had their heads together, laughing at the same silly things, swapping pre-war memories of pranks and picnics, house parties and games. Sadie was less comfortable about being paired with Ivo. She liked him very much, but Diana didn't know about John Courcy, and she suspected her sister's motives. Ivo was attentive to her, told her she looked very pretty, fetched her wrap, sat next to her in the theatre and in restaurants, and held her closer while dancing than was strictly necessary. She didn't feel she could tell John about that. It was bad enough writing that she had had a lovely time in London, when he was still stuck out in Le Touquet and working too hard.

But when he wrote back, all he said about it was *I'm glad you went to London when your sister asked you, and I'm glad you enjoyed yourself. You've worked so hard through the war, and you deserve some fun. If she asks you again, you should go. I wish I could have been with you, but the time will come, my dearest Sadie, and we will have fun together, I promise you.*

'I'm glad you're back,' Beattie said to Sadie, 'because your aunt Addie's coming to visit, and I shall need your help. Normally, Antonia would have done everything for me, but . . .'

Antonia was still an invalid, and was only out of bed for an hour or two a day, and then only to lie on the sofa in the upstairs sitting-room. Dr Postgate had ordered complete rest for the rest of her pregnancy. Even if he hadn't, she had no strength for anything else.

'Of course I'll help,' Sadie said. 'Is it just to get a room ready for her? How long is she coming for?'

'A week or two. And it's not just the room.' Beattie hesitated. 'Everything's so drab and miserable since the war ended. Your going to London was the first bright thing that's happened. I thought we might have a dinner party for her.

I'm sure everyone needs cheering up.' She looked at Sadie questioningly.

'Oh, what a good idea!' Sadie said.

'We used to have such lovely parties before the war,' Beattie said. 'And I never see anyone now, unless it's on a committee.'

'It'll be strange without Father, though.'

'David can take his place. But it will be hard to get the numbers right, with so many females – you and me and Addie. And Diana must come. I must have a little glamour at my table. But that's another female.'

'I'm sure Diana can bring a suitable man,' Sadie said, thinking of Guy Teesborough. His mother had been Rupert's godmother, so he was practically family.

'I'd better have Cook in to discuss the menu.'

'She'll be pleased,' Sadie said. 'She's had nothing but war cooking for such ages.'

Cook returned to the kitchen in a near frenzy. 'Quick, quick, my recipe books!' she flung at Eileen. 'Don't just stand there, fetch 'em to me! Oh my! Twenty people – a proper dinner – just like the old days.' Eileen was still staring at her with her mouth open. 'Though I don't suppose *you*'ll be much help,' Cook told her. 'I wish Emily was here. She knew my ways.'

Ada came in with her housemaid's box in one hand and a china shepherd in the other. 'There's a tiny crack down this, I just noticed it. I don't know who's done it. It wasn't me, I do know that. I suppose it must have been Beryl, and she didn't dare say.'

'Never mind that!' Cook said excitedly. 'Lady Carbury's coming to stay, and the missus is going to have a dinner party for her – a proper slap-up, sit-down, six-course dinner, twenty at table.'

Ada's face brightened. 'Ooh, just like the old days! We'll have to get the dining-room and drawing-room done out extra well.'

'She says she'll hire waiters to serve at table, so you'll be able to help me in the kitchen, won't you, Ada dear? I got to get out a menu for her to approve. Oh, I do hope I can find the ingredients,' Cook concluded, her mind a kaleidoscope of dancing dishes, moulds, glazes, sauces, exotic presentations. After years of making do, rationing, war recipes, and no one at home . . . She was almost panting with desire.

'What a shame Mrs David's not well,' Ada said, following her own track. 'She could have decorated the table – she's got such a light hand with flowers and such.'

Beattie's sister Adelaide looked so like her there was never any doubt they were sisters. Addie had always been a little taller, a little thinner, her hair a shade less fair and her eyes a shade less blue; and in her, Beattie's perfect features had a slight, though attractive irregularity. In their youth, Beattie had been the beauty, and also the clever one and the vivacious one; Addie had resigned herself to being a slightly faded version of her younger sister. Sir John Carbury, baronet, had been selected for her as a suitable husband, and she had had the good fortune to fall in love with him. Jock and Addie had led a very happy life together, despite the unrest and dangers of later years in Ireland. His only fault lay in dying too soon.

Beattie saw the effect of that bereavement. She hadn't seen her sister since before the war, and the difference was marked: Addie was too thin, almost gaunt in the face, and her hair had turned grey. She look ten years older, not four.

'I'm so glad you've come,' Beattie said.

Addie had been inspecting her, too. 'I'm so sorry about Bobby. If anything had happened to one of mine . . .'

'Let's not talk about that,' Beattie said, taking her hand and folding it under her arm. 'Let me show you to your room. You can take off your things and tell me how long

139

you'll be staying. I'm hoping it will be months. I've missed you.'

It was true: she was discovering how lonely she had been, with the estrangement from Edward, and now his long absence; Bobby's death, and David's wounding; and the loss of Louis, which had to remain a secret. She had borne all these things alone. She was not unique in that, she knew – all over the country women toiled silently under a burden of grief that could not be shared. But the very sight of Addie reminded her of their girlhood together, when they had shared everything from fans and artificial flowers to dreams and confidences.

'I wish I could stay longer,' Addie said, 'but my passage is booked for the thirtieth. I shall have to go straight from here to Southampton. I could have caught the boat at Queenstown, but I wanted to see you before I went so I booked it from Southampton. It's a bit more expensive, but it's worth it. I hope you'll come down on the train with me to see me off?'

'You're going to America?' Beattie had worked it out. 'But you didn't say!'

'Didn't I? I'm sure I put in my letter—'

'No, not a word.'

'Oh dear, I'm sorry. I seem to be getting very vague these days. Since Jock died, I don't sleep very well, which makes me stupid all day. I forget whether I've done something or only *thought* about doing it. Just last week I thought I'd refused Lady Newbridge's invitation to tea when I hadn't, and she waited and waited, and was quite annoyed. It was very embarrassing.'

They reached the bedroom that had been prepared for her, and Beattie noted with approval the nice arrangement of flowers, the clean towels, the writing paper, the fire in the grate and the biscuit tin on the overmantel. Sadie had done a good job. She helped Addie off with her hat, gloves and fur, and saw with distress how the old-rose woollen dress hung on her sister's frame. *I could get Nula to take it in for you,* she thought, but did not say it aloud.

'So you're going over to visit the boys?' she said instead.

Addie sat down on the edge of the bed, and felt with almost transparent fingers to see if her hair was still neat. 'It's more than that, Beattie dear. I really thought I'd told you. I'm going to live over there. I'm not coming back.'

CHAPTER ELEVEN

'Addie! You're emigrating?'

'Don't say it like that. You make it sound as if I'm dying.'

'But I'll never see you again,' Beattie cried. She had lost so much in the war. Now this?

'You might come and visit one day,' Addie said uncertainly. They both knew it was highly unlikely. Then she looked up pathetically. 'I half don't want to go. It's so far. It'll be so strange. But I've nothing in Ireland any more, now Jock's gone.'

'But the boys—'

'That's the thing, Bea. They're not coming back. They love it over there. They say there's no future for them in Ireland – and I think I agree with them. It's not the place it used to be. There are opportunities in America. It's a fresh young country.' She gave a despondent look. 'At their age, they *want* everything to be different. When you get to our age, all you want is for things to stay the same.'

'But what about the estate? Johnnie is Sir John Carbury now. Surely he can't just leave the land, his inheritance?'

Addie sighed. 'He's not interested in land. Or titles. He says they don't count for anything in America.'

'They count for something anywhere,' Beattie said firmly.

'Perhaps. But he doesn't want to be a farmer. He's going to sell the estate and use the money to get into minerals.'

'"Get into minerals"? What on earth does that mean?'

'Invest in them, I think. And minerals seem to be things

like copper and iron ore, and – and is there something called bauxite?'

'Darling, I have no idea.'

'He thinks it's going to be important, anyway. He says minerals are the future.' They looked at each other in bewilderment for a moment. Addie went on, 'He'll have to come back for a short time to wind everything up, of course, and to see about the sale. Meanwhile, the steward is going to run everything – he's very reliable. Jock trusted him.'

'The house? The furniture and so on?'

'The house is being sold with its contents,' Addie said. She didn't look happy about it. 'I've picked out a few things I wanted to keep, and they've been packed up with my clothes and personal effects to be shipped out. I'll be staying with Cousin Richard and Miranda in New York to begin with, but Johnnie's going to get a place of his own and I'll keep house for him.'

'In New York?'

'I suppose so. That's where these minerals are, from what I can gather. Or the investing side of them, anyway. I expect he'll travel a lot, though. Americans seem to travel all the time. Well, that will be nice, I suppose.'

Beattie looked at her sister's drooping mouth. Obviously there was no turning back now, so Addie would have to make the best of it. And Beattie must encourage her. 'I'm sure you'll enjoy New York,' she said. 'Wonderful shops. The theatres and so on. Lots of society. You were always so fond of society.'

'When I was young, I was,' Addie said. 'Once I married Jock, I got used to the quiet of the country. Not that it was quiet towards the end, with the rebels and everything.' She sighed. 'But you're right. It will be an adventure for me.'

They left it at that.

William received an invitation from Considine at last, and though Aunt Addie's visit had a week still to run, she insisted

143

he not turn it down for her sake. 'I've seen you, dear, and that's the important thing. You have your own life to live. Perhaps one day you'll come to America.'

'I'd really like to, Auntie. I'd like to travel everywhere in the world. And just think – one day in the future you'll be able to fly across the Atlantic in a day, instead of taking a week on a ship.'

Addie shuddered. 'The very idea! You'd never get me to go up in one of those things. *Much* too dangerous!'

'You're thinking of the early aeroplanes. They're much safer now,' William asserted. 'I'll fly to America one day, Auntie, I promise you, and come and see you. And take you up for a trip.'

Considine met William's train on a motor-bicycle.

'Jolly beast, ain't it?' he demanded, shoving the goggles to the top of his head. 'Bought it out of my last RAF salary. Second hand, but she goes a bit. Just the job for pottering about.'

'It looks super,' William agreed. It certainly made enough noise. 'But I thought you had a motor-car.'

'Yes, but she's not a taxi. Can't make a racehorse pull a milk cart, you know. Come on, hop on. Leave your bag. Our postman'll pick it up on his way past and drop it off. Oh – just a warning. Keep your mouth shut if you don't want it full of flies.'

William had to keep his eyes almost shut, too, for the same reason. But it was fun roaring through the narrow, winding country lanes, between hedges coming into full leaf, seeing cows leap away snorting, sending birds up with panicking cries. They pulled up a short time later in front of a pretty, modern house, with a big pink blossom tree in the front garden, and masses of tulips lined up like guardsmen on either side of a crazy-paved path.

Inside the house was modern too, with parquet floors and

light furniture and lots of floral-patterned chintz. Mr Considine was very dark, rather formidable-looking: a tall, bulky man with heavy glasses and a blue chin. He was in banking, and asked after William's father. 'Met him once, many years ago. He wouldn't remember me. I believe he's a big man now at the Paris conference?'

'They keep him very busy,' was all William could find to say. 'We don't hear from him very often.'

Mrs Considine was smart, well-dressed, with tightly curling grey hair done in a bun behind, and her glasses had thin gold frames. She greeted him kindly and said, 'Harold's told us so much about you. I've put you in the room next to his. I hope you'll be comfortable.'

And then she turned and introduced him to Eva.

William tried not to gawp.

'We're having an early tea,' Mrs Considine said, 'because I know you boys will want to go straight off to the airfield.'

Tea was served in a large, light room, with French windows onto the rear garden, by a neat parlourmaid in a frilly cap and apron. William was gaining the impression that everything in the Considine household was done with a high regard for propriety. Nobody looked at the maid or spoke to her, except for Mrs Considine saying, 'Thank you, that will be all.' He guessed the servants here would not be old family friends like those at The Elms.

He listened to the polite conversation that went on over tea (a good one, by the way, with very thin bread and butter and two different jams, cress sandwiches, muffins in a chafing dish, and both fruit and plain cake) and tried to respond politely when he was asked questions, but mostly he was trying not to stare at Eva Considine. She had black hair like her father's, curly and cut in a short crop, and dark brown eyes, whose lashes were so dark and thick they made them look enormous. Her skin was delicate and white, and her prominent cheekbones made her eyes seem slightly slanted and gave her an almost exotic look. When she caught him staring at her, she smiled at him: her lips were full and her smile was beautiful, so it didn't help much.

And then, when she carried round second cups, she changed her seat and sat next to him on the sofa and undid him completely with her first remark. 'I ought to be very cross with you, because I can see that while you're here I shan't be riding on the motor-bicycle at all. Usually Harry takes me on the back when he goes to the airfield.'

'Are you interested in aeroplanes?' William asked her, hardly believing his luck.

'How can anyone not be?' she said. 'As soon as they start up civilian flying again, I'm going to learn.'

Mr Considine overheard the remark and said, 'On that subject, I heard yesterday that that the change to the Air Navigation Regulations will certainly go through next week, and civil flying will be authorised from the first of May.' He adopted a stern scowl in his daughter's direction. 'And you will certainly not be learning to fly, young lady.'

But she only laughed and blew a kiss at him. 'Darling Papa, you know you can't refuse me anything.' She turned to William. 'Is flying the most divine thing, or is it? I've only been up once on a half-hour trip, before the war, but I loved it like anything. Don't you love it more than anything in the world?'

'I do,' William said, his heart lost. Those smoky eyes, that white skin, that cloud of dark curls – *and* she loved flying! And riding on motor-bicycles! And she was talking to him like a proper person. Having gone into the service virtually from school, his experience of women had been limited to his sisters and the servants, to whom he had always been a little boy. 'You feel so free,' he added, hoping to keep her talking.

'That's what I want!' she said energetically. 'To get away from this crabbed, cramped life down here on the ground. To soar! To fly! To travel! The whole world—'

'I suppose it will mean your wearing trousers,' Mrs Considine interrupted, bringing the flight of fancy crashing down. 'I must insist that you have them properly made by someone who knows what they are doing. I saw Lady Elsie Barton in trousers during that hospital rally last year, and I must say, though I rather abominate the whole idea, she did manage to look very elegant in them. You should find out who made them for her, Evaline, and go to the same dress-maker.' She put a hand to her cheek. 'Or would one call them a dressmaker, if they're making trousers? Oh dear, I foresee so many complications in this new world of ours. I wish things wouldn't change.'

'The war has changed everything, Mary dear,' said Mr Considine with a kind look.

'Except the capacity of a teapot,' said Mrs Considine. 'Ring the bell, Evaline, I must have another cup. You'll have another, won't you, Mr Hunter?'

'Th—' William began.

But Considine jumped in. 'No time for that, old chap. We have to be going, Mama, if we're to have a meaningful time at the airfield.'

'What time is sunset?' Mrs Considine asked. 'You know I don't like you riding about these lanes after lighting-up time. It's so dangerous.'

'Eight o'clock,' Considine supplied. 'Ten past, in fact.'

'Oh well, it doesn't matter, then. Dinner is at eight, and you'll have to be back by seven-thirty to change. The Dursfields are coming.'

William looked worried. 'Oh gosh, I'm frightfully sorry, I'm afraid I didn't pack any evening things.'

'We won't dress,' Mrs Considine said graciously. 'The Dursfields are old friends – they'll understand. But you'll be covered with dust when you get back. You'll want to wash and change into something more suitable.' Like Considine, William was dressed in flannel bags, shirt and a sleeveless pullover.

147

Considine was on his feet. 'Yes, yes, Ma, we know all that. Come *on*, Hunter, or there'll be no time left.'

William got up, casting apologetic looks around, and Eva Considine intercepted one and said sweetly, 'Don't let my brother bully you, Mr Hunter. It's awfully bad for him to get his own way all the time.'

William, virtually dragged away, had no time to answer, even if he could have thought of something sufficiently witty and arresting to say. He didn't want to appear like an idiot to her.

Edward had never been so busy. He looked back on his civilian days with a kind of astonishment, unable to believe there had been time to read newspapers, hold social conversations, drink sherry. Even the war had been leisurely in comparison: short bursts of wild activity, yes, but punctuated by long periods of tedium. Who was it who had said war was an organised bore? But now he was being appealed to from all sides for information, opinions and rulings, while trying to ascertain facts and figures from a variety of sources that ranged from the unhappily vague to the deliberately opaque.

The conference had formally opened in the Hall of Mirrors at Versailles, on the 18th of January. That was the anniversary of the proclamation of Wilhelm I as Emperor of the newly united Germany in 1871. From that event, popular opinion in France believed, all the evils of the war had sprung.

But the heads of state of twenty-seven nations were only the beginning. They attracted prime ministers and foreign ministers, diplomats, industrialists, academics, scientists, lobbyists for every popular cause from women's rights to national independence, and each orbiting satellite was surrounded by aides and advisers and secretaries as thick as meteors around Saturn. And the whole boiling was further surrounded by what Lord Forbesson called 'a plague of journalists'. The conference seemed to suck in more people and more causes by the week.

There were fifty-two separate 'commissions' to discuss different aspects of the peace settlement and prepare reports on the various topics, each with its own office in the Quai d'Orsay, which had been given over for the business of settling the treaty. Edward was staying at the Hôtel Duc de Bourgogne, and he had arranged for a private office there on the ground floor as well.

'You've got yourself holed in nicely in your dug-out here,' Lord Forbesson said when he visited Edward on his way to a meeting. 'I've always said, any fool can be *un*comfortable. I'm at the Normandy – fairly decent billet. Seen much of Paris?'

'Nothing,' Edward said. He was vaguely aware that some-where 'out there' was Paris, city of pre-war dreams, but he never had time to visit the sights, partake of the entertain-ment that was burgeoning again in response to the influx of visitors, or even eat in a restaurant. 'I go to bed late and rise early, and generally have my meals brought to me on a tray at my desk.'

'Oh, dear me, that won't do,' said Lord Forbesson. 'Surely you're entitled to some time to yourself?'

'I think mine is the busiest commission, what with war debts, fees, fines, valuations, reparations. Finance is the topic closest to everyone's heart.'

'And, of course, you've made yourself a slave to vested interests,' Forbesson said sternly.

Edward gave a faint smile. 'It's hard to do anything else. Here they all are, you know.'

'Yes, and I can't help thinkin' that Paris is to blame. If they'd held the damned conference in – oh, in Plymouth or Peterborough or Penge, all these johnnies wouldn't have been so damned eager to come to it, or hang around so long when they got here.'

Edward laughed. 'You may be right.'

'I know I am. Besides, there's no need of them. England and France should be sorting it all out between us.'

'What about America?'

Forbesson waved a hand. 'Of course they helped out at the end. But now they're pumped full of these high-minded ideals about a new world order, universal peace and brotherhood and such. All very well, but that's not how things get done. League of Nations indeed! They're just slowin' us down. As for the rest of these hangers-on – Austria, Hungary, Japan, the Balkan states . . .'

'The questions have to be dealt with,' Edward protested mildly. His aide came in just then with a tray of coffee and a pile of correspondence tucked under his arm. 'Ah, thank you.' He looked at Forbesson. 'Have you met Lieutenant Duval? His parents are French, but he was brought up in England.'

'Yes, I know his people. He went to the same school as my son Esmond. How are you, my boy?'

'Very well, my lord, thank you. I was at Harrow too,' he explained to Edward, 'but in the year above.'

'He looks after me very well, as you can see,' Edward said. Duval was a fine, intelligent young man, and he was becoming fond of him. He reminded him a little of young Peter Warren, his confidential secretary before the war, who had been like a son to him and had fallen at Passchendaele.

'I see that,' said Forbesson. 'And that smells like damn good coffee. Where did you get it, Duval?'

'I'm afraid I'm not at liberty to divulge my sources, my lord.'

Forbesson gave a bark of laughter. 'Good for you! Because if you did divulge, you'd be priced out of the market before you could wink! Good coffee's damned hard to find. The stuff the French drink is vile. Now, look here, Hunter, I'm at the Quai this afternoon and I know you are because

150

we're on the same committee, but I'm determined to take you out to luncheon beforehand. Damnit, a sandwich on a tray is no life for a man, particularly in the heart of Paris.'

Edward looked at Duval. 'What is my schedule for today?'

'You have an hour free between one and two,' Duval said, 'but I was going to try to squeeze in the head of the Paris branch of the London County and Westminster Bank. He's been pressing to see you. I thought he could talk to you over luncheon.'

'Luncheon – as in, sandwiches at the desk?' Forbesson put in.

'Yes, sir – my lord. Otherwise—'

'No, I've decided,' Edward said, suddenly rebelling. 'The bank will have to wait. Today, Sir Edward Hunter is going to lunch with Lord Forbesson of the War Office.'

'Very good, Sir Edward,' said Duval, serenely. 'And shall I warn the Mexican chargé that you might be late? You have him at the Quai at two.'

'Cancel him,' Edward said, a wild feeling of festival coming over him. 'Find some other time to put him in.'

'Good fellow!' Forbesson said, with a wide smile. 'I shall call for you at one sharp. I look to you to get him up to scratch,' he told Duval. 'Don't let him cry off.' And he drained his coffee, and sauntered out.

Duval closed the door after him, and brought forth the sheaf of correspondence. 'All these are for signature, Sir Edward. Nothing that need concern you. This letter I haven't opened. I think it's personal. It's from England.'

He placed the envelope before Edward, who recognised Beattie's script. 'It's from my wife.'

'Very good, sir. The ambassador will be here in fifteen minutes,' Duval said. He rearranged the letters on the desk and slipped quietly out. By the time he closed the door, Edward was deep in the letter.

It was not the usual fare from Beattie, who kept up a

151

dutiful correspondence with him, simply telling him what was going on at home. In this letter, she spoke of herself, and it was from the heart.

She spoke of her sister's visit, and the fact that she was emigrating to America. *I don't know why it has affected me so deeply,* she wrote.

Addie and I haven't seen much of each other over the years, but I always knew she was there, and that I could go to her if I wanted. Now I shall never see her again, and it's like another death. I feel as though everything is being taken away from me. And it makes me think of you, Edward, and our marriage. I know I did a terrible thing, and perhaps you can never forgive me. But we go on living, and one day the war will really be over and you will come home, and what then? I think if we tried we could still make a good life together. Do you feel the same? If there is any tenderness left for me in you, perhaps I could come over to Paris, and we could spend a little time together – to get to know each other again. Perhaps in a place where neither of us has any memories, it might be easier to get over our difficulties. May we try? I know I deserve nothing from you, but you are the very best of men, and I appeal to your goodness, your kindness, and the love we used to share. Please answer me soon – I am in torment until I hear from you.

He read the letter twice, his heart painfully torn. He was starting a third reading when the door opened and Duval looked in to say the ambassador had arrived. Edward held up his hand in a staying motion. 'If I wanted to take a few days off,' he said, 'would it be feasible?'

Duval looked at him kindly. A letter from his wife, and only now he wanted a holiday! Many of the principal players in the conference had brought their wives over, and sight-seeing with them was a second industry. Many others had established mistresses in Paris. Few were as conscientious as Sir Edward, who did not seem to have a selfish bone in his body, and gave himself too readily, in Duval's opinion, to be pecked to death by everyone with a footling demand.

'Whatever you wish can be arranged, Sir Edward,' he said. 'Your timetable is at your own disposal.'

'But there is so much to do,' Edward began doubtfully.

'The conference has been going on for over four months, and there is no end date set. All business must be attended to – but it needn't be attended to today or tomorrow.'

Edward smiled. 'In that case, perhaps you can arrange two free days for me – no, three days. Three full days. With evenings.'

'Of course, Sir Edward. And accommodation for Lady Hunter?'

'Yes. Not in this hotel.'

'No indeed. I shall make sure that no one but me knows where you are. Shall I bring in the ambassador?'

He went out, with a small private smile to himself. Three days? He would arrange four without engagements – and make sure those on the fifth day were postponable, just in case. Sir Edward deserved a holiday.

In a world of change and disappointment, the Ritz was always reassuringly the Ritz. Beattie sat with her back to the wall, facing Beth, and could see beyond her in the body of the restaurant the usual sober mix of respectable middle-aged women, elderly civilians and men in uniform, topped with a froth of young people enjoying their freedom – celebrating a warrior's return, perhaps, or an engagement. Some of the young men bore the evidence of wounds. She was reminded suddenly of Edward telling her that his club had mounted a nailbrush on the wall above the basins in the lavatory, so that members who had lost an arm in the war could still scrub the nails of the remaining hand. She gave a little shiver.

Beth was cutting the meat from the bone of her lamb cutlet and didn't notice. When she looked up, she said, 'A trip to Paris! I'm delighted for you. And envious. I should so love to travel again. I feel as if I've been shut in a prison for four years.'

'I feel the same. But it must be worse for you – you always travelled so much before the war, you and Jack.' They had been dedicated to walking and climbing, and had sought out mountains all over Europe.

'We used to talk, when he came home on leave, of what we'd do after the war,' Beth said. 'A long motor-tour, the first thing. We even talked of taking flying lessons and buying a little aeroplane, so we could travel further.' She sighed. 'Now I can't get him to leave the house. He won't even go to the pictures. Whatever film I entice him with, he says, "You go, dear. I'm a bit tired."'

'He's bound to be tired,' Beattie said. 'I remember when David—'

'David was wounded,' Beth said.

'But the whole experience,' Beattie said slowly. 'We can't imagine, really, what it was like for them, but it must have been shattering. Like a dreadful illness. It will take a long time to convalesce. You have to give him time.'

'You're right; I know. But I've longed and longed to have him back, and now all he does is potter about the house like an old man, and fall asleep in his chair. He doesn't even read. He'll sit with the newspaper open for hours, but never turns a page.'

'Perhaps he's afraid of what he'll see in it. Of what he'll be reminded of.'

'I want to help him,' Beth said, meeting her eyes urgently. 'I *do*. But how can I help when he won't talk to me? He won't discuss the war or his experiences at all. If I ask him a direct question, he makes a silly joke of it. Treating me like a child. And if I persist, he gets angry and walks out of the room.'

'It's something we'll have to learn to live with,' Beattie said. 'At home, I'm dealing with it every day – women coming to me for help because their men can't settle back in. Some are violent, others just closed off and silent. Some drink themselves stupid, or get into fights.' She thought a moment. 'Sometimes the worst ones are those who seem to be coping, but their wives know they aren't really there at all. And that sort, when they eventually break . . .' They had had three suicides in the village now. But she didn't want to bring that up with Beth.

Beth changed the subject with a determined smile. 'It's wonderful that Edward's invited you – no doubts about *his* dedication. And how exciting to be over there with all those kings and princes and so on!'

'I don't suppose I'll see much of them. But Paris – well!'

'Yes, it's enough on its own, isn't it? Goodness, the lovely times Jack and I have had there. But my dear, what will you do for a maid? And travelling alone? Before the war you'd have had a courier as well.'

'I'm quite capable of handling the journey,' Beattie said. 'Edward's secretary is booking everything for me, right through. First class on the train, and a deck cabin on the boat – though I think that's an extravagance, when the crossing is so short.'

'You might be glad of it, if it's rough,' Beth said wisely.

'Then I'll be met at the Gare du Nord, and taken to the hotel. As for a maid, I haven't had one since before the war, and there are always chambermaids at the hotel.'

'Bravely spoken,' said Beth. 'But when Edward's back home for good, you'll have to think about a maid. Sir Edward and Lady Hunter will be expected to put on a bit of style.'

'I'll cross that bridge when I come to it.'

'Any idea when that will be?'

Beattie shrugged. 'None. The conference seems to be self-perpetuating. I wouldn't be surprised if it went on for ever.'

155

Dr Postgate listened for a long time at Antonia's chest. 'Keep absolutely still and quiet,' he had told her. She kept still, and listened to the quietness of the house. When the flurry of excitement and movement caused by Beattie's departure for Paris had died down, it had left a very a depleted company, now that Lady Carbury had gone and William was away in Surrey.

'Don't worry about anything,' she had assured her mother-in-law. 'Sadie and I will look after the house and David will look after us. Go and enjoy yourself. I envy you. I've always want to see Paris.'

It wasn't quite true. She *had* always wanted to see Paris, but she didn't envy her. That long journey, the foreign porters, the fear of lost luggage, the strange hotel and the chamber-maids who wouldn't speak English. The sheer effort involved! Antonia was so tired, all the time, that even contemplating it daunted her.

She hadn't told David how tired she was. Whenever he asked how she felt, she spoke cheerfully, and pretended lying on the sofa all day was a trial to her. But the truth was, she was fit for nothing else. Even having Marcus brought to her exhausted her. She thought Ethel knew that because she took pains to keep the child entertained during those visits and to spare Antonia from talking much. But David mustn't guess. She couldn't let him down – it was hard enough for him, worrying about her being bed-bound. She wouldn't have him troubled by her stupid weakness.

Postgate sighed, and felt her pulse again. Then he removed the stethoscope from his ears and looked at her, a kindly but grave look that gave her a cold feeling, like a piece of ice going down her throat.

'What is it?' she asked.

He hesitated. 'Perhaps it ought to wait until your husband is here.'

Her lips seemed suddenly dry. 'That sounds as though

156

it's bad news. Come, whatever it is, tell me straight out. I'm not a child.'

'But you are *with* child,' Postgate said. He sat on the edge of the bed – a breach of protocol that warned her more than anything that trouble was approaching – and took hold of her hand. 'Very well,' he said. 'I know you are a sensible woman. Just remember that you must keep calm for the baby's sake.'

'Is something wrong with the baby?' she asked anxiously.

'No, it's not the baby, it's you.' He became brisk. 'Your attack of influenza has weakened your heart. It's a not uncommon side effect. Normally, a long period of rest and care would be prescribed, and in time, the heart might repair itself, grow stronger. But in your case, your heart is already having to do the work of two, supporting the baby, and when the time comes to give birth . . .' He sighed again. 'I'm afraid the strain of the birth process could prove too much.'

'You mean . . .?' She couldn't immediately say the words. 'You mean, I might die?'

He looked at her carefully as if gauging whether she could bear it. Then he said, 'It is a possibility. A danger.'

'I might die?' she said again. Even from within the cushioning cocoon of her tiredness, she felt a sharp surge of urgency. She didn't want to die! She was too young! She had a husband and children. Life was sweet, as sweet as the smell of a baby's head, as sweet as the warmth of a man's arms around you. She wanted her life – she was entitled to it.

Postgate's fingers were on her wrist. 'Don't get agitated. Take a deep breath.'

'I don't want to die,' she whispered.

'I had to make you aware of the risk. If you weren't already pregnant, I would advise most strongly against your becoming pregnant, given the condition of your heart. As it is, there is nothing to be done but to go through with it, to give you every possible care, and to hope for the best.' He watched her face struggling with it, measuring the beat of her pulse. 'That's why I wanted to wait until your husband—'

'No,' she said sharply. 'He mustn't know.'

'Now, Mrs Hunter, I really—'

'Promise me you won't tell him.'

'You will need his support. And if the worst comes to the worst, he will know anyway,' Postgate pointed out.

'But I might be all right – isn't that true? You only said it – it was a possibility.'

'Yes,' he admitted.

'Then I won't have him worried unnecessarily. He's been through so much. And perhaps it will all be all right. You won't tell anyone. Is that clear?' Her voice was firm now, her gaze direct and stern.

Postgate almost shrugged. 'It is your right to keep it secret,' he said, 'but I don't advise it. You will need support.'

'I shall have it,' she said, suddenly exhausted. She let her weight back onto the pillows, her eyes feeling like lead coins. 'Promise me.'

'Very well,' said Postgate. 'But I do advise you have a trained nurse to attend you for at least the last month. Six weeks would be better.'

'We'll see,' she said, her eyes drifting closed.

CHAPTER TWELVE

Every now and then, in a life spent with horses, you come across one so beautiful it makes your heart ache. The gelding was an English Thoroughbred, dark bay with black points and a long mane and tail; and while many horses could be described thus, there was some extra dimension of beauty to this one, a fineness, a harmony, a grace that made him stand out from the rest. When he turned his head to look at Sadie, she felt a pang at his perfection that was almost sorrow.

She had given him the name Allegro for his light, swift step. 'I know we aren't supposed to name them,' she had said apologetically to Mrs Cuthbert, 'but—'

'He's likely to be here a long time,' Mrs Cuthbert anticipated, 'so a name will be convenient.'

He had come to them in a batch for finishing and selling, with a healing scar from a shrapnel wound on his quarters, and some deeper wound to his mind which was not immediately apparent. He was good to handle, once he had settled in, and was, in Sadie's verdict, 'divine to ride', but he was unpredictable. He would go along steadily for some time, but then something would set him off. A sudden noise: a vehicle backfiring, a pigeon clattering unexpectedly out of a bush, the lid of the feed bin clanging shut, a distant gunshot in the woods – these were understandable irritants. But sometimes it was a paper bag blowing across the yard, or a jacket left across a gate, or something discarded and half hidden in the grass beside the ride. And sometimes it was impossible to tell what had done it. Then he would buck, rear, or try to bolt in panic. If he was confined in the stable, he might rear, bite or kick.

'Dangerous,' Captain Casimir had said. 'We can't sell him, not with that fault. He'll have to be put down.'

And Sadie had turned to him with a passionate denial. 'He's too good to give up on! I can reschool him – I *can*! Only give him time.'

Casimir continued to shake his head. 'We can't be sentimental in this business, not with tens of thousands of horses to deal with. Keeping him here costs money. He'll fetch five pounds from the knacker.'

Mrs Cuthbert had intercepted Sadie's look and realised that this was something out of the usual. She knew Sadie had come to terms with the necessity, at times, of humane dispatch; knew she was aware that thousands of horses were going for meat in France. Some things had to be borne. But for some reason this horse had crossed the border from a general love of horses to a particular. 'He *is* very handsome,' she said slowly. 'Slaughter would be an awful waste, if something could be done with him.'

Sadie's face turned to her in an agony of hope.

'I doubt—' Casimir began.

And Mrs Cuthbert interrupted. 'Suppose I buy him from the army?' she said. 'I'll give you the knacker's price. If we can cure him of his bad habits, he'll make me a pretty profit. If not . . .' She shrugged. 'There's always a gamble, when one deals with horses.'

Casimir had raised no objection, and the bay became Mrs Cuthbert's official property, but Sadie's in everything but name. Mrs Cuthbert left him to her care, reasoning that a constant relationship with one person was more likely to cure him than anything else. He had a jump in him, and a

160

turn of speed, and he'd make a fine hunter, or even steeple-chaser, if he shaped up, she thought.

Allegro had kicked Podrick, narrowly missing his knee, and bitten both the boys, Brian and Cyril – Cyril several times. He hadn't bitten Mrs Cuthbert yet, but that was because she kept a wary distance from him. Usually you could tell when a horse was going to bite, but Allegro didn't give you warning – another reason he was dangerous. But with Sadie he was better. Perhaps she really would be able to 'cure' him.

She was lungeing him in the paddock one Saturday after-noon in May: a fine day, with a light breeze ruffling his mane and her hair, and blowing the liquid call of wood pigeons down from the woods on the crest of the hill, and the smell of lilac from the hedgerow. A day for happiness. Allegro seemed content, and was trotting out beautifully with his ears at a relaxed angle. Then suddenly they shot forward and he gave a breenge that almost snatched the rope from her hand.

'Silly, it's only Mrs Cuthbert,' she told him, bringing him to her. He peeped about, fidgeting his forefeet as though contemplating flight. She put her hands to his muzzle and let him snuff her palms, and he consented to be reassured, and nudged her hard in the chest. It was a habit of his. She had a permanent bruise there.

She led him towards the gate. Mrs Cuthbert seemed agitated: she called something Sadie could not catch, and gestured with one hand; but there was no smile. Allegro caught her mood and would not go closer. Sadie's heart faltered. She hadn't heard from John for over two weeks. She struggled to control the horse as he snorted and pulled backwards. 'What's happened?' she called.

'It's John Courcy,' said Mrs Cuthbert

'Oh God,' Sadie cried softly.

'No, no!' Mrs Cuthbert called. 'He's *here*!'

'Here?'

'Up at the house – talking to Horace,' said Mrs Cuthbert, as if this detail would cut through the bewilderment. 'He's come home.'

She had to put Allegro away first and, having caught the general excitement, he played up all the way. Fortunately Mary was in the yard. 'I'll take him. You go,' she said.

The track up to the house seemed steep, effortful in the sunshine, in her heavy riding boots, as she tried to run. *He was home? Why hadn't he told her he had leave?* From under the surprise, a warmth of joy was rising. It was the first time she would welcome him back since he had proposed, the first time she would greet him as his avowed love, with the right to be glad, to be embraced. At every other meeting in the past she'd had to hide her feelings.

She found them in the small sitting-room at the back, with the French windows open to the neglected garden. With a cigarette, and a cup of tea on the table beside him, he sat facing Mr Cuthbert; Mrs Cuthbert was still standing, just inside the door. Both men rose as Sadie appeared. Her eyes were for Courcy alone. Love made a huge knot in her throat: she couldn't speak; she could hardly see.

He said, 'Sadie.' Just that. She crossed the room to him, and his arms came out jerkily, to enfold her. They held each other, quite still, for a long moment. Sadie had never imagined giving a display of affection in public like that; but there could hardly be anyone in Europe now who would be surprised to see a soldier embracing a girl.

Behind her, she heard Mr Cuthbert clear his throat. 'Perhaps we should . . .?'

And, cheek against John's chest, she felt as well as heard him saying, 'No, please, I want to talk to you all.'

He released her, and she felt oddly naked without his arms, oddly embarrassed. He had gestured to Mrs Cuthbert

162

to sit and, when she did, resumed his own armchair. Sadie hovered, unsure, ill at ease. Now, for the first time, she really looked at him. Before, she had seen only 'John'. Now she saw a man who had suffered too much. His hair was speckled grey all over, like frost; his face pale, too thin, and marked with the deep, fine lines of pain; and there was that indefinable look she had seen before, many times, in the hospitals she had visited, the look of someone who had been ill to the brink of death.

He looked at her at last, and tried to smile, calling her to him, so she perched on the arm of his chair, glad to be near him, wanting to touch him but not quite daring.

'I should have told you I was coming,' he said, addressing Mrs Cuthbert mostly, 'but there was so much to say, too much to put in a letter. And as you always said I was welcome to come here on leave—'

'Yes, indeed,' said Mrs Cuthbert with emphasis. 'You don't need to wait to be invited.'

He nodded thanks. 'So I thought it best just to come, and do all the explaining in person.'

'No explanation necessary—' Mr Cuthbert rumbled.

Courcy cut him off. 'It isn't leave, you see. I've been discharged.'

Sadie's heart jumped so hard it hurt her. 'You're home for good?' she cried gladly.

He looked at her. 'Discharged because of ill health. Sadie – please. Let me say it all.' He put his hands over his face and rubbed his eyes wearily. When he lowered them, he seemed brisker, as if determined to get through something. 'When I was ill in February, it wasn't influenza. It had similar symptoms, and with so many of us ill at the same time, it wasn't surprising that everyone thought it was. It was unpleasant while it lasted, and left me feeling weak and tired even after I was discharged as fit. But then, so does influenza. Then I had another bout of it a month ago, and this time

I saw a different doctor. He diagnosed it as undulant fever. Out there, they sometimes call it Malta fever, because so many of the troops in Malta suffer from it.'

Mr Cuthbert spoke for all of them. 'I've heard of Malta fever, but I don't know anything about it.'

'It's also called Mediterranean fever, because it's endemic all round the Mediterranean,' Courcy went on, in a matter-of-fact voice, as though discussing someone else's ailment. 'They don't know what causes it. It isn't infectious, apparently, so they think it's probably contracted through contaminated water or food. Well, there's plenty of that over there.'

'And the symptoms are like those of influenza?'

He nodded. 'Superficially. Fever, sweats, debilitation, nausea, headache. Pains in the joints and muscles – those are particularly unpleasant. Also back pain. And it seems that once you have had it, it recurs periodically – like malaria. There's no cure for it, and recurrences can continue for years, perhaps for life. So, despite needing all the vets they can get out there, they decided I was no longer fit to serve, and gave me my discharge.'

'You're out? Completely? You never have to go back?' Sadie asked urgently.

Now he looked at her. 'I'm not even bound to the reserve. I am a civilian again.'

Sadie was too overcome with joy to speak. She saw how ill he had been and how tired he looked; but now he was home they would care for him and feed him up. Rest and quiet would restore him.

Mrs Cuthbert said, 'Will you have to go to Edinburgh?' His father, an Edinburgh physician – his only relative – had died there the year before. As far as she knew, it was the only place where he had had ties.

'No,' said Courcy. 'The solicitor wound up the estate and sold the house. There's nothing for me to do there.'

'Then you must stay here,' Mrs Cuthbert said firmly.

'I can't impose on you for long,' Courcy began.

But she interrupted. 'Nonsense. It's no imposition. You know what this house is like – the more the merrier. You will look upon this place as your home, if you please, for as long as you wish.'

'Hear hear,' said Mr Cuthbert, getting to his feet. 'And now I think we should celebrate your freedom with a bottle of something agreeable.'

'Indeed,' said Mrs Cuthbert quickly. 'And there shall be a gala feast tonight. Sadie, you'll stay for dinner? You're not expected home? I can telephone and tell them.'

Husband and wife had exchanged a look. They both realised there was trouble ahead. But they had also seen Sadie's ecstatic face, and decided the time for revelations was not yet. Let there be pleasure and celebration while it lasted.

It was a good time for William to be at Brooklands. The *Daily Mail* had offered a prize of £10,000 for the first flight across the Atlantic within seventy-two consecutive hours, and Harry Hawker, the chief test pilot for Sopwith's, was going to take up the challenge. Accompanied by navigator Kenneth Mackenzie Grieve, he was going to fly a biplane, based on the Sopwith B1 bomber, from Newfoundland to Ireland, and the flying community at Brooklands talked about little else. The aeroplane, named the Sopwith Atlantic, had been extensively tested at Brooklands before being dismantled and shipped off to America. It had a deeper fuselage than the B1, to house a gigantic fuel tank; the wheels were designed to be jettisoned after take-off to reduce drag, and a boat was built into the fuselage decking behind the cockpit, in case of ditching at sea. The attempt ought to have taken place in April, but terrible weather in Newfoundland had prevented the *Atlantic* from taking off.

'So you haven't missed it after all,' said Considine. 'The *Atlantic*'s bound to be flown back to Brooklands afterwards—'

'— and we'll be here to see it,' William concluded. 'We might get to shake their hands!'

'What a thing!' said Considine 'To be able to say for the rest of our lives, "We were there."'

Meanwhile, the lifting of the restriction on civil flight meant an increase of opportunity for two earthbound ex-RAF flyers longing for change. They were accepted with brotherly ease round the sheds, and soon became such familiar figures that no one questioned their presence. They could take part in earnest discussions, stick their heads inside engine cowlings, wield a spanner, help trundle out a machine, generally make themselves useful; and trust that eventually, gloriously, someone would take pity on their envious faces and allow them to take one up.

The transatlantic attempt eventually took place on Sunday the 18th of May. The *Atlantic* took off at three-thirty local time, the information relayed by radio to Brooklands where everyone hung around the office waiting for news. But all went silent; and after many hours of painful hope, they realised something must have gone badly wrong. The likelihood was that the biplane had failed and crashed into the sea, or gone so far off course she had run out of fuel and come down. Either way, it was most likely that Hawker and Grieve were dead.

It brought home to all concerned that flying was still a dangerous business, especially when attempting to break records. Many flyers had been lost trying to cross the Channel in the early days, but now it was quite a routine thing. One day, men would fly non-stop across the Atlantic as if it were nothing, and the names of those like Hawker and Grieve who had failed would be forgotten, as were all but Bleriot for the Channel. But they were Brooklands men, it had been a Brooklands attempt, and they were mourned as flyers mourned: brisk and brotherly, and looking straight away to the next thing.

A week later mourning turned to relief and intense interest, as the news arrived on Saturday the 24th that a Danish cargo ship, the *Mary*, had put in to the Butt of Lewis with Hawker and Grieve on board. And, over the next few days, the story filtered through. The attempt had been going well until around nightfall on the first day, when the engine had started to overheat, probably because of a blockage in the water pipe. Attempts to repair had failed, and the flyers had been forced to alter course so as to reach the shipping lanes where they could put down with a hope of rescue. Having landed on the water, they were picked up by the steamer, but as she had no radio, there was no way of telling anyone where they were until she reached land.

'I think it's jolly decent of the *Daily Mail* to give them five thousand pounds anyway,' Considine said, as he and William strolled towards the sheds the following day. 'They deserve a consolation prize. They would have made it if not for that stupid pipe.'

'I'm just glad they're safe,' said William, because that was what Eva had said the night before at dinner. ('You can always build another aeroplane, but you can't replace people. And Mr Hawker is so *very* nice. And awfully handsome.')

Considine's attention had been distracted. 'I say, look, isn't that Colin Burgess?'

'I don't know,' said William. 'You mean the chap with the big 'tache? Who's Colin Burgess?'

'Oh, he was well known here before the war. One of the pioneers. Had his own company, BAC – Burgess Air Company. Flying lessons, pleasure trips, competitions. He was always damn nice to me, never told me to push off when I was hanging around asking questions. I wonder what he's up to now.'

'Wasn't he in the war?'

'Failed the medical for flying, poor fellow,' said Considine with considerable sympathy. 'He worked for de Havilland on research and development instead.' He had been walking briskly in the direction of the moustached one as he spoke, and now hailed him.

Burgess spotted him and smiled. 'Young Considine! Fancy seeing you here.' He offered his hand. 'I gather you had a decent war. Glad you made it out in one piece.'

'My friend William Hunter,' Considine said. 'We were in the same squadron in France.'

'Ah, another flyer? How do you do? I never could keep young Harry here off my buses. He used to bunk out of school and come down to the sheds in his uniform.'

Burgess was a pleasant-faced man in his mid-thirties, with keen blue eyes, and thick dark brown hair that matched the moustache – a real flourisher.

'Grand news about Hawker and Grieve, isn't it?' Considine said.

'The very best. We shall have the whole story before long – they're bound to come back here first thing. Did you hear their bus has been picked up? An American steamer found her floating, intact, so they'll be able to find out what went wrong. What are you two young heroes doing these days?'

'Nothing much,' Considine said. 'The RAF didn't want us.'

'Looking for a job?'

'Yes, sir, if it's a flying job,' said William. 'Trouble is, there don't seem to be many of them about.'

'And talking of buses, what have you got now?' Considine asked. 'I bet you're up to something. Is one of these sheds yours?'

Burgess brushed his moustache, looking at them speculatively. 'Tell you what, come and see. Mine's the one at the far end.' They started walking, and he said casually, 'You might be just the chaps I need.'

In the shed, a couple of middle-aged fitters in overalls looked up from what they were doing as the three men

168

appeared in the doorway against the sunlight. 'Fred Wake and Andy Boyle,' Burgess introduced them.

William exchanged a polite greeting, but his eyes were all for the strange-looking craft in front of him. 'It's a DH9, isn't it?' he said.

'That's right. A DH9C, in fact,' said Burgess. 'The RAF had any amount of 'em, and they're flogging 'em off cheap – ideal for my purposes. I bought three, but we're just working on two at the moment.'

It was obvious to William, now he'd got his eye in, what they were doing: a cabin was being constructed behind the pilot's seat, all the way to the rear, covering the bomber's seat as well. There were two windows cut out of the side of the new housing, which meant that it was not for carrying cargo.

'You're turning it into a passenger carrier,' he said.

Burgess grinned. 'Full marks to that boy! Yes, I've had the itch to try this for – well, since before the war, really. Couldn't have done it then, but we've jumped ahead a decade in aircraft design, and these Airco buses are reliable as the Bank of England. Now the war's over, people are going to want to travel again, so I'm going to start up a passenger service. The future is civil aviation, boys! You heard it here first.'

'A passenger service?' Considine said, walking round the craft inspecting it. 'How many will it carry?'

'Three. Two side by side in the main body, plus one behind in the bomber's seat. And there's room for their luggage behind the pilot's seat.'

'And where will you fly to?'

'Well, I thought, to begin with, one service to Manchester and one to Birmingham. All those industrialists eager to get Britain moving again. But it depends what people want. I'll take them anywhere.'

'When will you start?' Considine asked.

'If I can find a couple of pilots, next Friday or Saturday.

The buses are all but finished. We'll need to do a few test flights next week, see they handle all right with the cabins, make sure nothing drops off.' He gave the fitters a grin. They looked back phlegmatically. 'But I've got a couple of customers lined up – chaps with an adventurous spirit, who want to say they were the first. Plus a couple of journalists – that's very important. Get the word out. So what do you say? Do you fancy a job?'

'Gosh, *yes*!' William cried. 'Really?'

Considine grinned. 'I've been aching to get airborne again. It'll certainly beat being a clerk in my dad's bank.'

Burgess stroked his moustache again. 'I must be honest with you boys. I can't pay you much, not to begin with. Once the service is on its feet and the passengers are lining up, I'll review it, of course. But we're in an experimental stage at the moment – you understand.'

'Oh, quite. Quite,' said Considine.

William had hardly thought about money. His needs were few. But he said, 'If you're flying from here, I suppose I'll have to find lodgings of some sort.'

Considine threw an arm over his shoulder. 'Nonsense, you'll stay with us. You're comfortable enough in that spare room, aren't you?'

'Yes, very – but your mother—'

'We'll ask her tonight. She won't mind. I've often had chaps to stay.' He flung out a hand to Burgess. 'We're your men! Whatever the pay.'

They all shook. And William, with bliss in his heart, had a job.

With her parents away, and David preoccupied about Antonia, Sadie felt able to skip church, and went straight up to Highclere after breakfast. As she wheeled the bicycle down the path, Nailer appeared from under the hedge and stood before her, wagging not just his tail but his whole

170

rear half in pleasure at this early start. She picked him up to hug him and whisper into his surprisingly velvety ear, 'John's home. He's back for good.' Nailer seemed uninterested in the news, and wriggled to be put into the basket. The indignity of being lifted off your feet was only acceptable in a practical cause.

The evening before had been a joy. The six of them – Mary and Winifred had joined them – had chatted comfortably, and Sadie had been so happy just to be near John, that she hardly noticed he spoke very little. It had broken up early, with Mrs Cuthbert saying that John was obviously tired from his journey, and bustling Sadie off home.

Today, she thought, as she pedalled down the Rustington Road, they would have a long talk. It would be time, surely, to tell Mrs Cuthbert what she must in any case have suspected, that they were engaged. Should she write to her parents, or would it be better to wait until Mother got back? She was of age, so she didn't need parental permission, but it would never have occurred to her, any more than it would to any other well-brought-up girl, not to ask for it anyway.

She was free-wheeling down the hill now. Nailer's ears were streaming back and his eyes were half closed against the wind of passage. But he still spotted a labourer on a bicycle toiling up the other way, and barked officiously at him, his whiskers bristling. *My road! Mine! Mine!* The labourer grinned, and touched his cap to Sadie, and Nailer subsided, satisfied in a job well done.

When would they get married? Sadie wondered. John would have to get well again. Rest and good food at Highclere would do the trick. Would a month be enough? She didn't care about a grand wedding, and didn't suppose her parents would care, either. She was Sadie. She wasn't Diana. Something simple at All Hallows. If her father's work in Paris wasn't finished, he could come over, surely, for the weekend.

He wouldn't make her wait until the Peace was signed and he was back for good, would he?

She crossed the canal on the little bridge, waving to a narrow-boat going by underneath. The woman at the tiller had a baby at her shoulder, and made it wave its fat hand in response. Then through the quiet streets of Rustington, up the steep hill the other side, and past the railway sidings to Highclere, to the glorious smell of horses, and the whinnies of welcome from her favourites. Nailer sprang from the basket before she'd even stopped and scurried off to hunt rats; and Sadie, not wanting to talk to anyone before John, propped the bicycle against the paddock fence and hurried up the track to the house. This time, her feet didn't feel heavy at all.

She went straight round to the back, and saw John in a deck-chair on the lawn, his face to the sun, conveniently alone. She stood a moment to look at him, like someone stealing a secret pleasure. The sunlight falling on his face made it all hollows, and for a moment he looked like an old man. She had been going to creep up and surprise him, but now she thought better of it. She called him from the corner of the house, to give him time to wake up.

It seemed to take him longer than she, in her youth and health, could understand; and then he struggled to get to his feet – but it was never easy to get out of a deckchair. She wanted to run to him to be embraced, but he did not hold out his arms to her, and though he smiled, it seemed a troubled smile.

'You're not at church,' he observed, as she came up to him.

'I preferred to be here,' she said. She was going to say, 'Aren't you going to kiss me?' but changed her mind. He seemed closed off to her this morning. She couldn't find the way in. So she said, 'Did you sleep well?'

'Like the dead,' he said. 'You?'

'I always sleep well.'

172

'Your family – all well?'

'Mother's gone to visit father in Paris.'

'Oh yes, so you said. I'd forgotten.'

'And William's visiting a friend, so there's only me and Peter, and David and Antonia at home.' Why were they talking like strangers? She drew a breath and began, 'John, we ought—'

And he interrupted: 'Shall we go for a walk?'

'Yes – if you like. Or we could ride – it wouldn't take me a moment to tack up a couple of horses.'

'I don't think I've got the energy to ride,' he said. 'Walking makes it easier to talk.'

'Yes,' she said. She wanted to talk. But why didn't he smile, take her hand, kiss her? 'Is everything all right?' she asked falteringly.

'Let's walk,' he said, and started off across the lawn to the gate at the end, into the coppice. She fell in beside him, and tentatively put her hand on his arm. He drew it under and pressed it against his side, and relief flooded her. It was all right. He was just tired, and sick. Of course it was all right.

They walked without talking, following the meandering path until it came out at the top of the wood onto the patch of bare turf where the hill ended in a steep drop, and a view over the valley, and the rolling hills beyond. From here you could see the spire of the church on top of Harrow Hill. The sun made shadows of cobalt and indigo under the trees that covered the hills; it sparked off the river down below, and the occasional moving motor-car, winding along the valley road.

'It's so beautiful,' he said at last. 'England.'

'Yes,' she said, and waited.

'Men make such ruin. They destroy whatever they touch. When you think of France – so much of it is . . .'

173

She pressed his arm, trying to find the way into his thoughts. 'It was hard for you – over there,' she said.

'Yes,' he said, and his mouth was grim.

'The horses,' she began.

He shook his head, as if to stop her. 'I can't talk about that. It was more horrible than you can imagine. Than I hope you can imagine. It – it scars your mind. You can never forget something like that.'

'But you can put it aside. Eventually, you won't think about it. Like – like Bobby. I used to think about him all the time, but now it's only every so often.'

He turned to look at her, and she read in his eyes as clearly as if he had said the words, *It's not the same thing.*

'I'm sorry,' she said humbly. 'I know none of us back here can really understand.'

'Oh, Sadie,' he said, and his voice was full of despair. He turned to face her, taking both her hands, examining her face with a searching look as if – yes, as if it was for the last time.

Tears jumped to her eyes, 'Don't,' she said helplessly, as if warding off a blow.

'Sadie, I have to talk to you. Please, will you just listen? If you say anything, I might not be able to get to the end.'

Would that be such a bad thing? she wondered. But she just nodded, to help him.

'This undulant fever – I've told you that once you have it, it keeps recurring. I didn't tell you everything last night. I didn't tell you how devastating it is, when you're having an attack. The pain in the spine, and the joints, and the muscles. How weak and depressed it leaves you. You can't bear to have people near you. You feel utterly miserable.'

She opened her mouth to speak but he shook his head at her, and she closed it again.

'They discharged me from the army because I'm not fit for it. I'm not fit for anything.' He made a rueful shrug. 'I

174

certainly chose the wrong profession if I'm going to be chronically ill. Handling horses takes a lot of strength and energy, and I have neither.'

'There are other animals,' she began, unable to stop herself trying to help.

'I couldn't run a practice. Don't you understand? For the foreseeable future I'm going to be subject to periods of intense illness. I don't know, in fact, what sort of work I *could* do. Where would I find an employer willing to put up with my absences? I should only be able to earn a pittance, and with the likelihood at any time of being dismissed. I can't – do you understand this? – I can't support a wife.'

'Didn't your father—?'

A look of bitterness crossed his face. 'He left almost everything to the university library, in token of his disappointment in me for becoming a vet instead of a doctor. The very little he left me is a cushion, but it will soon be gone. I can't marry you, Sadie. We can't be married.'

No! she cried inside. *Don't say that!* She held his hands tighter. 'Don't you – love me any more?'

'Oh, Sadie,' he said feelingly. 'I love you more than life itself. If only that were enough.'

'But if you love me, everything will be all right,' she said urgently. 'I can work. I can get a job. Between us we'll manage. We don't have to—'

'You don't understand. Even if I could allow you to keep me like that, even if your parents would agree for an instant to such a marriage, you couldn't cope. How could you nurse me if you had a job? There would be doctor's fees – how could you pay them? And things will probably get worse. The intervals of illness may get longer and more frequent. There can be collateral effects – on the heart, the organs. The spine. I may end up a cripple.'

She stared, feeling as if she had been torn open and was

175

bleeding, there on the hilltop, with the sweet breeze stirring her hair, bleeding to death onto the turf.

He looked at her with an awful pity. 'I can't do it to you, my Sadie. I won't tie you to a hopeless invalid. I know you love me, God knows why, but how long would that love last, living in poverty and nursing a useless man who could never really be a husband to you? You would grow to resent me, eventually hate me.'

'No! Never!'

'And I'd grow to resent you. How could I live with what I'd done to you? I'd hate myself. We'd have no life. No, my Sadie, it breaks my heart, but I have to let you go.'

'No! John, no!' She was crying now.

'We have to say goodbye. Let's do it here, and now. A clean cut heals better. We mustn't drag it out.'

'No! I can't! I love you!'

He drew her into his arms, and she clung to him. They were folded as close as two bodies could be. She felt his thinness under the clothes; smelled the scent of his skin, his own smell. 'I love you, too,' he said. 'So very much.'

They were silent, holding each other, while the world went on around them: little rustlings and bird calls; a distant aeroplane droned towards Coney Warren; far away and tiny, a dog barked. She wanted to die, here in his arms, where she was happy. She wanted no more of life if there was not that.

After a long time, she had no idea how long, she felt him sigh. He kissed the top of her head, and loosened his arms, putting her gently back, and when she looked up into his face, she realised the decision had been made in that timeless time. It was over.

'What will you do?' she asked in a small, despairing voice.

'Go north,' he said. 'Back to my own country. I can't stay here. To be near you would be torture. For both of us. I'll try to find a job of some sort to support myself. It's all I can do.'

She saw the truth of it. And there was nothing she could say, nothing she could do, or suggest, or contrive, to change anything. It was as absolute as if he had died over there, like Bobby. The war had taken him, another victim. *I'm alone*, she thought, in a horrified realisation. *I shall be alone for the rest of my life. And so will he.*

He was trying to read her face. 'You'll be all right,' he said, and it was half statement, half question.

'I wish I was dead,' she whispered.

He hugged her again, light, tight and short. 'No, my Sadie. No. You're young and strong and clever and beautiful. You'll do wonderful things with your life. And marry one day – yes, you *will*! – and have children, and be happy.'

'Not without you,' she wept.

He was crying too, and it hurt her almost more than anything.

'We'd better go back,' he said, turning away, brushing his eyes with his sleeve. 'I'll leave tomorrow, first thing. We had better not see each other again before then. Go home, when we get back. Cut clean – it's the best way.'

'Hold my hand then. All the way back,' she said defiantly. He took her hand and their fingers intertwined fiercely. She saw how tired, and old, and wounded he was, and how the sorrow for him was worse than for her, far worse. He loved her: she must let him go easily.

'Do they know?' she asked suddenly, as they began their last walk together.

'Not – all this. I shall have to tell them.'

'That will be hard,' she said. 'I'm sorry.'

It didn't seem far, going back. Not far enough. They reached the coppice gate too soon. He was going to open it, but she pulled back, and he turned to look at her.

'Kiss me,' she said.

He took her face in his hands and kissed her, a long, long kiss. Tears squeezed out under her eyelashes. But she must not make it harder for him. When the kiss ended, she looked one last time into his face – he seemed exhausted, almost dazed – and inside, without words, she said, *Goodbye, my love*.

Aloud, she said, 'I'm ready.'

178

CHAPTER THIRTEEN

The railways had been hard used during the war, and now the system was creaking at every joint. Several times on Beattie's journey, the train had to slow to walking speed while it passed gangs of workers busy with track repairs, and the carriages were showing their age. Even in first class, the upholstery was shabby, the woodwork scuffed and the floor covering worn to holes.

In Victoria station, as she went through to her train, she saw a middle-aged woman at the next barrier holding up a photograph of a young man in uniform. There were still a lot of soldiers coming back from France, and she was asking each of them if he knew anything about the fate of her son. It was estimated that about half of those who had fallen on the Western Front had no known grave: they were just 'missing'. Every day there were advertisements in the newspapers, asking for information about this or that beloved son; families wrote to former comrades in the hope that someone, somewhere, might know something of how and where he had died. This poor woman was pursuing a last forlorn hope.

Recently, two Northcote women had come to Beattie for help, one for a missing son and one for a missing husband. There was little she could do, other than help them write to the official bodies, the War Office, the War Graves Commission and the Red Cross. They would probably never know where their men lay; the spark of hope that drove them was more a torment than a comfort. At least Beattie knew what had happened to those she had lost.

It was a fine day, with a light breeze, and the sea was calm and sparkling under a blue sky when she boarded the ferry. Her spirits lifted. It was years since she had gone away on a holiday, and the war had been a hard and horrible grind. Whatever awaited her in Paris, she was going to enjoy the sheer novelty of being somewhere new. She could not bring herself to go inside, into the cabin, but stood by the rail the whole way across, enjoying the fresh air and the movement, and the insolent stare of the cruising gulls, riding the air above, or settling for a rest on the superstructure before lifting off again. She couldn't see what benefit there was to them from travelling with the ship, and concluded that they were simply enjoying the trip, as she was. The notion made her feel absurdly cheerful.

From Victoria to Paris, everything had been arranged for her by Edward's excellent aide, Duval, and at the barrier in the Gare du Nord, a fresh-faced young man in uniform met her, told her that Sir Edward had sent his apologies for not meeting her in person, but assured her that he, Lieutenant Lambert, was there to see her safely to her hotel. He dealt with her luggage, acquired a taxi, and chatted to her lightly and amusingly, pointing out places of interest that they passed. She appreciated his attentions but would almost have preferred to do without them, for she wanted to stare undisturbed. The city seemed as dirty and shabby and, in places, as knocked-about as London, but it was *Paris*, and had that undeniable look of foreignness that the traveller longs for: the traffic, the buildings, the clothes, the shops and restaurants – simply, they were *different*! She was *abroad*!

They passed from wide into narrow streets, and halted at last before the Hôtel Rive d'Or, which looked alarmingly grimy and poor from the outside, but which her escort assured

180

her was very exclusive. Inside, there was a great deal of mahogany panelling and red plush, and the ceiling of the foyer was painted with gauze-clad ladies, ribbons, flowers and cherubs in a way that reminded her comfortably of the Ritz in London. Lambert was handing her over to the hotel staff, and assuring her that Sir Edward would call for her in two hours, at six-thirty, to take her to dinner, and her heart was sinking just a little at the thought of reviving her schoolroom French, when there was a little flurry behind her, and suddenly Edward was there.

He bowed over her hand and kissed it, and said, 'My dear, I'm so sorry I couldn't meet you at Calais, or even the Gare du Nord, but I've been tied up all day in committees that I simply couldn't get out of. But I've managed to escape early, and I'm at your command from now on. Did you have a good journey? Did Lambert look after you properly? Thank you, Lambert – I'll take over from here.'

Lambert departed, and Edward went on, 'I was assured this was the best hotel in this arrondissement. Duval looked into it for me. Slightly old-fashioned, but everything done in form. And it's only just around the corner from the Duc de Bourgogne, should they need to contact me. Though I've made Duval swear he won't unless the sky is falling.'

Beattie had never known Edward to chatter like that, and realised belatedly that he was nervous. Well, she was feeling uncertain herself; and a question rose to her lips that had to be asked, though it went rather too directly to the heart of the matter.

'You have not booked me into your own hotel?'

He stopped in the middle of the new sentence he had begun about taking time off, and looked at her seriously, a look that was stripped to the bone. 'I wasn't entirely sure what you wanted,' he said bluntly. 'It seemed too pointed to take a separate room for you in my hotel, and too presumptuous to assume you would share mine.'

'I see.' Her voice had a downward sigh.

He hurried on: 'It wouldn't be very comfortable in the Duc de Bourgogne anyway, with so many conference people there – they'd be forever buttonholing me. So I bespoke a suite here, which has two bedrooms and a sitting-room. I thought that gave us the most – flexibility. Beattie, I know this will be awkward – for both of us,' he said.

'Yes,' she said. And they hadn't even got further than the foyer!

'I wanted to give us the best possible chance to – to work things out. I've taken leave. And if you don't want me to stay in the suite here, I can go back to the Duc.'

'It was a good idea,' she said, to save him more embarrassment. Inside she felt a tremor – of hope, was it? Or apprehension? Well, perhaps a little of each. 'Shall we go and look at it?'

Now you are really alone, Sadie thought. There was no one she could talk to. No one had known about her understanding with John. She stood in front of the bathroom mirror, arrested in the action of brushing her hair, and suddenly saw herself. A stranger looked back at her: thick dark-brown hair cut in a bob, a thinnish face, straight nose, melancholy brown eyes, a mouth turned down at the corners. Who was this person? All the Sadie *she* knew was inside. But this reflected image was other people's daughter, sister, helper, friend, or just 'Miss Hunter', someone who passed by on a bicycle, was seen in a shop, sat in the third row back at church on the decani side. John had known the inside-Sadie, and loved her. And he was gone. It was Monday morning, the beginning of the rest of her life, in which she would be alone. She noticed that the outside-Sadie wasn't crying. She remembered her mother's stoicism when Bobby died. Some things went beyond weeping.

She couldn't go up to Highclere, to endure the sympathetic

eyes of Mrs Cuthbert. John would have told her everything. But she could not stay at home, either. She needed something to do, to take her away from the pain in her mind and – yes, her heart. She knew it was only imagery, but there was a pain in her chest. It caught her when she breathed deeply. *No self-pity!* she told herself fiercely, turning away from the mirror.

Outside the bathroom door she almost tripped over Nailer, who looked up at her from under his eyebrows and wagged his tail uncertainly. He had been sticking close to her ever since she had left Highclere the day before. She squatted to rub his cheeks. 'I'm not upset with you,' she said. He tried to lick her face. He rarely did that – he was not a licker. She felt the traitor tears prickle her eyes. *No, none of that!* She would go to Dene Park. 'You can come with me,' she told the dog. 'I expect they'll be glad to see you.'

Dene Park now housed mostly convalescents, along with one or two hopeless cases who were waiting to die; and since the convalescents had been there a long time, boredom was a real presence. Some were depressed, which took a variety of forms: a blank withdrawal, bouts of weeping, fits of anger, or over-boisterousness, which could lead to reckless behaviour. Some of them were worried about the future, wondering how they would be able to fit in, anxious about finding a job. Some were grieving lost comrades. Some had nightmares about shelling and gunfire. But all of them, in one way or another, were bored.

Sadie was impressed by the way Diana had thrown herself into the business of diverting them. When Sadie arrived on Monday morning she was already on the ward, perfectly dressed and coiffed, in a neat grey wool dress and a single row of pearls, helping to clear breakfast trays, chatting to the men and pausing to light the cigarettes of those for whom it was difficult. She was so involved with what she was doing that she evinced no surprise at Sadie's sudden arrival, only said, 'Can you go round with the teapot? They all like a second cup.' Then she saw Nailer, and frowned. 'What's that dog doing here?'

'I thought the men might like to see him. I expect a lot of them had dogs at home.'

'It's unhygienic. This is a hospital ward,' Diana said. She had never been a dog person, and was certainly not a Nailer person.

'But they're all convalescing,' Sadie pointed out. 'No open wounds or fevers.'

Diana might have put her foot down, but the man in the nearest bed was already calling Nailer to him with a look of intense pleasure, and the sister – a comfortable-looking, middle-aged army nurse – came up behind them and said, 'It won't do any harm, my lady, and it might cheer the men up. You know how they love seeing his little lordship.' Diana's eyebrows shot up at the implied comparison between her elder son and a scruffy mongrel, and the sister hastened to add, 'Anything that takes their minds off their own troubles, my lady, is very healing.'

'Oh well, if you say so,' Diana replied, and turned to Sadie with a sharp look. 'But you're responsible for him. And if he makes a mess or starts barking . . .'

'He won't,' Sadie said defiantly, but she soon saw that Nailer here was a different dog from the fighting, rat-catching, bitch-chasing, care-for-nothing the rest of the world knew. He went from bed to bed, quietly and politely, patiently allowed any amount of patting and stroking, and raised to the wounded men's faces eyes of liquid sympathy and understanding.

'I think he knows,' Sadie said, as she passed Diana later.

'Knows what?' Diana asked distractedly.

'That they're hurt.'

'Who knows? Who's hurt? I haven't got time to talk nonsense with you now,' Diana said, and moved rapidly on.

There was plenty to do, from simply sitting and talking to helping with letter-writing, reading aloud, fetching and carrying, lighting cigarettes, helping some of them move around. One officer persuaded her to try her hand at cutting his hair, which he said was a disgrace. 'None of the nurses or visitors will have a go,' he said beguilingly to Sadie. 'But you look like a straight woman to hounds. I'm sure you won't be afraid.'

'I'll risk it if you will,' Sadie said, laughing. 'I've clipped horses and pulled them, but I've never cut human hair.'

'You can't make it any worse,' he said, and picked up a magazine to show his complete confidence in her.

She had a game of dominoes with one man, and was soon being begged to play cards with three others. Before she knew it, it was lunchtime, and she was helping to hand round the trays. The morning had flown by. After lunch there was the compulsory nap for the patients, with the blinds drawn and silence imposed, and Diana invited Sadie to come to her private apartments for luncheon. So reconciled was she to Nailer, after his exemplary morning, that she even said he could come too; but Sadie thought there might be limits to his angelic behaviour, and let him out into the park for a run. He could find his way home from there, or come back to the house for her, as he pleased.

But the break in the pattern had let unwelcome thoughts back in, and as she walked up the stairs after Diana, her misery rose up again and choked her. She wanted to lie down on the beautiful stair carpet and die. Only thinking about the young officer who was blind, and who lay silently in his dark prison and had told her with heartbreaking politeness that he didn't need anything, thank you, stiffened her spine.

As they stepped into the sitting-room, Diana thought at last to ask, 'So what brought you here this morning? Shouldn't you be at Highclere, playing horses?'

'I'm not needed there every day,' Sadie said. 'I thought I'd come and play nurses instead.'

Diana went and pulled the bell and, standing by the empty fireplace, said, 'It isn't a game, Sadie. These men have very serious problems to face.'

'Do you think I don't know that?' Sadie said. 'I was visiting hospitals before you even thought of it.'

It might have been an awkward moment, but before any more could be said, a maid came in – too soon to have been answering the bell – and said, 'Beg pardon, my lady, it's Lord Teesborough for you.'

'On the telephone?'

'No, my lady, he's here.'

'Well, don't keep him waiting, show him in at once,' Diana said tersely. 'New maid,' she remarked to Sadie when the girl had gone out again.

Then the girl was back, with Guy Teesborough behind her, and at the sight of him, Diana's vestigial frown fell away and her face lit with such gladness, Sadie was reminded all over again what a great beauty her sister was.

'Guy!' she exclaimed. 'How good to see you. You've come for lunch? Lay an extra place,' she told the maid, before he could answer, 'and tell Worrell to choose a good claret.' Then, as the maid backed out, she extended her hand to Guy in a superb gesture that Sadie decided she had copied unknowingly from the old dowager.

Guy came forward to kiss it, then turned to Sadie and shook hands with her. 'What a pleasant surprise. I wasn't expecting to see you here.'

'She came to help cheer the men up,' Diana said.

'My mission as well,' said Guy.

Sadie had noticed something. 'You're not using a stick!' she exclaimed.

'First day I've gone out without it,' he admitted shyly. 'I thought I should take the plunge – one can get reliant, you

186

know. Left the bally thing at home, and came to show Diana I can do it.' He dropped Sadie a wink. 'Comforted, of course, by the idea that, if I find I've been premature, there'll be plenty of sticks here I can borrow.'

'No backsliding,' Diana decreed.

'It isn't sliding on my back, it's falling on my rump I most fear.'

'You're doing awfully well,' Sadie said.

'Thanks. I've left it aside for short periods before, but this is the first time I've ventured out into the big wide world entirely without it.'

'Big wide world,' Sadie said blankly. Yes, it was big, and wide, and a great swathe of it separated her from the one person she wanted to be with. *Oh, John! Where are you now?*

Guy was still speaking. 'I'm awfully glad to see you,' he said to Sadie, 'because I'm here with a request to Diana to come up to Town next weekend for the Roseberys' ball. It's in a very good cause, wounded servicemen, and deserves our heartiest support. My brother particularly asked me to ask Diana to persuade you to come, too. Now I can do it in person.'

'A ball? Oh, I don't think—' Sadie began.

'You made quite an impression on Ivo,' Guy went on relentlessly. 'Diana, tell her she must come. There's such a thing as duty, you know,' he added, with mock severity.

Diana was examining her sister's expression. 'If she doesn't want to, I won't make her,' she said. 'Don't tease, Guy.'

But Sadie had gone through a number of thoughts, from revulsion at the idea of dancing and merry-making, to real-ising that, like the wounded in the ward, she needed to be distracted. Noise and movement could not heal a broken heart, but they could stop you listening to the pain. In the silence at home, she would hear it all too clearly.

'No, I'll come,' she said. 'Thank you.'

He looked pleased, and he and Diana went on talking

about the affair, where they would dine and with whom, and what else they might do, now there would be four of them. Luncheon was served, and conversation became more general. They wondered about the progress of the conference in Paris, speculated on when the treaty would be concluded.

Then they discussed the ideas of the Peace Committee, which had been meeting since the 9th of May under Lord Curzon to plan some sort of celebration in London. A four-day gala had been mooted, with a victory parade and a river pageant, theatricals, tableaux, a ball and fireworks in the park. Sadie ate, and listened. When the treaty was signed, there would be jubilation, and the nation would be entitled to rejoice; but there would be many who would feel, besides relief, only sorrow.

The luncheon party was broken up by the arrival of a nursery-maid with young George, the two-year-old Earl Wroughton, fresh from his nap, and baby Amyas, who would be one in July. The men in the ward would also be waking up now, so it was time to go back down, taking George with them, because not only was he a popular diversion to the men, it was also *his* favourite pastime. Sadie saw how he disported himself like a young prince and, given the competition for his attention, she thought he must be in danger of being spoiled. But his childish prattle and delicious chuckle plainly did the men good.

Sadie lost herself once more in the business of being useful. By the time she went home, she felt tired enough to sleep right there and then. But Peter, back from a day at school, wanted her attention, and she had to see how Antonia was, and talk to David, and answer the servants' questions. And there was a letter from William saying he had been offered a flying job, and ought he to ask Father's permission, though he was nineteen and, after all, if he had been old enough to fight in the war he should be old enough to decide his own future, what did Sadie think? And a note from

Mother, saying she had arrived safely, and giving her direction in case it was wanted.

So her evening was busy; but out of the corner of her eye, she saw the shadow of her pain, waiting until she should go to bed and be defenceless. Then there would be nothing to do but think of John, wonder where he was, how far he had got, where he would lay his head, what he would do – whether he was thinking of her. She saw him in some meagre narrow bed in an inn or lodgings, lying sleepless, staring at the ceiling, silent and alone. Like her, most of all, alone.

Beattie and Edward were having breakfast in the dining-room, when a thin, brown-complexioned woman with very short-cropped hair came up to their table and exclaimed, 'There you are! I've been asking for you at the Duc de Bourgogne!'

'Laura!' Beattie exclaimed. 'I wasn't expecting to see you.'

'That much is evident!'

'Have you eaten?' Edward asked, rising to kiss her. 'Have something with us.'

An extra place was laid. Laura poured herself coffee, and continued cheerfully, 'One would almost think you didn't want visitors, since you never told a person where you were. I didn't even know you were coming, Beattie. It was Beth who told me you were having a jaunt to Paris, and an officer friend told me the finance committee were lodging at the Duc. But the staff there were reluctant to admit either of you existed, until a charming young man called Duval intervened and sent me here. So, Lady Hunter, how are you liking Paris?'

'Very much,' said Beattie. 'We've been to the theatre, the ballet, the opera, and an art gallery. And we were just discussing a visit to Versailles. What brings you here? Where are you living these days?'

'I'm still at Étaples, driving my ambulance with Ronnie

189

Mildmay. We ferry patients and various personnel to and from Boulogne. Like your peace conference, there doesn't seem any end to the medical work. When *will* the war really be over, I wonder?' Jim Ransley's contract had ended in April, but he had been persuaded to sign on for another six months, since there was a desperate shortage of doctors out there. He had been apologetic when he told her, but just for a moment she had felt a reprehensible small surge of relief; since then, she had wondered if he had felt the same when they asked him. It would be such a huge change for both of them, to give up their work, to return to England, to 'settle down'. Was she even a settling-down sort of person? Was he?

While Laura talked on lightly, with anecdotes about her work, Beattie's mind drifted to the subject that preoccupied her most – her relationship with Edward. So far her visit had been pleasant – sight-seeing by day and entertainments by night, meals in the best restaurants, a little shopping – and Edward had been a charming and attentive companion. But there was a barrier between them, and though she suspected they both wanted to break through it, neither of them seemed to know how. At the end of each day, they would face each other in the sitting-room of their suite, and the tension would rise; but they would say goodnight, formally and a little awkwardly, and go to their separate bedrooms.

It seemed absurd for people who had been married for so long to be shy with each other; but so much had come between them, and they had been living virtually apart for years. The step back into intimacy seemed as impossible as taking off one's clothes in a public place. It was a guilty relief to her that they were not left alone together very much: everywhere they went, Edward was recognised and accosted; everyone seemed to like and admire him. People joined them to walk along with them on sight-seeing trips; at the theatre they were bound to be sitting next to someone who knew

190

him; even in restaurants distinguished men and their wives begged to join them at their table. It had been something of a jolt for her to realise how eminent her husband now was, how respected in high government and diplomatic circles. She was proud of him – but it did not make him any more accessible to her. She was afraid that she would leave Paris no more reconciled than she had arrived; that the rest of their lives would be spent at arm's length from each other. And she knew that she would not be able to bear it. Under her serene outer carapace, she was a passionate and needful person. The war had frozen her outwardly, but it had not changed her at the core.

Laura was looking at her curiously, and she realised a question had been asked, though she had no idea what it was. Laura laughed. 'You were miles away. I've been boring you to death with my tales of derring-do.'

'No,' she protested foolishly.

Laura waved that away. 'I was offering myself as chauffeur, if you would like to take a trip out of Paris.'

'In your ambulance?' Beattie said doubtfully.

'I told you she wasn't listening,' Laura said to Edward. 'No, dear, I borrowed a motor-car from a doctor in Étaples to come here. Ronnie's got Matilda.'

'But Edward has an official car and a driver,' Beattie began.

'I shall begin to think you don't want my company,' Laura said severely. 'Edward oughtn't to take his official motor on a pleasure jaunt, and in any case, I shall be a much more agreeable and knowledgeable courier. So, where would you like to go?'

Beattie didn't hesitate. 'To see Bobby's grave.'

Laura nodded. 'Then go and put on your hat, and we'll set off straight away.'

It wasn't quite as straightforward as that. Bobby's last squadron had been based near Doullens, which was about twenty miles north of Amiens; Amiens was about ninety miles from Paris. Laura would indeed have leaped into the car and driven off, but Edward pointed out that it was rather too far to go there and back in one day, especially if one was to have a decent and reflective time at the graveside.

'Well, then,' said Laura, 'we had better stay the night in Amiens. It's still a nice town, not too knocked about, and I know one or two jolly restaurants.' She gave her brother a narrow look. 'It will do you good to get away from here for a couple of days. You have a pecked-to-death look about you.'

'I'm quite all right,' he said automatically, but he would not be sorry to get away. There was indeed too much of 'If I could disturb you for one moment, Sir Edward,' and 'I'm glad I bumped into you, Sir Edward,' which he felt was hindering his desire to reignite his relationship with Beattie. Perhaps in a town where no one knew him – and where she was not constantly pushed aside by matters of mere international importance – she might warm to him.

So, instead of simply a putting-on of hats, there were overnight bags to pack, and a message to send to the Duc de Bourgogne, and it was an hour before they were back downstairs to meet Laura in the foyer. While Laura and Beattie stood to one side of the street exit, talking about the route to be taken, Edward stopped at the desk to explain that they would be away for the night but would be retaining the room. As he turned to join his wife and sister, his eye was drawn to someone coming in through the revolving door. She passed Beattie and Laura without a glance, occupied with undoing the large buttons on her fashionable pale blue duster coat; a burly, prosperous-looking man followed her. She looked up, and straight into Edward's face. She coloured, hesitated the merest fraction of a second, so little it would not have been perceptible to her companion, and walked past Edward to the desk.

He could not help himself – he turned his head to watch. She reached the desk and said *bonjour* in a pleasant voice, and then the man joined her and said, in French, 'We have a reservation. Mr and Mrs Bricourt.'

The man had taken off his hat, revealing grizzled hair and a balding top. He seemed in his sixties. The woman, thirty years his junior, was Élise.

CHAPTER FOURTEEN

The borrowed car was a Renault tourer, and the weather, on the cusp of June, was fine and warm, so they drove with the top down. Beattie said she would prefer to travel in the back seat, so Edward sat up front with Laura and consulted the map, though it was more or less a straight road from Paris to Amiens. They chatted at first, but it was too noisy in an open car to converse comfortably, and they soon lapsed into silence.

During the war, Edward had marched extensively across northern France, along just such roads as these. The straight French roads, lined either side with poplars, were so typical they could have been anywhere; the sunlight flickering between the straight trunks was mesmerising; he could hardly help drifting, tired as he was from months of war followed by months of diplomacy.

And he could hardly help thinking about Élise and her companion. She had looked a little pale, he thought – but that might have been travel-weariness. Had they just arrived from England? *Mr and Mrs Bricourt?* She was married, then? He had not written to or heard from her in many months. He had resolved, when he first left for the Front, to cut himself out of her life, for her own sake as well as his. Even so, he was surprised that she had married without telling him – he was her financial adviser, after all. And how had she come to appear at his hotel, just like that? She had looked startled, as though she had not expected to see him. Was it pure coincidence? He didn't know what to think.

They slowed to pass through a village. A few houses, a bar, a small farm with a woman leaning, arms folded, on the top of the gate; behind her geese, strutting across the yard. A mere glimpse as they passed, but he saw her lined and defeated face, her hair descending in weary wisps from the clumsy bun she had pulled it into that morning. In all probability, her husband and sons were dead, perhaps her father and uncles too. Probably she was alone. War had been hard on women.

'I thought we'd stop in Beauvais for luncheon,' Laura said, bringing him back to the present. 'There's a nice little town square where we ought to find a restaurant.'

'Good,' he said. When they did stop, he jumped out of the car quickly, to open the door for Beattie, to hand her out, to offer his arm as they followed Laura. *I must try harder*, was his thought. Half their time together was gone already. If he missed this opportunity, who knew what would happen?

Bobby's RFC base had been on a farm on the edge of Doullens, and the mess hut was still there, though the tents and aircraft sheds had long been dismantled. The farmer – an old man, too old to have fought – showed them the hut without interest or comment, and there was nothing to see inside. It had been stripped back to the bare wooden walls and floor. Beattie stared around and tried to imagine it full of lively young flyers, but no image came. There were some holes in the walls where things had been affixed – notice boards, perhaps – and a distinctive pattern of pinpricks suggested where there had been a dartboard. There was nothing here, nothing.

A stanza of poetry came to her from her schooldays – Thomas Gray, she thought.

The boast of heraldry, the pomp of pow'r,
And all that beauty, all that wealth e'er gave,
Awaits alike th' inevitable hour.
The paths of glory lead but to the grave.

The boys who had laughed and drunk and sung here in all their youthful beauty and strength had gone. There was nothing but the grave.

The graveyard was a short distance further out of the village, down the same lane: the usual sort of plot, a square fenced off from the surrounding farmland, with a large cross mounted on a stone block at the far side from the entrance, and flanking the path to it, on either side, a neat disposition of graves. It was obviously well-tended by the local people, and someone had planted a little square of scarlet geraniums at the foot of the cross, blood-bright in the afternoon sunshine. The kindness of them brought Beattie near to tears.

They found Bobby's headstone – as simple as the others, with his name and rank, followed by the letters RFC, and below that the date of his death and his age. Those twenty years were all he had to lay claim to, all he had ever owned, or ever would. Beattie tried to call him back to life in her mind, but it remained stubbornly blank. She remembered the fact of him, but could not conjure the reality. Under this turf was a huddle of bones, and they were not Bobby either. She wanted nothing to do with them. He was gone; she couldn't get him back. She should not have come here. It had only made her feel old.

We should have brought flowers, Edward was thinking. *Something, anyway*. Bobby, his son. Bobby whom everyone loved, the lively one, the joker, the one who thought up games and arranged family fun. Animals always went to him, and small children. He had loved flying. Edward understood the passion – William had it too. The longing to be up in the sky and free. Bobby would not have regretted anything he did. And he would never have thought about death at all. War was a young man's game: that was what they said. And it was because, in their own minds, young men were immortal. Only older men, like him, anticipated the consequences.

The sky was clouding over, and a little breeze had got up, ruffling his hair. He turned to Beattie and saw her shiver. He tried to read her face, but it was blank – determinedly so, he thought. She had always concealed her feelings: he couldn't imagine what they were at this moment, faced with the grave of the child she had borne. You weren't meant to outlive your own children: nature revolted at it. He put his arm round her shoulders, and for an instant she was stiff; but then she yielded to him, and he heard her sigh.

'It's going to rain any moment,' he said. 'We should go.'

'We should get back to Amiens,' said Laura. 'I don't know about you, but I could do with a drink.'

Then Edward thought, *We shouldn't decide for her. Everything in war has been decided for her, and all to her loss.* He said, 'Do you want to stay longer? There's no hurry, if you do. We can stay as long as you like.'

'No,' she said, without hesitation. Then she looked up at him, a searching look, as though trying to fathom his thoughts.

'What is it, darling?' he asked gently.

'Nothing,' she said, then drew a breath, as if talking were an effort that she was determined to make. 'I thought I could find him here, to say goodbye. But he's not here. There's nothing here.'

She let Edward turn her away and guide her down the path, his warm heavy arm still around her. *Nothing here*, she thought. *Not even prayer. Not even God.* But Edward was solid and warm, and there was comfort in his touch, in his mere presence. That was something to take away from this empty

197

place. Edward was alive – and he was still here, with her. That was a great deal. That was everything.

Over dinner, Laura said, 'This trip has given me an idea.' Her companions seemed sunk in thought, or gloom, and she said, 'Shall I tell you it, or shall I just shut up? I understand if you don't want to talk.'

Edward roused himself. 'Do go on,' he said. The last thing he wanted for Beattie was more brooding silence.

'Well,' said Laura, 'I've been thinking about what to do next.'

'Come home and set up respectably, I would hope,' Edward said.

'Respectably!' Laura chuckled. 'I rather fancy the definition of respectability has changed somewhat since 1914. And if you're thinking that I might spend the rest of my life arranging flowers and sitting on charity committees until I dwindle into the grave—'

'I never thought that,' Edward said. 'You're too energetic to do nothing. What's your idea?'

'Guided tours,' she said. 'People are going to want to visit graves and battle sites, and they'll need a driver and courier, people who know France, can speak French and arrange everything for them – make it all as easy as possible.'

'You wouldn't tackle it alone?' Edward said.

'I'm sure Ronnie will want to come in on it too. And we have Matilda. It wouldn't take much to convert her into a charabanc for, say, six people, possibly eight. Large enough, anyway, for a family party, or a group from a club. Last time I was in Ypres, there was a party of nurses being shown around by a FANY – they were going to be taken out to the places they'd heard of from their patients. I'm sure there'll be other groups.'

'Yes, I can imagine trips like that being organised by church societies and so on,' Beattie said. Mrs Fitzgerald, their rector's wife, would throw herself into such a scheme.

Edward said, 'I'd be worried about your doing it without a male escort. There are all sorts of undesirables wandering about, you know – deserters and rogues and madmen. Nowhere is really safe any more.'

'Dear Teddy, you gave me shooting lessons and bought me a gun, don't you remember? Besides, it would take a determined robber to tackle Ronnie and me together. We're a formidable team.'

She changed the subject, and soon afterwards Beattie stifled a yawn and Edward said protectively that she was dead tired. 'And you must be too, after all that driving.'

'Oh, I can drive all day – I'm used to it,' Laura said. 'But I do feel quite sleepy. Must be all the fresh air.'

Laura had automatically reserved them a room together. When they were shown into it, Edward started to say something, but Beattie silenced him. It was not a large hotel, and it seemed full – there might not be another room. And she did not want speculation to be aroused, not least in Laura.

When they were alone, Edward said, 'I'm sorry. I should have thought to say something. But don't worry – I'll sleep on the sofa.'

Beattie looked at his tired, kind face. Her husband, who had always been good to her. To whom she had borne six children. She looked at his hands, and shivered, remembering. She had taken great pleasure of his body, and he of hers. War was loss, and death, and coldness, a child's bones under the clay. She longed for life, for the warmth of physical contact.

'There's no need,' she said.

She met his eyes, and a flush of hot, embarrassed blood rushed through her, as though she were an inexperienced girl, not a matron in her forties. She saw his longing. He *wanted* her, and at the realisation she felt the twinge inside she had forgotten about for so long. He was in the vigour

199

of life, a good-looking, distinguished man – and he was an accomplished lover. Oh, she remembered that! Let their bodies say what words could not.

He was shy, though, and she would have to help him. 'Come to bed,' she said.

He crossed the room to her. 'Beattie,' he whispered, his lips against her hair. 'I've missed you so much.'

In the dark, forgiveness came to lie with them. In the meeting of lips and hands, in the remembered ballet of their bodies, was neither passion nor awkwardness, only quietness. There was a sense of ending, as though some long struggle was over.

Afterwards, Edward fell instantly, heavily asleep, and she realised again how tired he was. She lay awake, thinking not of him, not of Louis, of Bobby, of David, not of the long fractured past, not of what the future might hold. In this act they had taken possession of an empty house: they must furnish it together in the weeks and years ahead, or what would become of them? But for now, there was only silence.

She lay holding him, and thought of nothing.

Sadie could not say that she enjoyed her weekend in London. There were times when she forgot for a few moments, but that only made the pain of returning memory sharper. She did her best to hide it from her companions, so as not to spoil their fun. They seemed in tearing high spirits – indeed, all the young people around them, released from the tensions and privations of war, seemed bent on having the wildest good time possible. In such a frenzy of noise and movement, her stillness might go unnoticed.

They went to a very silly musical farce called *Kissing Time*, with Phyllis Dare and George Grossmith Jr, full of mistaken identities and people popping in suddenly through side doors. Its frivolity seemed to capture the mood of those same young people perfectly. The war was over, and it was time to laugh, as often and with as little provocation as possible. She watched it with a blank amazement that such things could be.

They lunched with a noisy group of acquaintances, had tea with more of the same, dined and danced at a nightclub with what Diana called 'a jolly crowd'.

On Sunday she and Diana lunched with Beth and Jack, and Sadie was glad to see that, though still very thin, Jack did look better. For a while conversation was comfortable and easy. Diana talked about her children. Sadie told news of home. Beth and Jack spoke tentatively about future travel plans. But then – they were lunching at the Ritz – a group of young people came in, spotted Diana, and dashed over to exclaim, question and invite. In the clamour, Sadie relaxed her guard a moment. Beth leaned over, under the cover of the noise, and said, 'Sadie, dear, are you all right? You've been very quiet. You look as though something's troubling you.'

At another time, in another place, she might have been tempted to tell. But what could Beth offer, anyway, but platitudes like 'It was for the best'? She could get no comfort that way. There was no comfort to be got, for her.

She stitched on a smile and said, 'Too many late nights, that's all. I'm not used to it.'

Beth smiled. 'Jack's the same. He can't bear a lot of noise now. Look at him glaring at Diana's friends – poor darling!'

And so the moment passed.

In the motor on the way back to Northcote, Diana was preoccupied in thought, and Sadie was able to lean against the glass in pretence of gazing at the scenery and let her misery prevail. She was roused only when they were passing through Westleigh and Diana said, 'Sadie, what do you think of Guy Teesborough? Do you like him?'

'Very much,' Sadie said. Her sister appeared to want more, so she added, 'He seems quiet and thoughtful.'

'Yes, he is. And brave, too,' Diana said. After a pause she added, 'He's very good with my boys.'

Is she thinking of him for a husband? Sadie wondered. Had he already proposed, perhaps? He *was* very attentive to her. But it didn't do to read too much into that – he had been Rupert's best friend, so he might just be taking care of his best friend's widow. 'Do *you* like him?'

'Yes,' said Diana, 'but . . .'

'But what?'

'Oh, nothing. I don't know. Everything's so mixed up. The war, Rupert. So many of our friends are gone, or terribly injured. There's James Eynsham who's blind, and Jolyon Pargeter, Bobby Pargeter's brother, who's lost a leg. One doesn't know what to think. It seems almost wrong to be having fun.'

Sadie roused herself to do her best for her sister. 'I think you ought to have fun, if you can. The boys who died would have wanted it.'

Diana nodded thoughtfully, and lapsed into silence.

Sadie thought of Guy Teesborough, and how good he would be for Diana, if anything came of it. 'Guy is kind to Nailer, and I like that,' she said.

'Oh, Sadie!' Diana said reproachfully.

'No, I mean it. People who are kind to animals are generally kind to people, too.' Understanding animals, being able to handle them, winning their trust – all things she had valued in a man. In one particular man. Tears rose and choked her throat. It was lucky that Diana had done with talking.

There was a note waiting for her at home, from Mrs Cuthbert. It was typically to the point.

> *Dearest Sadie,*
>   *Please come back. Allegro misses you, and no one else can further his education.*
>   *Your devoted friend,*
>   *Annabel Cuthbert*

Sadie read it standing in the hall with Nailer pressed against her legs, desperate for her not to get away again. Ada, passing through, said, 'Oh, Miss Sadie, I hope that dog's all right. He wouldn't eat last night, nor Saturday night, and you know what he's like usually for his grub.'

Sadie bent to look at him, and the small dark eyes stared back from under the frosty hedges of his eyebrows. He wagged encouragingly. 'Let's see if he'll eat now,' she said to Ada. 'Are there any scraps in the bucket?'

'We'll find something,' Ada said.

In the kitchen they both watched as Nailer emptied the bowl in record time, polishing it with his tongue to gather the last lingering savours. Bread crusts, cold potatoes and cabbage, a bit of fish that Cook wasn't sure about, and a couple of spoonfuls of left-over gravy to help it down.

'He seems all right now,' Sadie observed. 'Perhaps he just wasn't hungry.'

'He's always hungry,' Ada said. 'I've seen him come back begging after Frank Hussey give him a whole rabbit.'

'Well, perhaps he's been missing Mother,' Sadie said. 'She'll be back tonight.' She glanced at the clock. 'I think I'll go up to Highclere for a bit. He can come with me.'

More like it was you he was missing, Ada thought. But that was Miss Sadie all over – always setting herself back. It was a crying shame she hadn't met some nice officer, with all her hospital visiting. Spent too much time at those blessed stables. She'd never meet a man up there.

Edward saw Beattie off after breakfast, and went back to work at his office in the Duc de Bourgogne, but his mind kept straying. Their night together in Amiens had not magically changed everything on the instant. There was still a tension between them. They did not converse freely; they were extra polite and careful with each other, like people who had only just met. He did not know what she was thinking.

203

But it had been a beginning. To be received back into her arms, to pour himself into her, was joy and relief. And when they had got back to Paris, she had slept in his bed, and he had woken in the morning with his wife beside him – something so simple that he had taken for granted all those years. It was a setback that she was going home without him, but he felt they had made something to build on when he finally returned. He hoped so, at least.

He managed at last to concentrate on the paperwork in front of him, and was surprised, when Duval interrupted him, to discover that it was past one o'clock.

'There is a lady here for you, sir,' Duval said, with a slight air of constraint. 'She says she is engaged for luncheon with you.'

Edward frowned. 'I don't think—'

'There is nothing in your diary, sir. A French lady, sir – a Madame de Rouveroy.'

Oh, Edward thought, enlightened. Duval was thinking he had only just got rid of his wife and was preparing to cavort with a paramour. Edward certainly had no engagement with Élise – but did not feel quite able to expose her in front of his secretary.

'I'm sorry,' he said. 'It was very vague – not fixed – or I'd have mentioned it. I had better see her. She is a client of mine, from London, from the bank.' He was aware he was talking too much, not the best way to lull Duval's suspicions. 'I had better take her out and feed her,' he concluded, trying for lightness.

'You're going out for luncheon, sir?'

'Have I any appointments?'

'Nothing until four o'clock. The French treasury. But there are papers to read for it.'

'I will be back in plenty of time,' Edward said, grabbed his hat and escaped.

* * *

204

Élise was waiting in the foyer, attracting a good deal of attention. She was elegantly dressed in striped silk of cream and beige, a light summer tippet at the neck, a large hat of ecru lace, with cream-coloured ostrich feathers drooping over the brim. She looked gay and modish, and nothing so attractive had stepped into the foyer in months.

As he approached, she extended her hand with a mischievous smile. 'You are cross because it is not *comme il faut* for me to come to call for you. I see it in your eyes. The great Sir Édouard wonders, *oh, la la,* what will people think?'

'They will think you look very beautiful and *à la mode,*' he countered.

'I am a week in Paris and have not seen you. I could not wait longer, so I came to – to *winkle* you out. Is that correct?'

'Quite correct.' She was not speaking *sotto voce,* and he took her elbow to turn her gently and usher her out into the street. There was too much intimacy in her tone, her choice of words.

'Where do we eat?' she asked, quite unabashed. 'I am hungry, me.'

'I *will* take you to luncheon—' he began.

She pretended alarm. 'Oh, so grim! You say it like a threat: bad woman, you shall be fed! *Voici Paris, mon ami,* where one eats for pleasure. Luncheon is not a punishment.'

'You enjoy misunderstanding,' he said, hailing a taxi. 'But you know very well what people will think when I lunch alone with a beautiful woman.'

'Pah! Parisians will think nothing at all but of your good fortune. *Enfin,* if you fear your English colleagues,' she added with a mischievous look, 'we had better find *un restaurant discret – presque caché.*'

'We shall do no such thing,' he said firmly. 'We shall lunch in the full glare of public view, and make sure everyone knows we have nothing to hide.'

'But it is true, we '*ave* nothing to hide,' she said, eyes wide. 'And we shall keep it that way.'

He took her to the restaurant at the Crillon, which had very good food – he knew she would expect that – but was very public, being the hotel where the American delegation was staying. It was flattering that the *maître d'hôtel* recognised him, and created a little flurry of bows and compliments to escort him to a good table. It was true, Edward saw, that he made nothing of Élise, other than to treat her as he would any fashionably dressed lady. Élise, still with mischief in her eyes, asked for champagne, and when they were finally left alone with the menus, he said to her in a low, exasperated voice, 'Very well, you have had your pantomime. Now tell me, what are you *doing* here?'

'*Je suis parisienne* – where should I be?'

'There is the little matter of your husband, madame – whom I don't see here with you today.'

'Can it be that you are jealous, Sir Édouard?' she said, fluttering her eyelashes.

'Of course not – only surprised that you did not tell me you were getting married. There would have been financial considerations to discuss.'

'Ah,' she said, and was instantly serious. 'In fact, I am not married.'

'But I heard you – at the Rive D'Or – Monsieur and Madame Bricourt—'

'Even in Paris, one may not register as unmarried people.' She sipped champagne. 'You looked shocked.'

'Not at all.'

'*Tiens,* I will tell you all. Gilbert Bricourt was a business friend of my husband's.'

She broke off as the waiter returned for their order. She chose efficiently, and he ordered the same for quickness' sake, and they were alone again.

She resumed. 'Gilbert was a friend of my Guillaume. His wife is dead and he has no children, so when the war was over he decided to have a holiday in England. We met, quite by accident, in Oxford Street. He was glad to see a familiar face, and wished to have time to talk to me. We met for dinner, and then again, and so it goes.' She shrugged to indicate there was no need to go into details. 'We are grown-up people, Édouard, a widow and a widower.'

'I'm concerned for you, that's all,' he said stiffly.

'Oh, is that all?' she mocked him. 'Well, so that you shall not think I am being – what is it? – led in the garden, Gilbert does wish to marry me. He has proposed in the proper form, and disclosed to me his financial worth, since I have no father to enquire for me. His business is in good heart, and he will provide for me correctly, and I think will be a kind husband.'

Edward digested this, examining her as she picked apart a fillet of sole. Her dress was expensive but not showy; she wore a strand of pearls, and pearl earrings, and her fur appeared to be mink. Her maquillage was discreet, her perfume expensive. She looked prosperous and elegant, and he could have taken her anywhere. She looked like a wife, not a mistress – and, in any case, it was none of his business.

'Well, I'm very happy for you,' he said at last. 'But I ask again, why are you *here*? Why did you wish to see me?'

'You said yourself I should consult you before I marry again,' she countered.

He studied her. 'We cannot very well discuss finance in a restaurant. And I am no longer completely *au fait* with your investments. But I can send to the bank for the figures, if you wish.'

'Oh, Édouard,' she said sadly. 'You are so *English*. You 'ave no imagination. I wish to ask you if I *should* marry Gilbert, of course.'

'I can have no opinion on that,' he said awkwardly.

'No? Will you be 'appy to see me married to an old man, and taken to France where I shall never see you again?'

'You said he was kind—'

'But *old*. We sleep together, but that is all it is. *Pour dormir, seulement*. Must I say it in French, that you understand?'

He felt himself blushing. 'Élise,' he began in a low voice.

'We were much to each other, you and I,' she said. 'I cherish the memory of that night. I 'ave 'oped so much there would be others.'

'I'm married.'

'I know that. But for you – for you I would accept that I can be mistress only. For you, my dear. If you want me.'

This was agony. 'Élise . . .' he began again.

But she read his face and put up a hand to stop him. 'I understand. No need to say more.'

'I'm sorry,' he began foolishly.

But she shook her head. 'Don't,' she said. Then, 'That was her, was it, that I saw you with? I 'oped it was another mistress. But I knew, really.' She sighed. 'So I shall marry, and be Madame Bricourt, very respectable and dull with Gilbert, and you will be the important Sir Édouard, very respectable and dull with Mrs – no, that is wrong – with Lady Édouard?'

'Lady Hunter.'

Her mouth drooped. 'C'*est la fortune de la guerre, n'est-ce pas?*' Then she seemed to brace herself. 'Ah well, let us enjoy the *ris de veau* that the Crillon does *à merveille*, and talk of other things. Tell me, how goes the conference? Shall we have a peace treaty soon?'

He allowed her to change the subject, and talked of the conference while they ate. But when they finally put down their forks, he said, 'Élise, will you really marry him?'

'Really,' she said. 'I see you are thinking, *but you don't love him*. Well, I like him, and that is much, in a marriage. We are practical people. I am lonely, and wish to have security and a name. Gilbert will give me those things, and be kind, and not trouble me too much.'

'And you'll live in Paris?'

'Gilbert wishes to retire, to enjoy his new young wife. And I wish to come home. I shall open my own ballet school, and teach now and then, and be a great patroness of the arts. And,' her eyes twinkled again, 'in time I expect very discreetly to take a lover. Gilbert will never know about it. I will make him happy. It is the bargain understood. But what of you? Will your cold wife, who betrayed you, love you properly, as you should be loved? As I would have loved you?'

'We are going to try,' Edward said, and he could hear how cool and English and inadequate it sounded, even before she laughed at him.

Sadie leaned the bicycle against the fence and went straight to Allegro's box. He whickered when he saw her, and came bustling up to shove his head over the half-door and investigate her. She stroked him and murmured, and he nibbled at her hair and her buttons with delight, then banged a forehoof impatiently against the door. *Let's go out!*

The noise brought Mrs Cuthbert out of the stable block. She came over. Sadie gulped. 'I'm sorry I've been—' she began, and couldn't go on.

'John told me everything,' Mrs Cuthbert said. 'Oh, Sadie. I'm so sorry.'

Sadie's eyes filled with tears, and somehow she was in Mrs Cuthbert's capable arms and was weeping onto her solid shoulder.

'My dear,' said Mrs Cuthbert, patting her kindly. 'My dear.'

Sadie got control and pulled back, and a handkerchief was thrust into her hand. She wiped her eyes and blew her nose. Mrs Cuthbert said, 'I'm more sorry than I can say. But he was right, you know. He did the right thing. And one day you'll know it. And that's all I'm going to say.'

Sadie shoved the handkerchief into her pocket and turned away to rest her cheek against Allegro's warm face. He allowed it for a moment, then jerked his head away. 'Have you been exercising him?' she asked, and was amazed at how normal her voice sounded.

'Not enough,' said Mrs Cuthbert. 'Why don't you take him out now for a good long run? It'll do you both good.'

To be alone with the horse and far away was what she craved most, as Mrs Cuthbert understood. But this was Allegro, and Sadie had to ask. 'What if he throws me?'

'You'll get up again,' Mrs Cuthbert said wisely.

CHAPTER FIFTEEN

'Well I never!' said Cook admiringly. 'Just look at that!' Ada was peering over her shoulder as she examined the photograph of William standing beside an aeroplane, with the headline FIRST PASSENGER SERVICE TO NORTH OF ENGLAND BEGINS. 'We seen Miss Diana in the papers a good few times, and you was in once, Miss Sadie, with your horses, but I never thought to see Mr William in.'

'So handsome as he looks,' said Ada. 'Ever so like the master, when he smiles.'

'It says here he wears his brother's watch for luck, what was a flying ace in the war,' Cook noted. 'That's Mr Bobby's, God rest his soul.'

William's letter had been short on detail. He had sent the copy of the newspaper – a local one, which they would not otherwise have seen – and said that he would be staying with the Considines for the time being. He hoped everyone was well and asked when Father would be coming home, and that was all.

'He doesn't mention any salary,' Beattie had commented, when she read it at breakfast. 'I suppose they must be paying him something.'

'Surely he wouldn't call it a job if he didn't get paid?' Sadie hazarded.

'I'd do it just for fun,' Peter said, 'and I bet William would, too. All he wants is to fly.'

211

'But you're still at school and don't have to make your way in the world,' Sadie pointed out.

William and Considine had test-flown both the converted DH9Cs several times before the official first passenger runs on Saturday the 31st of May, to check for any faults and to get the feel of handling them. A fighter pilot during the war had only himself to worry about, and comfort was not a priority, but with a passenger on board, bumps and sharp turns had to be avoided.

'You can't throw the passengers about,' Colin Burgess had warned them. 'If they don't get a smooth ride they'll soon tell everyone, and that'll be the end of the business.'

On the Friday, there had been a trial run, William taking one machine to Birmingham with Fred Wake on board, and Considine with Andy Boyle taking the other to Manchester. Burgess had arranged with the press to cover the official inauguration on Saturday, but quite a few journalists were around on the Friday, and one from *Flight* magazine persuaded Burgess to let him go along on the Manchester run.

In the event, William was glad he had not had the journalist on board, because only a few minutes out, a heavy knocking sound started, and he had to find a field to put down in so that Fred could discover what was causing it. It proved to be a loose hose connection and was easily fixed, but it would not have looked good written up for the country's premier air magazine.

Furthermore, William had never flown to Birmingham before. The usual method of navigation was to follow the roads and railway lines, but in the tangle coming out of London William picked up the wrong line and was concentrating so hard he didn't notice immediately that he was heading west instead of north-west, until Fred recognised Reading beneath them and tapped him on the arm. William was glad not to have a reporter witness his error, or the difficulty he had in finding his destination airfield, which involved much circling and considerable head-scratching.

Still, he knew the way now, and after a stop for lunch and to stretch his legs, he flew confidently back with no more difficulties.

On the Saturday, there was a gala feeling at Brooklands, and dozens of well-wishers had swelled the normal Saturday crowd of amateurs, enthusiasts and little boys. Mrs and Mrs Considine and Eva had all come, and while William was sure Considine's parents were there to wish their son well, he had a small and secret hope that Eva had come at least partly for him. She did head straight for him when they arrived, and shook his hand and wished him well. She was wearing a pretty pink shantung outfit and a particularly fetching hat.

'You ought to have a uniform,' she said to William.

'It's early days yet,' he answered. 'I expect if it really gets going, it might be thought of.'

'I shall speak to Mr Burgess about it. Something in dark blue with gold braid would look well.'

William grinned. 'I should look as if I was in the navy. Anyway, a leather jacket and flying cap is a *sort* of uniform, isn't it?'

Later, a reporter came up to ask him about Bobby's watch. He wondered how the man knew about it. 'Oh, a little bird told me,' the reporter said with a wink. 'It's the kind of detail the public likes to read about. You were an air ace during the war, weren't you?'

'I wasn't an ace,' William said. The public generally had a much looser definition of the term than did flyers.

'But your brother was? How many Germans did he shoot down? Were you ever wounded? Your father's Sir Edward Hunter, isn't he? Do you have a fiancée?'

He hardly had time to answer one question before the next was shooting at him, and photographs were being taken

213

from every angle. But the crowds around Considine were greater and in the event, it was his picture that appeared in the national papers, while William's only graced the *Surrey Advertiser*.

He had only two passengers for his first flight, an air enthusiast who was just going for the interest, and a factory-owner who had been pushed into it by his son and was extremely nervous, never having flown before; so Colin Burgess took the spare third seat. He told William he might as well see how the thing worked. Now he knew the way, William had no problems, and over the engine noise he could hear the factory owner chattering excitedly to the enthusiast, who kindly told him what places they were flying over.

'It all looks so different from up here!' the industrialist cried, as artlessly impressed as a child. He handed round a bag of barley sugars, and lamented loudly when he was told they were approaching landing. 'It's so quick! I wish it'd taken twice as long.'

The new superstructure made the DH9C heavy, and awkward to land. William had to concentrate hard to get down steadily. When they disembarked, his passengers shook his hand and thanked him, and the factory-owner in particular was thrilled with the whole experience and promised to tell all his acquaintances how marvellous it was.

'And quick!' he added. 'You could come up for the day and be back home for supper!'

'That's the idea,' Burgess said, beaming.

There were two passengers booked for the return flight, but at the last moment an interested bystander – an air enthusiast – asked if he could take the flight. Colin Burgess accepted at once, and said aside to William, 'I'll go back on the train. I'm not going to turn down a paying customer. You did well, lad – I'm satisfied you have a handle on the job.' He shook William's hand. 'Once the bookings flow in, I'll go to two services a day. Then I can put up your wages.'

William hoped that would happen soon, because although he was comfortable at the Considines', and could see Eva every day, he was aware that his friend's parents had not been entirely thrilled at the idea of a permanent guest. Mrs Considine's smile had been slightly forced when Considine had gaily announced it, and Mr Considine had asked only this morning whether William's family mightn't be missing him.

It would be better all round if he moved into lodgings – there were plenty of cheap ones to be had near the airfield – before he wore out his welcome; but Burgess had promised him only a pound a week to begin with, and even with his limited experience of budgeting, he knew it would be hard to manage on that.

In the upstairs sitting-room, the sun had gone round, and with the windows open to allow in the breeze it was cool, with a sweet smell of lily-of-the-valley – Sadie had brought up a bunch that morning for the little green glass vase on the table by the sofa. It was quiet, too, with only the occasional passing traffic to disturb the air. On the sofa, Antonia was writing, and her pencil made no sound; at the round table by the window, David was reading Livy and making notes for his next pupil.

In fact, Antonia was not writing a great deal that morning, and Ben the Circus Pony's adventures were not progressing much. Her pencil rested idle for much of the time, as she daydreamed, and gazed at David: the strong line of his neck as he bent his head over the paper, his hawklike profile, the softness at the base of his throat where his neck disappeared inside his open shirt . . .

He looked up and caught her watching him. 'Something wrong?'

'No, just resting my hand.'

'How far off finishing are you?'

'Close. Another week or so.' She smiled. 'You're impatient.'

'Of course I am,' he said. 'I was in at the beginning and mean to be in at the end. Then we shall see about getting it published.'

'Better wait and see if it's good enough,' she said.

He stood up and went to the window to stare out. He still limped as he walked – he always would, she thought – but he moved now without thinking about it. As she watched him he shoved his hands into his pockets and whistled under his breath. It was good to see: the sort of thing a normal, happy man did, a man who had never been grievously injured and in despair of ever walking again. There were darknesses inside him, and they would probably always be there, and might come out from time to time in moodiness or bad temper or nightmares, but he was as close as possible to being whole again. And impatience was a symptom of that. He had been taken out of the flow of life for a long time, and he wanted to get back in. The world beckoned; and she – well, she suspected she would be left behind. She had been the wife of his disability: he might not need her when he went out into the world. But she must not hold him back: that would be fatal. As soon as he decided the direction he wanted to take, she must—

She gasped, the thought ending abruptly as a sharp pain went through her. David started talking again, something about his father and the Peace Conference, but she was unable to listen, concentrating on her inner sensations.

He turned at last, hearing no response, and said, 'Are you listening to me? I said—' And then he broke off, seeing her expression. 'What's the matter?'

'I think it's beginning,' she said.

The doctor's little motor-car stood outside again. 'I don't like to see it there,' Ada said, coming into the kitchen. 'It's like bad news.'

216

'Posh folk have doctors to them for babies, my mum says,'
Aggie offered. 'Ordin'ry folk just have the midwife, or they
does it theirselves. Mrs Bean next door had a baby Christmas
Day, and Mr Bean had to help her. He borrowed Pa's big
carving knife, what Pa was just going to carve the pork with,
and when he brought it back—'

'That's enough of that,' Cook interrupted sharply. There
was no knowing where *that* story might go.

'The missus looked worried,' said Eileen, 'and when Mrs
Wilkes come she was whispering away to her, like there was
something wrong.'

'Don't you talk about something being wrong, or you'll
feel the back of my hand,' said Cook. It wasn't lucky to talk
like that. 'The missus and Mrs Wilkes between 'em have
brought dozens of babies. They'll see to everything all right.'

'So what for did they call the doctor?' Eileen said simply.

Cook met Ada's eyes. The same question had occurred
to her. You didn't get the doctor in right away, not for a
second birth. And he didn't stay on like that.

'Push that kettle back over to boil,' she said, instead of
answering. 'You never know when they'll want the hot water.'

'She kept it to herself,' Beattie was saying to Nula. 'All that
time – she didn't want to worry David. I suppose she thought
if she told me, I'd feel I had to tell him.'

'You would have,' Nula pointed out.

'Poor thing, it must have been a strain, living with the
worry.'

'Not so much of a strain as living with *his* worry,' said
Nula. 'Well, it doesn't matter now. We just have to help her
as best we can. The doctor's here, and fair play to him, he's
not leaving until it's over.'

Sadie had persuaded David out into the garden, where he'd
be less likely to hear anything from the bedroom. 'You're

'completely transparent, you know,' he'd said angrily, but he went anyway. He didn't *want* to hear anything.

'You can't help,' Sadie said. 'Better to keep out of the way.'

'You women think we're all made of glass. You forget the sort of things we saw—' He was going to say 'in the war', but stopped short, because he didn't want to remember.

'It's not the same,' Sadie said, and left it at that.

Out in the garden, she tried to get him to talk about something else, anything else. His interest in horticulture was almost non-existent, but she got him as far as Munt's shed, and started a conversation with Munt about vegetables. Munt, perfectly well aware of what was going on, addressed himself to David and asked him for instructions on several points, 'seeing as the master's away, and you're making the decisions'. So David was drawn in, and kept occupied at least for a little while.

Dr Postgate looked worn out. 'It was touch and go,' he said. 'But we got through it.'

'And she's all right?' Sadie asked, since David didn't seem to be able to speak.

'She's resting now,' Postgate said, 'and that's the best thing for her. Plenty of rest. It was a considerable strain on the heart. You must keep her quiet at all costs – no agitation.'

Sadie noticed that he hadn't answered the question, and glanced at her mother. Beattie's mouth was set in a hard line. Beyond her, Nula caught her eye, and said, 'She's all right for now. And we'll nurse her up, get her fat and well again.'

'Can I see her?' David asked.

'Of course,' said Postgate. 'But remember what I said. No upsets or excitements.'

'A little girl!' Cook exclaimed in pleasure. 'Well, now! The missus'll be glad it's a girl, her other grandchildren being boys.'

'Nula said she's perfect, and healthy as can be,' Ada said.

'What'll they call it?' Eileen asked, poking her head out of the scullery.

'Haven't said yet,' Ada answered. 'I dare say they'll name her after Mrs David, or her mother. That's traditional.'

'I'd give her a special name that was all her own,' Eileen said. 'Like . . .' her mind worked feverishly '. . . Redempta.'

'That's not a name,' Cook objected.

'It is in Irish,' Eileen said. 'I've a cousin called Assumpta.'

'You're as bad as Emily with your nonsense,' Cook said, with a little pang of wondering what had happened to her former kitchen-maid. It was horrid, not knowing. Like all those poor boys over there who were just 'missing'.

'Anyway, Doctor says she should have something light to eat,' Ada went on.

'A drop o' consommy,' Cook said at once. 'That's the ticket. And a little egg custard for after – lots o' nourishment in that, and it slips down easy.'

David felt he would never forget how utterly flattened, exhausted, wiped out Antonia looked. Propped up on the pillows, and tidied up by Nula's careful hand, she seemed too weary even to smile. He bent over and kissed her cheek, and it felt cold and damp, which startled him.

'A girl,' she said faintly. 'I hope you don't mind.'

'I'm glad it's a girl,' he asserted. 'One of each. A boy to play cricket with, and a girl to make a pet of.' He sat beside the bed and took hold of her hand. 'Postgate says there aren't to be any more,' he said gently. 'It would be too dangerous.'

If Nula and Postgate hadn't already told her, Antonia would have known that for herself, anyway. She didn't need to be told how nearly she had died. And she didn't want to die. Whatever the future held, she wanted to be with David for as long as God allowed. She would preserve her life with great care – do whatever was needed. Her analytical mind had jumped ahead already to consider that, if there were to be no more babies, there would probably be no more lovemaking; and a vigorous young man like David would sooner or later be tempted to find release elsewhere.

'But we don't need any more,' David was saying. 'Two is enough.'

'Did you tell Daddy?' she asked.

'Mother telephoned him. He's coming tomorrow.'

'Good,' she said. Her eyes closed of their own volition and she drifted a little. It was good to feel David close, holding her hand. Just for now, he probably loved her as much as he ever would, and she was happy.

'Are you going to sleep?' he asked, and she felt him begin to withdraw his hand. She would have loved to sleep, but not if it meant he went away.

She opened her eyes, and made herself speak. 'What shall we call her?'

'Would you like to name her after you?'

'I've never liked the name Antonia,' she said. 'It's too hard for a little girl.'

'She won't always be little. How about Antoinetta?'

She shook her head. 'That's worse.'

Ethel came in, with Marcus by the hand, and a white bundle in her arm. 'He wanted to see you, madam,' Ethel said. Marcus's eyes were red and swollen with weeping. 'He thought you'd gone away.'

'Come here, little man,' David said, holding out his arms.

But Marcus ignored him and went to the other side of the bed. He did not fling himself at Antonia, but stood just beside her, examining her seriously, and then reached out a forefinger and touched her hand, as if to check that she was real. She smiled at him. 'It's all right,' she said. 'It really is me.'

He nodded, satisfied, and went back to Ethel and tugged her skirt. 'Can I play with my train?'

'In a minute,' said Ethel. 'Did you want to hold the baby, sir?'

'Let me,' Antonia said. Ethel brought the white bundle and laid it carefully in her arms; but she remained on the spot, aware of how tired those arms were.

Antonia looked at her small daughter, determinedly sleeping: the amorphous nose, the tiny pink triangle of a mouth, the faint tracery of eyelashes. So new – so defenceless. A whole world lay ahead of her, a very different world from the one Antonia had grown up in. But she would have plenty of champions, including an older brother, something Antonia would have loved. She would be all right.

'Alice,' she said. 'She looks like an Alice.'

David considered. 'I like it,' he said. 'She shall be Alice, then.'

Antonia threw a glance of appeal at Ethel, who stooped to gather the baby up. 'Come on, Marcus, Mama wants to sleep. You can see her again tomorrow.'

David was sleeping in the spare room for the time being. Postgate had recommended engaging a trained nurse, but Nula said she would stay for a few days and see how they got on, and they had moved in the folding bed for her so that she could be on hand in the night. She was roused by the sound of the baby crying, and a moment later Antonia's voice in the darkness said, 'Are you awake?'

So she switched on the bedside lamp and got up, slipped on her dressing-gown and went over to feel Antonia's forehead – cool – and her pulse – faint, but slow. 'Don't you get agitated, now,' she said.

'I won't. I expect she's hungry,' Antonia said.

Nula nodded. It would do the baby good to get the pre-milk, and wouldn't do the mother any harm. Suckling was well known to promote calmness and well-being. She helped Antonia to sit up, propped her with pillows, and said, 'Stay quiet, and I'll fetch her to you.'

Soon the wailing ceased, leaving a blissful silence. Young Alice seemed to know exactly what to do, and latched on right away. A good sign, Nula told the mother. 'She's lusty for life. They're the sort that do well, and live long.'

'I hope Marcus won't be jealous of her,' Antonia said, cradling the tiny head close.

'You should get a proper nanny for him now,' Nula said. 'Ethel's a good hand with a baby, but she can't mind two when he's the age to be running about everywhere. And she's a nursemaid, not a nanny.'

Antonia gave a tired smile. 'I wish you could be their nanny.'

'I've had my turn,' Nula said. 'Don't you fret, we'll find someone good. Let's put her on the other side, now.'

She effected the change, and stood by, watching. The baby's sucking slowed, and finally stopped. She was asleep. Nula knew how precious such moments were, and waited; but after a moment, Antonia made a strange small sound, like a gasp. Nula looked up from the baby and met her eyes, and Antonia gave her an agonised look, and whispered, 'Take her.'

Nula put the baby down in the armchair, and ran. Sadie's room was nearest. She banged on the door and went straight in. Sadie sat up in alarm, wide awake at once. 'Ring for the doctor,' said Nula, 'and then wake your mother.'

She ran back to the bedroom, checked the baby was still safe in the depths of the armchair, then went to Antonia and felt for the pulse in her neck. Antonia's cold fingers fumbled for hers and grasped them. 'Daddy,' she gasped.

'He's coming today,' said Nula. 'Don't try to talk. Just lie still and breathe.'

In the little upstairs sitting-room, Beattie sat in the armchair beside the unlit fire and rocked the baby in her arms. June dawns come early, and it was still only half past seven, though it felt as if a whole day had passed.

Ethel appeared in the doorway, with Marcus by the hand. 'I'm taking him out for a walk, madam,' Ethel said. Marcus's thumb was firmly in his mouth. Ethel saw Beattie looking and added defiantly, 'I'm letting him, just this once.'

Beattie nodded wearily, and they went away. The sun was pale gold and sweet outside, but the house felt heavy and dark.

After a while, Sadie came in. Her hair was unbrushed and there were dark shadows like thumb marks under her eyes. She wasn't a child any more, Beattie realised. She was thoroughly a grown woman. Where had the years gone? They had lost them in the war – years of innocence and years of childhood. 'Nula's just finishing,' Sadie said. 'D'you want me to take the baby while you go and see?'

Beattie shook her head.

'She looks very—' Sadie was going to say *peaceful*, but it wasn't true, was it? Dead people didn't look anything, just dead. 'Nula's made her look nice,' she said instead.

How old are you, Sadie, Beattie wondered, *talking so calmly about laying-out, taking control instead of me? But I can't get up. I can't move.* The new baby slept solidly in her arms, and she fancied there was something of Louis about the shape of her eyes and forehead. So much death; too much death. She needed the baby as a counterweight.

'I've sent a wire to Father,' Sadie went on. 'I don't know if he'll be able to come. And I telephoned Mr Weston. He was getting ready to leave. He's still coming, of course. I'll tell Ada to get his room ready. I expect he'll want to stay a few days. The rector's coming at eleven.' She passed a hand over her face to aid memory, discovered a loose end of hair and pushed it back behind her ear. 'Oh yes. I rang the undertakers. And I've sent telegrams to the Palfreys and to Beth and Jack. Was there anything else?'

223

'Sadie,' Beattie began, wanting to say something kind to her.

But Sadie held up a hand. 'Don't,' she said abruptly. 'I'll cry if anyone's nice to me. They're all crying in the kitchen. I'll go down and make them start breakfast – give them something to do.'

Beattie nodded. Then she said painfully, 'David?'

'He hasn't come out of his room yet.'

'I should go to him,' Beattie said.

'Not yet,' Sadie said. 'He won't want anyone yet.'

And though Beattie was his mother, and ought to know him better than anyone, she accepted Sadie's judgement. In any case, what comfort could she give him? She thought suddenly, longingly, of Edward. She hoped he would come back when he got the telegram. She needed very badly to have him here.

Later, Sadie wandered out into the garden, having nothing specific to do until the rector called, when she would be needed as a buffer between him and her mother and David, neither of whom would be able to bear too much religion at such a time. On the stretch of gravel behind the house, Ethel was playing catch-ball with Marcus. He was too young to catch a ball, and his fat little hands, clapping clumsily together, closed on air every time, unbalancing him so that he sat down hard on his padded rump. Munt had not yet restored the lawns, so the gravel was the only open space to play.

She went down the garden, and Nailer appeared from under a bush and trotted beside her, not looking up – just being there, good, silent company. They found Munt tying in the runner beans, pruning-knife in hand and a ball of string bulging out of his pocket. He stopped what he was doing and turned to her as she approached.

Sadie stopped too, and they examined each other for a long time. In the strong June sunlight, Munt looked old, the lines in his face cruelly thrown into relief, his milky eyes set deep in wrinkled pouches. Nailer picked a spot halfway between them and sat down, then hoicked a hind leg and scratched long and furiously behind one ear.

The movement seemed to set them going. 'You saw it coming?' Munt said.

'Not really,' Sadie answered. 'Death is so – *surprising*, isn't it?'

'That's 'cause you're young. You keep on thinking that way, while you can.'

'You'd think, after the war—'

'Nothing don't seem real in a war. It's all like a sort o' story. You think when you close the book things'll go back to normal.'

'Yes,' said Sadie, wondering how he knew.

He seemed to consider whether to go on, then, straightening painfully with his hands in the small of his back, he said to the air, 'Lorst a son in the South Africa war. He'd a bin thirty-seven now. Still expect him to come walking back in, whistling like he always done.'

'I didn't know you had a son.'

'Only the one. We don't never talk about it.'

Sadie considered. 'So it doesn't get any better?'

He looked at her now. 'Lorst is lorst. *That* don't change. You get on with it, that's all.'

'What was his name?' she asked shyly – but he seemed, just for once, to want to talk.

'Albert,' said Munt. 'He was tall – taller'n me. Strong, too. Useter pick his mother up round the waist. Lifted her right orf the ground, he did, and she'd shriek like—' He turned his head away and scratched behind his ear, under the rim of his cap, a defensive action. 'When a young man wants to go for a soldier, you can't stop 'em.'

'I know,' said Sadie. 'David and Bobby were like that. And William.'

He turned his head back, and his eyes were suddenly direct. 'What happened to your'n?'

She was startled. 'What?'

'You had someone you was in love with, didn't you? War's over and he's not come back.'

'He came back,' she said, 'but—' She didn't know how to explain the nature of the problem. She didn't know that she wanted to.

'None o' my business,' he said, pulling the string out of his pocket and cutting a new length to indicate that he would probe no more and she was free to go.

She heard the church clock ring the three quarters, and realised she had better get back to intercept the rector. She turned away, not wanting to go back into the house, where everything was dark and miserable and lonely with death.

Behind her, Munt said kindly, 'You're a right one. Pick o' the bunch, I allus said.' She paused but did not look back, and as she began to move again, he said, 'Life's a lot longer'n what you think. You'll see. Someone else'll come along for you one day.'

Tears filled her eyes. *But I don't want anyone else*, she thought.

Nailer, who had been digging under the runners, realised she had moved, and scurried with a hop and a jump to catch her up.

CHAPTER SIXTEEN

Eileen, going out to the dustbin, walked into a big man in khaki and let out a shriek.

'Now then,' he said, catching her by the elbows to keep her upright. 'No need for that. You know me.'

She squinted up at him nervously, then her expression cleared. 'You're Cook's – f-friend.' She had been going to say 'fancy man' but changed it in the nick of time. The 'f' did for both.

'Right you are. What's going on?' There were motor-cars parked outside, and through the window he had seen a mass of people inside.

''Tis the funeral,' Eileen said, with big eyes. 'Poor Mrs David, she had a baby and died of it. Oh, it's so sad! They buried her today and all these people came back. Twice as many as Missus expected, so we're all to pieces. Aggie's gone down the village for bought cakes, there's no time to make more.'

'I see. Well, off you go, then, whatever you were doing.' He put her to one side and went in, and saw his betrothed at the kitchen table buttering bread with an air of panic, and two strange maids loading trays and filling teapots.

Cook looked up, expecting Eileen, and she shrieked too.

'Don't worry,' he said, 'I'm not AWOL. I'm out, finished – discharged. Two weeks' demob leave and then I hand back my greatcoat.'

'You're demobbed?' Cook said. 'Why ever didn't you let me know?'

'Wanted to surprise ya,' he said. 'I can see I did that all right.'

'I've got no time for you now,' she cried, leaning away from him as though she expected to be seized and ravished. 'We've got a death in the house.'

'I know, the kid told me. Damned shame.'

'She was a fine, good lady. And now I've got dozens to feed. We didn't make near enough sandwiches. So many people came to the church, and Missus had to ask 'em back, or how would it have looked?'

'Don't worry. I won't get in your way. I'll help.'

'You – help?' she cried. 'What can you do?'

'Fill that kettle for a start,' he said, and took it from the thin elderly maid who was struggling with the weight. 'I'm Fred McAusland,' he told her amiably.

'She's Betty, maid from up the road, helping out,' Cook intervened distractedly. Fred grinned at Betty, completing her rout, filled the kettle in the scullery and pushed it back onto the heat.

'Now, then,' he said, looking around. There was a whole ham, in cut, on the table. 'This for the sandwiches?' he asked. 'All right, I'll carve for you.'

'Gotter be thin slices for the ladies and gentlemen,' Cook warned.

He had picked up the long ham knife, and now flourished it at her with a hurt look. 'I'm a butcher, remember? I know more about cutting meat than you'll ever forget, Margaret my girl. Just you get on with buttering your bread, or I'll overtake you. Thin slices – my word!' he added under his breath, but loud enough for her to hear. 'There'll be some apologising to be done when this lot's over.'

She looked on suspiciously as he trimmed the edges and put the fragments in his mouth, but when he had cut – with unnecessary flourish – two delicate slices, she relaxed and turned again to her own task. 'Don't call me Margaret in front of the others,' she hissed. 'Nobody but you calls me that.'

'That's the whole point,' he said.

Antonia, it seemed, had touched many lives. Everyone came to her funeral – not just the family, but all the local gentry: the Olivers, the Cuthberts, the Covingtons, Hardings, Latterys, Woodwicks and Farringdons, Dame Barbara Woodville of the Red Cross and Mr Whiteley the MP. And the other people came, the Church End and Old High Street people, those she served in the Hastings Road canteen and on various committees, but many, many more whom she had helped and given advice to without anyone's knowing. Her short life had been a rich one.

Mr Weston, grey in his agony, took comfort from the many who praised her to him, and even more from those who sidled up, too shy to speak, but to give him a speaking look, sometimes through tears.

She had been a casualty of war, in her way. The village had lost so many, for whom there had been no funerals: Antonia's sending-off, Sadie decided, had taken on some sort of symbolism, as if it was a chance to mourn all the lost. Northcote had taken her to its heart, but that day she represented more than herself: she was the whole village.

Sadie was glad her father had been able to come home, and William: they should all be together. Diana came, eerily beautiful in black, bringing her children to stay in the nursery with Antonia's while everyone went to church – bringing her nursery maids, too, so that Ethel and Nula could attend the service with the other servants.

Afterwards, when so many, many people came back to the house, David stood like a granite cliff while people said things at him, and Mr Weston trembled and had to sit down. Mrs Weston bit her lip and couldn't help him. Sadie was glad of Beth, and Audrey and Mary Palfrey, to help her protect them from the well-meaning. And she was glad of Laura, who fortunately had been in England, seeing to the conversion of her ambulance, and who undertook the protection of Beattie and Edward without being asked.

For herself, Sadie had cried herself out in the nights following the death, and if some of the tears had been for the loss of John, Antonia would have been the last to blame her. Now she felt as though she would never cry again, for the whole of the rest of her life.

On the Sunday, there was a languor over the house.

Diana came over again for the day, with the children, having had the hint from Sadie that they would help distract people. George seemed to take an instant liking to Mr Weston, and consented to sit on his knee and chat to him. Laura, who had gone home to her own house, came back in the late morning, and took pity on Peter, who was being painfully good and helpful, and played serial games of cribbage with him quietly in the corner.

After luncheon they said goodbye to the Westons. Beattie had urged them to stay as long as they liked but was inwardly relieved that they declined. Mr Weston shook hands with David but neither of them could find anything to say.

When Sadie accompanied him to the door, he asked her, 'Did she finish her book? The – the adventures?'

'Not quite. Almost.' Sadie paused. 'I don't know if David will do anything with it. He's very down. He may not have the heart.'

Weston nodded, but said, 'It ought to be published. She'd have wanted that. I could help. If David would send it to me . . .'

'I don't know how he'll react if I mention it,' Sadie said. 'He's hard to talk to.'

'I understand,' said Mr Weston. 'I'll leave it to you to

230

choose a moment. If he's willing, I'll do everything. He needn't be troubled. I'll even pay to have it published, if necessary.' He raised haunted eyes to hers. 'I always hoped she'd be a writer one day.'

'She *was*,' said Sadie.

William had a telephone call. He went out into the hall to take it and, coming back, seemed excited. Sadie raised her eyebrows at him, and he beckoned her out, and into the morning-room where they could talk. As soon as she shut the door, he said, 'They've done it! They've done it! Non-stop across the Atlantic! Of course, it's wretched that Harry Hawker wasn't the first after all, but at least they're our boys and not French or American!'

'What are you talking about? Who was that on the telephone?'

'My friend Considine. He's been down at the sheds, and the news came in this morning, so he had to let me know as soon as possible. It'll be in all the papers tomorrow. Jack Alcock and Teddie Brown have won the *Daily Mail* competition! You remember, flying across the Atlantic in less than seventy-two hours.'

'Do you know them?'

'I know *of* them – they were both pilots in the war, both got shot down and taken prisoner. They've been working with the Vickers team at Weybridge, converting a Vimy twin-engined bomber. They took off yesterday from Lester's Field in Newfoundland. Apparently had a lot of engine trouble, and terrible weather – first fog, then snow – but they kept going. They made landfall in Galway about half past eight this morning.' He grinned. 'Apparently, they saw what they thought was a nice flat green field to land on, but it turned out to be a bog and she tipped on her nose and broke a wing. But they weren't hurt. Lord, what I'd give to have been with them!'

231

'It *is* very exciting,' Sadie said, 'but don't go back into the drawing-room with that face.'

'Oh, I know. But I had to tell someone, or I'd have burst. Considine says everyone's going mad at Brooklands. They're saying the King's going to knight them both for it. That's on top of the ten-thousand-pound prize. Under seventy-two hours?' he scoffed. 'They did it in less than sixteen!'

'And how is your job going?' she asked him, hoping to calm him down. 'Isn't it rather boring flying between the same two points every day?'

'Flying is never boring,' he asserted. 'It's different every time. You should let me take you up one day – I bet you'd love it.'

'I bet I would, too,' she said.

'Anyway, the job's going all right. We're getting more passengers, and Burgess has put my screw up to thirty bob. So I'm looking around for lodgings. I can't sponge off the Considines for ever.'

The decision that it was the right time to move had been aided by his growing awareness of a certain Miles Drago, one of the enthusiasts at Brooklands, who had bought a two-seater Pup from the RAF for his private use. Drago was tall, good-looking, independently wealthy, had auburn hair, and seemed to attract females like moths to his flame. There were always several fluttering around his shed. He was the sort of confident, outgoing chap William had always longed to be. And on Friday evening he had called to take Eva out in his motor-car. She had gripped William's arm as she passed and whispered, 'Isn't he *wonderful*? Aren't I lucky?' and even he couldn't pretend that the grasp was anything but sisterly.

Now he said, 'I've heard of a decent place, room with breakfast and supper for seventeen-and-six. I reckon I could manage all right on the rest.' He frowned in calculation. 'There's laundry, that's four bob, then there's ciggies, lunches

232

and the occasional pint of beer. Haircuts. Shoe repairs. Can't think of anything else, much. Oh, coal's extra at Mrs Hudson's, but I won't use a lot – I'll be out all day. No, I think I can manage pretty well for now.'

'What about fares?'

'I'm going to take my bicycle back with me on the train. It's only a couple of miles from the airfield.'

'What about train fares to come and visit *us*?' Sadie asked. Diana was gone, Bobby was gone, now William – and she was left behind with the sadness. What was going to happen to her? Now the war was over, her job couldn't last much longer. And then what?

William said, 'Don't worry, old thing, I'll still come and see you.' His eyes were alight with dreams and plans, and though he put a loving arm round her shoulders as he said it, she knew he wasn't wondering about her future. He assumed she'd always be here, at home, with Mother and Dad.

And perhaps she would.

Edward had gone to his study to look through some papers. He had telegraphed Duval to say that he would be returning on Monday. He would spend another night here, then go up to Town first thing to call in at his office, and catch the boat train around noon.

He hoped that perhaps there would be time this evening to talk to Beattie. With so many people about, it had not been appropriate or even possible to be alone with her. Last night he had slept in his dressing-room: at the door of the bedroom, Beattie had turned an agonised look on him, and he had known she could not bear any intimacy. It was wretched that he had had to be away while all this was going on. He hoped it had not set them back. The tension between them was palpable, but it was not good tension. Perhaps tonight she would let him go into the bedroom with her –

233

just to hold her, for comfort. If she could not take comfort from him, what hope was there for them?

He unfolded some papers and forced himself to concentrate on them, until David knocked tentatively on the half-open door and said, 'Can I talk to you?'

Edward away pushed the papers, not without relief. 'Come in,' he said. 'Come and sit down.' He watched his eldest son across the room and said, 'You're hardly limping at all. Does it still hurt?'

'If I use it too much,' David said, 'it aches. And if I bang it or jar it, it hurts like the Devil. But I try not to do that.'

'Of course.'

'Antonia—' He stopped as if he had not meant to say her name, then started again. 'Antonia used to massage it for me. When I was tired and aching.'

'David—' Edward began.

But he put up his hand to stop him. 'Don't, Dad. It's all been said. Don't say any more.'

'All right,' Edward said. He cleared his throat. 'What did you want to talk about?'

'I've been thinking – ever since it happened – about the future. Well, I was thinking about it before that. I was going to talk to Antonia once she was – back on her feet.' He made a flat gesture with his hand, as if suppressing any comment. 'As you've noticed, my leg's pretty sound now. I mean, I can get about, and do a day's work, as long as it's not all standing. I'll never be an athlete, but—' He shrugged.

Edward studied him. He was – what? Twenty-five? Twenty-five, but he looked ten years older. There was grey in his hair, silver threads among the bronze, and lines of pain and experience round his eyes and mouth corners. He was a widower with two children. No, he would never be an athlete – or a fresh-faced young man again.

'So what have you been thinking?' Edward prompted him.

'I can't go on doing what I'm doing,' David said, 'cramming

234

little boys. It hardly pays for my food, and now I've two children to support, and my leg's more or less all right, I have to get on with my life. Term ends in a week or so, and I'm not going to take on any more pupils. I want a proper job.'

'Teaching?'

'We talked about it, Antonia and I, because her father was in the business so I suppose it seemed obvious to her. And it might have made sense, as a housemaster in a residential place, with accommodation thrown in for her and the children. But my heart was never in it. I don't . . .' he met his father's eyes with the confession '. . . much like children.' Edward smiled in response. 'Also, to be frank, I don't feel it's – well, *enough* for me.'

'You have ambitions?'

'Is that ridiculous? I want to make more of myself than that – fading into some old pipe-smoking dominie, cut off from the real world. So I thought – I wondered – could you put me in the way of something?'

'You want a job at the bank?' Edward was surprised, but not displeased. He had always hoped one of his boys would follow him into the profession.

'Is that possible? I've always been pretty good at maths, and even though I didn't finish university, I've got a good grasp of history and politics and so on. I'd work hard, Dad, I swear, and not disgrace you.'

'I know you wouldn't disgrace me. I've always been proud of you, David. And I won't pretend I haven't had ambitions for you.'

'So – can you do anything for me?' David asked eagerly.

Edward hesitated, saw his son's mouth turn down, and hastened to say, 'Yes, I can find something for you – get you into a billet of some sort, where you could prove yourself. After that, it would be up to you to make something of the opportunity.'

235

'I would, I will. Why do you sound as though you're going to say, "but".'

'I'm only wondering if it's too soon,' Edward said. 'You've so recently been bereaved. You've a new baby, and a little son. Perhaps you ought to give it a few weeks before you add another strain to your system.'

'It was Antonia who had the weak heart, not me,' David said, with a bitter look. 'As for being bereaved – thousands were, during the war. They didn't take time off. They just got on with it.'

'That was wartime, and they had to.'

'Don't you understand?' he said, clenching his fists with frustration. 'I've been sitting on my rump for three years. Being waited on. Being pitied. Not a real man any more. I can't sit still any longer. I want to work. I *have* to work. I can't sit around in the house until the Fitzgeralds of this world agree that I've done a proper amount of mourning!'

'You misjudge me. That was never on my mind. I just don't want you to take up a job in haste, under the influence of grief, then find it's not to your liking.'

David gritted his teeth. 'Just get me a job, and I'll show you. I'll do it, whatever it is. And I'm thinking perfectly clearly, Dad, whatever you believe. I've had enough grief in my life to know. This is not that.'

Edward wanted so badly to put his arms round his son, and hold him as if he were eight years old and had skinned both knees. Such defiance in the face of pain never failed to call to the father in him. 'Very well,' he said. 'You can come up to Town with me tomorrow morning and I'll see where I can place you.'

'Tomorrow?' David looked like someone who had pushed at a door, believing it to be latched, only to have it swing open. 'Really? You mean it?'

'Do you have a decent suit to wear?'

David grinned with relief. 'I've got one – don't know

236

how decent. I think I've rather changed shape since I last wore it.'

'Well, after we've been to the office, you can go to my tailor and get yourself measured.' Something occurred to him. 'You won't be leaving home?'

David looked embarrassed. 'I wasn't thinking of it. I mean, I have two children. Who would look after them? I was hoping I could stay here. I'll pay for their keep, of course, – once I'm earning enough.'

'Don't think of leaving,' Edward said. 'It would break your mother's heart. And the children belong here. You think you'll manage the journey up and down every day?'

'Of course,' David said. 'It's all sitting down.'

There was more to it than that, for a man whose femur had been a jigsaw puzzle, but Edward was not going to say anything more to discourage him.

Laura persuaded Sadie to go for a walk round the garden with her. 'I want another cigarette, and the air inside is so blue, with everyone smoking so much, I feel guilty,' she said.

They walked down the main path, between what had once been the lawns. 'This used to be such a pretty garden,' Laura lamented.

'But we grew a lot of vegetables for a lot of people. It was the right thing to do,' Sadie said.

'Oh, quite – but the war's over now. Isn't one allowed a little bit of grass to walk on?'

Sadie said, 'Munt is with you. He can't wait to get to work on it, though he says it'll be twenty years before it's a proper lawn.'

'How old is he? I wouldn't have thought he had twenty years in him.'

'I expect sheer stubbornness would keep him going,' said Sadie. 'If he started a lawn, he would simply refuse to die until it was perfect.'

Laura stopped to light her cigarette. 'I didn't like the look of David,' she said, blowing the first smoke skywards.

Sadie was surprised. 'But he's ever so much better.'

'I mean his mind, not his body. So much anger!'

'That's the way it takes him, I suppose,' Sadie said doubtfully. Yes, now she thought about it, it was a kind of rage. Against God for taking Antonia? Or against Antonia for being taken? 'But if it helps him get through . . .'

'Yes. But I wonder if it will. It can be so debilitating.' She smoked for a moment in silence. 'I was pleased to see those Palfrey girls so well settled, though. Did you know Audrey's going to university?'

'No,' said Sadie, surprised. 'After practically running the factory all through the war, I'd have thought she'd carry on, or do something similar. Surely Uncle Aeneas didn't make her give it up?'

Laura snorted with amusement. 'He'd have liked to, but he has a healthy respect for that little girl. No, it was her choice. She told him, now she's proved that she can do anything a man does, she ought to have her choice, and her choice is to go to university.'

'And then what?'

'An academic career, I suppose.' Laura shrugged. 'And then there's Mary, happy as a lark preparing to marry her Clive, looking forward just to being a wife and mother. Twins, but so different from each other. Women continue to surprise me. We're much less homogeneous than men, don't you think?'

Sadie didn't know the word but guessed what she meant. 'I expect men hide it more,' she said.

Laura turned to look at her. 'And what about you, Sadie? Wouldn't you like to go to university?'

'Me? I don't have that sort of mind.'

Laura's eyes narrowed. 'I think you could do anything you wanted to.'

'Well, it's not always up to one, is it?' Sadie said. 'David and William got the brains in this family. And Peter, too, I think. He wants to be an engineer. Or an explorer. He hasn't made up his mind.'

'Wise boy!'

'They got the brains, and Diana and Bobby got the beauty. I'm just Sadie-in-the-middle. Nothing very much of anything.'

'I think you're very much of a great deal,' Laura said sternly, 'and if you don't make something of yourself I shall be very cross. I suppose your horse job can't last much longer.'

'I suppose not,' Sadie said glumly.

'Then you must find something else to do. I don't want to see you sink into obscurity as the daughter-at-home. You can't want that.'

What I want is John, Sadie thought before she could stop herself. She had made it a rule with herself not to think of him, but sometimes he slipped through her guard. If she only knew where he was, and that he was all right . . .

Edward, too, had noticed the anger in David. He knew it was one of the ways David reacted to anguish. It was better, anyway, than the black gloom: at least anger kept you moving forward. Whether David could control it was another matter. Directed, it would give him power; undirected, it would destroy any possibility of a career. Edward had already decided that he would give David into the care of old Murchison, his clerk, to learn the ropes for a few weeks. That would be a severe test of his patience. If he came through, he would have proved he had mastered himself. If he blew up – well, it wouldn't hurt Murchison, and it would show David he hadn't the temperament for banking.

He explained all that to Beattie, when they were alone in the drawing-room, after everyone had gone home or to bed.

She looked worried. 'It's too soon,' she said. 'Barely a week since his wife died.'

'Men don't take time off work when they're bereaved,' Edward pointed out.

'But he's not—' She stopped.

'Yes, he is a man,' Edward said, guessing what she hadn't said. 'He's twenty-five, not your little boy any more.'

'I know that,' she said irritably. It was difficult, discussing David with Edward. Dangerous.

'He needs something to do,' he said. 'This will get him out of the house and occupy his mind. And if he fails – I'll set it up so there's no damage done.'

'It would damage David, to fail,' she said. And there was in her look both hostility and the old wariness, and he knew he would not be holding her in his arms that night. It hurt him more than he had expected to have David come between them as an object of contention.

'You have to let him go, Beattie,' he said quietly. 'He has to live his own life. You can't live it for him.'

She gave him a hard, bright look, and seemed about to speak; but she turned and left him without a word. He listened to her light step across the hall and up the stairs. Tomorrow he would have to go back to his hotel room in Paris. It was difficult to repair a marriage when you were not there, on the spot. *And David was*, came the unbidden thought. But he would not be jealous of his own son. That way lay madness.

CHAPTER SEVENTEEN

In the kitchen, the same languor prevailed. There had been extra washing-up to do from the party, and seldom-used crockery to be packed and put away. And then servants' dinner and upstairs luncheon to get and, given Miss Laura and Miss Diana were staying, Cook put herself to the trouble of making fresh rolls to have with the soup, and did a beurre blanc with the turbot. Thank goodness there were strawberries coming in from the garden, and nothing made June strawberries any better than having them fresh, with cream. When all that was done and cleared away, Ada went to her room and Aggie and Eileen went out to see their respective families. Ethel, of course, was upstairs with her babies, and Nula went home to her neglected husband.

Cook sought her armchair in the servants' sitting-room, and had just eased her feet onto her battered footstool when Fred came in like a whirlwind – not noisily, but seeming to displace a great deal of the world just by his presence.

'All alone? That's good! Give us a kiss, and then put your best hat on – I'm going to take you out for a posh tea.'

Cook turned her head away as he bent over her so that he only got her cheek, and said fretfully, 'Oh, not now, Fred! It's not the time.'

'Sunday afternoon's when you're off, isn't it?' he said, remarkably untroubled by her rebuff. 'Right! Come on, then. Best bib and tucker!'

'With all this trouble in the house?' she said. 'Haven't you got no sense of propriety?'

That stung him. He straightened up. 'Now look here, my girl—'

'Don't you "my girl" me. We've had a death in the family, and the least you could do is act respectful.'

'It's not your family, it's not your death, and there's nothing disrespectful about expecting your intended to go out to tea with you. I'm not asking you to cavort in the street wreathed in feathers.'

'Not my family? Whatever are you talking about?' Cook said angrily.

'What are *you* talking about?' he countered. 'You're a servant in this house, that's all. I don't doubt she was a nice lady and you're feeling a bit shocked and sad about it, but life has to go on. *Your* life – not theirs.' She glared at him, unable to think of the right words. He saw he had really annoyed her, and sat down in the armchair opposite, leaning forward, his long forearms on his knees and his hands dangling before them. 'Come on, now, Margaret – I've put me big old foot in it, haven't I? I'm sorry if I spoke a bit strong. But you and me, girl – we've got things to do. You don't have to go into mourning for someone in your employer's family—'

'You don't understand,' she said. 'I've been with them twenty-five years. They *are* my family – all the family I've got.'

'What about your sister and her lot, down in Folkestone?' Fred said, and saw her look guilty, because she had forgotten them in the heat of the argument. He went on, 'I expect you're fond of them upstairs, in a way, but you got me now, and we'll be leaving soon to start up a new life in sunny Australia. Where you'll be Mrs McAusland, and a respectable married woman at last – after all these years of calling yourself "Mrs" for no reason!'

242

He had hoped to make her laugh, but what she picked up on was 'soon'.

'What d'you mean, leaving soon? You never said anything about that.'

'I'm saying it now. Well, I was hoping to talk to you more civilised, over a fancy tea, with your best hat on, but I suppose it'll have to be here, now. I've booked two passages on the *Orsova*, sailing on the thirtieth, and since I reckoned it wouldn't suit your dainty ways to travel with a bloke you weren't married to, I also bought a special licence, so we can get married any time you like. That gives you two weeks to pack your traps, pick a wedding day, and say bye-bye to gloomy old England.'

'Two weeks?' Cook gasped. Inside, she was trembling with alarm and doubt, but outwardly she let it turn to anger. 'You come marching in here, telling me I got two weeks to marry you and leave my home and traipse off across the world with you, like I was a – a . . . Is that what you call giving me notice? Who do you think you are, Fred McAusland?'

'I think I'm the bloke that's been engaged to you for two long years,' he said sharply, 'while I served me King and Country, just waiting for the moment I could come home to my best girl and start a new life with her. You knew we were going to get married and go to Australia when the war ended. Blimey, it's seven months since the Armistice – I'd have thought seven months was enough notice.'

'But you never told me you were out, or coming home, or anything. You just turn up on my doorstep—'

'Whose doorstep should I turn up on?' he asked. 'Anyway, it's not your doorstep. It's theirs. I'm offering you a doorstep of your very own, and you're giving me the old acid.'

'But I can't just walk out,' she said plaintively. 'Not just like that. What would they do without me?'

'Blimey, girl, you don't get it, do you? You're the cook. You're not their bloody ewe-lamb! It won't break their hearts

243

when you go. You leave, they'll get another cook. That's how it works.'

'It's not like that,' she said tearfully.

'Yes, it bloody is!'

'Don't swear!'

'It's enough to make a man swear. I've waited two years for you. What's all the bloody palaver for now? You trying to back out or something?'

'I just don't see what all the rush is about. Why can't we take our time, catch another boat? Give me time to prepare?'

'Look,' he said reasonably, 'in two weeks, the army stops paying me. I've got money saved to start up my business in Australia, and my demob money, to pay for our passages and a nice wedding for you. But if I hang around in England, what am I going to be living on while you're packing your lingerry and sobbing on your so-called family's bosom?'

'Fred!'

'"Bosom" isn't a rude word. I'm not going to spend my savings hanging around here while you make your mind up. Are you coming with me or not?'

'I *want* to come with you,' she began wretchedly.

'Well, then,' he said, and looked at her, eyes narrowed. 'Have you been stringing me along? There's a word for women like that, and it ain't a nice one.'

She gasped. 'Don't you talk to me like that!'

'I'll talk to you any damn way I want!'

'And I suppose that's what you'd be like if we was married – all lovely-dovey before, but once the ring's on my finger, it'd be swearing and bullying and shouting—'

He looked surprised. 'I'm not like that.'

She turned her head away. 'Seems to me that's exactly what you're like.'

He looked at her for a long moment. Then he breathed out hard and said, 'You never meant to marry me, did you? It was all some bloody game with you.'

'No, Fred,' she said, alarmed, looking at him now. 'I meant it – course I did. But you're rushing me. I got to have time to get used to it.'

'There isn't any time! I've bought the bloody tickets!' She didn't answer, and he stood up. 'I tell you this, girl, I'm gonna be on that boat. So you can come with me – or I'll go on my own.'

She folded her lips. 'You'd better go on your own, then. I'm not going to be talked to like that.'

'Right,' he said. 'So I know where I stand.' He started for the door. 'Pity you weren't a bit more honest with me before, 'stead of making a fool of me all this time,' he added, without looking round. 'Seems I'm well out of it.'

And then he was gone. And there was nothing for Cook to do but release the flood of tears that had built up inside her – tears of anger, trepidation, hurt and, yes, regret.

On the 21st of June, shocking news came of the scuttling of the German fleet, which had been interned at Scapa Flow. It had been moved there in November while it was decided what to do with it. Much of the crew had been repatriated, but morale among those remaining was low: they were not allowed ashore, or to visit other ships; food sent from Germany was monotonous, and with too little to do and no recreation, discipline had fallen to pieces. The German admiral in charge, von Reuter, had decided that scuttling the fleet was a more honourable end than rotting at anchor. Secret orders were put in place, and at 11.20 a.m. on the 21st, a code signal was sent, and the crews opened the seacocks and flood valves and smashed internal water pipes. Portholes and watertight doors had already been opened, and in some ships holes had been bored through bulkheads. By the time the British guard ships became aware of what was going on, it was too late. A handful of ships were towed to shallow water or beached, but fifty-two of the seventy-four vessels sank.

Edward heard the news from Duval, who brought in a signal just as Edward was leaving the office for a reception at the Elysée. At the reception it was, naturally, the foremost topic of conversation. There was considerable indignation against von Reuter, because scuttling was specifically forbidden under the terms of the Armistice. But some, especially from the naval side, had sympathy with him, and felt he had kept his dignity in an impossible situation, depriving the enemy of a valuable resource. They, they indicated without actually saying so, would have done the same.

'It's a mess,' said Lord Forbesson, who was over for another series of meetings. 'Not least because we'll have to treat all those sailors we picked up as prisoners of war, which means we'll have to keep 'em and feed 'em instead of sending 'em home. And what do we do with von Reuter?'

'He'll be a hero in Germany,' Edward commented.

'He'll be a thorn in our side.'

Edward lowered his voice. 'From my point of view, sinking those ships is a blessing in disguise. You know the French and the Italians have been agitating about them – they each wanted a quarter of them for their own navies.'

'But that's the last thing we want! It would dilute the advantage our fleet has over other navies.'

'Yes, so Admiral Wemyss was saying only last week. Well, this way, there can be no more argument about it. Shocking as it was, I'm glad they're gone. It's saved me a lot of work. Whenever anybody thinks someone else is doing better than he is, he ends up complaining to the treasury committee. We're the repository of last resort for all complaints.'

Forbesson grinned. 'You're a national hero, Hunter – always knew you'd turn out a very handy feller to know. When all this is over, there'll be a cosy billet for you in Whitehall.'

'Thank you,' Edward said, with a shudder, 'but I'd rather crawl back into my bank and pull the covers over my head.'

They chatted about other subjects for a while, and then Forbesson said, 'By the way, I popped into the bank the other day and I feel sure I spotted that boy of yours, passing down a corridor.'

'You may well have,' said Edward.

'Thought I wasn't mistaken,' said Forbesson. 'Distinctive-looking chap, with that profile and that hair. Leg all right now?'

'Good enough to get about on,' said Edward, and yielding to Forbesson's naked curiosity, he explained, 'He wants to get started on a career, and I've put him in at the bank just to get him into the way of working, and to see what he's good for. Murchison is teaching him the basics.'

'What's his background?'

'He was reading Greats when the war broke out and he volunteered. But he did all the usual subjects at school.'

'Cricketer?'

'Pretty handy with the bat,' Edward said, with an inward smile.

'Sounds the right sort of chap,' said Forbesson, without defining for what.

'We'll see how he does,' Edward said. 'It's early days yet.'

David was trying really hard. The basic routines that Murchison had been tasked with showing him he quickly grasped; and the basic tenets of banking, as far as Murchison was able to explain them, led him only to ask more questions. There was nothing wrong with his brain. The trouble was, there was not enough in following Murchison around to keep it occupied. The old man was so slow, and his explanations were so repetitious, David was often on the brink of shouting at him in frustration: 'You've told me that already, you stupid old man!' He kept his temper with difficulty, occasionally escaping into the lavatory to bang his head against the panelling until he calmed down.

Matters were not helped by the discovery that it was harder on his leg than he had anticipated, and he was often in pain. When he got home in the evening, after that long train journey – which seemed to get longer as the week went on – he was so tired he didn't want to eat, and only forced a few mouthfuls down because otherwise he would have had his mother hovering about him. What kept him going was the knowledge that he was on probation with his father. If he failed this first test, Dad would give up on him.

Fortunately for his sanity, after the first two weeks Mr Cruickshank, who had taken over his father's office for the duration of the war, stepped in. Though Edward had not said anything to him, he had decided for himself that Edward expected him to take David under his wing and make sure he got on. And seeing that David was far from a fool, and discovering that he had a good grasp of figures, he took him over from Murchison and began showing him the real work.

With something intellectual to grapple with, David calmed down. Some of the red mist dissipated from behind his eyes, and he began to feel that there was a possibility here of earning his keep. He was introduced to another young clerk, Eric Findlater, to learn about the stock market, and here David found much to engage him. He was able to forget himself, the war and his troubles for long periods while reading up on the performance of companies and matching it to their share price. Once he came back from a long spell of concentration to see the black armband on his jacket and wonder for a fraction of a second what it was for. He often forgot he had two small children: lost in the world of numbers and finance, he could be twenty-five again.

The Treaty of Versailles, officially ending the war between Germany and the Allies, was signed in the Hall of Mirrors on the 28th of June, exactly five years after the assassination of Archduke Franz Ferdinand, which was often regarded as the event that had precipitated the war. Treaties between the Allies and the other powers that had fought on Germany's side had yet to be concluded. The main thrust of the treaty was the requirement of Germany to accept full responsibility for the loss and damage of the war. It was required to disarm, concede substantial swathes of territory, and pay billions in war reparations.

The news of the treaty was received euphorically in the newspapers in England, especially the bit about 'making Germany pay'. The more thoughtful editorials might murmur that Germany was a trading partner of Great Britain and that crippling its economy would do no good to anyone: the part the people liked was good old Lloyd George demanding that British war pensions and widows' pensions should be included in the sum Fritz had to cough up. That'd show 'em!

Now the way was clear to talk about Peace Day, which was set for Saturday, the 19th of July. Lloyd George had been impressed by the French preparations for a celebration on Bastille Day, involving a Victory March of troops past a great catafalque, saluting the memory of the dead. Edwin Lutyens was called in to Downing Street and asked to design a suitable structure for the Peace Day parade in London.

Time was short, but within hours he had come up with a simple and elegant design, which could be constructed quickly out of wood and plaster: a pylon that rose in a series of set-backs to an empty tomb on the top, which he called the Cenotaph. Lutyens had come across the word when designing a garden bench for Gertrude Jekyll in the 1890s: her friend Charles Liddell, who was a librarian at the British Museum, had used the term for the tomb-like block. The only dissent in the cabinet came from the classicists, who argued not about the word but its pronunciation. Since it came from the Greek *keno*, empty, and *taphos*, tomb, it should clearly be pronounced 'keenotaph', not, as Lloyd George anglicised it, 'sennotaph'. But he was prime minister, after all. He had his way.

Not everyone liked the idea of Peace Day. There were some letters to newspapers saying that the money 'wasted' on it ought to be distributed among the demobbed soldiers who couldn't find work; others that the war had been fought to end militarism, not to see it celebrated. But the protests were drowned by far more enthusiasm: if the war was really over at last, there ought to be a festival.

'Will the master be home in time for it, madam?' Ada asked, as she cleared breakfast on the Monday before it. Everyone else had left; Beattie was lingering over the newspaper. There was so much she ought to be doing, but she was finding it strangely difficult to make decisions, these days. The turmoil of her feelings over Antonia's death, and her ongoing worry for David, had left her feeling limp and weary, as though she were convalescing from an illness.

She dragged her mind back to the question. 'I'm afraid not,' she said. 'The peace treaty is really only the starting point. There is so much still to do.'

'Oh, what a pity, madam,' Ada said. She waited with a receptive look until Beattie, noticing she had not gone away, realised what she was waiting for.

'Naturally you will all have the day off, if you wish to attend the parade,' she said.

'Oh, *thank* you, madam,' Ada said. 'It's a once-in-a-lifetime thing, isn't it?' And she went off to the kitchen to tell the others the good news.

She noticed that Cook did not seem to be particularly excited. Now she came to think about it, Cook had been in a bad mood for weeks now. She had always been quick to take offence, and irritable of temper, but you could usually tread your way round it, if you knew her. Just lately, though, she'd seemed almost to be looking for things to be angry about. She had even sided with Ethel – practically unheard-of – in objecting to the idea of hiring a nanny for the children. 'Waste of money,' she had snapped, and 'Load o' snobbish nonsense,' which was not like her. 'We don't want some snooty dragon in a uniform looking down her nose at us, getting under my feet, demanding fancy foods on top of what I got to do already.'

Later in the day, Ada happened to find herself alone with Cook, who had just finished a batch of fruit cakes and put them in the oven, and was listlessly wiping the same bit of table over and over with a cloth. So she said brightly, 'Time for a cuppa?'

Cook looked up impatiently. 'Haven't you got work to do?'

'Come on, five minutes,' Ada said, wheedling. 'Do us good. I'll make it. You sit down. You been on your feet all morning.'

'On my feet every morning,' Cook said. But she pulled out a chair with an enormous sigh and sat down.

Ada quickly made the tea, and sat down opposite her. 'Can't beat a nice cuppa tea,' she said. 'I'm parched.' Cook didn't respond, but she sipped the tea, staring gloomily at nothing.

Ada gathered her courage. 'I couldn't help noticing,' she said, 'that you don't seem very happy lately.'

'Happy?' Cook responded sharply. 'We've had a death in the family, in case you haven't noticed. Am I the only person in the house that remembers poor Mrs David?' she went on, with rising wrath. 'People seem to think as soon as you've planted someone you can forget 'em and go straight back to making merry and prancing about wreathed in feathers like as if nothing had happened. Well, I happen to think she deserved a bit more respect than that, thank you very much!'

Ada contemplated this outburst and couldn't make sense of it, especially the feathers. There was something going on all right and, as Cook's closest friend, she felt it was up to

251

her to get to the bottom of it. She took a sip of tea to fortify herself, and said, cautiously, 'Haven't seen much of your Fred lately, have we? Is he—'

'He's gone,' Cook said.

'Gone?' Ada asked in surprise. 'Gone where?'

'Back to Australia. He sailed on the thirtieth. And that's that.'

'Oh no,' Ada said softly. 'Did you two quarrel?' Cook was staring at her hands and didn't seem to want to answer, but Ada pressed her. 'You got to tell me,' she said. 'Whatever in the world did you quarrel about?'

'He was all in a rush, thought I could just pick up and go without notice, didn't have no respect for my feelings, everything I had to do, arrangements to make, can't just up sticks in five minutes and . . .' Her voice trailed away.

Ada tried to pick her way through the jumble. 'Did you change your mind, then? Not want to go?'

Now Cook looked up, and there were tears in her eyes. '*Course* I wanted to. *Course* I did. But – I was scared, Ada.' Saying the word seemed to release the flow. 'It was all new to me. I never been anything except in service, I never lived outside, I never been married. I was *scared*. And it's so far away, Australia. Foreign. I don't know what I'd find there. What the people'd be like. I don't know even if they speak English. Supposing I was to hate it – how could I come back? It takes *months* to get there on the boat, that's how far it is. If I went, I'd never get back.'

'But you'd be married, you wouldn't want to come back,' Ada said. Cook only shook her head, her lips tight to stop herself crying. 'Did you say all this to Fred?'

'Never got the chance. Before I knew it, we was quarrelling. He said – he said I'd just been toying with him. He got angry.'

'Well, he would. A man would. But you weren't, were you? Toying with him?'

252

'I don't know,' Cook said miserably. 'I never been married, I don't know what it'd be like.'

'But you meant it when you said yes?'

'Course I meant it. I just – got scared.' Cook stared at her fingers, anxiously pleating the dishcloth she had picked up again. Such clever fingers with pastry. She could fillet a fish in two lovely movements. She could make delicate icing-sugar roses for a wedding-cake or bone a leg of lamb. She knew several hundred sauces. She could make a sponge cake so light it near lifted off the table. There was nothing she couldn't do, when it came to cooking. But that was all she knew. Those fingers had never undressed a man; and even thinking about Fred's body under his uniform made her face go hot and prickly. She looked up into Ada's calm, sad eyes, and knew that here was the one person in the world who might understand. 'How did you do it, Ada?' she asked. 'Men are so – *different*. When it came to it, with your Len – how did you do it?'

'I don't know,' Ada said. 'I just sort of jumped in. I mean, he was so lovely, my Len, and sort of gentle, and I wanted to be with him. When it came to it, it was that or grow old all alone, without him, so it wasn't really a choice.' In the end, of course, she would have to grow old without him anyway. But there was no need for either of them to say that. 'I'm glad I did,' she concluded. 'I wouldn't have missed that for the world, short as it was.'

Cook nodded. 'I sort of felt that way about Fred. He was – sort of big. And strong. Like he'd take care of you, and you'd never be worried about anything if he was there.' She used the cloth to wipe her eyes. 'And now it's too late. He's gone. I'll never be married now. I'll be all alone. And what'll happen to me when I get too old to work?'

There was a silence as they sipped their tea. It was everyone's fear – penurious old age. You got your Lloyd George when you reached seventy, but that was only five bob a week, and how could you live on that? And what if you couldn't keep working until seventy? It was something too frightening to contemplate: you just kept your mind turned away from it.

Then Ada said, 'We're in the same boat, you and me. Except – well, I got my war widow's pension. I been saving it up – haven't needed to spend it. I should have a decent bit put away by the time I have to stop work. What about you and me sort of joining forces?'

'Joining forces?' Cook didn't think she had any force.

'When we're old, we could live together, share what we got, sort of look after each other.'

Cook's eyes moistened again. 'You'd do that for me? Share your savings and everything?'

'I don't want to be alone,' Ada said. 'And we known each other a long time.'

Cook was remembering all the times she had snapped at Ada, the times she had criticised her, belittled her, not appreciated her. She remembered especially that she had discouraged Ada from walking out with Len. 'I don't deserve a friend like you,' she mumbled.

Ada gave her a painful smile. 'I didn't deserve my Len, but I got him anyway. If we all got what we deserved, it'd be a funny old world, wouldn't it?'

Cook nodded. It was a funny one anyway, she thought, but she knew what Ada meant.

'So is that a bargain, then?' Ada went on. 'You and me – sort of pledged? We'd do all right keeping house together. You could cook and I could clean. We could have a little garden and grow vegetables to eat. We could even keep chickens, for the eggs.'

That was a touch of poetry too far. 'Nasty dirty things, chickens,' Cook said, snapping out of her reverie. 'I can't abide the smell of 'em. What are you thinking? You'll be saying we should keep a pig, next.'

254

'Good for eating up leftovers,' Ada said.

'There won't be any leftovers in *my* kitchen,' Cook pronounced. 'We'll be eating 'em. I didn't learn all that wartime cooking and economy to be throwing good food to chickens and pigs. You talk as if we'll be made o' money. A strict budget, that's what we'll have, and good food without any waste.'

Ada smiled inwardly. There was no doubt who would be giving the orders in their shared household.

CHAPTER EIGHTEEN

'So you were planning to keep me a secret until – when exactly?' Ransley asked Laura over an early breakfast on the 19th of July.

'Now don't be offended,' said Laura. 'Isn't one allowed to have a delicious secret one keeps to oneself, to increase the savour?'

'Oh, I'm delicious, am I?'

'Don't fish! I said the secret is delicious. But as it happens . . .' She reached across the table and let him squeeze her hand.

She hadn't been planning on coming home for Peace Day – she felt she could live happily without seeing another formation of soldiers ever again – but Ransley had received an invitation from a friend who was high up in the Ministry of Health to bring a party to watch from the windows of the building on Whitehall.

'Do you realise,' he said, 'what most people would give for a place at a Whitehall window?'

She saw he was serious. 'You really want to see it, don't you?'

'I do. I shan't be able to convince myself it's really over until I see the King take the salute.'

'Very well, I shan't spoil your fun. I shall come with you and be suitably awed – and probably moved, as well.'

'If you shed a tear, all will be forgiven. Who shall we invite? Welford says I can have six places.'

'Don't you have any friends?'

'I have you – that's enough.'

Laura thought. Ronnie was still in France, and Annie was very ill – failing, it seemed, of something the doctors could not identify. Laura had discussed it with Ransley, who again wondered whether her having spent so long in an enclosed space with all those X-rays bouncing back and forth could have caused it. Laura was desperately sorry about Annie; Ransley was desperately grateful that she, Laura, had been only the driver.

In the absence of her two best friends, Laura thought of relatives, and said, 'Well, then, Beth and Jack, if you please.'

'And two more. Your brother's in Paris still, isn't he? What about your sister?'

'Hmm. Sonia is not whom I would choose for company for the day. But on the other hand, she is probably the person who will be most impressed by the invitation.'

In the event, Aeneas said he would be in Scotland that day, and Sonia begged to give up her place to two of her children, who would enjoy it so much more than she would without the support of her husband. The two chosen were Audrey, who – Laura told Ransley – would be excellent company, and Duck, who was just finishing school and would be going up to Oxford in the autumn. 'He was always an ingenious boy, and he'll have plenty to say, all of which will be intelligent. And he'll love being there, so you won't feel you've wasted the honour.'

In relaying the invitations, she had been obliged to mention that they came from 'my friend Major Ransley', and though no one was vulgar enough to ask any more questions, Laura felt the nature of their relationship was bound to be fathomed with a whole day of exposure. 'I'm not sure I can sustain an air of indifference to you,' she said, 'let alone restrain myself from touching you at any point.'

'Wanton harlot,' he said with a grin. 'We had better get

across the night before so that you can work some of it out of your system.'

'As long as you don't give away the fact we stayed together at my house,' Laura stipulated. 'I don't want to shock them.'

'I thought you'd relish being a fallen woman.'

'I relish *being* one – not being *known* to be one,' Laura said.

It was only a short walk from her house in Westminster, and they strolled happily, enjoying the sunshine. The Park was already crowded, and people were slowly pushing towards the parade route, looking for vantage points, but they didn't encounter any real crush until they got to Admiralty Arch, which was a bottle-neck. Trafalgar Square was already packed, and it would have been impossible to get across it, had they needed to; but they had only to turn into Whitehall, which was closed off and guarded by mounted policemen. They were let through, and walked down the empty street to the Ministry, pausing to admire the Cenotaph, which had been unveiled in a quiet ceremony the day before.

'It looks amazingly solid,' Laura said. 'Quite like stone.'

'The sides are not actually parallel, you know,' Ransley said. 'I read about it. If they were extended they would meet at a point nine hundred and eighty feet above ground.'

Laura put her hands over her ears. '*Please* don't tell me. I know Duck is going to explain every aspect of the thing to me at great length and with great enthusiasm, and the least I can do for him is to pretend I'm surprised by the information.'

On the opposite side of the road from the Ministry of Health was the Foreign Office, a massive building in the classical style with a multiplicity of windows. Here Guy Teesborough had secured places in a room for his party, which included his mother, back at last from Malta, his brother Ivo, Diana and her sister Sadie, Bobby Pargeter and Lady Helen Hale, the Earl and Countess of Hexham, who were cousins of

258

Diana's by marriage, though she'd never met them, and Oscar Mainwaring, the long-term companion of Guy's mother in her widowhood.

It was a company calculated to make Sadie shrink to the back and efface herself – though the whole point was to be at the front by the windows. The view could not have been better – right opposite the Cenotaph and above the dais where the King would take the salute. But she felt awkward and out of place, though Diana's maid Padmore had come to help her dress that morning at Park Place, in one of the outfits from her previous jaunts. Padmore had trimmed her hair and curled it, and slyly recommended a touch of lipstick and a little brush of powder; and had assured her she looked 'very nice'. Still, despite the overpowering honour, she half wished Diana had left her out of it.

A fine breakfast of cold cuts, rolls, cakes and fruit, prepared on the assumption that none of the guests would have had time to eat before coming, was laid out on a table at the back of the room, along with coffee and champagne, and a girl and a man to serve it. The other guests all knew each other very well, and chatted nineteen to the dozen as they ate and drank. But the dowager Lady Teesborough was too good a hostess to let Sadie be left out. She made a point of talking to her, and chatted so sensibly about horses and Highclere and hospitals that Sadie began to feel much more relaxed – particularly when she had finished the first glass of champagne. It seemed to her an excellent accompaniment to breakfast. She wondered why it wasn't more generally served.

Ivo Rainton had come up to listen to their conversation, and was about to say something when Lady Teesborough fixed him with a stern look and said, 'Now, Ivo, I've just got Miss Hunter comfortable. Don't tease her or she'll bolt.'

Sadie couldn't help smiling at that, and said, 'I think I'm quiet enough for a loose rein, now, ma'am.'

And Ivo said, 'I'm not going to tease her, Mama – just make sure she has a good view. Come and see,' he went on to Sadie, 'and let me tell you all about the Cenotaph. I have some astonishing figures at my fingertips with which to dazzle you.'

'Oh dear. If you dazzle me, I may bolt after all,' Sadie said.

'That will never do. I'll talk about Mr Lutyens instead. Did you know he once designed a gazebo for Mama, at Stockridge?'

'That's your country seat, isn't it?' said Sadie, who had heard Diana mention it.

'Yes, in Hampshire. The gazebo was based on the temple of Hercules in Rome . . .' With the lightest touch on her elbow, he guided her to the window.

Aggie and Eileen went with their own families to the local celebrations in Northcote, to which Beattie took Peter; Ethel was not interested at all, preferring to stay with her babies. So Ada and Cook went to London together. They caught the earliest train they could manage, but on arrival, they realised they would have had to start out much, much earlier to get a place on the main route. Indeed, thousands had come the day before or by the night trains, sleeping in the parks or on the pavements to be sure of getting a good position. Kensington Gardens were out of bounds, having been turned into a military camp: the troops taking part in the parade were mustering there. The other parks and open spaces were crammed by nine o'clock.

But it was fun wandering along and looking at the decorations – flags and bunting, ribbons and flowers everywhere – and feeling the atmosphere of excitement and happiness. The pubs were doing a lively business, and people had spilled out onto the pavements with their drinks. Faces lined every window, and people stood on the leads of buildings, had climbed on statues and railings, and had even shinned up lampposts for a view. There were military bands playing in the parks, and other, less official, musicians – barrel-organists, fiddlers, fifers – blasted away in various spots on street corners and at the entrances to stations. Ada bought a souvenir programme for a penny, and Cook bought a bag of peanuts in the shell to munch as they squeezed along.

'Tonight,' Ada read, 'they're going to light a chain of beacon fires all over England. It says here, they did it in 1588 to warn about the Armada coming, and that was on the nineteenth of July as well. Isn't that a coincidence?'

The bodies along the pavement edge were an impenetrable wall, leaving just a narrow passage behind it. 'I'm sick of being jostled and trod on,' Cook complained. 'Let's try and get into Hyde Park. We're never going to get anywhere near the parade.'

'Well, I suppose it'll be on the newsreel at the cinema,' Ada said philosophically. 'We'll be able to see it that way.'

Duck made nothing of being introduced to 'my friend Major Ransley', being young enough to find the personal affairs of his elders of no interest. Audrey, Beth and Jack were too polite to show anything. Jack immediately got talking to Ransley about medical facilities at the Front and what was going on out there now, and the two men seemed to be getting on extremely well together.

The others clustered by the window with the rest of the guests – Ransley's friend had his own party – and admired the look of the Cenotaph, so pristine and white in the sunshine. There were one or two dabs of colour on its steps – little bunches of flowers people had left to remember their dead.

'Strange idea,' Laura said. 'Like putting flowers on a grave, I suppose, except that it isn't one.'

'But their dead probably don't have graves, or if they do, they're too far away to visit,' said Beth.

261

'Ah, well, I shall do something about that, with my guided tours,' said Laura.

'Only for the well-to-do,' said Beth. 'Look at those flowers – they aren't from florist shops. They're from poor people's gardens, tied up with string. Awfully pathetic, somehow – they look so small and insignificant on that huge monument.'

'The Cenotaph is for them – for all the small and insignificant people,' Ransley said, rejoining them.

'Aunty, did you know that the straight lines in the Cenotaph are not really straight lines at all,' Duck said enthusiastically. 'The horizontal surfaces are actually sections of a sphere . . .'

She moved over to let him come next to her and tell her all about it. Ransley came up behind her. 'They'll be here any moment,' he said. And down low, where no one could see, she slipped her fingers into his.

First came the three Allied commanders, Pershing, Foch and Field Marshal Haig, riding side by side. Their horses stepped daintily, necks arched against the curb, ears flirting nervously because of the huge crowds on either side. And then came the servicemen from the three arms, and from all the allied countries, including the Empire. There was no music then: they marched in silence, the only sound the clump of their boots striking down in perfect unison, regular and uncanny as a heartbeat. So many of them, a solid mass of humanity moving as one. No one among the spectators had ever seen so many soldiers together – even Laura, who in France had watched from the side of the road countless times as companies swung by, once even a battalion. Fifteen thousand, it said in the programme. It made the hair rise on the back of her neck: the column was like a many-legged beast, something beyond human.

The spectators might have done anything in response – applauded, perhaps, or cheered, or chattered in wonder; but they were silent too, held in the supernatural strangeness of the moment; probably every one of them thinking of someone lost, someone who had not made it back from those foreign fields. And behind the heartbeat of the march, almost but not quite simultaneous, there came to be perceived another sound, the faint, hollow echo reflected from the tall buildings, so that it seemed a ghostly army of the lost marched along with their brothers, unseen, only felt deep in the blood and the nerves.

Laura found herself looking at a woman, down below in the crowd and opposite her, beyond the moving column, whose face was awash and contorted with tears, and yet who held herself straight, as if she were on parade too. Husband, brother, son – whom had she lost? In a moment of searing enlightenment, Laura understood the real meaning of that empty tomb on top of the monument. She understood what Ransley had meant, that the Cenotaph was for the small and insignificant people, for all of them together, and for each of them, like that weeping woman, in particular. All deaths were one death; each of them had been bereaved of every single soul lost.

There were, to console the many who had failed to see the parade, a variety of entertainments in the parks that went on all afternoon: military bands playing popular and patriotic selections; tableaux organised by the League of Arts; acts from Shakespeare performed by the National Organisation of Girls' Clubs; choirs ranging from harmonic quartets to church choirs and philharmonic societies. And that was apart from the informal entertainments of jugglers, stilt-walkers, mimes, barrel organs and Punch and Judy booths. Later there was a grand open-air concert in Hyde Park, with ten thousand voices and the massed bands of the Brigade of Guards, at which the King and Queen made an appearance, to rapturous applause.

263

So Cook and Ada had 'got their money's worth' by the time they took the train home, footsore and weary but generally satisfied.

'Well, we gave that old war a good send-off,' Ada concluded as they edged with the crowd along the platform towards the exit at Northcote Station.

'I don't know why,' said Cook, 'but I'm ever so hungry. All those bits and pieces we ate, you'd think . . .'

'That sort of stuff doesn't satisfy like a proper dinner,' Ada said wisely. 'I'm hungry too. And thirsty – I'm pining for a cup of tea.'

'Soon as we get in,' said Cook, 'I'll get the kettle on. And then what do you say to a nice Welsh rarebit? I could—'

'Ooh, yes – with a bit of onion to it,' Ada began, and then realised that Cook had broken off in mid-sentence, and was staring at something ahead of them, arching her neck this way and that to try to get a better view. 'What is it? What you seen?' she asked in concern, for Cook was looking shocked rather than pleased.

'I thought—' Cook began in a husk of a voice. She wetted her lips, and gave a little awkward laugh. 'Seein' ghosts, that's what it is. It's nothing.'

'Who was it?' Ada persisted.

Cook looked at her for an instant, and then away again. 'I thought just for a moment I saw Fred. Course, it wasn't him.'

Ada slipped a comforting arm through hers. 'We all do that,' she said kindly. 'Practically every week I think I see Len across the street or going into a shop.'

'Oh, Ada! You never said. I'm sorry,' Cook said.

Ada shook her head and smiled. 'Doesn't matter. I'd sooner see him that way than never.'

The Teesboroughs' Town house in Park Street had been requisitioned by the government during the war and was still occupied, but Guy's party had been invited to take supper at the house of his friend Lord Tonbridge round the corner in Mount Street. If Sadie had felt out of her depth before, she was positively drowning in the glittering company gathered there. She was impressed with how insouciant Diana seemed amid all the titles and grandeur – forgetting that her sister had grown used to moving in those circles.

It was actually, if she had not been too disturbed to realise it, an informal gathering: Tonbridge had provided a buffet supper and people had not dressed. The idea was to eat, chat, and then watch the fireworks together – a grand display was to be held in Hyde Park to round off the day's events. The buffet, however, was on a scale befitting a wealthy earl, and it would have gone ill with Sadie, who was starving but too shy to push herself forward, had Ivo Rainton not come to her rescue, and forged a way for her through the crush to the table. There, he guided her through the multiplicity of choices, and then carried both their plates away and found places for them at a table already occupied by four smart young people.

'Ivo, darling, I haven't seen you in an age,' said a very beautiful young woman with blue eyes and fair hair. 'Not since the hospital in Le Touquet. How's the arm?'

'Good as new,' said Ivo.

'And how's poor Guy? I thought I saw him earlier.'

'Oh, mending. He's here somewhere, escorting Diana Wroughton. This is Diana's sister Sadie – Sadie, Diana Manners.'

The cool blue eyes surveyed Sadie briefly, and she received a nod, before they returned to Ivo. 'Bad boy! I've been married a month, don't you remember? It's Diana Cooper now.'

'Sorry. Where *is* Duff?'

'Somewhere about. You know Fuzzy Branksome and Adela Grange, don't you? And this is Oliver Winchmore, who was a doctor at the Front – did you ever come across him?'

It transpired that Diana Cooper – who was *Lady* Diana Cooper and a duke's daughter – had nursed at the Front, as had Adela Grange, and there was some war talk and swapping of names that made Sadie feel like a spectator at a tennis match. Oliver Winchmore had some amusing stories – he seemed rather a joker – and Fuzzy Branksome laughed heartily at everything he said, without contributing much himself. Sadie was quite glad not to have any attention directed towards her, and had drifted rather, when Lady Diana's beautiful eyes suddenly swung towards her like two blue lamps and she was asked, quite abruptly, 'Did you nurse, Miss—?'

'Hunter,' Ivo supplied, and seeing that Sadie had been taken by surprise and had no words ready, he answered for her: 'No, she's been busy the whole war with breaking and schooling horses for the army.'

'Goodness!' said Adela Grange, wrinkling her nose in distaste

But Lady Diana's face lit with interest. 'How too divine! I love horses, don't you? What got you into it? Wait, I'm sure I remember seeing something in the newspapers about it. Was that you? Didn't they give you a medal, or something?'

Sadie didn't like talking about herself, but she never minded talking about horses; and from there the conversation went on to Diana and her hospital, and Guy, and some other friends of the present company who had been treated there, and she was able to join in and feel more natural.

When it was time for the fireworks, Lady Diana suggested they went up onto the leads to watch them. 'I'm sure you can see the Park from up there. We should have a fine view.'

The word went round, and eventually most of the young people went up, some of them thinking it was quite a lark and seeming rather more excited than Sadie would have thought necessary. She supposed they did not often do unconventional things like climb a ladder to a trapdoor, and she worried a little for their fine clothes. Guy declined to go and Diana stayed with him. Sadie would have remained with them, but Ivo caught her elbow and said, 'Come on! I'll make sure we get a good spot.'

'Won't it be cold?' Diana objected on her behalf.

But Ivo said, 'No, no, it's a warm evening.'

Northcote's proximity to London meant that most of the eminent people of the neighbourhood were going to the national celebration, which made the local event rather low-key. A temporary monument – a large cross on a plinth – had been set up on the green opposite the station, and here the rector held an open-air service of thanksgiving, and many people laid wreaths or bunches of flowers on the monument's steps. The shops and houses in the centre of the village were decorated with flags and bunting, and the camp at Paget's Piece, though gradually winding down, provided a body of soldiers to head the parade. Following them was a formation of convalescents from all the local hospitals, representatives of the local schools, a contingent of nurses, troops from the Boy Scouts and the Boys' Brigade, and even one of former munitionettes from Darvell's. Behind them came various local tradespeople on decorated carts and wagons. Hymns were sung by the combined choirs of all the local churches, and music to march up and disperse to was provided by the brass band of Northcote High School.

Afterwards there was a fair, set up on the field opposite the Red Lion, with all the usual sideshows and opportunities to eat and drink, finishing as dusk fell with a firework display which, while it did not match the one in Hyde Park, was certainly as well received. Despite feeling tired from standing and walking all day, Beattie thought it must be rather flat for Peter in the evening, so after partaking of the cold supper that had been left ready in the kitchen, she played cards with him until bedtime. Left alone, she sat for a while, staring at nothing, trying not to think. It was finally all over, then. This was, officially, peace. She felt as if a huge section had been taken out of her life, leaving an unbridgeable gap: it seemed impossible to marry the two ends, the Beattie who had existed in 1914 and the life she had lived, with the person and the life there was now. There seemed no meaning to any of it. Bobby and Louis were dead. She had seen Bobby's grave; she had no idea where the hospitals buried their dead. They were gone, but nothing felt finished. She felt adrift, a boat without moorings and without sails.

But there were new lives, too. She mustn't forget that. She went upstairs to look at the babies sleeping, and found Ethel sitting under a lamp, sewing, and felt an unusual surge of pity for her. If she, Beattie, felt incomplete, it must be even worse for Ethel, who had no family, no friends, nothing. Ethel got to her feet as Beattie came in, and Beattie said, 'You don't need to stay in this evening. I am here to watch the babies. Why don't you go out?'

'Out, madam?' Ethel said blankly.

Beattie made an effort. 'There's a dance at the Station Hotel. I'm sure you'd enjoy that.' She remembered that the maids had gone to dances there before the war.

'No, thank you, madam,' Ethel said. 'I'm quite all right here.'

So she left it at that.

CHAPTER NINETEEN

The stream of horses passing through Highclere had left some casualties behind – horses that could not be brought up to the standard to be sold. Some had physical disabilities, such as partial blindness or deafness, broken wind, recurrent lameness; some were too old for hard work; and others were so mentally disturbed by their experiences that they were unreliable or, in the worst cases, unrideable.

Mrs Cuthbert was not sentimental. Some of the horses that could not be sold it was a kindness to put down. But there were others she could not bear to think of being sold for dog meat, and she had got into the way of hiding them from Captain Casimir when he came to inspect. There was plenty of grazing at Highclere, and more than enough stables, and all her staff were happy to go along with the unspoken policy. 'The Crocks', as she tended to call them, faded into the background, hidden in plain sight among their fitter fellows.

But now the stream of horses had slowed, and they'd been told it was nearing the end. Casimir was coming this afternoon, and the Crocks were going to stand out like sore thumbs.

'What's going to happen to them?' Sadie asked. They were leaning on the paddock rail, watching half a dozen Crocks grazing.

'It's a worry,' Mrs Cuthbert sighed. 'I bought Allegro

because he was too good to be let go, and you've done wonders with him. But some of them, like poor old Jingle here . . .'

Jingle had wandered up when they arrived and was standing close to Mrs Cuthbert, having the spot behind his ears scratched. He was almost completely blind, but he had adapted his behaviour to navigate by sound, and would come so readily to call that Sadie believed he liked human company and perhaps felt safer near people.

'I suppose you can't buy all of them,' Sadie said, with a hint of a question mark. 'If they're only good for slaughter the army couldn't want much for them.'

'I think Horace would have a fit at the idea,' said Mrs Cuthbert. 'And, besides, then what would we do with them?'

'Give them a decent retirement, a bit of peace, and some affection,' Sadie suggested, and Jingle turned his head towards her, nostrils flaring to catch her scent, then gave a contented grunt, stamped a foot to shake off a fly, and turned back to Mrs Cuthbert's ministrations. How could you possibly put down such a dear old fellow? Sadie thought.

She hung about while Casimir did his round, fearing the worst but unable to bear not knowing. She wished desperately that she had money, so that she could have bought at least one or two to save them from the knacker. When they got to the paddock and Betty, a brown mare that suffered from recurrent lameness, started hobbling eagerly towards them, Mrs Cuthbert turned to Casimir before he could speak and said, 'I suppose it's foolish to expect to appeal to the army's better feelings, but I do wonder if there isn't a little leeway for – well, some gentle deception?'

Casimir's face gave away nothing. 'What exactly do you mean? What's wrong with the mare?'

'Lameness in the tendons that comes and goes. When she's fit, she's fine, but one couldn't sell her as sound.'

'And the grey over there?' said Casimir. 'He looks more than fifteen.' Fifteen was the upper age the army allowed.

'We call him Captain. He's perfectly fit, but from his teeth, I should guess he's at least twenty,' said Mrs Cuthbert.

'Hmm,' said Casimir. 'I don't remember those two in the last batch. Or the chestnut over there. Or those two blacks.' He paused. Sadie looked at him, and got the suspicion he was enjoying himself. But why?

Mrs Cuthbert was too preoccupied to notice. She pulled herself up to her full height, and said, 'I suppose you could say I have defrauded the army, and if you want to move against me, I shall have to take my medicine. I've been hiding horses from you. I admit it freely.'

'I know,' said Casimir.

'You know?' Mrs Cuthbert looked startled.

'My dear ma'am, I'm not blind. I've known all along what you were doing, but I saw no harm in it. It's your fields they're grazing, and the army can afford the bit of extra feed you slip them. There's been enough waste of equine life in France, God knows, without hunting down these few poor fugitives.'

'But—' Mrs Cuthbert said, unable to reassemble her thoughts.

Casimir turned to face her squarely. 'The question is, what do you want to do with them now? Or, to be more accurate, what do you want *me* to do?'

'If you have to send them for dog meat, so be it,' Mrs Cuthbert said, 'but I wish you wouldn't.'

'Are you willing to keep them here?'

'Yes, I can give them a home. But I can't afford to buy them all.'

Casimir shrugged. 'That won't be necessary. Officially, they don't exist – they've fallen out of the system over a longish period, and there's no paperwork for them. On behalf of the heartless army, I give them to you. Take them with

271

my blessing. If horses could wish, they'd wish to spend their twilight years here. And these chaps have earned their retirement. I'm sure most of them deserve a medal, but I expect they'd prefer a nice quiet field and a few carrots. And Miss Hunter to pet them now and then.'

Sadie and Mrs Cuthbert exchanged a relieved look. 'Now I just have to break it to Horace that we have some long-term visitors we'll have to maintain,' said Mrs Cuthbert.

'Well, you can keep what's left of the feed and straw – that'll keep you going for a while,' said Casimir. 'I'm taking the rest of the viable horses today.' He held out his hand. 'It's been a pleasure working with you ladies. You've done a wonderful thing for your country, and the army thanks you.' He grinned again. 'These old Crocks are a queer sort of pension, but I'm afraid it's the only one you'll get.'

Mrs Cuthbert looked happy. 'I'm just glad the fields and stables won't be empty,' she said. 'I've been dreading that. And I think Horace was too. Perhaps he won't begrudge me my Crocks. One has to have a hobby. There are women who breed cocker spaniels.'

As she helped load the departing horses into the railway box later that afternoon, Sadie thought that the Crocks would also give her something to do to ease her into the world of post-war idleness. They would still need grooming and exercising – but it was not war-work any more. Not work at all, just a hobby.

Edward stepped out of the house and paused in the hazy August sunshine to light his pipe. He couldn't remember the last time he had smoked one. It was a thing for leisure: it couldn't be hurried. Pipe-smoking had largely disappeared during the war, hustled out by the convenience of cigarettes. But this morning, after waking early, he had been rummaging in a drawer in his dressing-room and had come across an unopened tin of his favourite tobacco, and the longing had come over him for the ritual and the fiddling about and the slow, hands-in-pockets comfort of his old pipe.

He was on leave. He had neither felt the need for it, nor wanted to take it, having too much to do, but the army could be rigid about such things. So he went home, remembering there were many things he needed to check up on, and hoping that he could further his campaign with Beattie. *That* had not gone well: it seemed impossible to revisit the atmosphere of those few days in Paris. Here, at The Elms, Beattie seemed distracted, shut off, enigmatic; he was diffident, afraid to push when he would so soon have to go away again; the atmosphere between them was awkward. He was still sleeping in the dressing-room, and when they were together they were formally polite to each other. So he was glad to have the bank to flee to every weekday – even if little messages from the Treasury and the War Office interrupted him too often there.

Pipe drawing satisfactorily, he strolled down the garden. Munt was digging a strip of earth in front of the hedge that divided what had been the pleasure garden from the kitchen garden. He rammed the fork upright and straightened as Edward approached.

'Morning, Munt. Fine day.'

'Warm,' Munt allowed. 'Blackfly weather.'

Edward removed the pipe from his mouth and waved the stem at the turned earth. 'What's this for?'

'Got a nice load o'manure what Miss Sadie got for me from her stables to dig in.'

This struck Edward as evasive. He sought to be specific. 'What's going *in* here?'

Munt looked defiant. 'Roses. Got a dozen bushes on order. Get 'em settled in so's they root up nice before winter.'

'Roses?' Edward smiled. 'Don't worry – I don't mind the expense. The war's over. We can have roses again. We can have all sorts of flowers.'

'Didn't know what plans you had,' Munt said cagily. 'You being abroad an' all.' He coughed. 'Going to be much longer out there?'

'I don't know,' Edward said. 'It could go on for some months yet. But there's no reason you shouldn't think about getting the garden back to normal.'

'Been thinking already,' Munt admitted, looking as pleased as his craggy face would allow. 'Once the taties is up, I wouldn't mind getting a start on me lawn – persoomin' you want it back?'

'What's an English garden without a lawn?' Edward said agreeably.

'Good to get a start while the soil's warm, then it gets a bit of a rest through the cold months, all ready to go come springtime.'

'Good. And while you're doing it, we might make improvements to the layout. There's that patch over there that gets shaded by the tree and never does very well. Now, if you took the lawn across *there*, and cut a new bed out of the corner over *there* . . .'

It was a conversation to delight the hearts of two enthusiasts. They walked round the garden together, Edward proposing, Munt disagreeing, alternative plans arising, compromise being sought and found. They were standing by the edge of the wilderness looking back when Edward said the thing that took Munt's heart by storm, and confirmed Edward in his esteem as 'the master', a title he had hesitated to give anyone since his apprentice days.

'With all this work you'll need more help than a part-time boot-boy. I think we should employ a full-time gardener's boy. With the men coming home and taking back the factory jobs, it ought to be easier to get one. Would you like to ask around? I dare say you have friends in the same line who would pass the word.'

'I'll do that,' Munt said. He cast a sidelong look at Edward, and said gruffly, 'Glad you said that, about a boy. Garden like this deserves t' be treated right. Plenty o' scope here to make it proper splendid. Bit o' the right help, and I'll make you proud of it.'

'I know you will,' Edward said. A cloud passed over the sun, and his pipe had gone out, and the garden suddenly looked autumnal and sad. He thought about his trouble with Beattie, of David, of poor Antonia's death, and Bobby's. He remembered the work piling up in Paris for him; but at least for a little while in discussing plans with Munt he had forgotten it all. A garden would do that for you.

William came home for the weekend, to Sadie's surprise. 'Not that I'm not glad to see you, but I'd have thought you'd have more customers at weekends. Can they spare you?'

'I had to come and see Dad, didn't I?' William said, hunching his shoulders and sticking his hands into his pockets. With his long legs and his elbows out, he looked like a depressed heron.

'What's the matter?' she asked. 'Are you getting tired of the job?'

'No, just the opposite,' he said quickly. 'Trouble is – well, they *can* spare me, you see. There aren't enough customers. Burgess is talking about closing down.'

'Oh, William! I'm so sorry!'

'He can't pay four of us to keep the service running if no one's buying tickets. He's talking about selling one of the buses, but I don't know who'd buy it, when you can get all the little machines you want for next to nothing.'

'But if he keeps *one* going . . .'

'He'd ask Considine, in that case. He's known him longer, and he's a local man. But I don't think he can keep even one going.'

'So what's the problem?' Sadie asked. 'Why don't people come?'

'I suppose they aren't used to going places by air,' he said. 'They just don't think about it, when they've always gone by train.'

'So what will you do?'

'Come home, I suppose. I'll have to break it to Mother and Dad. And then try to get another job. But it's hard, with so many of us chasing the same few.'

'So I imagine,' said Sadie. She sighed. 'There's a lot of us in the same boat.'

William examined her expression. 'You too?'

'I'm afraid so. The last lot of horses went on Friday. They're closing us down.'

'So what will *you* do?' He gave her question back to her.

'I don't know. It's harder, being female. At least there are openings for men.'

'I thought there were for women, too, these days.'

'During the war there were. But now everyone expects us to give up our jobs and go back to dusting the dining-room and arranging flowers—'

'Or getting married,' William suggested.

'That's not for me,' Sadie said quickly.

He looked at her critically. 'I don't see why not. You're quite pretty really, even with your hair short. And you're awfully jolly to talk to.'

'There are too many of us and not enough chaps,' Sadie said shortly. 'And I wouldn't marry just to leave home. I'd have to love whoever it was.'

'I know what you mean,' William said, thinking of Eva Considine – who was going out regularly with Miles Drago. Another good reason for coming back home – to get away from her influence. His first attempt at falling in love hadn't gone well.

The rector and Mrs Fitzgerald were away for the bank holiday weekend, in Aylesbury at the wedding of her nephew Dolly

Beamish to a local girl, leaving the curate in charge of the service. Beattie took the opportunity not to go to church on Sunday morning; Edward had never intended to go. It was rather pleasant having the house to themselves, to sit and read the papers in companionable silence.

The peace was broken by the door bell. Edward rattled his paper with annoyance. 'Now, who can that be? You aren't expecting anyone, are you?'

'At this time on a Sunday? No, of course not.' She sighed and got up. With the servants at church along with Sadie, William and Peter, and David lying late in bed, there was no one to answer the door.

She was surprised, when she opened it, to see a dishevelled, poorly dressed woman, her face smeared with tears and her hair coming down. She recognised her belatedly as Mrs Spauling, who lived in Dog Kennel Lane. She had come to the Soldiers' Families' committee several times for help. But she should not have come to the front door. Beattie recoiled from her and was about to say so, when she noticed that one of Mrs Spauling's eyes was blackening, and there was blood in her hair.

'Oh, ma'am, I'm sorry,' Mrs Spauling said, with haunted eyes. 'I went round the back and knocked but nobody come, and I'm that desperate. I went to the church but Rector's away and I can't talk to that curate. He looks at me funny. So I thought – I thought—' She seemed to sway on her feet, and a drop of blood trickled from her scalp down the side of her face.

'You'd better come in,' Beattie said resignedly. She led her into the servants' sitting-room. 'Are you hurt?'

'I'm all right,' she said automatically. But she put a hand up to intercept the drop of blood and looked at it vaguely. 'He pulled my hair,' she said. 'Pulled a lump right out.'

'Let me see,' Beattie said, made her sit down and parted her hair. A piece of scalp had been ripped out with the hair, and it was oozing. She fetched a clean tea towel from the kitchen, wetted it, and wiped the blood away. 'It's not too bad,' she said. 'The bleeding is stopping. Who did this to you?'

'My Gab,' she said miserably. Gabriel Spauling had been the delivery man for Jackson's hardware and lumber yard before the war. He had been a good worker, but was fond of his beer on a Saturday night, and sometimes on a Sunday night too, and he hadn't the head for it. He had frequently been late or absent entirely on a Monday, and had been in trouble with the police several times for brawling. When he had come home from the war, Jackson had been glad enough to have a reason not to give him his job back: he'd got a fifteen-year-old who was just as good and much more biddable. But it left Spauling out of work, with a wife and three children, and a reputation that made it hard to get another job.

Mrs Spauling had supplemented the family income during the war, working as a barmaid in the Red Lion, but with the return of their barman she'd lost the job. Spauling was furious on two counts: that she no longer brought in money, and that she had taken the job in the first place. His experiences at the Front had not sweetened him: he was moody and quick to explode, and Mrs Spauling had more than once sported the trophies of his temper. But now he had got it into his head that she had been 'carrying on' while he was away.

'He thinks I took the job at the Red Lion to meet men,' she said, her lips pale. 'He won't listen to reason. I only done it for money for the kids, but he says – he says I'm a loose woman. Oh, ma'am, I never done nothing like that! I never would! But there's no talking to him. He was down the Lion last night, and had a bit too much and come home in a rage. I thought he'd sleep it off, but he was still drunk this morning and started on about Len Tupper, what was drinking there last night, making out I'd been carrying on with him. Len Tupper! He punched me in the face, and then he swung me about by my hair and kept hitting me.'

She had managed to escape, and had come to Beattie because she'd always been kind, and she didn't know what else to do. 'It's not his fault,' she excused her husband belatedly. 'It's the war done this to him. He's a good man, really.'

'Where are your children?' Beattie asked.

'Sunday school,' Mrs Spauling said. 'That's why I come up the church, but when I see it was that curate . . . He's got a down on me because he come to the Red Lion one day when I was working there and he saw me take a sip of beer. He thinks beer is the Devil's Work. And he don't approve of women working outside the home.'

Beattie knew the sort. She was not fond of the curate either. She offered to help Mrs Spauling complain to the police, but she was too frightened of Gab to do that, and refused absolutely. There was not much else Beattie could do for her, except listen and offer sympathy. The woman wouldn't leave her husband because she had nowhere to go. Pressed by Beattie as to what she wanted, it seemed she had hoped Rector would talk to Gab and make him stop. Beattie didn't think it would do much good: Gab would heed the words while he was sober and perhaps feel ashamed of himself, but the next time he drank it would all be wasted air. But she promised to talk to the rector as soon as he was back, and saw the poor woman out.

Edward found her sitting on the bench outside the back door, and sat down beside her. 'What was all that about?' he asked. She told him. 'It's monstrous that you should be bothered like that on a Sunday,' he said, seeing how weary and distressed she seemed.

'You don't know – you've been away,' she said. 'They come at all times. With all sorts of problems. But the worst to deal with are the women whose husbands have come back strangers. They're not all violent, like Spauling. Some are depressed, and some are just so withdrawn there's no way to reach them. And there are one or two who've come back to find a child too many at the hearth.'

'Ah,' said Edward. 'Not a good situation.'

'It feels as though there's no end to it. Blind men and maimed men in the streets everywhere, men out of work – they come knocking at the door here, asking for odd jobs, anything to earn a few pennies. And the women are at their wits' end. Then to add to it all, there's going to be a surge of births at any moment – all the women and girls who got pregnant on or around the Armistice, and not all of them are happy about it.'

'I can't make the trouble stop,' Edward said. 'I wish I could. But I let me take you away from it for a few hours. Dinner, up in Town, somewhere smart. Would you like that?' She hesitated, and he added, 'We could invite Beth and Jack to join us.'

He thinks I don't want to be alone with him, she thought. She wanted it more than anything, but somehow or other she could not break through the barrier the war, and Louis, had placed between them. But he was making an effort, and she must at least show appreciation. 'Dinner with you would be nice,' she said. 'I'd love to see a play, as well. Is there anything good on?'

He seemed delighted. 'I can find out, and reserve tickets. What about Tuesday? I'll have to go into the office for a while, but you can come up and meet me in the afternoon. We can have an early dinner, then go to the show, and perhaps have a nightcap afterwards.'

'Sounds lovely,' Beattie said, and tried to smile. But the image of Mrs Spauling's bleeding scalp arose and spoiled the moment. She really *did* need to get away from this house.

On Tuesday morning Sadie was grooming Allegro – something they both enjoyed so much she always took her time over it

– when there was a sound of hoofs in the yard, and she looked out over the half-door to see an elderly countryman leading a bay vanner on a rope halter. She hurried out to intercept him.

'Good morning,' she said. 'Can I help you?'

The old man pulled off his cap, revealing sparse threads of grey eked over his scalp. His face was nut brown and creased, except where the white whiskers were coming through – farmers traditionally only shaved once a week, for church. His jacket was frayed at the sleeve ends and there was a mended tear in the breast; under it he wore a collarless shirt, and his ancient trousers were held up with binder twine around the waist. He looked to Sadie as though he was barely making ends meet; but the vanner was groomed to a shine, though it looked as old in horse years as he was. There were deep 'salt-cellars' over its eyes, and so many grey hairs among the brown, it was almost roan.

'Morning, miss,' the man said humbly. 'Are you the boss, so to speak?'

'No, that would be Mrs Cuthbert, but she's busy at the moment. Perhaps I can help you?' He hesitated, his eyes flitting about nervously. To get him along, Sadie said, 'Is he yours? He's a nice-looking fellow.'

The old man's eyes lit. 'Best ol' horse that ever lived, is Bingo. Had him since he was a foal.'

'How old is he?'

'Guess.'

'Well, I can see he isn't young. Nineteen, twenty?'

'He's twenty-eight, miss. Twenty-nine next January,' the old man said proudly. 'That's how come the army didn't take him when they come round in nineteen fowerteen. I farm round t'other side of the hill, miss, at Overcroft. Breakspire's my name. Army took my other horses, Boxer and Beauty, but they said Bingo was too old. He's had to do all the work, along of Blossom, that'd be the mule they give me instead. But he threw hisself into it, miss. Never one to shirk, my Bingo.'

'He's a grand fellow,' Sadie said, stroking the bony nose. The vanner sighed and settled its weight. 'But I'm wondering why you've brought him here.'

Mr Breakspire twisted his cap round and round. 'Well, miss, it's like this. Old Bingo, he's gettin' too old for the work. He'll never give up, but it breaks my heart to see him struggle, and so tired at the end of the day he can hardly eat his feed. The missus says we should get another mule to go with Blossom – the army's sellin' 'em off cheap, and we could get a bargain. But then what about old Bingo? I can't afford to keep feeding him and another mule as well. And I couldn't let him go to the knacker-man. Had him since he were a foal,' he said again, his voice wavering. The vanner turned its head and nudged him companionably. 'Couldn't do that, miss, not to old Bingo.'

'No, I quite understand,' said Sadie.

The old man lifted hopeful eyes to her. 'Then I heerd that the lady here had a rest home for old army horses. Well, Bingo here warn't in the army, but he helped raise food for it, and that's just as important, i'n't it? So I wondered if she could find a place for him. He's a good horse and no trouble and . . .' His voice trailed away and hope faded from his eyes. 'I couldn't pay nothing, miss, that's the trouble.' He looked ashamed now. 'I'd give anything to see old Bingo comfortable, but I've not got anything to spare.'

Sadie couldn't bear to see him humbled. And surely one more Crock wouldn't make any difference? 'I'll go and fetch Mrs Cuthbert,' she said. 'You wait here – and don't worry, I'm sure it will be all right.'

Mrs Cuthbert was up at the house, wrestling with accounts. She did them unwillingly and rarely, but the withdrawal of the army contract had required her at least to create enough order to see where they were starting from. She was happy to be interrupted, and listened to Sadie's narrative attentively, with sympathy that turned at the end to slight anxiety. 'I wonder who told him I was running a rest home for old horses,' she said.

'Oh, things get about like wildfire,' Sadie said. 'And it's not far from the truth.'

'Far enough,' said Mrs Cuthbert. 'Your Mr Makepeace –'

'Breakspire.'

'– he may be just the first off the sprinting-block.'

'He doesn't look as though he's got a sprint in him.'

'Don't quibble, Sadie. I'm worried. If we take his horse, and he spreads the word around, what's to say we won't be inundated with everyone's old and lame animals? They'll think, "Oh, Mrs Cuthbert's a soft touch. Why should we pay to keep old Dobbin at home if she'll do it for us?"'

Sadie looked doubtful. 'He does look very poor – I really don't think he can afford to keep Bingo, and it would break his heart to sell him to the knacker.'

'You're not looking at the bigger picture,' Mrs Cuthbert said impatiently.

'Well,' said Sadie slowly as she thought it out, 'if someone came who obviously could afford it, you could make them pay, like a livery stable. Or at least give a donation – like a charity.'

'I'm not planning to take *anyone*'s—' Mrs Cuthbert began, then paused thoughtfully. 'A charity, eh? Wait a minute, that might bear thinking about. We've already got the Crocks to support. Supposing we *did* make it a charity, advertised for donations – the Highclere Home of Rest for Horses. People are very sentimental about animals. They'd give freely for something like that. I've heard the Blue Cross always does very well when it has a flag day.'

'Oh, I'd forgotten the Blue Cross. They already rescue old horses.'

'But obviously not enough of them, if your Mr Spokeshave

has had to come to me. There's room in this country for another rescue trust, don't you think?' She jumped up from the hated paperwork, her face alight. 'And Horace would like it, I'm sure – putting the Crocks on a proper basis. Let's go and see your new friend. Don't worry, whatever happens, I'll take his Bingo. Can't turn him away after making him wait so long. I'll talk to Horace tonight. He has a much better brain for organisation and finance and so on than I have. Oh, Sadie, I was dreading the end of our work here! I couldn't bear the idea of going back to doing nothing, being a lady of leisure, having no purpose. This could be the answer for me!'

Sadie almost said, 'For me, too,' but at the last moment held off. She couldn't help feeling she needed more.

CHAPTER TWENTY

The show, a romantic opera called *Monsieur Beaucaire*, was quite long to begin with – three acts – and it overran, so that when they stepped out of the Prince's Theatre onto Shaftesbury Avenue, Beattie said, 'We had better hurry, or we'll miss the last train.'

'I don't want to hurry,' Edward said. 'I've enjoyed this evening so much. Wouldn't you like to go to the Café Royale and have a brandy and watch the dancing?'

'We really would miss the last train, and then what would we do?'

'London is full of hotels,' Edward pointed out. 'We'll go and stay at the Ritz.'

Her eyes widened. 'But we haven't any things with us. What would they think?'

He laughed. 'We're Sir Edward and Lady Hunter. What on earth *could* they think?'

She didn't speak. He seemed so relaxed – she had not seen him like this for a long time, not really since before the war. She thought of the long train journey out into the cold dark countryside with revulsion and, suddenly, she didn't want to go home. Home seemed not like a haven, but like a prison. Here there were lights and people and movement and no one knew her or wanted anything of her. She felt – free. And strangely happy.

He had been watching her face, and added, temptingly,

'They're quite accustomed to providing the necessaries for last-minute guests. And we aren't in evening dress.'

The last was a telling point. Because they'd had an early dinner, they had not dressed – rules for the theatre had relaxed perforce during the war – and Edward was in lounge suit, Beattie in a silk afternoon dress and coatee. They would not draw unwelcome attention when they stepped out of an hotel in the morning.

'The Café Royale it is, then,' she said. 'But not brandy – champagne.'

'You shall have whatever you like,' he said, and as their eyes met, a frisson ran through both of them.

It was a wonderful night – better than in Paris. There was no awkwardness between them: Beattie's feeling of holiday, of freedom, allowed her to relax.

It was as good as the best had been, in the middle years of their marriage, when they had first gone to Northcote and his spirit had revived, and she had conceived Peter. When she lay in his arms afterwards, her face against his neck, she drank in the remembered smell of him, which had once spelled comfort, safety, and pleasure. And in that moment, she thought about Louis without regret, and was able to forgive herself. She had done what she'd had to at the time, but it was over, gone, and must be forgotten. Life was not over: there could still be good things in it. And Edward wanted to share them with her. Gratitude made her press closer to him, and he folded his arms round her more tightly and grunted – a small, comfortable sound that touched her so much she wanted to cry. Except that she didn't.

In the morning, he would have taken her to the station, but he was only steps away from his office, and she told him it was foolish and she could get a taxi.

'If you're quite sure,' he said; and he lifted her hand to his lips and kissed it. 'You look beautiful,' he said.

'So do you,' she replied. She hadn't known she was going to say that, and it was foolish, but it was also true. There was something – had always been – something essentially *good* about Edward, and wasn't goodness a beautiful thing?

'I wish I didn't have to go back to Paris,' Edward said. He examined her as she stood in the sunshine: as composed as always, a faintly smiling enigma; but there was, somewhere deep in her eyes, a spark of warmth that had not been there for a long, long time. It was a connection, a promise that when he came back, she would still be there. It was a light at the end of the tunnel.

He hailed her a taxi, saw her in, and walked away. Beattie settled back in the leathery stuffiness, and thought about home, and the warm, comfortable feeling began to leach away. Everything she didn't like about life at the moment – the aftermath of the war, the problems she was expected to solve, the tedious routine and, yes, the boredom – was waiting for her there. And what was to be done about that?

Seeing how hard William had been trying, Edward had reinstated his allowance while he was at home, until he was able to find new employment. William was grateful, and it was not purely for pleasure that he spent some of it on going to the Hendon air show. He hoped he might meet someone there who would offer him a job; but he could not pretend it was not bliss to be around aeroplanes again, to smell the tang of burning fuel, to hear the roar of engines, to see them bump over the grass and lift like eager birds, and remember with every nerve ending what it felt like to be at the controls. He wandered and gazed, watched the aerobatics, and inevitably found himself veering towards the sheds like a moth to a lamp.

There were stewards preventing members of the public from getting too close and being in the way, but after hovering for a while, William spotted Colin Burgess within the sanctified area, talking to a tall, rangy man with a genial aspect and a wide mouth that seemed designed for smiling.

William called. 'Burgess! I say, Burgess!'

Burgess turned, grinned and beckoned him in. 'I thought I might see you here,' he said, shaking William's hand cordially. 'Can't keep away from the old buses, eh? Do you know Fred Handley Page?'

William shook the other man's hand. 'I've heard of you, of course, sir.'

'Don't "sir" me, for goodness' sake,' said Handley Page. 'Makes me feel ancient. Flyer?' he added, looking William over keenly.

'Yes, sir – sorry, I mean, I was with the RAF. Applied to stay on but they didn't take me.'

'Shame. Who could have guessed they'd run down the service so quickly?'

'He's been flying my Birmingham passenger route,' Burgess explained. 'I was sorry to have to let him go. It seems we were ahead of our time there. Have you found anything else yet?'

'No,' said William. 'I suppose in the end I shall have to look for a job that's not flying. One has to earn a crust. Have you heard anything of Harry Considine?'

'Oh yes, he still hangs around Brooklands. Takes someone up on a pleasure flight now and then, to keep his hand in.'

'Lucky pup,' said William wistfully.

Handley Page looked at him critically. 'Hunter,' he mused. 'Are you related to Sir Edward Hunter, by any chance?'

'He's my father.'

'Indeed? I was thinking you look damned like him. I see his name on documents all the time – you know I run a London to Paris service for government servants and mail?'

'Yes, sir, I did know. You use converted O/400s. Eight-seaters.'

Handley Page grinned at Burgess. 'He knows his stuff. Like to come and have a look at one?' he offered William.

288

The three walked over to the Handley Page shed and had a satisfying inspection and discussion of the converted bomber – at the time of its design, the largest aircraft in the world. Then they talked about aircraft design in general. William, though naturally retiring, forgot himself when talking about his favourite subject, and asked eager questions about the leading edge slot, which HP were developing to reduce stall speed. To William, Fred Handley Page, who was fifteen years his senior, was a grown-up in the same way that his father or a schoolmaster was, but when talking about flying and aeroplanes he forgot the difference, and the three of them might have been of one generation. He had missed that sort of comradeship of equals when he left the RAF.

When a natural pause occurred, Handley Page patted the wing of the 0/400 they were standing beside, and said to William, 'Think you could handle her in the air?'

'Oh yes,' William said simply. 'I can fly anything.' As soon as he said it, he blushed, because it sounded boastful, and he hadn't meant it that way.

Fortunately, Handley Page took it well, and laughed. 'I like confidence. Look here, can't do anything today, with the air show going on, but come and see me tomorrow, and you can take her up and see how she handles. And then, if you like her and I like you, I might offer you a job.'

William, starry-eyed, could only say 'Gosh!'

'I need another pilot for my Paris service. We're expanding it, in conjunction with Airco – not just diplomats and mail-bags, but ordinary passengers too.'

'Where will you find them?' Burgess said. 'There don't seem to be many people around with money to spare for flying.'

'Paris is a different proposition from Birmingham,' Handley Page said. 'The journey by train, then boat, then train again is much more tedious and inconvenient. And Paris – well, it's a lure, isn't it? If people are going to fly for pleasure, they need a pleasant destination.'

Burgess laughed. 'You've got a point there. Birmingham can't really compete.'

'I'll be carrying a certain amount of light freight to help cover my costs,' said Handley Page. 'Newspapers, for instance, and perishables, things that need quick transit. And luxury goods. There's still a lot you can't get in France – and some things you can get in France that people want here. Like perfume.'

'And cheese,' William added without thinking, and made them all laugh.

'A good ripe French country cheese would certainly make the flight back interesting,' said Handley Page. He clapped William on the shoulder. 'Come and see me tomorrow. I think we're going to like each other.'

The new nanny started with great efficiency on the 1st of September. She came highly recommended, having worked for Lady Hadlicott at Northcote Manor, and was leaving her service only because her one son was going off to school.

She was a big woman, not fat but tall and bulky, in her forties, with grey-speckled hair crimped in front and screwed into a tight bun behind, and in her blue uniform dress with white cuffs and collar she looked like a tightly packed monument to cleanliness and discipline.

Cook had soon taken a dislike to Nanny Woods, which put her in the rare position of agreeing with Ethel. She was so uncomfortable at finding herself there, that she compressed her lips and declined to mention Nanny in front of Ethel, but to Ada she griped openly. 'Her with her airs and fancies! Looking down her nose at us – as if Lady Hunter wasn't the equal of Lady Hadlicott any day of the week!'

'But Lady Hadlicott's the wife of a Lord,' Ada pointed out in fairness, 'which makes her higher than the wife of a Sir.'

'Higher *maybe*,' Cook snapped, as though there might still be some doubt about it, 'but not better.'

Nanny Woods was a whale on discipline, order and routine, which she found sadly lacking in the nursery at The Elms.

'It's no wonder things are slack,' Nanny Woods said, 'leaving the nursery in the hands of a maid, instead of a trained professional.'

Ethel had got into the habit of regarding the little ones as her own, and had cared for them in her own way and, she felt, satisfactorily. They were healthy and happy, and that was all that mattered. She didn't have time to be fussing about cleaning the rooms. Aggie and Ada were the housemaids and they did the cleaning, and the nurseries fell to Aggie's part. Ethel admitted that Aggie wasn't the world's most thorough; but when Nanny Woods ran her finger along the top of the door, or pointed out dust mice under the cots, or streaks on the window glass, she looked sternly at Ethel as though it were *her* fault. With a seventeen-month-old toddler and a motherless three-month-old baby to take care of, she had had plenty on her hands, and it was only when they were both taking their nap that she'd had a chance to sew and mend their little things and do other essential tasks. She hadn't got time to be chasing about after Aggie and running *her* finger along mantelpieces and such.

'Which is exactly why I have been brought in,' Nanny said magnificently, when Ethel managed to convey some of her resentment. 'Things have got into a poor way, but I shall put them right.'

And putting them right, Ethel discovered, meant that she was demoted from taking care of the children to menial work, wiping things down, washing baby clothes, mending and fetching and carrying. She was supposed to *wash* Marcus's toys – who ever heard of toys being washed? *Marcus*, whose favourite occupation was 'helping' Munt, which meant playing with mud and getting it everywhere, and sucking his muddy fingers, and eating anything he discovered, not just grass and daisies but worms and woodlice. There was an old

291

saying, you had to eat a peck of dirt before you died, and Marcus was getting his peck in early. Dirt never hurt anyone – not *clean* dirt. But Nanny Woods wanted to see 'her' little boy spick and span every minute of the day, which wasn't natural in a child. Same with Alice – whom she always called just 'Baby', as if she didn't have a name. If Alice sicked up on her dress, even the slightest bit – and what baby didn't? – she had to have all her clothes changed and washed.

And Nanny expected Ethel to wash the baby things herself. 'They mustn't be put in with the rest of the laundry. They must be done separately, and carefully. Cleanliness is not only next to Godliness – with little children it has to come first.'

Ethel could not resist reporting this sentiment in the kitchen, where it was seized on, as she knew it would be, by Cook.

'Blasphemy!' she hissed, with great satisfaction. Now she was licensed to hate Nanny Woods – she would have anyway, but at least now she knew she was right to do so.

It wasn't just her general 'putting on airs', and her habit of saying snootily, 'We didn't do things *that* way at Northcote Manor. Lady Hadlicott was *most* particular.' It wasn't just that she kept referring to Lady Hadlicott as 'a superior person', as though *their* mistress was somehow inferior. It wasn't even that she refused to eat with them in the servants' hall but demanded all her meals be taken up to the nursery, 'As if she was the blessed housekeeper!'

No, the thing that really got Cook's goat was that she came into the kitchen and *interfered*. She ran her finger along things and tutted. She looked pointedly at blemishes such as a patch of grease on the floor that Eileen hadn't got round to wiping up yet. She said to Cook, 'Do you always keep the butter on the same shelf as the meat?' and 'Surely you don't use the same pot for my children's meals as for your own?' – as though the staff were covered in sores or

292

something. She had the cheek to send back an omelette as 'tough' and demand another – when omelettes in any case were upstairs food, everybody knew that, and not to be whipped up for a servant, which was what Nanny was, though she didn't know it.

Of course, there was nothing to be done about it, unless Nanny was discovered drunk, entertained men in the nursery, or dropped Alice on her head. Whenever she spoke to anyone in the family, she was charm itself (though Cook couldn't understand how she managed charm with a face like that) and they were perfectly satisfied with her. The children were sparkling clean whenever they were presented to Mr David or her ladyship, and Nanny spoke highly of their intelligence and beauty, which was what parents and grandparents wanted to hear. Once or twice, when Cook dared to voice mild dissent to Lady Hunter during their daily séance about food, the mistress didn't even seem to notice.

So they were stuck with her, and Cook could only express her feelings by a subtle campaign to thwart and discomfort Nanny in any way that presented itself. It was surprising how often a tiny slug found its way into Nanny's lettuce, or a hair into her egg custard, or how an unavoidable problem in the kitchen delayed the serving of her meal until it was tepid. Nanny relentlessly fought back, returned burned toast and cold tea, demanded another breakfast egg that wasn't rock hard, and sent back the next for being too runny. She was aware that Cook had been a long time in the household and was treasured. Complaining about her wouldn't get her dismissed – would only make her, Nanny Woods, look like a troublemaker.

So the warfare between them continued under the surface of the household routine, and in a strange way both of them enjoyed it, especially Cook, who at last had someone to vent her spleen on, the spleen that had built up since Fred ran out on her. Not that she would ever have admitted enjoyment.

The person worst affected was Ethel, who was hardly allowed to touch the children, except to change their nappies and wash them. Nanny was continually pointing out, by word and action, that Ethel was only the nursemaid. She would have liked to quit in protest – that would show them all! – but then she'd never see her babies again. And her babies were all she had. She hadn't seen Frank Hussey in months, but she had heard a rumour that he had been walking out with a local girl and they were planning to get married. She had spent the whole war rejecting him, so what did she expect? But it hurt, all the same – even if she couldn't have accepted him had he asked. It still hurt.

David came out of Baker Street station onto the Marylebone Road in the sweet, buttery sunshine of a mild September day, having decided on a whim that he didn't want to go down into the Tube: he would take a taxi to Piccadilly, and hang the expense for once.

Someone hailed him. 'David! David Hunter!'

He turned, and saw Christopher Beresford hurrying towards him. With his eager, freckled face and wiry fair hair, he looked much younger than his age, too young to be a Member of Parliament.

'I thought it was you,' Beresford said. 'Can't mistake that height or that profile! How are you?'

'I'm pretty well, thanks. Congratulations, by the way, on being elected.'

'Oh, the party did all the work,' he said lightly. 'I just had to make speeches at the hustings – tremendous fun!'

'Don't you mind the heckling?'

'Not at all! It's like a jolly good game of tennis! How is everyone at home? Your mother well?'

'Yes, thanks. Busy as always – with the returning soldiers and their families.'

'Yes, I wish we could do more for them,' Beresford said,

'but the economy's in a mess. But we're working on it. Your father's doing great things at the Quai d'Orsay, I hear.'

'I wouldn't know about that. He never talks about it. I only know what I read in the papers.'

'And Sadie,' Beresford said. 'How is Sadie?'

David smiled. It was odd, he thought, that it felt as though the rest of the conversation had been leading up to this point. 'She's well,' he said. 'Just the same Sadie – she never changes.'

'Doesn't she? That's good. She's a grand person – wouldn't want her to change.' He cleared his throat awkwardly. 'Haven't read anything in the papers about an engagement or marriage.'

David took pity on him. 'She isn't even going out with anyone, as far as I know.'

Beresford brightened. 'Look here, have you time to come for a cup of coffee? It would be good to chat.'

'I'm afraid I'm on my way to work,' David said. 'My father got me a billet in his bank in Piccadilly. I'm on probation, so it wouldn't do to be late.'

'Oh, I see! Well, I'm getting a taxi, so let me give you a lift. I can drop you off, and we can talk on the way.'

In the taxi, the conversation blossomed. Beresford was easy company, and his association with the Hunter family meant they had enough memories in common not to be strangers to each other. And David discovered a deep desire in himself for contact with another man – for friendship. He had not had a friend since Jumbo died.

After a brief time at university he had gone into the army, where after another brief period he had been wounded, invalided out, and had seemed to be shut in a dark cave with his pain and incapacity thereafter. Before the war he had been a normal, cheerful youth. Since taking the wound, he had talked to no one but his family, and the little boys he had tutored. Even now, at the bank, they were mostly old fellows of his father's generation.

But Beresford was accessible, sensible, pleasant, and seemed just as eager to befriend him as he was to be befriended. The taxi journey was not long enough, but during it, David managed to touch on his dissatisfaction with his current position and his restless desire for change. 'I know it's good of Father to have me put on, so I have to do my damnedest to give satisfaction, but it all seems so—' He hesitated.

'Fusty? Boring?' Beresford suggested.

David laughed. 'Oh, I wouldn't go that far.'

'Of course *you* wouldn't. But *I* can.'

'Finance *has* a fascination,' David said. 'I've glimpsed it – but it's not at my level, and who knows if I'll ever get high enough up the mountain to breathe in its heady scents?'

'I say, that's very good,' Beresford said. 'You have a way with words. Seems a shame to waste it. Are you fit now? I mean, the leg not troubling you too much?'

'Oh, I can get about all right,' David said. 'Aches a bit if I overdo it, but to all intents and purposes—'

'Ah, this is your stop.' The taxi had halted outside the bank, and stood ticking, waiting for further instructions. 'I'd love to have a longer talk with you. Would you be willing to meet me after work one evening? Don't have to be home by curfew or anything?'

It was said lightly, but it reminded David of something he'd forgotten for the last few minutes. 'I've no one at home. My wife died in June. In childbirth.'

Beresford looked mortified. 'I'm so sorry. Insensitive idiot that I am.'

David shrugged. 'But I have two children to support now, so I had better get to my desk. Thanks for the lift.'

Beresford said, 'Look here, do come and meet me. Have dinner with me at my club. I'd like time to talk to you properly. What about Wednesday?'

'Yes, I'd like that,' David said.

* * *

Mrs Cuthbert had made an arrangement to park the horsebox in the station yard, so they had only to lead the horses across the road to the green opposite. They had chosen Jingle, for his sweet temper, and Hazebrouck, a big black artillery horse, because he looked impressive. Mrs Cuthbert had suggested Captain, but Sadie had pointed out how hard it was to get a polish on a white coat. 'And we want people to see them at their best.'

They were both groomed up to a shine, with their hoofs oiled, and each wore a well-buffed halter with a red-white-and-blue rosette pinned to the browband. Hazebrouck had red-white-and-blue ribbons plaited into his mane, and Jingle wore a red ribbon round his neck with a large cardboard disc hanging from it, painted gold and with the word HERO written on it, which Mary had made.

Sadie, Mary, Winnie and Mrs Cuthbert had all come, two to hold the horses, and two to shake the collection tins. They had also made a placard which read in bold black letters:

WAR HEROES
DESERVE
OUR SUPPORT!
HIGHCLERE HOME OF REST FOR HORSES

The placard was fixed to a pole, which Podrick had sharpened at the other end so they could drive it into the grass.

They attracted plenty of attention from the moment they arrived, and soon there was a cluster of children was permanently hanging around, as well as the adults who stopped on their way past, and the usual village idlers who always swelled any crowd that formed. Both horses were gentle and liked to be petted, and Sadie had brought along a bag of carrot chunks.

Mrs Cuthbert explained the work of Highclere during the war and what it intended to do now. Even in the few weeks of its existence, the Home of Rest had taken in several more horses. There had been a child's pony, young and fit, but brought to them because the boy who had owned it had died suddenly of a brain fever, and his parents couldn't bear to have the pony around. 'It reminds us too much,' said the grieving father, 'but we don't want to sell it to a stranger. He loved it so. Could you just give the poor thing a home?'

An elderly lady had asked them to take her chestnut hunter, Sorrel, because she couldn't ride any more and it wasn't fair to keep it in a stable all the time, and she had no grazing.

An old man brought an ancient carthorse – he was retiring from his fruit and veg round and couldn't afford to feed it. A very poor farmer brought a plough horse that kept going lame.

A prosperous-looking woman asked if they could take her son's pony – but he would want to come and ride every evening and at weekends. She was turned away. Mrs Cuthbert decided she was simply hoping to have the pony's keep paid for by someone else, and felt sorry for the son, having a parent so penny-pinching.

But on the plus side, Mary's parents had sent a cheque for a hundred pounds to get them started, while Sorrel's mistress and the dead boy's parents had both made donations.

Sadie told the horses' stories, and related the histories of other horses which she had read in the papers or been told. Some she had heard from John Courcy, and she thought about him all day, on and off, longing for him, wondering where he was, how he was managing, whether he was well.

People dropped coins into the boxes, and took a flag to pin to their lapels, which would spread the word further. Most people were supportive – everyone liked horses, and nearly everyone knew the contribution they had made to the war, and the great sacrifice it had cost. But there were one or two dissenting voices. One woman called out that it was a disgrace to be begging for money for horses when there were so many men out of work. Another woman, well-dressed and with a piercing voice, harangued Mrs Cuthbert on the same subject, and objected to the placard, saying that horses were dumb beasts and only men could be heroes.

And a group of rough-looking men shouted about the cost of war in general and to them in particular and called them stupid women and sentimental fools. One of them even threw a stone, which hit Hazebrouck, not hurting him, but startling him so that he backed several steps and bumped into a pram, almost knocking it over. Things might have turned nasty, but a veteran in a wheelchair, with no legs below the knees, wheeled himself up to Hazebrouck and made a fuss of him, and Police Sergeant Whittle took the opportunity to go quietly up to the rough men and suggest they move away.

A reporter from the *Westleigh Herald* came (Mrs Cuthbert had organised that, too) and interviewed them, and his photographer took a nice shot of the two horses and three women, the placard and the interested crowd standing around. That aroused the commercial instincts of Mr Evanton, who had a photographic studio just down the road, next to the Windmill Café: he left his assistant in charge of the shop, brought a camera and tripod down to the green, and suggested to Mrs Cuthbert that he took photographs of people standing with the 'war heroes' and made a donation to her fund for each he sold. At first, there were not many takers, until one little girl asked if she could sit on the nice horsey. Sadie lifted her up, and she looked so thrilled sitting astride Jingle's warm shiny back that Sadie suggested to her mother that a photograph would be a nice memento. After that, a stream of children came up, and both photographer and the fund did very well out of it.

Ethel had walked into the village, and wandered over to see what the crowd was staring at. She was watching as Miss

Sadie lifted another child onto the brown horse's back, and thinking disconsolate thoughts, when suddenly she felt cold all down her back, and turned her head to find Frank Hussey standing just behind her.

'Oh,' she said. She had forgotten how tall he was, and how big – not an ounce of fat on him, of course (in fact, his face looked thinner than she remembered), but big with bone and muscle, and with something that came from inside him: when Frank was there, you didn't look at anyone else. He was dressed neatly in corduroy trousers and a blue shirt that made his eyes look bluer in his brown face.

Since he had abandoned her because of her continual rejections, she would have expected him to be righteously angry, or at least stand-offish – he had every right – or, well, to be honest, she didn't know what she would have expected. But not this, him looking down at her with such kindness, and the same warm interest, just like in the old days. In her confusion, she fell back on her practised sarcasm.

'Well, well, look what the cat's brought in!' she said.

'Hello, Ethel,' he said. 'I wasn't expecting to bump into you here.'

'Why shouldn't I be here? Free country, isn't it?' She couldn't meet his eyes, and lowered hers. His shirt was open at the collar on this warm day, and she found herself looking at the patch of delicate skin at the base of his strong neck where his pulse beat. She wanted unaccountably to press her lips to it.

'Course it is,' Frank said, staring at her so intently she felt as if he was looking inside her as well as out. 'Just a lucky coincidence. I don't often come into Northcote, and I didn't think you did, either.'

'Got sent on an errand,' she said, and her irritation burst out. 'Me, sent on an errand! And on my afternoon off, too.'

Frank glanced around. 'You here on your own?'

'What's it to you?'

'I'd like to talk to you,' he said, 'but not here, standing out in the street. Let's go and have a cup of tea and a bun at the Windmill, and be comfortable.'

She gave him a cold look. 'Won't your young lady object, you taking other females to cafés?'

'What young lady would that be?'

'I heard you was walking out, engaged and everything, practic'ly married.'

'Don't know where you heard that,' he said. 'There isn't a young lady and never has been.' He thought. 'I walked home from church one Sunday with Bessie Cheeseman, maybe that's what the gossips picked up on.'

'Who's Bessie Cheeseman?'

'Works in the kitchen at the Hall. Pantry-maid. Nice girl, but dumb as a post, and shaped like a pumpkin.'

'I have no interest in Bessie Cheeseman,' Ethel said loftily.

'Nor have I,' said Frank. 'So come and have tea with me – do! I want to hear how things are going with you.'

'Can't. I got to get back.'

'You said it was your afternoon off.'

It was – and resentment rose to bolster curiosity and a simple desire to be near Frank. 'All right then,' she said, with a parade of reluctance. 'But I can't stay long.'

And Frank smiled as though it were the most gracious acceptance ever.

CHAPTER TWENTY-ONE

In the café, with a pot of tea in front of her, Ethel felt like a valued person for the first time in ages, and it didn't take Frank many questions to break through her resolve and get her talking. Resentment of Nanny Woods was stronger than resentment of Frank's abandonment.

'Sent down to the village to buy gripe water, as if I was the under-housemaid! Me, that looked after Mr David all those months! And cared for little Marcus, and then him *and* baby Alice, single-handed. *I* didn't have anyone to boss about and run errands for me. Gripe water, she wants, and a packet of Farley's rusks! And them rusks are not even for the babies!' Ethel cried in indignation. 'She eats them herself! I've seen her dipping 'em in her tea when she thinks no one's watching. I've a good mind to tell Cook.'

'Why would Cook mind?'

'Because she's always made the children's rusks herself, going right back. It'd peeve her no end to think a Hunter baby was being given bought rusks. She'd snatch that old nanny bald-headed if she knew.'

'You don't like her, then, this nanny?'

'I hate her. I'm not allowed to look after my children any more. I'm just a skivvy. I'm hardly allowed to touch them.'

'So you're not happy at The Elms?' he asked.

Ethel almost answered, then narrowed her eyes, sensing a trap. 'What you been doing all this time?' she asked. 'One

302

day you're there, the next day you're not. You might've been dead for all we knew.'

'It was hard for me to stay away,' he said.

'Didn't look like it,' she retorted. 'We never heard a word from you. I'd've thought at least you'd be grateful to Cook for all them Sunday dinners.'

'I was grateful, and I do miss my Sunday dinners,' Frank said, 'but even more, I miss all of you. You were like a family to me.'

Ethel tossed her head. 'Nobody was stopping you coming.'

'Well, I was ill for quite a while,' he said. 'I had that Spanish flu quite bad, had to be sent to the fever hospital, there being no one to take care of me. I was away six weeks. But Sir Martin was very good, kept my job for me.'

'Oh.' Ethel was caught wrong-footed. She saw him lying alone in a narrow hospital bed, with no one to visit him, no one to know even if he died. It affected her too much, and she took a sip of tea to cover her confusion. 'We didn't know you were ill, did we?' she said harshly.

'Course you didn't. I lay no blame. But you see, I had a lot of time to think in the hospital. You'd made it clear you didn't want me, and I thought p'raps it was time I took you at your word and left you alone. I didn't have the heart to come and see everybody else if *you* were giving me the cold shoulder. So I thought I'd better stay away and try to forget you.'

Ethel looked down at her cup, and fiddled with the teaspoon. She didn't want to ask, but she couldn't keep it in. 'And did you?'

'No,' he said. 'I can't get over you, because you're my true love. If you were just any girl, I could have put you out of my mind in the end. But you only get one true love in your lifetime, and you're it.'

She wouldn't look at him. She felt her cheeks burning. He reached across the table and took the hand holding the teaspoon, stilling it. She let the spoon go and, after a moment of resistance, allowed her fingers to curl around his warm strong ones.

'I think about you all the time,' Frank said. 'I can't seem to stop.'

Ethel said nothing, but she didn't remove her hand. She felt him looking at her, as if it was a physical touch. 'I always believed you cared for me a bit, underneath, in spite of what you said,' he went on. 'Was I wrong?' He squeezed her fingers. 'I want to marry you. More than ever now. Just seeing you standing there today brought it all back to me. Oh, Ethel.'

Such a longing came over her that she thought it would split her apart, like an apple. She couldn't speak.

'I know I'm no great catch,' he went on, 'but I've got a steady job. Now Sir Martin's back, Mr Orwell's retired and I'm head gardener, with the bigger cottage. I can support you properly. I'll take care of you, I promise, and love you always. Will you marry me?'

'I can't,' she said wretchedly, pulling her hand away.

He shook his head. 'I might take "won't" for an answer, but not "can't". Why can't you? The only reason I can think of is you're married already, and it's not that. Is it?'

'No,' she said, still looking down.

'Then what is it? *Do* you care for me?' he asked.

The answer was a long time coming, and it was almost inaudible, but it came with a nod of the head. She was near to tears.

'Then say you will, dear, and let's be happy,' he said gently. 'I know you always said you couldn't leave little Marcus, but now this new nanny's stopping you minding him, and you're not happy in that job any more. Marry me and have a little boy of your own. Two if you like,' he added, smiling at the top of her head. 'I love you, Ethel. Say yes. Let me see your face.'

She looked up reluctantly, knowing the sight of him would

304

undo her. 'I want to marry you,' she admitted – for the first time. Joy leaped to his eyes. She went on quickly. 'But I can't.'

She saw him take it like a blow, and his expression grew firm. 'Then you must tell me why.'

She shook her head.

'Yes,' he said. 'It's only fair.'

She fumbled in her pocket for a handkerchief. She dried her eyes and blew her nose, and all the while he waited patiently – as he would always wait, she thought. There was something immovable about him, like a great tree rooted deep in the ground. You might beat your fists against the trunk, but you'd never make it sway.

'Tell me why,' he insisted. 'Maybe it's something we can get over.'

'Let it be, Frank,' she said wearily. 'I can't tell you why. Not here. Not now.'

He considered that. 'But you *will* tell me one day?'

'Maybe.'

'And you do love me?'

'Maybe.'

And, after a moment, he smiled. 'Good enough for now,' he said. 'Finish your tea and I'll walk you home.'

David sat in his father's study, writing-paper before him, pen drying in his hand, assembling his words, thinking back to the evening meeting with Christopher Beresford at his club. Any diffidence he had felt had melted away within minutes: Beresford was so affable, so easy to get on with, and seemed, quite simply, to like him.

They had discussed general topics at first – the progress of the talks in France, the situation in Afghanistan, the probability that British troops would be pulled out of Russia, leaving the fighting there to the Russians. 'There's really not much we can do any more. Russia's ungovernable.'

They talked about Ireland, and the latest idea for settlement – separation, with two Home Rule parliaments, one in Belfast and one in Dublin. 'But with an overarching Council of Ireland to work on a plan for unity.'

They talked about Beresford's particular interest, the Town Planning Act, which was to provide a government subsidy to local authorities to build council houses in great numbers. 'Half a million by 1922, that's our target. The first necessity of a decent life is a decent place to live. We can't leave it to chance and private landlords any more.'

'Homes fit for heroes?' David suggested.

Beresford smiled tightly. During the general election, Lloyd George had promised 'a land fit for heroes', and the words were used every time some patently unfit aspect was pointed out. It had become a political thorn in the side. 'Why not?' he said. 'The trouble is, everything like that takes time, and the people want it done now, if not sooner. And when it isn't, they think we aren't trying, or didn't mean it.'

'But you do mean it?'

'With every fibre of my being,' said Beresford, and David liked him even better.

And then, by dint of asking a few well-chosen questions and being interested in the answers, Beresford got David to talk about himself and, to David's slight surprise, everything came pouring out: his sorrows, his frustrations, his ambitions. He told him about the time in 1914 when he and Jumbo had sat beneath the tree in the Oliphants' garden and talked about doing something noble and heroic. 'When the war broke out, we thought we'd found it, God help us. But there's nothing noble about war – though sometimes there is heroism. But it's not the heroism of St George in polished armour killing the dragon with a clean thrust to the heart. There was nothing clean out there. St George lived in mud and lice and stank to high Heaven. And the dragon didn't die well.'

Occasionally during the evening David heard himself talking and thought he ought to shut up, because he was saying too much, but every time he stopped, Beresford would slip in another question and he'd be off again.

'I'm not usually such a gabbler,' he said at last, when the coffee was brought. 'You must forgive me. I don't know what's come over me.'

'Nothing to forgive,' said Beresford. 'We're friends, I hope, and what are friends for?' He went on quickly before David could wonder. 'So, given that you're not happy at the bank, have you thought what you'd *like* to do?'

'These days, with so many looking for work, you have to know someone. My father's a banker, but I don't want to be a banker. My uncle Aeneas is the Palfrey of Palfrey's Biscuits, but I don't want to be in commerce. I've tried teaching and I don't want to be a teacher.' He smiled apologetically. 'That's an awful lot of "don't wants".'

'Never mind the actual job – what would you like to achieve?' Beresford asked.

David thought. 'To make a difference,' he said. 'To make the world a better place, even if it's only in a very small way. I suppose that's the old "something noble" ambition revisited. But I hope I'm more down-to-earth now. No grand gestures. I'd just like my children to have one thing to be proud of me for.'

'It sounds to me as if politics is your natural home,' said Beresford.

'Is that why you went into it?'

'Into politics? Yes – because how else can one change things? Unless one is a millionaire philanthropist. Look here, why don't you come and work for me? I need a confidential secretary, and we seem to get on well and have similar views.'

David was doubtful about the word 'secretary'. 'What would I have to do?'

Beresford read David's thought. 'I have a very competent

young woman who does shorthand and typing and takes care of my correspondence. That wouldn't be your worry. A lot of your job would be research – finding out facts and figures for me, and getting them into a digestible state. Looking into problems I'm interested in, talking to people who have solutions and testing how feasible they are. Keeping a finger on the pulse at Westminster and in Whitehall and keeping me informed about what's going on. There'd be a certain amount of travelling – when I'm out and about, I'd need you with me to furnish me with information. When I give speeches, I'd need you out there to tell me how the audience received them. Oh,' he laughed, 'and I might need you to help me *write* those speeches! You have a great way with words. But I can't tell you everything you might have to do – let's say you'd be my right-hand man, and my *Encyclopaedia Britannica*. What do you think?'

'Well—' David began.

Beresford was off again. 'In return, you would be at the heart of affairs and in a position to do a great deal of good. I'm ambitious, I don't mind telling you. I mean to get a ministerial post very quickly, and then into cabinet. And at some time in the future, if your ideas ran that way, I'd be in a position to help you get put up for a seat.' He looked at David, bright-eyed. 'You can't change things from the outside, only from the inside. Well? Will you join me?'

'Yes,' said David, carried away by the eloquence. 'Yes, I think it's exactly what I want to do. To be at the centre, to *know* what's going on, and to influence it.'

'Then it's settled.' Beresford thrust his hand across the table, and they shook.

'Oh,' said David, his grin fading a little, 'but I'd have to ask my father. He went to the trouble of finding me a billet, and I wouldn't want to seem ungrateful. But as long as he doesn't mind . . .'

'I've worked with your father, and I'm quite sure he'd

308

never stand in your way. You can tell him from me I'm sure you have a fine career ahead of you. And now,' Beresford went on, 'let's have a brandy to celebrate. And you can tell me more about Sadie's new venture with the horses.'

Digesting all these memories in his father's study, David looked at the blank paper and thought that here was an opportunity to practise his précis skills and pretend he had to write a persuasive speech. And as he began to write, he was aware of a very small thought in the back of his mind, which he quickly banished. Beresford might still be interested in Sadie, but he wouldn't go so far as to offer a fellow a job just in the hope of exploiting his influence with her.

Ransley had borrowed a motor-car from a colleague, and he and Laura were pottering along the coast road through what the painter Levêque had named the Côte d'Opale for its soft milky skies and lambent light. The weather was so sweet and benign it seemed a crime to go indoors to eat in a restaurant, so they had decided on a picnic among the dunes, and as Ransley had acquired the car, Laura had taken on the duty of providing the comestibles.

'Glorious, isn't it?' Ransley said. The first post-war harvests were in, and there were fields of golden stubble in the background, but also the green of fallow fields. It did not do to wonder whether they were fallow because the men who should have tilled them were all dead. Or to reflect on the tales that were heard all too often, about what farmers were turning up when they ploughed. Today was a day for pleasure. And, Ransley thought with a certain firmness, for decisions.

'Glorious,' Laura agreed. 'It's good to be away from the battlefields for a change. 'I wonder how long it will be before the trees grow again. Those splintered stumps give me the shivers.'

'I didn't think anything troubled you, O level-headed one.'

309

'I profess to some sensibilities.'

'Those I know about, I'm glad to say.'

'But it's amazing how many people have come back to Ypres already, even though there's hardly one stone standing on another,' Laura went on, following her own thoughts. Since July, the Belgian government had offered a subsidy to anyone who wanted to go back to the city and rebuild their property, but there had been people returning long before that, almost as soon as the Armistice was announced. 'They live in cellars, and sell goods from wooden stalls set up in the rubble. The resilience of humanity is astonishing.'

'What about here?' he asked, pulling into a wider space at the side of the road. 'Those dunes look inviting. And there's a path, so it won't be so much of a scramble.'

With blanket and basket they followed the sandy path through the dunes until they came to what was evidently a favoured spot, since it had been flattened, and someone had imported three large stones whose scorch marks showed they had housed a cooking fire. It was a good place, with marram-covered dunes behind and to the windward, and a fine view over the empty beach to the empty sea, which lay, as calm as sleep, grey-blue to the horizon.

'England's just over there,' Ransley said, as Laura spread the blanket. 'If we were a bit higher up, we'd see the white cliffs.'

Laura laughed. '*Wiv a ladder and some glasses we could see to 'Ackney Marshes*,' she teased him. 'Are you feeling homesick?'

'Yes, I am, as a matter of fact,' he said. 'Aren't you?'

'Well, of course,' she said, realising he was serious.

'No, I don't think it is "of course" with you. I was ready to go home in April, I can tell you, but I had to stay on when they asked me. You could have gone home any time.'

'I do go.'

'I mean, and stay there.'

'And leave you out here?' she said lightly. 'I'll lay out the food while you open the wine. There's cheese and sausage and – mmm, this bread smells wonderful! Some grapes. And will you look at these peaches! It seems almost a crime to bite them – they have cheeks like little children. And some chocolate, for afterwards. The war has left me with such a craving for chocolate.'

'You've practically lived on cocoa, as far as I can gather,' he said, drawing the cork with a satisfying *plop*.

'That's how I've become addicted. You can't get chocolate poisoning, can you, Doctor?'

'Not without really trying,' he said.

They sat, and ate, and drank, in companionable silence, gazing out at the moveless sea and relishing the sweet air, the gentle salty breeze, the dazzling white of the occasional cruising gull turning peacefully against the opalescent sky.

At last, Ransley said, 'How are you enjoying your tourist trips?'

Laura didn't answer immediately, and he wondered whether she was going to dissemble, because he knew the answer. But she said, 'Not as much as I expected to, I must confess.' There had been two in July, four in August, two already in September.

'I thought as much. You'd have talked about them a lot more if you'd enjoyed them. But tell me why.'

'There seems to be an awful lot of weeping. I try not to get involved, just concentrate on the driving, while Ronnie deals with the customers.'

'Poor Ronnie.'

'She's very robust. She doesn't mind.'

'I bet she does.'

Laura ignored that. 'I thought I'd meet lots of new, interesting people and have lively conversations, but they don't seem to want to talk. And when we get there, they cry. Anyway,' she shook herself, 'Matilda's not enjoying the roads

311

over here. Her springs are in a frightful state – not fair on the customers. I think if we go on we'll have to think about getting a big touring car.'

'You said, "if we go on",' said Ransley, leaping on his chance. 'So there is some doubt about it?'

'It wasn't that kind of "if".'

'That's pure defiance. I can just see you as a schoolgirl, hands behind your back, chin stuck out, refusing to admit you'd hurt your knee.'

She laughed. 'How well you know me! But your questions do not quite sound random to me. What's on your mind?'

'I simply want to know if you would be sorry to give up the sightseeing trips.'

'Are you thinking of making me?'

'I'd never try to make you do anything. But I've had an offer of a post at St Thomas' Hospital, both operating and teaching. They're particularly interested in having someone who has learned new surgical techniques at the Front. It's a very good position, and if I accept, I would be taking it up in October – as soon as my army contract runs out, in fact.'

'*If* you accept?'

He grew serious. 'I want to do this, Laura. Surgery in a clean operating theatre, with plenty of time to do it. And no shells. And teaching vital skills to a new generation. I have no children,' he added, with a simplicity that was more affecting than pathos. 'To teach is my chance to pass on something of myself.'

'My dear,' Laura said, 'if it's what you want to do, how could you think I'd stand in your way?'

'I know you wouldn't. But I want to settle down. I'm tired of living in a tent and trekking from place to place. I want a house, a home – a wife. And,' he went on, seeing her about to answer, 'I want them very soon, not in some distant golden future when you've got the itch out of your feet.'

312

'Oh, Jim, am I cruel? I'm sorry.'

'You are cruel, and you're not sorry,' he said, with a smile to remove the sting, 'but I'm going to be crueller, and I'm not sorry either. Marry me, Laura – and within the next few weeks. The Thomas' professor of surgery should be a married man. We can live in your house in Westminster, if that suits you – it's very well placed for the hospital. Speaking of which, I have another proposition.'

'Tell me,' she said, with a look that revealed nothing.

'They have a vacancy for a lady almoner. I know you will need something to do when we go home, and it occurred to me that it might suit you very well.'

She wrinkled her nose. 'Quizzing people about their income to check whether they can pay for treatment?'

'There's so much more to it than that, these days. Yes, you'd be looking into their home circumstances, but with a view to giving them advice as well, directing them to the services they need, making sure they get help. You could make such a difference to so many poor people's lives.'

'You think I'm so much of a philanthropist?'

'I know you are. Would I love you so much otherwise?'

She laughed. 'Blackmail! Now I have to do what you want or lose your respect.'

He knew she was joking. 'Just think how much we'd have to tell each other in the evening when we came home. We'd never run out of conversation. You'd have a staff of two assistants and a clerk, and your office, I believe, has been improved to a tolerable level. The first lady almoner had to work out of a cupboard.'

Laura saw the trap that had been laid out before her, so obligingly unconcealed. Marriage, a home, a job, all in the same place. No more restless change, no more dashing about. Could she bear to be – oh so kindly and gently – tied down? Would loving Ransley be different when their moments were not snatched from the jaws of desperate danger? When they

313

travelled home on an omnibus instead of treading a narrow line between shell holes, dodging air raids? She had loved him in war – could she love him in peace? Could she cope with ordinary life?

She looked at his thin face, read the humour in his eyes that said he knew exactly what ailed her, and she discovered that there *was* a longing in her for home. She was tired. Taking people to see where their loved ones had fallen had given her a revulsion for the battlegrounds she had driven over with such resilience during the war. Without the ongoing heat of conflict they were old and cold and stale and revolting. Yes, she wanted to go home. And who was to say that the sheer novelty of being married wouldn't be excitement enough?

'I suppose any job can be interesting, if you make it so,' she said. 'When do you want to get married?'

His face split in a grin. 'Is that a "yes"?'

'It does seem to be, doesn't it?' she said, and leaned forward to kiss him.

It was unusual enough at any time in the servants' hall to get a picture postcard. In the old days, Cook had sometimes got a card from her sister in Folkestone, when she couldn't be bothered to write a whole letter, but that was a long time ago, before the war.

Eileen carried it in on the flat of her hand with the reverence due to a holy relic. 'Who's it for?' Aggie demanded.

'I don't know,' she said. 'The postlady just give it me. Isn't it grand? It's a lovely picture.'

Ada took it from her. It showed a seaside scene, a long, slightly curving beach with a town behind it, and distant blue mountains. She read aloud the words printed along the bottom: '"Bray, County Wicklow". That's Ireland, isn't it?'

'I don't know,' Eileen admitted, shamefaced. 'I've never been.'

'But you talk all Irish,' Aggie objected.

'Everybody does at home. I was only a babby when Ma and Pa come over. They were from County Clare.'

'Well, read it, for goodness' sake,' Cook said impatiently, looking up from boning beef. 'Who's it for? Nobody here don't know anyone in Ireland.' She had a sharp little hope that it was from Fred. Maybe he'd stopped off at Ireland on his way to Australia. Or – on his way back?

Ada turned it over. 'It's for you,' she said, and Cook's heart jumped. 'It's addressed "Cook, The Elms, Northcote, near London". Lord, it's a miracle it got here!'

The little hope died. Fred knew the proper address, and he never called her 'Cook'. 'Read it to me,' she said. 'My hands are all sticky.'

Ada read: '"Dear Cook and All at Elms, I hope you are well. I am well. I am on the honeymoon. I am Mrs Hugh Malone now." Then it gets all squashed and tight because it's run out of room. I think it says, "The weather is fine." And the signature's all scrawly and half off the bottom.' She raised her head and looked at Cook. 'It looks like it might be "Emily".'

'Good gracious!' Cook said, the knife arrested as she stared back. 'Emily? That girl! All this time and not a word to us, and then just a postcard, cool as you like!'

'Is that her that was kitchen-maid before me?' Eileen asked with interest. 'Who's this feller then?'

'Hugh Malone,' Ada supplied. 'Not anyone I've ever heard of. She never mentioned him, did she?'

'Never mentioned anyone,' Cook said, 'except her mum and dad and any number of aunties and uncles that was always having accidents and seeing ghosts and suchlike.'

'Did *she* see ghosts?' Eileen asked, round-eyed. 'Did she see 'em in this house? I'm afeart of ghosts. They foretell your doom, so they do.'

Cook rolled her eyes. 'Not another one of you! There's no ghosts here and, anyway, there's no such thing as ghosts. Fetch me that big plate off the side there, for this beef.

315

Is that all she says?' she urged Ada. 'Not a postscript or anything? Does she give an address?'

'Nothing. That's every word. I wonder how long it's been in the post. Could be weeks, without the proper address.' She turned the card over, looked at the picture. 'Seems like a nice place.'

'Married!' Cook said. 'I can't believe it. Who'd marry a scatterbrain like her? He must be off his head.'

'Hugh's a nice name,' Ada said. 'And he's taken her on honeymoon, so he must have a bit of money.' She thought a moment. 'Emily couldn't read and write, could she?'

'That's right,' Cook said. 'I wonder who wrote the postcard for her, then?'

'It must've been him, I s'pose. Which'd be kind. So maybe he's nice.'

'Well, she's someone else's responsibility now, and I wish him luck of it,' said Cook. 'Put it on the mantelpiece in the other room, Ada, where we can look at it. It *is* a nice picture.'

'It's a mystery, though,' Ada said, walking away. 'Why didn't she come back from holiday, and where's she been all this time, and how did she meet this chap? I'd love to know the story.'

'Well, I don't suppose we ever will,' said Cook. 'Anyway, now I can stop worrying about the silly girl, so I don't care.'

Ethel came in through the back door, looking flushed and strange – almost dazed.

'Where've you been?' Cook snapped. 'We've had that Nanny Woods down here twice asking why you weren't back with the gripe water. Wouldn't be surprised if it wasn't for her. She'd give herself the gripes all right, sour-faced old bucket!' She noted the lack of parcels in Ethel's hands. 'Where is it, then? Where have you been?'

'Haven't got it,' Ethel said. 'I been at the Windmill, having tea.'

'Having *tea*? When you was on an errand?'

'It's my afternoon off,' Ethel said. 'She'd no right sending me down the shops.'

'Well, I hope you tell her so plain, my lady, she'll be glad to know,' Cook said, with round sarcasm. Her attention sharpened. In the old days, Ethel had always been slipping off to meet men – a different one every time, from what Cook had gathered. Don't say she'd started up her old ways again. 'Having tea with who?'

'Someone you know. I've brought him back to see you.' Ethel stepped to the back door and beckoned, and Frank came in, ducking under the lintel, and smiled around, very much at home.

'Afternoon, everybody.'

'Frank Hussey!' Cook exclaimed. 'Well, I'll go to the foot of our stairs!' She didn't know whether to be delighted that he had returned or offended he had stayed away so long, and between the two she was rendered speechless for just long enough for Ethel to knock her for six – right over the boundary, as Peter would have said.

'Frank and me,' Ethel said with a hint of defiance, 'are engaged.'

Instead of walking back by the streets, Frank had taken Ethel along the footpath that ran between and behind the built-up parts of Northcote and across the green bits in between. It was mostly narrow, and often muddy in the winter, but just now it was dry and pleasantly secluded. He had taken her hand to help her over the stile behind the village school, and had somehow forgotten to let it go, taking it back through the crook of his arm.

There was a place were the path was running between the back hedges of two big houses and had to tack round an enormous oak tree, making a little square no man's land in the shade of the branches. Here Frank had stopped, and when she turned to look at him, he had taken both her hands and said, 'We're as private here as we'll ever be. So tell me why you can't marry me.'

And suddenly she couldn't fight any more. She looked at him with a misery that clutched his heart like a cold hand, and told him: that the woman she'd called 'Ma', who had brought her up, was in fact her grandmother. That the woman she'd thought was her sister Edie was in fact her mother.

'But that happens a lot,' Frank said, tightening his hold. 'Girls get into trouble and families have to do the best they can. There's many a lord, even, that only has his title because his ma went astray. You shouldn't worry about that: I wouldn't.'

'You don't get it. I haven't told you who my father was.' She swallowed and forced herself to go on. 'The man I called my brother Cyril – he wasn't my brother. But he *was* Edie's brother.' She pulled her hands away from him and covered her face. 'I'm an abomination,' she said, muffled by them. 'I can never marry anyone.'

Frank took his time, knowing that the wrong answer could push her over the edge. 'Did you always know? Since I first met you?'

She shook her head. 'When Ma was dying, she told me.' She lowered her hands, but turned her head away from him. She couldn't look at him. 'She told me about Edie, but she wouldn't say who my father was. But she left letters that had Edie's address on. So I went and found her. Asked if it was true. And asked her – the other thing.'

'I remember, you went away for a while,' Frank said. She'd come back heavily pregnant, and agreed to marry him. 'When you lost the baby, you changed your mind about marrying me. Was that why?'

She nodded miserably. 'I'd said yes because of the baby, because I was scared, and a baby, well, you owe it a good life, if you can. But when there was no baby, I – I couldn't

318

do it to you. Not tie you to someone like me. You'd been good to me. You're a good man. So now you know, you can forget me and marry someone else. Someone that's not . . .' she paused a long time, and when the word came, it was very low, almost inaudible '. . . unclean.'

He took her by the shoulders. 'You're not unclean! Don't you say that! Ethel, look at me. *Look at me*. Where did you get such a crazy idea?'

'It's in the Bible,' she said. 'I'm the child of incest. I'm accursed by sin.'

'But it wasn't your sin! How could you help what those people did, before you were even born? *You*'ve done nothing wrong. You say I'm a good man – well, could a good man love you, if you weren't good?'

'You *can't* still love me. Not now you know.'

'It makes no difference to me. I don't care who your parents were or what they did. It's *you* I love, and I know you, and you're not accursed.' He pulled her against him, and she let him. He felt her trembling, but she was pressing herself to him. 'You should have told me this a long time ago.'

'I couldn't,' she said, muffled now by his chest. 'I was so ashamed.'

'Don't you ever be ashamed,' he said, almost angrily. 'Not of something other people did.'

'I thought you'd hate me.'

'Didn't I tell you you're the love of my life?' He released her, pushed her a little back so he could see her face. She looked dazed. Gently, he moved a strand of hair away from her eyes. 'So is that all?'

'All?' she repeated. Wasn't it enough?

'You've no other reason not to marry me?'

'What about – if we had children?'

'I hope we will. Ethel, please believe me when I tell you, there is nothing wrong with you. Look at you – you're beautiful! You haven't got horns and a tail, or six fingers! And any children we have will be half me. Aren't I normal enough?'

'I don't know. I can't think. I'm so—'

He saw her confusion. She had carried this for such a long time, and it would take a while to adjust. 'Don't think. There's no need. Just say you'll marry me, and everything will be all right. I'll look after you. I'll make you happy.'

'Happy?' she said, as if it were an alien concept.

'Say you'll marry me. Say it.'

And she said it. Like someone speaking from a trance, she said, 'I'll marry you.' And gave a trembling sigh that had, as yet, little happiness in it.

But it would come. He held her again, for a long time. Then she struggled free to look up at him and say, almost frantically, 'You won't tell? No one else can know – not ever! I couldn't bear it!'

'Of course I won't tell. There's no need for anyone ever to know. It's our secret. You're safe, Ethel. Safe with me.'

And for a wonder, she did feel safe – for probably the first time in her life.

CHAPTER TWENTY-TWO

Mary Russell, up at Highclere, announced that she was leaving to get married.

'We didn't know you were walking out with anyone,' Winnie said. They were all gathered in the tack-room drinking tea.

'I wasn't, really,' Mary said. She was perched on the low rickety stool, and Nailer had his forefeet up on her knee, having his head scratched. 'Miles is my cousin – well, second cousin, actually – and I've known him all my life. He was in the war and lost a leg.' She took a breath. 'There aren't so many of our set who came back at all.'

There was a little silence as they digested this. So many girls had lost their fiancés, and the death toll had been higher among the officer class so there was much less chance now of finding someone. Sadie had once seen an advertisement in the newspaper that said, 'Lady, fiancé killed at the Front, will marry blind or disabled officer, for mutual comfort.'

Mary went on, 'There's really not enough work to do here any more.' It was true. Most of the Crocks lived out most of the time. 'Mummy and Daddy are getting on. They won't always be there to support me. Miles has a private income.'

It was Sadie who asked what was on all their minds. 'But you do love him?'

Mary smiled. 'Of course. I told you, I've known him all my life. We played together in the nursery. He's talking about setting up a publishing house. I could help him with that. It would be interesting.'

Mrs Cuthbert cleared her throat. 'His – er – leg won't trouble him?'

'Oh, he has a false one. They're very good nowadays.'

It was time to be happy for her. They clustered round with congratulations. But afterwards Sadie thought again about there not being enough work. Mostly, these days, she came up to ride and school Allegro. Mrs Cuthbert had taken a shine to the chestnut hunter, Sorrel, who was a kind and steady horse, and loved being ridden. Allegro liked him and he was a steadying influence, so Mrs Cuthbert often went out on long rides with Sadie. She was talking about hunting this winter, assuming the hunts were back in business. Sadie insisted they did some road work, since Allegro wouldn't be any use for hunting if he wasn't safe with traffic.

'But I shall be hunting Sorrel,' said Mrs Cuthbert.

'Yes, but he's fifteen, he won't be able to go all day. You'll need a younger second horse if you want to stay out.'

But while riding Allegro was a joy, it was not work, and the rest of her life seemed to stretch in front of Sadie as a straight, empty road between bare fields, featureless, and with no destination in sight. What was she to *do*? The war had given her occupation, and that had been taken away. It had given her John, and taken him. She ached for him, longed for him, and sometimes she was so angry with the fate that had torn them apart that she wanted to scream and break things. There was a hole in the centre of her life, and she didn't know what to do to fill it.

She decided it was time to take Allegro out on the road alone – without Sorrel. 'I have to do it some time,' she said to Mrs Cuthbert, who had come to the door of the box, 'and he's been going so well lately.' She thought Mrs Cuthbert would object, and added, 'I'm sure he'll be good. And if he seems too fidgety, I'll come back by the fields.'

But Mrs Cuthbert only said, 'Mmm, yes,' as if her mind was on other things.

Sadie dropped the hoof she was picking out and said, 'Is everything all right?'

Mrs Cuthbert hesitated, then drew something out of her pocket. 'I don't know if I'm doing the right thing,' she said. 'I hope I am. This came yesterday and I've been wondering whether I ought to tell you. It's a letter from John.'

Sadie whitened, and put a hand on Allegro's neck for support. He looked round and shoved her companionably with his muzzle. She couldn't speak for the pain of hope.

'He promised me before he went away,' said Mrs Cuthbert, 'that he would write to me now and then, to let me know how he's getting on. He said it wouldn't be right to write to you, and I agreed with him, because you ought to have every chance to forget him. I think he assumed I wouldn't tell you about our correspondence. But . . . I don't know. Would it ease anything for you to know how he is?'

Sadie was staring blindly towards her. 'I want to know,' she said with an effort.

'He writes that he's living in Edinburgh now. He says he's got a room in a lodging-house, and he's got a job assisting a veterinary surgeon. He does the small-animal work at the surgery while his senior does the farm work, so it's not too much of a strain on him. It doesn't pay much, but the man is understanding about his illness and holds the job for him, which is everything. He's had several bouts of the fever, but once his landlady understood it wasn't contagious, she let him stay, and even looked after him. So you see,' she concluded, searching Sadie's face, 'it isn't too bad. He's all right.'

Sadie stared at nothing. *All right*. In a way. As far as it went. *Oh, John!* It wasn't meant to be like this.

Mrs Cuthbert broke the silence at last. 'Was I right to tell you? Sadie? Did I do the right thing?'

And Sadie said, on an outlet breath like a sigh, 'Yes. I'm glad you did.' She tried a smile, to reassure Mrs Cuthbert, but it didn't really work. 'It's better to know things.'

'That's what I always feel,' said Mrs Cuthbert. 'Are you still going out? Do you want me to come with you?'

'No, thanks.' She wanted to be alone.

Allegro walked along briskly, glad to be out, ears everywhere. The streets of Rustington were narrow and full of people and quite a few motor-cars, but he didn't mind them, and Sadie had no trouble until they were out of the village at the bottom of the hill and came upon a road-mending crew. There, Allegro took grave exception to the steam-roller, dug in his toes and refused to move. But he didn't bolt, and when the flagman came and took the rein he allowed himself to be led past the steaming dragon with no more than a bit of skittering when it sighed. Sadie patted his neck as they rode on. 'You're a wonder.'

There was a lot of traffic up the long hill to Northcote, but having passed the worst, he seemed settled, and only started once when a labouring van backfired. She put him up on the grass verge and they swung along gaily; and when they reached the gates of Dene Park she decided he deserved a good stretch, and turned in.

Riding in the park, away from the traffic, she could relax, and think about John. She imagined the surgery like the one in Northcote Old High Street: poky and dark, a narrow waiting room with four wooden chairs, and the surgery beyond, cramped, smelling of disinfectant, the examination table in the centre and shelves behind with boxes and bottles of pills and potions, and a glass-fronted case of instruments. She imagined John there, tending people's cats and dogs and cage birds: patient, kind, his sure hands calming the nervous animals; but weary, low, unwell, with no resort at the end of the day but a narrow bed in a rented room, and no comfort in his illnesses but the grudged attentions of a busy landlady. But perhaps, she told herself, she would not be grudging; perhaps she would be kind.

Sadie swallowed the sickness, the frustration, the blind longing, and, desperate for some release, put Allegro into a gallop, barely seeing where they were going, trusting him to avoid trees and other hazards.

When he slowed of his own accord, she pulled up, slid off him, buried her face in his neck, and cried hot, angry, miserable tears.

Like a thunderstorm, it passed, leaving her feeling scoured empty. She remembered that when Bobby had died, a time had come when she had stopped thinking he might come back, when the wound had become a scar. She understood at last, really understood, that she would never see John again. She was like all those other girls whose fiancés had fallen in battle. As from death, there was no way back. But it was harder, in a way. If he had been killed, she might have wished to die too; but he still lived somewhere, and so she had to live, too. It was like carrying a burden that was too heavy for you: the time came when, though every step still hurt, you stopped thinking about it. You just trudged on, because nothing would change.

She mounted again, and cantered on, and the passing air felt kind as it dried the tears on her cheeks.

Across the luncheon table at the Meurice, Edward began to smile. 'Really? Truly? I'm so pleased for you.'

'You needn't look so surprised,' said Laura.

'My dear girl, I'm not surprised that someone has recognised your fine qualities,' Edward said. 'Only that you are willing to go in harness. I never thought you would.'

'It took the right man to handle the reins,' Laura said. 'And now can we drop the metaphor before it gets insulting?'

Ransley was grinning to himself. There was a lot that was

325

alike between brother and sister. 'I love her to distraction,' he said, 'and I'm immensely flattered that she's agreed to marry me. All we need is your consent as head of the family.'

Laura rapped his hand. 'Not consent! For goodness' sake, I'm a grown woman.'

'Well, what then?'

'Blessing,' Laura said.

'You certainly have that,' said Edward. 'A man willing to take on my sister must be a man of character, and I presume you have means – though she has a little money of her own.'

They told him about the Thomas' jobs. 'I start on the twentieth of October,' Ransley concluded, 'Laura the following week. So we would like to be married very soon.'

'And I'd really like you to give me away, since we have no father,' Laura went on. 'If you can get away from Paris for the occasion . . .'

'I'm finishing here at the end of the month,' Edward said, 'so I shall be in London from the beginning of October. I can guarantee I shall keep clear whatever date you select. Where is the deed to be done?'

'We talked about a register office, given our advanced age,' Laura said, 'but in the end there were so many people we both wanted to invite, it seemed more . . . gracious to do it in church. St John the Evangelist is my parish church in Westminster. But I do refuse to wear a long white gown and a veil.'

'And afterwards?' Edward said. 'The wedding breakfast?'

'A hotel, I suppose,' Laura said. 'My house is too small – that's where we'll be living. Jim hasn't any property.'

Edward nodded. 'The Savoy would be convenient. I'll get Duval to make enquiries once you've chosen a date.' Laura's eyebrows rose. 'And before you mention expense, let me say at once that I shall be paying for this wedding, and I mean to see you turned off in style.'

'But Teddy, dear—'

326

'You're a grown woman, I know. But regardless of age, the bride's father traditionally pays for the wedding and, as you've pointed out, we don't have a father so the pleasant duty falls to me.' He smiled. 'Don't worry about it. I've done rather well out of the war – after all, I could hardly pursue astute investments for my clients and not for myself, could I? I am now very comfortably off, and we shall not discuss the topic of money any further, lest Major Ransley decides we're a hopelessly vulgar family and runs away.'

Ransley put his hand over Laura's. 'Can't do that. She has something deeply embedded in my heart. A grapnel, I think. Pulling away would be death.'

'Pretty talk!' Laura snorted. 'I hope you're not going to turn sentimental on me now the war's over.'

'I shall be as cold and cruel as you want, my love. You only have to give me my instructions. Will you require regular beating, or just harsh words?'

'Idiot! I'll talk to Edward,' Laura said loftily, 'see if I can get sense out of him. So you'll be home in October? Is the conference over?'

'No, it will carry on for a few more months,' Edward said, 'but I've been ordered back to England.'

'How come?'

Edward told her.

He'd been at his desk, looking at something that had come in an envelope marked 'personal', which Duval had handed to him unopened on the top of the pile of correspondence. Inside the envelope there had been nothing but a handbill advertising the school of dance of Madame Bricourt, with an address near the Opéra, offering to teach all forms of dance to the sons and daughters of gentlefolk. It was tastefully done, and expensively printed, but there was nothing remarkable about it except that someone had underlined the word 'Madame'.

So she was married. He was glad for her, and glad she had an enterprise to keep her busy and happy. He hoped it would thrive. He had seen her only once since the time Beattie visited, passing in a taxi as he walked along the rue de Rivoli. He had begun automatically to raise his hand to his hat, but she had not been looking in his direction, and the taxi passed without her seeing him. He was glad Paris had not thrown them together so far; with luck, he might not see her again before he went home. The tender place in his conscience might now grow a callus and allow him to get on with his life.

Duval came back in, and he crumpled up the handbill and threw it into the wastepaper basket. 'Lord Forbesson is here to see you, Sir Edward.'

Forbesson was in genial mood. 'There's something about Paris,' he said. 'Can't think what it is – just a dirty, tumble-down city full of stinking motor-cars and truly dreadful plumbing, but when you're here, you know you're not anywhere else.'

Edward smiled indulgently. 'I can't say I've had much chance to notice where I am.'

'Yes, and that's just like you, Hunter. All work and no play.'

'Am I a dull boy?'

'That's the odd thing. You are of considerable interest to a great many people – which is rather why I'm here.'

'Not to sample the joys of Paris?'

'No, as a messenger.' He accepted the glass of sherry Duval handed him and waited until he'd left the room to continue. 'They chose me because – well, I've known you a long time. And they weren't sure you'd prove amenable – after all, this has been a long grind, and you've every right to be sick of it – but they think I'm a pretty persuasive fellow, so here I am to talk you into it.'

They were going to make him volunteer again, Edward thought resignedly. 'I hope I shan't disappoint you,' he said, 'but you may have to give me just a *little* more information if you want me to understand what on earth you're talking about.'

Forbesson gave a bark of laughter. 'There's that sense of humour. Glad it hasn't been beaten out of you. Never had the slightest wit myself, but I know it when I see it. Look here, I'll come to the point. There's a lot to be done now the war's over, a damned mountain of work to get things straight. We've got a huge programme of social reform to get through – decent housing, decent education, public health. Protection for agricultural workers. The women thing. Ireland. And National Insurance – we want to get an Act through next year if possible: unemployment insurance and old-age pensions for the working classes.'

'Excellent ambitions,' Edward said, 'but all that's going to cost a pretty penny.'

Forbesson snapped his fingers. 'You see? You've put your finger straight on it. Invaluable fellow. That's why I'm here. We need good men to get this off the ground. We want you in the government.'

Edward's eyebrows shot up. He hadn't been expecting that. 'In the government? You mean you want me to stand for Parliament?'

'No, that would take too long, and we need you right away.' He paused, distracted. 'Would you *want* to be an MP?'

'Not at all,' Edward said. 'I'm not a great persuader. I'm a back room toiler.'

'Well, we need your mighty brain, and your experience, but we need your vote in the House as well. So the suggestion is that you accept a peerage, and come into government from the upper house.'

'A peerage? You can do that quickly?'

'Nothing simpler. Into the House with a barony, one-two-three, attach you to the Treasury and we all sit back with a sigh of relief. Can you come home straight away?'

329

'I'm finishing anyway at the end of the month.'

'Excellent. The House returns on the fourteenth of October, but you might need a few days before that to find your way around. Oh, and the PM will want to meet you, and Chamberlain, to thrash out a few ideas. What do you say?'

'You said yes?' Laura asked.

'I had little choice,' said Edward.

'How exciting! What title will you choose?'

'That's a woman's question,' Edward said indulgently.

'Well, I am a woman. You could be Lord Northcote, I suppose. Or does someone have that?'

'There was a Lord Northcote, but he died in 1911 without issue, so it's free,' Edward admitted.

Laura grinned. 'So you *have* thought about it! Woman's question, indeed! Have you told Beattie?'

'Not yet. I want to tell her face to face. Don't say anything, please.'

'We won't tell until you say we can,' Laura promised.

Edward flew home, for quickness' sake. He had hoped William might be on duty, but he learned there was more than one crossing daily and William had flown another service. Flying was very convenient – his army car took him to Le Bourget, and Duval had arranged for a car to be waiting for him at Hounslow, and in between he had nothing to do but sit. But he couldn't say he enjoyed the experience. It was interesting when they took off to see the ground fall away beneath him, and he was almost excited when they banked and he spotted through the porthole the indisputable Eiffel Tower in the distance. The world looked different from the point of view of a bird. He could understand the fascination.

But the weather quickly turned wet and windy, and once they were over the Channel, there was nothing to see in any direction but greyness. He assumed it was the weather and not the pilot's incompetence that made the aircraft tilt about and judder so much, and occasionally drop sickeningly like a lift with the cables cut. The motion made him feel queasy, and the thoughtfully placed brown-paper bag did nothing to reassure. He couldn't help thinking how much nicer it would have been on a ship, where he could have been enjoying a civilised gin-and-tonic in the first class lounge at this moment.

But he lived to tell the tale, and as soon as he arrived home, he took Beattie into his study for a private talk. He wanted to tell her first, before the family.

When he told her about the barony, she put a hand over her mouth in a curious reaction, as though to bad news.

'It won't make that much difference to you, dearest,' he said. 'You're already Lady Hunter. You'll be Lady Northcote instead. That's all.'

'It seems like a big difference to me,' she said at last.

'It's a chance for us to make a new start,' he said earnestly. 'These five years have been very hard for you—'

'For you, too.'

'I think it will be good for us to make a complete break with the past.'

'How complete?' she queried.

'We'll have to move to London,' he broke it to her. 'Travelling in from Northcote every day will be too much of a strain, especially when there are late-night sittings. I don't want to find myself staying at the club instead of coming home to you. We'll have to sell The Elms and buy a house in Town.'

'Leave The Elms?' Beattie said. 'Leave Northcote?'

'I'm sorry. But I think it will be better for us.'

Beattie said, 'It will be a wrench in some ways, but . . . not all the memories here are happy ones.' He took her hand. 'And your family is in Town – Sonia and Beth and Jack – so we'll see more of them. And I suppose Laura will settle there eventually.'

Edward was glad to have Laura's news to tell her at that moment. It made the interview a more positive thing.

Diana came over for luncheon, bringing the children. 'I had to come when I heard you were home,' she told her father. 'And to tell the truth, I was glad for an excuse to get away. My mother-in-law is staying, and she's in a terrible mood.'

'A general one, or a particular?' Sadie asked, holding George on her knee. He was getting very heavy, and wouldn't stay there long – at two-and-a-half he wanted to be dashing everywhere.

'Oh, she's furious with me because I've been talking about selling Wroughton House,' Diana said.

'Why would you do that?' David asked.

'It's too big and I hate it. I've got Park Place for when I'm in Town. It costs a fortune to keep up, and there are lots of repairs that need doing but have been put off because of the war. Mother-in-law just expects them to be done, but Boardman's worked out an estimate, and it's huge. He says the money would be much better spent on the estate because *that* needs work too. Charles,' she added, with a conscious look, 'always wanted to bring the estate up to scratch. He said the land was everything.'

'It sounds a sensible idea,' Edward agreed. 'The land will give you a return, which a house won't. But would anybody buy it?'

'Oh well, you see, there's a new idea. Guy is selling Rainton House to this woman called Stephanie Spencer Bouvier. She's buying on behalf of an American millionaire, who's going to pull it down and build a block of flats instead.'

'Pull it down!' David exclaimed. 'And you want to do the same to Wroughton House? No wonder Lady Wroughton's upset.'

332

Diana shrugged. 'It's not her house to be upset about any more.' Sadie was impressed by her fortitude. She had used to be afraid of her mother-in-law. 'And I have to do what's best for the estate and George. You see, nobody wants these big old houses any more. Can't afford them. But they'll still want somewhere to stay when they go up to Town, so a really nice flat – spacious and elegant, but modern and convenient – will be just what they need. Stephanie's shown me some of the plans and I wouldn't mind living in one myself. Rich people in New York live in flats and don't think anything of it.'

'You've met her, then?' Sadie said, letting George wriggle down.

'Several times. She's really nice – and full of wonderful ideas.'

Edward caught Beattie's eye. 'I think Wroughton House is doomed.'

'It seems so,' Beattie said. 'Time to tell your news?'

'Yes, Dad,' said William. 'It must be something important for you to *fly* over.'

So he told them about the peerage. There was a clamour of congratulation.

'It's no more than you deserve,' Sadie said.

'I don't know about that,' Edward said. 'I hope to deserve it at some time in the future, by serving my country, but at the moment it seems I'm being rewarded in advance.'

'So what sort of lord will you be?' Peter wanted to know. 'A baron? Isn't that hereditary?' He hooted. 'That means David will be a baron one day!'

David looked blank. 'Good Lord!'

'And that means Marcus will be one too, eventually,' said Peter.

'George will outrank him,' Diana said, 'but they'll be in the House together – that will be nice.'

'Speaking of houses,' Edward said, and told the other half of the news.

333

'Leave Northcote?' Sadie said.

David was enthusiastic. 'I've been thinking I needed to live in London, with my new job for Beresford – the travelling is a real inconvenience – but I didn't know what would happen to the children. If they were here and I was there I'd never see them. But if you all come . . .'

Beattie looked at Edward. 'I suppose you'll want to be somewhere near Westminster. That would be good for David, too.'

'There are some nice houses in Belgravia,' Diana said. 'Guy has a friend in Eaton Square, and it's lovely.'

'It will be easier for me to get to Hounslow from London than from here,' William said. 'Fewer changes on the train.'

'But what about me?' Peter asked. 'I've just started a new year at school.'

'There are schools in London,' David said impatiently.

'Yes, but all my friends are at Lorrimers, and I'm probably going to be picked for the middle-school rugby fifteen this term.'

Edward had thought of that. 'Would you like to stay on as a boarder?'

'Gosh, yes! That would be topping! Rogerson's a boarder, and he says they have ripping times. Except London would be pretty super, too,' he added wistfully.

'How about being a weekly boarder, and coming home to London at weekends? That way you'd have the best of both worlds.'

Peter thought it an excellent idea. Diana asked her mother about the servants, and Beattie said they would probably want to come, but if they didn't, it wouldn't matter. They could be replaced.

'There's an agency I use in London, that gets me people,' Diana said. 'And I've just thought – why don't I ask Stephanie Spencer Bouvier to look for a house for you? She knows all the London property that's for sale. She could arrange several for you to go and look at, save you the boring part.'

'It will be lovely,' Beattie said, 'to have all the family together in one place.'

'And if you want to get out into the country at any time for a break,' Diana said, 'you can always go to Dene. Whether I'm there or not, you can always use it.'

No one had asked Sadie what she thought. She had listened to the conversation with her mind in turmoil. She had supposed they would live in Northcote for ever, and it was a shock. To leave would mean leaving Mrs Cuthbert and Highclere, where all her memories of John were. And Allegro. But Allegro was not her horse. In London, perhaps she would find something worthwhile to do with her life. Surely there would be more opportunities in the great capital.

'I wonder how Nailer will take to living in the city,' she said, but no one heard her.

Everyone else had gone to bed; Edward and Beattie were the last to walk up the stairs. 'You'll be going back tomorrow?' she said.

'I have to – so much to do before I leave Paris.'

'Such a short visit.'

'It would hardly have been worth it if I couldn't have come by aeroplane. But I wanted to tell you face to face. It wasn't something for a letter.'

'I'm glad you did.'

'And you're not too upset about London?'

'No. I think you're right – it will be a completely new start for us all.'

At the door to the bedroom they paused, and he looked at her uncertainly, unsure whether he was to kiss her goodnight and go on to the dressing-room. 'A new start for us,' she said. 'I think there is much to let go of. For both of us. It will be – a relief.'

335

'Yes,' he said. 'I'm tired, Beattie. I want to come home.'

'Come home, then,' she said, and took his hand to lead him into the bedroom.

Later, he lay in the dark holding her, his whole self, body and mind, thrumming with happiness. There had been Paris, and then London, but somehow here, in what had been their home, it mattered more. He had entered her with relief, and with tenderness, and with a certain apprehension because he had been rejected so often, but he felt she had been really *there*, for the first time since before the war. She had been trying, since Paris, to get back to him; but this night she had made it. He held her, and thought, *We're together again. And it will get better. This is only the beginning.*

CHAPTER TWENTY-THREE

William was going to be flying the aeroplane on which Edward went back to Le Bourget, and was excited and pleased about it. 'I'll make sure you get a smooth flight,' he said. 'You'll never want to travel any other way again.' He was even more pleased when Edward said they could ride to the airfield together, in his hired motor-car. It was such an awkward journey by train and bus, he had even thought of going into lodgings again.

'Are you enjoying it, though, your new job?' Edward asked.

'Oh, it's tremendous!' William said. 'They're talking about setting up some long-distance routes one day. Imagine flying to India! Even Australia!'

There was time after an early breakfast for Edward to look over some papers in his study. David came in with the baby in his arms. 'She's awake,' he said. 'You didn't really see her properly yesterday.'

The baby looked tiny against David's big chest, held in his big hands. He had never shown much interest in Marcus when he was young, and it touched Edward. 'How are you, my boy?' he asked. 'Are you – getting over it?'

'I'm all right, Dad,' David said. 'You needn't worry about me. This new job, it's just what I needed. To be doing something that matters. And when you come back, we'll both be working for the same ends. I like that.'

'Yes, I do, too,' said Edward. 'Would you think of running for Parliament one day?'

'I might,' David said. 'I can see that it's the logical end of it. And while I like Beresford awfully, I wouldn't want always to be the magician's assistant and never the magician.'

Edward laughed. 'Well put! Here, let me hold my granddaughter for a moment.' He took the tiny baby and looked down into the amorphous pink face, with the unfocused dark blue eyes, and smiled, imagining her growing up into a Sadie, or a Diana. Then, conscious of time fleeting, he handed her carefully back, and never once thought that she was not really his granddaughter. Louis had lost and he had won, but he didn't think that, either.

Beattie did not often go into the kitchen quarters. She was not the sort of mistress to be poking about in cupboards and checking on the servants. Cook and Ada ran that side of things and she trusted them to uphold standards. So her appearance through the door after the master had left warned them that something was up. She told them succinctly about the ennoblement, the necessity to move to London, and the consequent selling of The Elms. 'Any of you who want to come with us may keep your job. And if you don't wish to make the move, I will of course provide you with a reference.'

When she had gone, Eileen piped up, alarmed, 'I can't go to London! Da would never let me! And when'd I ever see Ma and the little ones?'

'You don't have to go,' said Ada soothingly. 'Didn't you hear Madam say she'll give you a reference so you can get another job?'

'But I don't want another job,' Eileen wailed. 'I like it here. Why can't I stay?'

Aggie took the news phlegmatically. 'I s'pose I'll get another place. One house is much the same as another.'

Cook looked doubtfully at Ada. 'I don't know if I want to go,' she said. 'London? It'll be a big upheaval.'

'We used to live in London,' Ada pointed out. 'We used to like it all right. There's more shops and more cinemas for when you've your time off. The music hall as well. And the nice parks, with bandstands.'

'That's all very well,' said Cook, 'but think of the trouble of packing up and moving. I don't like change.' She thought with dismay about getting used to a new kitchen, with different cupboards and pantries and never knowing where to put your hand to something. New staff, as well, and what if you didn't get on with them? A new kitchen-maid to train. A new stove – that was the hardest. It took years to learn all the little ways of an oven, and the prospect of week after week of failed cakes and undercooked meat was daunting.

'Well,' said Ada, 'change will come, whether we go with the family or we don't.'

Cook seemed to shrink. 'But I couldn't start working for a new family, not at my time of life. We'll have to go. We don't have any choice.'

Ada beckoned her into the sitting-room, away from other ears. 'We don't *have* to go,' she said uncertainly. 'You know I been saving up my widow's allowance ever since Len died, and there was the bit of money that came to me from him as well. I got nearly seventy pounds put aside now.'

Cook's eyes widened at the sum. 'Good gracious me!' She looked around to check no one was nearby. 'Where you keeping it?' she whispered. 'Not under the bed?'

'No, silly,' Ada said robustly. 'In the post office. Have you got any savings?'

'Nothing like that,' Cook said. 'I got a few pounds hidden away for emergencies, that's all.'

'Well, that's something. We talked about setting up together in our old age, but there's no reason we couldn't do it sooner if we wanted. And what if we rented a little house and took

339

in paying guests? With your cooking and my housekeeping we'd run it easy, and it'd pay its way with a bit to spare. What d'you think?'

Cook looked frightened. 'Oh, Ada, that's such a big thing! Going into business! What if it all went wrong and we was left with nothing?'

'Why should it go wrong?' Ada said calmly. 'Anyway, no need to decide straight away. We've time to think about it. But at least it gives us a choice, to stay in Northcote if we want.'

'Who would the guests be?' Cook asked, her curiosity aroused.

'Oh, there's all sorts of people who have to travel for their work – decent, respectable people, commercials and builders and engineers and suchlike. They'd love a comfortable house and good food when they're away from home. We'd never want for customers, I know that. But,' she went on, seeing how the whole thing had thrown Cook, 'just think about it, that's all. If you don't want to in the end, we can go to London with the family.'

Beattie went upstairs to tell the nursery staff. Nanny Woods listened impassively with her hands folded across her stomach – a posture she had copied from the stately hospital matron she had so feared during her early training. Nursing had not suited her temperament: there was too much skivvying, too much time to be served before the mast before you could reach a position of power. And adult patients were too unpredictable. Babies and small children could be moulded and intimidated into compliant behaviour. She had learned quickly how to win the approval of parents, and after a brief chrysalis stage as a nursemaid she had become the full-blown Nanny Woods so completely that it was impossible to imagine her as anything else.

When Lady Hunter had finished speaking, she said, with

340

a terrifying smile, 'I will, of course, be delighted to continue in your employ in your new establishment. I am devoted to the dear children, and I shall raise them to be a credit to you and Sir Edward.'

Beattie was satisfied not to have to look for a new nanny as well as all the other upheavals, and went away, only feeling later that she had been vaguely menaced.

Ethel had said nothing. She had not yet given her notice or mentioned her engagement to the mistress, and the other servants, despite their natural disposition to gossip, had closed ranks against Nanny Woods and kept her in the dark. Ethel was rather regretting having said anything in the kitchen, because it seemed there was a problem, and she could not see any way round it, which meant that the marriage would not happen, and she would be left looking a fool with her fellow workers. That was perhaps a small concern beside the larger one of losing Frank, but the new life he had offered her still seemed so dreamlike it was hard to believe in it anyway.

He had come round to see her on Friday night and she had put on her coat and hat and walked with him down the street so that they could have privacy. It had started to rain, a fine drizzle, and they had stood under the enormous oak tree at the end of the road for shelter while they talked about wedding plans – or rather, while Frank had talked and Ethel had listened as though to a fairy story.

And then he had punctured the bubble. 'I'll need your birth certificate,' he said.

She looked up at him. There were tiny rain droplets on his front hair and eyelashes. 'Haven't got one,' she said.

'What?'

'Never had one,' she said. Her lips tightened. 'I told you about how I come to be born. D'you think they'd've gone to the authorities and boasted about it?'

341

Frank laid a hand on her arm to soothe her. 'Don't get upset. I'm sure there's a way round it. There must be lots of people all over the country that don't have one.'

'Are you saying we can't get married without?' Ethel pulled away from his hand. 'I knew something'd come up! It was never meant to be.'

'Leave it with me,' Frank said, exuding reassurance. Ethel was like a wild creature, he knew, ready to bolt at any moment. 'Don't you know I can fix anything? Don't you trust me?'

'Don't see what you can do about it,' she said in taut tones. 'And if it comes out about – what I told you . . .'

'Just leave it with me,' Frank said again. And kissed her, to prevent further argument.

There was no question of Munt going to London. Munt came with the garden, they were all-of-a-piece with each other, and Beattie didn't even think to address him on the subject. It was Sadie who went down the garden, with Nailer at her heels, to tell him the news. 'It will be a while before the right property can be found, so it won't be happening tomorrow. And when The Elms is sold, Mother will recommend you highly to the new owners, so I'm sure they'll keep you on.'

He blinked at her slowly, digesting the information. He had got used to the Hunters and, though no one would ever have asked him such an absurd question as 'Do you like them?' he thought they were no trouble, on the whole.

They owned the house. The house had had a different owner before, and it would have a different owner again, and he was only mildly interested in the subject. But the garden was his. He had created it out of a bumpy virgin field when the house was first built, had tended it all these years, had overseen the destruction of his work to grow wartime food, was beginning the slow process of restoration now the war was over. He had plans for his lawns and flowerbeds, his roses and shrubs, his fruit trees and vegetable plots. How long any new owners might stay, or what they might be like, hardly mattered. *He* would stay with his garden, as long as there was breath in his body and sufficient mobility in his limbs.

But he discovered, slightly to his own surprise, that he would miss Sadie. He had watched her grow up, the middle child and always just a little left out, the onlooker who saw things others brushed past unnoticing. He had felt a little spark between himself and her. There had been times when she had come to sit on an upturned bucket to watch him at some task – potting on seedlings, say, or grafting roses – and he had permitted her presence because she kept silent or, if she asked a question, it was a sensible one. He had even sometimes felt that if he'd had a daughter, he'd have wanted her to be like Sadie.

Well, she would be going away, and there was nothing to be done about it. As well complain that rain was wet as fret about things you couldn't change. But he felt a strange, inexplicable urge to give her something to remember him by. Daft! Why should she remember him? Why should he want her to? But he felt in his pocket. Nailer, who had been sitting nearby scenting the air and watching Sadie, hoping she might feel the urge to go for a walk, stood up, wagging hard, in case the hand should emerge with something edible.

Munt held something out to Sadie and, puzzled, she took it and examined it. It had a bone handle that had worn and darkened over the years to a smooth amber colour, and a blade, slightly curved and wickedly sharp, which folded into the handle. Closed, the thing fitted comfortably into the palm, with a pleasant weight and balance.

'Your pruning knife?' she said. She had seen it in his hand a thousand times, cutting a stem or a length of string or a piece of tobacco for his pipe. It was such a useful tool that it was hard to imagine him without it. She looked up questioningly.

'Yours, now,' Munt said, and when her mouth opened, he forestalled her with 'Handy thing to have. Keep it about you. Never know when you might need it.'

'Thank you,' she said, profoundly. She understood how great a gift it was. 'I shall treasure it always.'

He sniffed. 'Keep it sharp, that's all I ask.' And he turned away, to signify the audience was over. There was only so much of that sort of thing a person could take.

But as he heard her walk away, he turned back to watch; and seeing Nailer prance after her, he called out, 'How d'you think that dog'll take to London?'

Sadie turned at once. 'I don't know. I've been worrying about that. He's used to roaming all over the country. I think he'll hate being confined to a garden.'

'Leave him with me. I'll look after him,' said Munt.

Sadie felt almost tearful. She understood that this was a gift, too. 'Would you really? I'll miss him frightfully, but I'm so afraid he'd escape and get run over. It would be much better for him here.'

'You can come and see him. 'T ain't the end of the world,' Munt pointed out.

Frank Hussey didn't come for Sunday dinner, and Ethel's heart sank. It seemed it was over already, the impossible dream. Cook had been expecting to set an extra plate for him, now he was back in Ethel's favour. (She couldn't believe a nice, good-looking chap like him was marrying a worthless baggage like Ethel! It was such a waste. On the other hand, it was good to be getting rid of her. If Cook did go to London, she didn't want *her* tagging along and souring the milk.)

'Where's Frank, then?' she'd asked. 'Aren't you expecting him?'

'Mind your own business,' Ethel had retorted.

'Don't you speak to me like that, my girl!' Cook had snapped, and there was an Atmosphere all through dinner.

But in the late afternoon, when Ethel came downstairs to wash out baby Alice's bottle, Frank was there at the table, drinking tea and looking as inscrutable as a cat. 'Come for a walk,' he said, getting up at once.

'I can't be long,' Ethel said, trying and failing to read his face. Good news or bad news? He would always be kind to her, that was the trouble. He'd try and make bad news tolerable.

'That old termagent's got no right to make you work on a Sunday afternoon,' Frank said.

'Babies don't take time off,' Ethel said, which was what Nanny Woods had said to her.

'Come on. Ten minutes, that's all,' Frank urged.

So they went out to walk in the gloaming, and as soon as they were clear of the house, he said, 'It's all right. I've sorted it out.'

'You mean . . .?' She hardly dared to hope.

'I mean we can get married, as soon as you like.'

'What've you done?'

'I've been to Goston,' he said. It was the village just across the fields from Northcote where Ethel had been born. 'I went to see the vicar, Mr Treadgold – remember him?' Ethel said nothing. 'And then I went to see the headmistress of the school, Miss Morton. Well, she's retired now, but she was headmistress twenty years ago.'

'What's that got to do with anything?' Ethel snapped. She was frightened. She hated even to think about Goston, and to have it brought back before her like this . . . To think of *him* there, poking about, asking questions . . .

'Schools keep registers, Ethel,' Frank reminded her patiently. 'That's official records. And what it comes down to is I've got two letters that the vicar promises me will serve instead of a birth certificate. He says there's a lot of people in your position.'

Poor people, the vicar had said, or actually, *the poorest people*, but Frank wouldn't tell Ethel that. They often neglected to register a child's birth: there might be so many of them, so little time to spare from work, the parents might be exhausted with labour and ill-health, or profoundly ignorant, and indifferent to formality. Generally, if there was a midwife, she would remind them, or bully one of the parents into doing it. But in Ethel's case, Treadgold seemed to remember, there had been no midwife. The mother had given birth with the help only of an older child. It was not her first – there had been several previous children, most of them dying early – so she knew what to do.

The letter, signed by the vicar, said *To the best of my knowledge and belief, Ethel Lusby was born some time in February 1894 at No. 4, Deede's Rents, Goston. Her mother was Mary, known as Annie, Lusby. Her father, Albert Lusby, a cowman, died some time in the winter of 1893–94. She attended Goston village school for six years.*

And the letter from Miss Morton said, *Ethel Lusby was enrolled in Goston Village School in September 1899 when to the best of my knowledge and belief she was five years old. She attended school regularly and left in April 1905 when she would have been eleven.*

Ethel read the letters, her hands trembling, then looked up at Frank, appalled. 'But it's not true,' she whispered. 'It says Ma was my mother and she wasn't.'

'You wanted your secret kept quiet,' Frank said.

'But it's a lie. What if it comes out?'

He took both her hands and gripped them hard. 'How could it come out? No one knows, only you and your sister, and she's not going to tell. You've got a sworn statement here from a reverend, and you can't get more solid than that.'

She looked wretched. 'But I know. And you know.'

'You don't know – not really. Who's to say your ma was telling the truth when she said that, or your sister? There's no proof one way or the other, is there? It's all hearsay, and if it comes to hearsay I'll take the vicar's word over your sister's. I want to marry you, Ethel Lusby, and I don't care where and how you were born. It's *you* I love – don't you understand that? Now, are you going to marry me, or not?'

It was a matter of whether she trusted him or not, Ethel thought. And if there had ever been anyone in the world you could trust completely, it had to be Frank Hussey. 'All right,' she said.

'You will marry me?'

'Yes – but not in a church.' She could lie to the government – what did that matter? – but not in front of an altar.

He grinned as though he read her thought. 'God's everywhere, you know. Even in a register office.'

For some reason, Sadie had expected Stephanie Spencer Bouvier to be young and tall and willowy and rather languid. Instead she was short, middle-aged and brisk, with a slight American accent. She was very plain, with a large nose and thin lips, black hair and a complexion almost swarthy; but she was dressed very elegantly, and to judge by her beautiful sable wrap and the many diamond rings she wore, she was very well off, which suggested she was successful at what she did.

Diana had persuaded Sadie to come and stay at Park Place for a few days and go with her to look at houses. 'I don't want to take all the responsibility,' she said.

Sadie was feeling unsettled since the news of her father's title and the move had been broken, and was glad to get away for a bit.

'Now this,' said Mrs Bouvier, managing a large key in a large lock with dexterity, 'is a little shabby, perhaps, but the proportions and size of the rooms are excellent. And it's no bad thing, in my view, to begin in a new home with a little redecorating.'

It was, like the other houses in the terrace, five-storeyed, the ground floor white stuccoed, with yellow London stock brick above. It had a pillared porch over the front door, and steps going down into a railed semi-basement, which housed the kitchen offices. The entrance hall was impressive, with a chandelier – bagged at present – in the centre, a fine staircase straight ahead, and rooms to either side. 'Morning-room and business-room,' said Mrs Bouvier. 'The drawing-room and dining-room are on the next floor – very handsome, ideal for entertaining. Four principal bedrooms on the second floor, five smaller bedrooms on the third, nursery above, and servants' rooms in the attic.'

She led them into the morning-room, which was nicely square, bigger than their morning-room in The Elms, and had a handsome marble fireplace.

'It's awfully dark,' Diana said doubtfully.

'It needn't be,' said Sadie. The walls were panelled to dado height in brown wood, and finished above in dark red damask, rather soiled and greasy-looking, and there were heavy red velvet curtains. 'If the panelling were painted cream, and that red damask replaced with, say, a pale green . . . The sea-green carpet from our drawing-room would fit nicely in here, and then you could have pale green curtains to go with the panels.'

'Yes, I see it all,' said Mrs Bouvier. 'You have an eye for this sort of thing, Miss Hunter.'

Sadie looked confused at being praised. Diana sighed and said, 'If a thing is one colour, I can never imagine it any other. The same with furniture. Rupert would move a console to a new position and the whole room would look different. I can't imagine it until it's done.'

'It is a talent,' Mrs Bouvier, 'and not everyone has it. Have

348

you thought, Miss Hunter, about going into my line of business?'

'I didn't know before that it was a business,' Sadie said. 'But I do think it's interesting. Isn't every little girl fascinated by the transformation scene in *Cinderella*?'

Diana was unmoved. 'I don't really notice what things look like in the house, unless they're actually broken or dirty. Then you have them seen to. Otherwise, I can't see the point of changing anything.'

'Many people feel like that,' said Mrs Bouvier, tactfully, 'but the war has changed others, and they want things to be different, including their surroundings. Miss Hunter, if you ever feel like taking up the challenge, come and see me.'

Sadie wondered whether this was something she could do with her life. Judging from Mrs Bouvier, it would pay enough to keep her independently, and would be interesting – different every day, not like going to work in an office.

When they came out into the street later, the first person they saw was Ivo Rainton, who was passing by, and stopped with a look of pleasure, lifting his hat to them. 'I didn't know you knew anyone here,' he said.

'We're just looking at the house,' Diana said, 'as a possible home for my mother and father. Father has to move to London, now he's going to be in the government.'

'Oh yes, Guy told me about the title.'

'What are you doing here?' Diana asked. 'I didn't know *you* knew anyone in Eaton Square.'

'I've been visiting a chum of mine from the army – old Bossy Freebody, splendid chap. Lost a leg at Messines. They fitted him with a jury one at Roehampton, but of course it doesn't end there. There's a splendid organisation just down the road here that helps chaps with false legs and missing arms – how to get about, cope with everyday tasks and so on. And the – er – mental side of it, too.' He looked slightly awkward. Men, especially ex-soldiers, didn't like to talk about

349

that sort of thing. You were supposed to get on with life and not admit you felt a bit glum.

'It sounds like a useful organisation,' said Sadie. 'What's it called?'

'Oh, they do sterling work. Bossy can't speak highly enough of them. Mostly volunteers, you know, though they have some medical experts on hand as well. Lady Farringdon's Trust for Aid to Disabled Soldiers, it's called. It's – er . . .' He cleared his throat. 'It's all too easy to forget chaps once they've been discharged from hospital, when quite a modest bit of help can make all the difference to how they live. Poor old Bossy was very down, even after he got the tin leg, but he's bounced back now he's had someone to give him a bit of a shove in the right direction.'

Mrs Bouvier had glanced at her watch, and Diana took the hint and said, 'We'd better get on. We've several more houses to look at.'

'I'll say good-day, then,' Ivo said, raising his hat again.

'But do come to supper tonight, if you're free,' Diana said. 'Guy's coming, and one or two other friends. Very informal – we won't dress.'

Ivo looked suddenly very much more cheerful. 'I'd be delighted to.'

Edward came home from France, but was so busy in Town it made little difference to the household – he was hardly ever there. He even stayed up at his club some nights when lamps were burning late at the Treasury, proving, if proof were needed, that the house move was necessary. Beattie had begun packing things, with Nula's help – linens and china not in daily use – and a very depressing job she found it. Moving house was always stressful – she still remembered when they'd moved to Northcote from Kensington – but this time it would be sadder because she would be leaving Nula behind.

'You don't need me any more,' Nula responded, when Beattie said something of this.

'I need you more than ever,' said Beattie.

'Ah, no, you think you do, but you've changed these last few years, Beattie Cazalet. You've outgrown me, so you have. You're all grown-up now.' She smiled as if it were a joke, but it wasn't.

'What makes you say that?' Beattie asked, curious, because she did feel different.

Nula looked at her a long moment, her head slightly on one side. 'You've woken up,' she said at last. 'All those years, you were sort of in a dream, not really with us. It was *him*,' she said, with a touch of acid. 'You were always half thinking he might come back, so you didn't need to live the life you had, cos you might be leaving it anyway.' Beattie wanted to protest, but there was a grain of truth in what Nula said. 'But now you've let him go, and not before time. Now you can stop looking over your shoulder.'

'I shall miss you dreadfully,' Beattie asserted.

'You won't. You'll be busy and happy, and that's the way it should be. I've my own life, and glad I'll be not to be minding you. Sure my husband'll think it's Christmas every day, having all my attention.'

The first thing I'll do when we're settled in London, Beattie thought, *is to go and see Louis's solicitor and sort out his estate.* Louis had left her his plantation in South Africa, which was being looked after by a manager and an agent, and was probably going to rack and ruin for want of an owner's care. She would sell it, she thought, and put the money into bonds, until a use should be found for it. Nula was right. She had let go. And it gave her a feeling of lightness and freedom she hadn't known since her coming-out days. The feeling that anything was possible; and that life on the whole was likely to be pleasurable.

* * *

351

The Dowager Lady Wroughton arrived at Park Place one morning in a taxi and a bad temper, which wasn't improved by having to wait because Diana was not fully dressed.

'I'm sorry, I wasn't expecting you,' Diana said, when she came eventually into the morning-room. 'Did they offer you refreshments?'

Violet Wroughton waved that aside. 'You are late rising.'

'We were late to bed last night.'

'Dancing, I suppose. All you young people seem to think about is dancing.'

'We went to a nightclub after dinner, so, yes, there was some dancing. It's a pleasant way to pass the time.'

'And no doubt you were escorted by Guy Teesborough?' It sounded like an accusation.

'My party included Guy,' Diana said. 'Why do you ask? Is my choice of companion any of your business?'

Lady Wroughton blinked in surprise. She was used to Diana accepting her criticism as everyone else did – meekly. She rallied. 'Certainly it is my business,' she retorted. 'The family's name, the family's credit are very much my business.'

Diana smiled. 'Well, I don't think there was any damage done to the family's credit. My companions were all very respectable, and the club is the one frequented by the Prince of Wales – in fact, he was there last night.'

Lady Wroughton waved that away as well. 'You are not to model yourself on *that* young man. I have no opinion of him, none at all. He has appallingly middle-class habits. Not that *you* would be likely to notice.'

The air froze. Diana bit down on her immediate response, and instead asked icily, 'Is there something in particular you wish to say to me, Mother-in-law?'

'Yes, there is,' said Lady Wroughton crossly. She sat down and waved Diana to a chair, as if it were her house. Diana sat, wondering if it was to be about Wroughton House again. She didn't want to discuss it. Stephanie

Spencer Bouvier was already talking to her American millionaire about it. The estate needed money spending on it and, if need be, she would invoke Charles's ghost, because the land was what he had always cared about, the thing he said would last, when buildings had crumbled away.

But Lady Wroughton had other things on her mind. 'What are your intentions concerning Guy Teesborough?' she asked bluntly.

'My intentions? Don't you have that question the wrong way round?'

'Don't trifle with me. Do you intend to marry him?'

'That's a question I will answer only to him, when he asks me.'

'So he hasn't asked you?' Diana was silent. 'He *has* asked you?'

'Not in so many words. But I know he wants to. He is being very correct, which should please you. I wasn't properly out of mourning until June, and he's giving me plenty of time, not rushing things, which is thoughtful and gentlemanly of him.'

'Never mind all that fiddle-faddle. Answer me straight. Do you intend to marry him?'

It was a delicate matter to Diana, because she had not entirely decided what her answer would be when Guy asked her, as she believed he would. She liked him very much, but she wasn't sure what more marriage would give her than their present friendship did. People of their rank did not live together hugger-mugger like mice in a nest, so it hardly mattered that they had two different houses. And she had not enjoyed the bedroom business with Rupert, which seemed to be the other big difference between being married and not. She liked dancing with Guy, and feeling his strong arms round her; and sometimes when he kissed her hand goodnight, she wondered what it would be like if he kissed her on the lips instead; but he had not pressed any attentions on her and she had not longed for them.

'I don't know,' she said, in answer to the question. And then, 'What is your objection?'

'The title is inferior to ours. A nineteenth-century creation – a *political* creation. The Wroughton earldom may be recent but the barony is ancient. You cannot wish to exchange being Lady Wroughton for being Lady Teesborough.'

'At least then you would be the only Lady Wroughton,' Diana said. 'Wouldn't that be an advantage?'

Lady Wroughton stared in anger. 'You *joke* with me? On a subject as serious as this? You have changed, Diana, and the change is not to your credit. You were never *quite* one of us, but you have coarsened still further. You are pert.'

Diana blushed with anger at the insult, but she was surprised at herself too. She had always been terrified of her mother-in-law, and would never have dared to answer her back or disagree with her. Her new fortitude, she realised in a flash of revelation, came from Guy: she wouldn't be afraid of things any more, because she knew he loved her and would always defend her.

Lady Wroughton went on: 'Your son is the Earl Wroughton, and the protection of his honour must be your only concern. To be presenting him with a step-papa, when he has no need of one – when he has a brother, and the succession is secured – would be an act of crass selfishness on your part. You are not to be putting your own comfort above your duty to the family.'

'I see. Anything else?'

The dowager reddened. 'And you are not to think of selling Wroughton House. It is *not* yours to sell.'

'You're mistaken,' Diana said calmly. 'I had it out with Boardman when Rupert died. It's not part of the entail. It would be wrong of me to sell it and spend the money on myself, but I have no intention of doing that. The money will be put back into the estate, into improving the land. As for doing my duty to the family, I have provided it with two male heirs. What I do now with my private life is my concern.'

'So,' Lady Wroughton glared, 'you are determined to be selfish. Tell me plainly, once and for all, are you going to marry Guy Teesborough?'

'Why shouldn't I? He is a man that any mother would think a suitable match for her daughter. And *I* think he is very nice and a good man.'

'Then there is nothing more to say,' said Lady Wroughton, standing up. 'I was prepared to invest a great deal of my time and trouble in guiding you and advising you, but you are obviously too mulish to listen to reason, so I shall save my breath. Kindly ring the bell.'

Diana didn't move. She said at last, 'I was engaged to one of your sons and married the other, and you never liked it, but I was a Wroughton by marriage, and you can't bear the idea that I'd take another name. You think I should be grateful to stay a Wroughton for the rest of my life, like a shadow of you. You think it's an insult that I want to be different from you. That's what all this is about – not the children or the estate, but your pride.'

Lady Wroughton did not answer. She gave Diana a look of measureless disdain, and saw herself out.

CHAPTER TWENTY-FOUR

Of the properties Mrs Bouvier showed them, Sadie thought the best was a house in Eaton Place, almost identical in layout to the one in Eaton Square, but in better internal condition, needing no redecoration. While she would have liked to have a hand in redecorating, she knew her mother would have hated the disruption. It had been empty for some time, the owners having moved permanently to the country when their only son was killed in 1917, so they were anxious to divest themselves of the lease.

'I want us to be a family again,' Edward said to Beattie. 'I don't like having to stay up in Town without you. If you favour this house, let's close with them and move as quickly as we can.'

So Beattie went to see it, and met Edward for luncheon afterwards. 'I like it,' she said. 'It's similar in style to our old house in Kensington, but larger.'

'Bigger than The Elms?'

'It has nine bedrooms instead of ten. And very little garden, of course. But the rooms are all bigger. And it's much grander.'

'Lord and Lady Northcote will need a grand house. Shall you be happy there?'

'It's a big step, moving back to London,' she said, 'but I think I shall be glad to have more to do. I've thought sometimes about my life before the war, and I've wondered how I got through the days. The war woke me up. It's woken all of us up. I don't think women will be able to go back to sleep.'

'Well, there should be plenty to do in London,' he said. 'Not just entertainments, but good causes to take up.'

'And Lord Northcote will probably be expected to entertain a great deal more,' Beattie added, 'so we shall have a busy social calendar.'

'Hmm,' he said doubtfully.

She laughed. 'Edward, you can't go back into your shell – you've accepted the title now! I shall have the harder task, you know, planning all the meals, to say nothing of endless fittings with dressmakers.'

He laid his hand over hers across the table. 'Shall we give it all up and run away? Live in a cottage and be plain Mrs and Mrs Nobody?'

'I believe you'd prefer that,' she said.

'In some ways,' he said. 'It would be nice to have my wife to myself.'

And for a wonder she didn't withdraw her hand and turn her face away. She was able to look straight into his eyes, and be glad that, after all that had happened, he still loved and desired her. Yes, she felt the desire like electricity running through their touching hands. And, with a little cold finger of sensation down the back of her neck, she knew she desired him, too. It was a long time since her body had been aware of its needs. Since their reconciliation they had been a little tentative with each other, and his absences in Town and his tiredness from the long journey when he *did* come home made it too easy for them simply to fall asleep. But when they were living together properly and things had settled down . . .

'Do you want to see the house first, or shall we take it?' she asked, and it was not a non-sequitur.

'I trust your judgement. Let's get it done.'

* * *

Peter was the first to leave. It was decided that it was better for him to start boarding as soon as possible after the start of term, so that he would not feel like an outsider. Edward, who had been a boarder at his school, knew that essential alliances were forged in the first weeks. Peter was hugely excited, and the sound of his feet racing up and down stairs became the heartbeat of each evening. He helpfully packed his trunk, and when Ada pointed out that heavy things like shoes and books had to go in the bottom, unpacked it all again, then decided on a completely different set of things to take. What he left behind had to be packed in a tea chest for the removers.

When he was ready to go, the sight of his empty bedroom gave Beattie a qualm. Her last little one, flying the nest.

'But I'll be back every weekend, Mum,' he told her, bestowing a rare hug. 'Here first, and then London. Unless,' he added an emphatic caveat, 'there's something really super going on at school. I *can* stay if there is, can't I?'

'If it's *really* super,' said Beattie. 'But we shall want to see you sometimes, you know.'

'Gosh, yes!' said Peter. 'There's lots of things I want to do in London.'

Ethel gave her notice.

'You don't want to come to London with us?' Beattie asked.

'I'm getting married, madam,' Ethel said, colouring slightly. 'To Frank Hussey.'

Beattie blinked in surprise. 'Oh, how – nice,' she managed. Ethel had been a difficult servant at times, though since becoming nursemaid she had settled down, and seemed to be genuinely devoted to Marcus and Alice. But they had been here before, expecting her to marry, then finding her back on their hands. Beattie did not want to expend congratulations on something that wasn't going to happen. 'When is the happy day?' she asked cautiously.

'Next Saturday, madam,' Ethel said. 'If it would be all right, I'd like to stay Friday night and leave Saturday morning. I'd have my bag packed and take it with me to the register office.'

'Yes, I suppose that's all right,' Beattie said. A week's notice was all that was needed on either side, but it was annoying to have to find a replacement in such a short time, especially with the added difficulty of the move: a locally recruited girl might not want to go to London – though it was easier that way round than taking a London girl to the country. She brought her mind back to realise that *something* more was needed than her muted response. Ethel had been with them for some years. 'Well, congratulations,' she said. 'I hope you'll be happy.'

Ethel hesitated, then said, 'I shall miss the children. Very much.'

Beattie hardly knew what to say. 'But you'll have some of your own soon, I'm sure.'

She thought afterwards that perhaps what Ethel would have liked to hear was that the children – or at least Marcus – would miss her.

Nanny Woods was elated. She had disliked Ethel on sight: too pretty, which in her mind equated to flighty and unreliable. Added to that, Ethel had a sullen demeanour; and, worst sin of all, called the little boy Marcus, rather than Master Marcus, and seemed to attract his affection. It was always the same, she thought, when you inherited a nursery rather than setting it up yourself. Things would be different in London. She would order things *her* way, and select her staff herself. After a conversation with Lady Hunter, she had it agreed that a temporary girl would be got in for the few weeks until the move, and that once they were in London, she should have *two* underlings, one to help with the children and the other to see to the cleaning, washing and general fetching and carrying. It was not safe, she intimated, to leave cleaning the nursery rooms to a general housemaid. Special care was needed, and special techniques had to be learned. And in a house with many stairs, a strong young girl was needed to run down to the kitchen and back the many times a day that would be needed.

The other servants had mixed feelings about Ethel's leaving. It was always sad to see a colleague go when you had worked beside them all those years.

'Not that it's always been a pleasure, as far as that young madam's concerned,' Cook added, though without her usual vehemence. She had other things on her mind.

'But it's lovely that her and Frank have got together at last, after all their ups and downs,' Ada said. 'I'm sure I hope they'll be very happy together.'

'It's a hope, all right,' Cook said. 'What's she going to do with herself, living in an estate cottage out in the country? Nothing but fields and cows for miles around. She'll go mad.'

'No, she won't. She'll have a lovely husband to take care of, and her own home, and I'm sure there'll be little babies to come. She won't want for something to do.'

Cook sniffed, unconvinced. 'Still, if anyone can keep her in check, it's Frank.' She put her hands to her cheeks. 'Oh dear, I've just thought, we'll never see him again, either! Oh, Ada, this move – it feels as if everything's coming to an end. Like a sort of doom. I feel all shook up inside. I didn't sleep a wink last night, for worrying about it all.'

'Have you thought any more about what I said?' Ada asked.

'Every time I think about it I get palpitations, like I can't breathe. It's all too much. I hate change.'

'Well, never mind now,' Ada said soothingly. 'Let's just get past Ethel's wedding, and then we'll talk some more. Has she thought what to wear? I don't s'pose the missus will give her an old suit, like she did me.'

360

'I should think not! Ethel's never earned that kind of favour.'

'But we have to help her look nice,' Ada said coaxingly. 'It *is* her wedding day, after all.'

Ethel was nervous enough about the wedding without having to worry about clothes. She, too, had wondered how she would take to living in the country. She would be alone all day while Frank was at work, and however little she had engaged with the other servants, they had been *there*. She imagined a small damp cottage, like the one she had been born in, surrounded by the silence of the country. She would have to clean everything, and prepare every bit of food. No clean sheets unless she washed them and dried them and ironed them. No roast pork and baked potatoes, no apple pie, unless she learned how to cook them. She might still toil all day cleaning the house and laying fires, but there'd be no sitting down afterwards to a dinner prepared by Cook and placed on the table by Eileen. The prospect was so daunting that she half wanted to call the whole thing off, and go with the family to London, where her work was defined, comfort was provided, and shops and buses, cinemas and people were all around. Only the satirical look in Cook's eye – she was still expecting the wedding to be called off at the last minute – stiffened her resolve. She would not give Cook the satisfaction. She would marry Frank Hussey if it killed her.

Nula, though not prompted this time by Beattie, helped with the clothes. She felt sorry for Ethel, whom she saw as a cornered fox, always defiantly facing her tormentors. Beattie had had Nula to take care of her: Ethel had had no one. Her sharp tongue and refusal to exhibit any softness towards anyone were her defences, all she had ever had. So Nula quietly tricked up a blouse of Beattie's that she didn't wear

361

any more, and steamed and pressed Ethel's navy skirt, and trimmed it – large pockets with buttons on them were the fashion at the moment, and easy to add. Ada lent her the hat she had worn for her own wedding, which had an artificial gardenia sewn on it. And Ethel had nice gloves of her own – one thing she had always taken care of.

So on the day, Ethel looked quite smart; she had always been pretty, so she made an attractive bride. She was late down to breakfast, having taken a long and tearful farewell of the children. She hated leaving them to Nanny Woods's tender mercies. Her bag was packed and sitting in the rear hall.

'You ought to eat something,' Cook said, seeing her pick at her plate. 'It'll be a long day. Have another bit of fried bread, at least. Don't want you fainting in the middle of the service.'

Ada came to Ethel's rescue. 'How you getting home after?' She poured Ethel another cup of tea – that, at least, she could stomach.

'Oh, the train, I s'pose,' said Ethel. Home? Yes, it would be her new home. What would await her there? Damp, mice, black beetles? An empty larder? An empty grate. A cold, neglected stove, caked in grease? She shook herself. Frank was kind and thoughtful. He would surely have a fire laid and a cold supper in, at the very least. And tonight, this very night, she would sleep in the same bed with him, up against his big, warm body. She shivered with anticipation. Unlike Ada, she would not approach her wedding night in ignorance. The act held no mysteries for her. But she had been fighting feelings for Frank for years, and she knew that with him it would be different. *I do love him*, she thought in surprise. And perhaps, then, it would be all right.

Cook, Ada and Nula went to the wedding, walking into the village with Ethel. Ada insisted on carrying her bag for her.

362

Ethel was silent all the way. *Nerves*, Ada thought. She thought about Len, her dear, kind Len, and wanted to cry. Well, she could cry at the wedding – that was expected.

Frank was waiting outside the register office, in his best blue suit, looking handsome and just a little nervous, which was nice. He had a surprise for Ethel: the warm weather had brought another flush to his roses, and he had a white rose in his buttonhole and a posy of pink and white ones for her. Ethel was more touched than she would allow to be known. She accepted the flowers, glanced up at him, and was almost paralysed by the smile he gave her, which seemed to promise such present happiness and future joy it frightened her. It could not be for her, all this bounty, not for the outcast, unwanted, unloved Ethel Lusby, whose very birth had been a mistake of the worst kind. But Frank took her hand and passed it through his arm and squeezed it against his ribs, and in that moment she was an ordinary girl going to her wedding like other girls did.

The service was short. She spoke the required words in a faint, wobbly voice. Frank's was firm, not overloud, just right. He would always know what was just right, she thought. He slipped a ring onto her finger, and it felt heavy. Real gold? Well, why not? He probably had a bit saved. And then they walked out into the hazy sunshine, and there was another surprise: a car to take them home. One of the estate cars, and the second chauffeur to drive it. 'It's all right,' Frank said, to her nervous look. 'I got permission.'

And now Ethel had to say goodbye to Cook and Ada and Nula, and to everyone's surprise, especially her own, she hugged each of them, and was hugged in return, and all four of them were crying. Then she and Frank got into the car and were driven away, and the other three waved it out of sight, and then looked at each other, feeling suddenly flat.

'Well,' said Cook.

And: 'Well,' said Nula.

'I s'pose it'll be all right,' said Cook, doubtfully.

'She's married Frank,' Ada said, and thought again, achingly, of Len. 'Course it will.'

'He'll mind her all right,' said Nula.

'I shall miss her, in a funny sort of way,' Cook said. 'Like that old Munt, you never knew what she'd say next. But it sort of livened things up.'

Cook and Ada sat up late, talking. When the sitting-room fire died down, rather than make it up they moved into the kitchen for the warmth of the stove – frugal habits learned from the war. The stove was kept in all the time, only allowed to go out when the chimney was swept. Ada made some more cocoa, and they sat at the kitchen table, talking in low voices – not that anyone else was around to hear them, but the quiet of the hour seemed to demand it. The clock on the wall in the sitting-room ticked softly, the stove hissed a little now and then, and Nailer, who had arrived when all the other fires had gone, snored a little on the rag rug in front of it..

'New nursery-maid will be coming Monday,' Ada said.

'And she'll be more trouble than she's worth,' said Cook. A local girl had been hired on a temporary basis. 'Won't know what to do, and not enough time to teach her.'

'Well, that's Nanny's problem, not ours,' said Ada

A silence fell. Cook sipped cocoa, and suddenly said, in a low moan, 'Everything's going. Oh, Ada, I got such a feeling of . . . Like something bad's going to happen.'

'That's 'cause you've not made your mind up,' Ada said soothingly. 'That'll always give you the whimwhams. Once you know what you're doing, you can face up to it.'

'I don't want to go to London,' Cook said. 'All that getting used to new things! And the missus said there'll be more staff hired, 'cause of it being a bigger house. Extra maids, and probably a footman or two. Even a chauffeur. I don't know how many I'd be cooking for. Lord and Lady Northcote! It'll be grand dinners every night and important people coming.'

'You used to like cooking grand dinners,' Ada reminded her. 'I remember when you complained there wasn't any dinner parties any more.'

'I was younger then. This war's took a lot out of me.'

'It has out of all of us,' Ada said with a sigh. 'But at least we've still got each other.' They both sipped. Then she said, 'You don't have to go to London. Let's talk about that. I looked in the estate agent's window on Thursday when I was out. There's a little house on Maxted Road, nice and handy for the station. Three bedrooms plus a big attic room, two rooms downstairs and the kitchen and scullery. Ten shillings a week. We could use our savings to furnish it up nice, buy the sheets and crockery and everything that we'd need. You and me could sleep in the attic, and we could have three guests. And I'd still have the rest of my widow's pension to tide us over until we got going.'

'Go on,' Cook said, looking more comfortable.

'You could cook lovely meals for them – your steak and kidney pie and your ragout and so on – and that'd make us famous. All the travellers would want to come and stay because they'd know they'd get good grub. And I'd keep it all spotless clean.'

'But, Ada, strange men!'

'Decent, hard-working fellows, far from home and lonely for their wives,' Ada said. 'Just wanting a bit of home comfort.'

'Tell me some more.'

'Well, there's two rooms downstairs, like I said. One would be the dining-room for the guests. We'd have to buy a table and chairs. We'd always have a nice clean tablecloth on, and maybe flowers in a vase for dinner – make it nice, like. And the other room, the smaller one at the back, would be our sitting-room, so's we'd have somewhere to go when we'd finished our work.'

'Two armchairs by the fire,' Cook offered. 'And a clock – could we have a clock on the mantelpiece?'

'We could have anything we liked. We'd sit there after we done dinner and do a bit of mending, say, and talk. Play a game of cards if we felt like it.'

'We could have a cat. I'd like a cat. They're no trouble, aren't cats – not like that old dog. And it's nice when they curl up by the fire. Makes it feel like home.'

Ada observed Cook's softened expression and dreaming eyes, and said gently, 'So we'll do it, shall we? We'll tell Missus tomorrow we won't be going to London.'

Cook almost quailed, but she thought about the clock and the cat, and Ada smiled at her and nodded so encouragingly that she swallowed hard and said, 'Yes, we'll do it. It'll be – an adventure.'

'Mother's terribly put out,' Sadie said, 'because now the only one of the servants who wants to come is Aggie, and she doesn't really want her.'

'In some ways,' said Mrs Cuthbert, pressing her legs to Sorrel's flanks to make him keep up with Allegro's long stride, 'it will be better to start with a clean slate. Transposing old servants often doesn't work. And as Lord and Lady Northcote they'll be living a different sort of life. They'll need servants who understand that and are up to it. London servants.'

'I don't think she minds particularly about losing Cook and Ada,' said Sadie. 'She doesn't really have any personal affection for them. It's the nuisance of finding new people and getting the new household set up.'

'I wonder she doesn't get a housekeeper to do all that,' said Mrs Cuthbert. 'She'll surely not want to be bothered by domestic matters – she'll have so much outside life to fill her time.'

'I don't think any of us knows how much of anything there will be to do, only that it will be different,' Sadie said.

'You sound glum,' Mrs Cuthbert suggested.

'I like Northcote, I like The Elms – I like Highclere. There won't be any riding in London. And what will I find to do?'

'Well, in the first place, Highclere will still be here, and you can come whenever you like and ride Allegro. It's only a train journey away. Goodness, one would think you were moving to the ends of the earth!'

Sadie smiled. 'Thank you. And, of course, you're right. Even if I got a job, I would still have weekends. It's only an hour on the train.'

'*Will* you get a job?'

Sadie told her about Mrs Bouvier's suggestion. 'I think it would be quite interesting.'

'How odd,' Mrs Cuthbert said, 'to be decorating other people's houses for them.'

'It's the coming thing, especially in London, where everyone's so busy all the time. It would be like playing doll's houses, but on a grand scale.'

'I can see the fascination. Would she pay you?'

'I imagine so. I haven't talked to her about it yet, but apparently she makes an awful lot of money doing it, so she could afford to. Apart from redecorating people's houses, she also fits out the new apartments that her millionaire friend builds, which in some ways would be even more fun because you could let your imagination roam free.'

'And would that be enough for you?' Mrs Cuthbert asked.

Sadie turned a lock of Allegro's mane the right way over, and he switched his ears back to her in acknowledgement. 'I don't know. I hope so. One must do something. Life is too long to be idle.'

'Not so long from my point of view,' said Mrs Cuthbert. 'It's amazing how quickly it passes. But you'll marry one day, Sadie – I know you think you won't,' she anticipated, 'but you're too lively and warm-hearted a girl to be wasted. Someone will come along and you'll wake up and live again, and that will fill the rest of your life, the part that isn't work.'

'And until then I just have to keep busy?' Sadie suggested mockingly.

'It's what everyone does,' said Mrs Cuthbert. 'You aren't the only one.'

'I know,' Sadie said humbly. They rode in silence for a while. Then she said hesitantly, 'When I come and visit, if you've heard from John, will you tell me?'

'It will be better for you not to keep being reminded,' said Mrs Cuthbert. 'That part of your life is over. You have to accept it and put it behind you.'

'I know. I am. But, if I could only know that he was all right . . .'

'My dear, you can't know that. You can't be with him. You have to keep moving forward.'

Sadie nodded, but her look was bitter. 'Then I have to find something more to do than decorating houses. I have to find something that matters.'

'I'm sure you will,' said Mrs Cuthbert.

Time was very tight for Laura's wedding to Jim Ransley, if they were to be married before he took up his new position. 'I'm afraid there won't be time for a honeymoon,' he said, when they discussed it.

Laura gave him an amused look. 'Some would say that, rather shockingly, we've already had it. I'm sure if the presiding minister discovers we're living together we'll be sent to the right-about and have to marry in a register office after all.'

'Well,' he said brazenly, 'we just won't tell him.'

She laughed. 'I'd marry you in a grass hut in Zanzibar if I had to, but my family would really enjoy seeing me turned off properly.'

In the end, they had to settled for Saturday, the 18th of October, with just the Sunday to enjoy the novelty of being married before Ransley started at Thomas' on the Monday. October had started as warm as September had been, but by the 18th it had turned colder, though it was still dry and sunny, with deep blue skies by day and the first touch of frost at night.

The family from The Elms was staying with Diana at Park Place for the wedding. On the morning itself, Sadie went over to Laura's house to help her dress. Ransley, for decency's sake, had spent Friday night in an hotel.

'Are you nervous?' Sadie asked.

'The answer should be, of course not,' Laura said, 'but as a matter of fact I am, strangely, just a bit. It's a big step. And the older you get – before you ask – the harder it is to take it. When you're a dew-fresh young girl, you don't see all the things that could go wrong.'

'I suppose not,' said Sadie. 'I remember what Diana was like – just wild to get married. She didn't seem to think about that would happen afterwards. But that was before the war. I wonder if any of us are dew-fresh any more.'

'Things will even out, eventually,' Laura said serenely.

'Perhaps for the next generation,' said Sadie. 'I think it's too late for us.'

'Goodness! You're supposed to be supporting me, not making me sad. Now, I'm all done under my dressing-gown. It's just a matter of putting on the top layer.'

Sadie helped her into her dress of pale blue chiffon velvet, which had a scooped neck and long sleeves, and a dropped waist with a broad, ruched sash around it, just on the hips. It was simple and elegant, and the colour suited her dark hair and brought out the colour of her eyes. To go with it she had a wide hat in a darker shade of blue, with the front brim turned up and pinned with an enormous white silk flower.

'What do you think?' Laura said anxiously. 'Too much?'

'You look – tremendous,' Sadie said. 'Any bride would be glad to look half as good as you.'

Laura laughed. 'At my age all one can ask is not to look foolish. Help me on with these.'

Sadie fastened her simple string of pearls round her neck: they were good pearls, given to her by her father when she was twenty-one. She put in her pearl earrings; and there was just her fur wrap to go over the top. 'This fur's as old as the hills,' she said. 'I can't think when I last wore it.'

'But fur doesn't go out of style,' said Sadie.

Diana's car, lent for the occasion, came to fetch them. St John's was a very large church, but the wedding party had managed to make it look full. Ransley's two elderly maiden sisters had come from Worcestershire, where they lived together with several dogs and spent their time walking them, and when indoors, making tapestry kneelers for their church. He had no other family except a few cousins, but he had many, many friends, both from the army and his civilian days. And Laura had a large family and had been collecting friends all her life.

It was quite a distinguished company, as the newspapers remarked, illuminated by Diana, who was escorted by Lord Teesborough; Lady Teesborough and Ivo Rainton had also been invited. Lady Overton came with her son Oliver Winchmore, the distinguished surgeon. To Laura's sorrow, Annie, by rights Lady Agnes Daubeney, a duke's daughter, was not there. She had died three weeks earlier, of the unknown sickness. But Ronnie Mildmay was there, and Louisa Cotton with her new fiancé, a handsome sea-captain who had sailed with her brother, and a whole slew of friends from the Women's Cause and from her time as a policewoman. The Palfreys were all there, and Beth and Jack.

Edward met Laura at the door, and when the great organ

sounded out he walked her slowly down the aisle to where Ransley was waiting for her.

'I never thought this day would come,' Edward murmured to his sister. 'I thought you were too wild ever to settle down. But I'm so glad you're happy.'

'I am,' Laura said. 'Scared, but happy.'

'It will be all right,' Edward said. 'Practically everything is, in the long run.'

Afterwards, there was a great deal of champagne and the wedding breakfast at the Savoy, and, in the modern style, after that there was dancing. Sadie found herself unexpectedly much in demand with the many young doctors who had served with Ransley in France and had come to see him turned off. She fox-trotted energetically and smiled at their jokes, and for a while forgot her cares, until one of them said earnestly that she was a splendid girl and asked if he could see her again. Her bubble burst. She told him that she had been engaged to someone in the war, and it was enough to make him apologise and leave it there. There was no need, these days, to be more specific. So many people had lost someone.

Later, when a waltz was played, Ivo Rainton came and asked her to dance, and she was glad to go with him because it was always easier with someone you knew, and you could sometimes get away without talking at all.

Indeed, they danced in silence for a while, and Sadie felt more comfortable. They passed Laura dancing with Ransley, and Sadie smiled to herself, because her aunt looked so happy. If someone so old could find love for the first time . . .

At the end of the room, when they turned, she saw Diana nearby, dancing with Guy Teesborough.

'You sister looks lovely today,' Ivo said.

'She *is* very beautiful,' Sadie agreed. Chaps had been saying that to her since she was fifteen.

'And happy, don't you think?'

'Yes. Your brother does, too.'

'They make a handsome couple,' Ivo said. 'Would you mind if . . .'

'If Guy asked her to marry him?' Sadie prompted. 'Why should I mind? Do you think he might?'

'I've never seen him so smitten.' He looked down at her with an expression that was smiling, but quizzical. 'If they did marry, that would make me your brother – sort of.'

Sadie coloured. 'I already have four brothers,' she said, without thinking. 'Three, I mean,' she corrected herself.

'Well, perhaps I can just be a friend – for now,' Ivo said.

'One can never have too many friends,' said Sadie.

The music stopped. 'Then may a friend take you to find another glass of champagne?' he asked.

She slipped her hand under his proffered arm. 'That would be nice,' she said.

CHAPTER TWENTY-FIVE

Mrs Fitzgerald was most put out that the Hunter family was moving. 'I had hoped you would be the leading light in our campaign to raise money for a war memorial,' she complained to Beattie. 'Especially with your new title. It would look so well at the head of the list – Lady Northcote.'

'I will, of course, make a donation,' Beattie said. 'Where would it stand?'

'It ought to be right in the centre of Northcote, so that everyone passes it every day. The green opposite the station would be ideal.'

'I suppose you'll have to get an architect to design it,' Beattie said. 'Just a simple cross, one imagines.'

Mrs Fitzgerald looked restless. 'That was the rector's suggestion. But I thought we should try for something similar to the Cenotaph in Whitehall. Not all those who died were Christians, you know.'

'I didn't know,' said Beattie, surprised. 'Who do you mean?'

'Well, that fellow Korder who sells Indian toffee, he had a son who fell at Loos. His real name is Khangorda, I'm told. He is a Sikh – they have their own religion, apparently.'

'I see. Who else?'

Mrs Fitzgerald avoided her eyes. 'I don't know of any others. But the number doesn't matter. The Cenotaph was for everyone, and so must our memorial be.'

Beattie said no more. The wood-and-plaster Cenotaph,

built in London for Peace Day, had proved so popular with the public that there had been agitation in the newspapers for it to be made permanent. The cabinet had finally announced on the 23rd of October that it would be replaced by a Portland stone version that would be a replica in every detail of the temporary structure. Rumour was that other communities were building their own scale models. Beattie suspected that Mrs Fitzgerald's desire for a Cenotaph-like memorial in Northcote had less to do with the sensitivities of the Indian toffee man than her own quest for distinction.

'Perhaps the people who buy The Elms will be amenable to campaigning with you,' Beattie suggested kindly.

It was comfortable to reflect that The Elms would not stand empty when they left. A family called Pendlebury would be moving in almost immediately. He was a solicitor in London, in search of a more rural home, from which he could still travel in to work. He had a wife and six children, ranging from fourteen to four, and they had all come and looked at the house and loved it. Beattie remembered when she had first come, how spacious it had seemed and how quiet and clean Northcote was compared with Kensington. The wife seemed a gentle, rather shy creature, ready to be pleased with everything. Beattie had recommended Munt, and Mrs Pendlebury had agreed eagerly to keep him on, as though she thought it was a condition of purchase. She would be easy prey for Mrs Fitzgerald: Beattie was hoping to scrape Aggie off on her.

Cook and Ada had walked into the village to look at the house Ada liked, but only from the outside. Cook had shied away from the idea of asking the agent to show them inside, in case it would commit them to taking it. Ada understood that she would only get her friend to move in small incremental steps. Each of them was, for Cook, a perilous leap.

They were just passing the green opposite the station when

Ada, glancing back, said, 'I do believe there's a man following us. Whenever we stop to look in a shop he stops as well, and when we move on, he moves on.'

'Oh, Lord! Don't say that!' Cook cried in alarm. 'What could he want with us? Does he look like a robber?'

'*I* don't know,' Ada said. 'He's a man in an overcoat with a trilby hat on, pulled down. I can't really see his face. My goodness, he's seen me looking. He's coming!'

'Quick, cross the road!' Cook urged. But there were motor cars coming in both directions, and by the time a gap appeared, he was almost on them.

'Ada – wait up!' the man called.

Ada pulled Cook back onto the kerb, and turned nervously; then as he pulled off his hat, her face cleared. 'Oh, Cook!' she breathed. 'It's your Fred!'

Cook's cheeks grew red and her heart pounded, but she didn't know whether it was from joy at seeing him or rage at his disappearance. 'He's not *my* Fred,' she objected. And as he reached them, she managed a cool and lofty tone as she asked, 'Well, when did you come back from Australia?'

He looked older, she thought, as though he had been finding life hard; his craggy face was thinner and there was a bit of grey in his hair, over his temples. He wasn't, she noticed, terribly brown either – wasn't it always sunny in Australia?

He twisted his hat round in his hands, without his usual bullish assurance. 'I never went,' he admitted.

'*Never went?*' Cook said in outrage. 'Well, where in the world have you been all this time? And what have you come back here for? I'm sure nobody here wants to see you.'

'Oh, Cook,' Ada breathed. 'Let him speak. I think he wants to explain.'

'I do,' he said gratefully. 'Explain and apologise. Look, I've been a fool, and I've paid for it, but I want you to know what happened. Will you let me explain?' He glanced around.

'Isn't there a little caffy somewhere about? I think it's coming on to rain. Let me buy you a cup of tea, at least.'

'Well . . .' Cook said, softening. She wouldn't mind a sit-down. And the grey November sky was lowering.

'I'll go home,' Ada offered.

But Fred said, 'No, I'd like you to hear as well. You must've been thinking all sorts of bad things about me.'

'Oh, I don't know about that,' Ada murmured.

'All right,' said Cook. 'You can treat us to a pot of tea and I'll listen to your story. But I can't think what excuse you've got – disappearing and then appearing again, as if you was Houdini or something.'

When they were settled in the Windmill, and the tea had been brought, Cook took charge of the teapot and said, without looking at him, 'Come on, then. Get it over with. Last I heard of you, you were getting on that boat without me, and using a lot of bad language into the bargain.'

'Aw, come on, Margaret, I was a bit miffed, I admit, but you know I never use bad language. That's a bloody libel!'

She didn't realise it was a joke. 'If you're going to start again, I'm leaving right now.'

'No, no, I'm sorry. Look, I'll tell me story straight, if you'll just listen. See, I thought you were giving me the brush-off that day, and I felt like a fool. Well, a man doesn't like to be knocked back like that. I went off to London in a paddy and got meself a room, and I went out that night and got good and drunk. Trying to get you out of my head, see?'

'Getting drunk's no way to behave.'

'Crikey, don't I know it! I'm not a big drinker, don't you think that. In normal times it's a beer to wet me whistle after a day's work, and that's good enough for me. But I was in a right state that night – just had me heart broken by me best girl, didn't I? I got drunk, and ended up playing cards in the back room of some pub or other. Well, I won't bother you with the sordid details. I lost and kept on losing, and when I woke up in the morning I was minus all me savings.'

'Oh *dear*!' Ada gasped.

He looked at her and nodded. 'Yeah, it was a bit of a shock. Couldn't go back to Australia and start up a business without it. Had to sell the tickets just to give me something to tide me over.'

'So what did you do?' Ada asked, seeing that Cook wasn't going to. She had her lips pressed into a tight, hard line, and her eyes were firmly on her teacup.

He shrugged. 'Had to get a job, didn't I? Started as a barman in a pub, because that came with a room. But then some joker come in that worked down at Smithfield, and he told me there were good jobs there for butchers. Oh my word! He wasn't kidding. I've never seen so much meat – and for a bloke who knows his way round a carcass and can handle a knife, there's good money to be made. I was always quick, but I promise you I got quicker! And that's where I been ever since.'

Cook still didn't speak, but Ada could guess what she wanted to ask. 'But why didn't you write and tell us?'

His eyes slid away. 'Tell the truth, I was a bit ashamed of blowing up the way I did. I dunno what came over me. I guess it was the war and everything – bit of a strain on the old nerves, eh? And I felt like a fool for what'd happened to me after. Anyway, I thought a certain person didn't fancy me any more. But once I'd settled down a bit, I thought, well, I got to redeem meself – couldn't come courting the way I was. Had to get the money together again. And then, well, I wasn't sure what sort o' reception I'd get. I was scared I'd get me head bitten off. So I kept putting it off. Anyway, I been working like a dog, every hour God sends, and living very frugal, and I've got enough now for the passage and a start over there. So I've come back to see how the land lies – whether I've still got a chance.'

377

Still Cook said nothing.

In a gentle, humble voice, he said, 'How about it, Margaret? Will you forgive me for being a big dope? Will you marry me and come to Australia with me, like we talked about?'

She looked up, and her lips trembled. 'I don't know as I can trust you.'

'Yeah, you can. You gotta give me another chance. Blimey, you don't give a bloke away for one little bust-up! I done me time – living like a monk, saving every penny, wondering if I'd lost the only girl I ever loved.'

'Girl!' she said in derision.

'You wouldn't believe how much I missed you,' he said. 'And it wasn't just your rock cakes.'

'Don't joke,' she said fretfully.

'Didn't you miss me at all?'

'Not a bit,' she declared.

'Oh, Cook, you did,' Ada said reproachfully. She looked at Fred. 'Our family's moving to London, and we decided not to go with them. So when they go, we'll be out in the big wide world, fending for ourselves. We thought we'd run a boarding house together. She's been ever so brave about it. But now we're leaving anyway, she can go to Australia with you instead.' She turned to Cook. 'You can! It'll be a much better life for you. You can't give up a chance like that. Oh, Cook, you got to forgive him! You don't get a man asking you to marry him every day of the week. I only got one chance, but I wouldn't have missed it for anything. Say you will – you must!'

Cook looked up. 'And what will you do if I go?'

Ada shrugged. 'It doesn't matter. I got my pension and my bit of savings. I'll be all right.'

'No,' Cook said slowly, 'that's not right. We been together all these years. You got to come too.'

'What?' Ada said in astonishment.

'She can, can't she, Fred? I mean, there's lots she can do over there, a smart, hardworking woman like her.'

'Course there is,' Fred said. 'Land of opportunity, Australia is.'

Cook nodded. 'And I reckon I could do with having a friend over there with me. It'll all be a bit strange, but having Ada there will make it easier for me.'

'I can see that,' Fred said, his mind working. 'Look here,' he said to Ada, 'you say you got some savings?' She told him how much. 'Blimey you're a rich woman! How about you come in with us, in the butcher's shop I'm going to open? Invest in it, like a partner.'

'I don't know – I've never done anything like that.'

'You can live with us, as well, and help out in the shop, if you like. And if you want to go your own way later, well, we can buy you out. And I tell you what: Australian men know how to appreciate a fine woman like you. If you're not married inside a year, I'm a monkey's uncle.'

'Oh, Ada, say you will,' Cook urged. 'Half the reason I was scared before was leaving you behind and not knowing anyone over there. Say yes! It'll be an adventure!'

'It'll be that all right,' Ada said. From what she was feeling now, she understood why Cook had been so scared. Right across the world, to a strange country, not knowing what you'd find there? But you could face anything better when there was two of you. And she didn't want to be all alone here in Northcote. She swallowed hard and said, almost breathlessly, 'I'll do it!'

'Good on yer!' said Fred. 'So does that mean it's a yes from you, my Margaret? You'll marry me?'

'I will,' Cook said, with almost as much of a swallow as Ada.

'Remember that phrase,' Fred said, grinning. 'It'll come in handy.'

On the evening of Monday, 10th of November, the King held a banquet at Buckingham Palace with the French president as guest of honour, to commemorate the anniversary of the Armistice. There were already unofficial plans in place for the following day: veterans' associations were organising marches of their members down Whitehall, and it was expected that thousands of people would gather at the Cenotaph. So an official act of remembrance was deemed appropriate. A guard of honour of soldiers and sailors was told off, and the prime minister was to walk there from Downing Street to lay a wreath. At the King's suggestion, there was to be a two-minute silence as Big Ben struck the hour of eleven, and everyone in the United Kingdom was urged to observe it, wherever they were.

Diana was once again with a party at one of the windows of the Foreign Office, along with the Teesboroughs, the Hexhams, and one or two other friends. When eleven struck, the crowd fell silent. All of London had stood still, so there was no background of traffic noise; the assembled soldiers stood to attention, people in the crowd bowed their heads; the only movement was the flutter of flags and the occasional stamp of a horse. Diana thought of her brother Bobby, of Charles and of Rupert. But the great enveloping silence stretched her mind to the millions who had given their lives, to the vast, incomprehensible sum of death, which had been the payment for peace. When the gun sounded, signalling the end of the silence, she felt scoured out by emotion, hollow and light. Life, the one gift that everyone present had received, regardless of merit; life, which digs its roots so deep in you, holding you to the earth, tenacious for survival; life had been taken so easily from so many. They had blown away like dry leaves, were scattered and gone. They would not come back. And those who were left owed it to them not to waste what they had.

They went out for dinner later, Diana and Guy. She had grown so used to his being around that she did not think anything of their dining alone together; and for once, no crowd of friends attached themselves as soon as they appeared in the restaurant. Tonight was one night when everyone wanted to be quiet; there was no mood for a party.

They talked of this and that, as friends do. 'When is your family moving?' Guy asked.

'On the twenty-first,' Diana said. 'At least, that's when the removal company is moving everything into the house. Everyone's going to stay with me for a few days while it's all sorted out. It will be hard for Mother because none of the servants are coming with her, except for the nanny, so she's got to get new staff, at the same time as settling into a new house.'

'It sounds like a nightmare.'

'Well, I don't envy her,' said Diana. 'She's got two house-maids and a cook engaged to be there on the Friday, and some more coming on the Saturday, I believe. And she's coming up to London tomorrow to interview housekeepers – none of those she's seen so far has been suitable. But they can move in without a housekeeper. Fortunately, Nula's promised to come for the first few days to supervise every-thing, so I expect they'll be living there properly from the Monday. There will be little awkwardnesses at first – but Sadie will be a great help. She's a very *practical* person.'

'I do like Sadie,' Guy said.

'I'm glad you do,' Diana said. 'I was used to thinking of her as just an annoying younger sister, but she's grown up quite well.'

'So in two more weeks your family will be settled into their new home, and you won't have any more distractions.'

'From what?' Diana asked, with a puzzled smile.

'Well, from me, principally. Selfish person that I am, that's uppermost on my mind.'

'What do you mean? I see you often.'

'Darling Diana, can you really be so detached? You must know that I love you madly, and that I want to marry you.'

381

She looked shy. 'You never said so.'

'Delicacy, that's all, I promise you. I didn't want to rush you. Poor Rupert – I didn't want to offend you by seeming not to care about him.'

'I know you cared about him. You were his best friend.'

She was still giving him no clues. Carefully he asked, 'Have you . . . sufficiently recovered? Are you able to think about marrying again?'

'It does seem very soon,' she said, frowning. 'And yet, at the same time, it seems such a long time ago. It's hard to believe it was only last year. Something very odd seems to have happened to time, these past years, don't you think?'

'It's because we've all had to live as though there'd be no tomorrow. Sometimes it was a lifetime in every hour, when you were going back to the Front and leaving behind the person you loved.'

'Yes, you're right. That must be it.'

He cocked his head at her, with a faint smile. 'You seem to be avoiding answering me. Is it because you don't want to hurt my feelings? If you don't care for me in that way, I'd sooner know, honestly. Better for both of us. Could you think of marrying me? Or does the prospect dismay you?'

'Oh, goodness, no! I mean, it doesn't dismay me. How could you think it? I do like you awfully. It's just – I wonder what people will think. It's only been a year.'

'Almost a year and a half,' he corrected. 'And I don't suppose people will think anything. They've seen us together for months now. I imagine they all expect us to get married. They might be more shocked if we don't,' he added with a smile. 'I'm already your children's trustee – what more natural than that I should become their stepfather?'

Diana smiled slowly. 'It would infuriate my mother-in-law.'

'All the more reason to do it, then. There's only one question that really needs answering. Do you love me? Do you *want* to marry me?'

'That's two questions.'

'Don't cavil. Answer.'

She looked at him, and felt a little shiver inside. There seemed in his eyes a promise of things undreamed-of by her. She had been married and had had two children – but what if that were not all there was? What if he knew things that Rupert had not? She had loved Rupert, but she had never understood him, or felt at ease with him or that he understood her. He had begun by despising and insulting her, and there had always been, deep and unacknowledged, a sense of unease in her at the sudden change in his attitude. What had he really felt about her? She didn't know. Was she 'over' him? Unnervingly, yes, she was. She had been shocked at his death, but he had passed into history, and could no longer touch her. Guy was here, real and warm and alive, looking at her in *such* a way . . . She wanted his kisses. And though the love-making had not been a pleasure to her before, she wanted to know if he knew how to make it different. Suddenly, she wanted that very much. It would be pitiful to go to her grave never knowing if there were locked rooms in marriage that she had never explored.

'Do you really love me?' she asked.

'Oh, Diana, more than you can imagine!'

Her smile was tremulous. 'Then let's get married as soon as possible.'

Sadie took one more walk round the house to check that nothing had been left behind. It looked bigger without their possessions, emptied out for the next owners. How strange to think of people who weren't Hunters living there. Unknown servants would answer bells and grumble about their employers in the servants' hall. Strange new children would run up and down the stairs. New little girls would sit on the top flight and nurse their dollies, new little boys play cricket on Munt's relaid lawn and accidentally hit the ball through the pantry window. And when they grew older, they would have tennis parties, watch the members of the other sex under their eyelashes, and dream of love. Please God they would never have their lives torn apart by war, as the Hunters had.

Well, she thought, the Hunters were moving on, had packed up their home and, she hoped, packed up their troubles too, and would have a fresh new start. She wouldn't shed tears over a house; she had done her crying when she said goodbye to Nailer. He had been upset, not because she was leaving, which being a dog he couldn't know or understand, but because she was crying. She had crouched to stroke him one last time, and he had licked the tears from her cheeks.

Munt had said, 'He'll be all right,' and 'You can always come and see him.'

And Sadie said, 'I'll come and see *you*.'

But they both knew she wouldn't.

The new house was grand, and a bit echoey, and she kept turning the wrong way out of doors and having to think which room was which. The body had its own memory. She stumbled on the top stairs more than once because the treads were a different height from those at home. No, she mustn't call The Elms home any more. Eaton Place was home now. Some of their furniture looked a little odd, and there wasn't really enough of it. There would be shopping expeditions. Father, it seemed, was quite wealthy now. So the expense of new furniture would not be a problem. It was interesting, she thought, how it was the more modern pieces that had been bought new for The Elms that didn't look right, whereas the old furniture Father had inherited from *his* father fitted in. There might be something in this decorating business after all. Sadie decided she would get in touch with

Mrs Bouvier as soon as the household had settled down, and see if there was a job for her.

A dark strip of water appeared between the ship and the crowded dock, and gradually widened. Cook stared, her mind a fog of fear and sadness, and thought, *I'll never see England again.* Her legs felt weak, and she might have sunk to the deck, were it not that Fred at her right side had his arm round her, pinning her to his big body, and to her left side Ada was clutching her hand as though she were drowning.

She was Cook no longer – she was not even Joan Margaret Dunkley. She was Mrs McAusland. She was going to Australia. Weeks aboard a ship, tossing on the winter seas – though Fred said it would be summer when they got there, a confusion too many for her already battered brain.

She was a married woman – she now knew what Ada knew, though she was sure her Fred was twice the man Ada's shrimpy little Len had been. With the aid of several glasses of sherry at the wedding reception, she had managed the business of getting undressed and into bed, and – well, what had happened after that was nobody's business! But she had been married nearly a week now, and she was beginning to get used to it, and once you got past the sheer *rudeness* of it – well – well – there were times when she almost enjoyed it. It was sort of nice to know that of all the women in the world, Fred only got that look in his eye when he looked at her. And it was lovely in the night to lie up against his hot body in the dark and feel safe. She had always been a chilly sleeper, needing two hot-water bottles just to get off. Fred was better than any number of 'em. He was like a furnace.

The fog was thickening, and now there was nothing to be seen but indistinct grey shapes and the oily-looking water. Dear old England was gone. Beside her, Ada said in a wobbly voice, 'Oh my! Whatever shall I do?'

Joan Margaret McAusland squeezed her hand, and said, 'We're going to Adelaide.' Adelaide, Fred had said, was a lot like London, with familiar-looking houses, and trams and bobbies and shops and parks. There was even a part of it called Kensington. 'We'll have a lovely house.'

'Yes,' Ada whispered.

'With a jacaranda tree.' That jacaranda tree was something that kept Mrs McAusland going when she got the collywobbles.

After a bit, Fred said, 'You're looking a bit chilly, Margaret my girl. Better go inside. You look as if you could do with getting a stiff one inside you.'

Diana telephoned – yes, they had the telephone at Eaton Place! – and asked Sadie to drop over. Sadie walked for the pleasure of being out. It was grey, drizzly day, with a low wet sky, and the air was clammily cold. Despite the size of their new home, there was little garden, and having nothing but streets outside made her feel confined. She supposed she would get used to it. When she got to Hyde Park Corner she went into the park and walked on the grass, under the trees, as far as The Ritz. It was balm to the soul.

Diana was looking radiant, more lovely than ever. Her announcement, when they had been a week at Eaton Place, that she and Guy were to be married, surprised nobody. They were so obviously suited to each other.

'What will happen to the earldom?' Sadie asked, as they sat in the window-seat of the morning-room.

Diana looked surprised. 'Why do you ask?'

'I was just wondering. All this is new to me, you know.'

'Well, George is Earl Wroughton, nothing will happen to that. I'll be Lady Teesborough, and if we have a son, he'll inherit Guy's title.'

'So poor Ivo will be disinherited?' Sadie joked.

'Poor Ivo doesn't care a jot,' Diana said sharply. 'He

doesn't want to be earl.' She softened. 'He has his own fortune, you know, from a collateral inheritance.'

'Collateral inheritance! You know all the proper terms, don't you? But won't it be awkward, having two lots of property?'

'Why should it? Guy is already trustee for the Wroughton estate, and he looks after his own as well. As long as you have good people under you, it isn't a problem.'

'And where will you live? Will you stay here, in Park Place?'

'I think so. It's comfortable, and big enough for now, and it couldn't be more central. Later we might move to something bigger. And we'll probably mostly use Dene as our country place, seeing as it's closer to London. But we'll go down to Stockridge too, for longer periods. And for the hunting. Which brings me to the reason I asked you to call. I want to learn to ride,' Diana concluded, looking a little self-conscious.

'You? But you always refused before! You don't like horses. You always said they were smelly and dangerous.'

Diana looked annoyed. 'Goodness, don't remind me of things I said ten years ago! It wasn't necessary for me to be able to ride before. Rupert was more of a Town person, but Guy loves country sports, and I'd like to be able to fit in. And, of course, I want George and Amyas to ride, and it would be better if I knew how before they start to learn.'

'Well, they're all good reasons,' Sadie said. 'And perhaps exposure to horses will make you love them. What did you want me to do?'

'Come with me,' Diana said. 'I really don't want to go on my own. And you know everything about horses.'

'If we were at home – in Northcote, I mean – I could teach you myself, up at Highclere.'

'I've too much to do to spare the time to drive out there for lessons. There's a riding school just started up again in Hyde Park that does private lessons—'

'Goodness! Where did they get the horses?'

'I haven't the least idea. Bought them from the army, I imagine.'

'They might even be horses I reschooled myself,' Sadie said, entranced with the idea.

'Oh dear, never mind the horses – will you come with me?'

'You mustn't say "Never mind the horses" – from now on you're a horse lover! And of course I'll come with you. The chance to ride – even if it's only in a park – how could you think I'd refuse?'

'Good,' said Diana. 'So we'll start as soon as I have the right riding clothes.'

'You can buy them ready-made from the Army and Navy,' Sadie mentioned.

'But I'd have to have them fitted, and all the seams gone over by hand,' Diana said.

'We live such different lives,' Sadie said, but she smiled as she said it.

Once the first lessons were over, and Diana had ceased to feel she might fall off at any moment, Guy and Ivo sometimes joined them. They were both very natural in the saddle, having ridden since birth, and Sadie welcomed their company, not least because Guy naturally stayed by Diana's side, which meant Sadie and Ivo could go off for a canter.

'It's lovely to be on a horse again,' Sadie said on one of those occasions, 'even if it is only a riding-school hack, and only along the tan in Rotten Row.'

'You must come to Stockridge,' Ivo said. 'Wonderful riding country.'

'That's where Diana and Guy are going on their honeymoon, isn't it?' She had wondered whether Guy realised Diana was not a woods-and-fields sort of person. She liked shops and pavements.

'For the first two weeks. Then Paris, Rome and Florence,' said Ivo.

'Oh, good. He does understand her, then,' Sadie said.

'Look, after the wedding, why not come to Stockridge too?'

Sadie raised an eyebrow. 'On the honeymoon? I don't want to be Mademoiselle de Trop!'

'In the first place, the house is big enough for everyone to be private. I shall be going, and I don't expect to be in the way. In the second place, my understanding is that ladies like to have other ladies to talk to, even on their honeymoon. And in the third place, I'll have estate business to conduct on my brother's behalf, which will be dull, and no one but the lovers to talk to in the evening, which will be duller. If you came, we could mix business with pleasure, do a lot of riding . . .'

'What if the weather's too bad?'

'Do you play billiards?'

'Rather well.'

'You see? And then there are card games, a gramophone, and lots of neighbours who'd love to be invited over for supper, bridge and dancing.'

She looked at his eager face, and smiled. 'All that for me? I'm not worth it.'

He grew serious. 'I know your heart is broken. I'm not the insensitive fool people think me. But life goes on, and since one has to live it, why not live it pleasantly, with people one likes?'

'I'll think about it,' Sadie said. 'But there are other things than pleasure, you know.'

'Good works, you mean? Well, I can provide you with an introduction to the Lady Farringdon Trust. There's a lot of good work to be done there.'

'Tell me about it,' Sadie invited, and he obliged. He was even better company, she decided, when he was being sensible than when he was being frivolous.

★ ★ ★

389

'It was a lovely wedding,' Beattie said, as she and Edward walked up the stairs to bed. 'I think she'll be happy with him.'

'He seems like a very nice fellow,' Edward said. 'Trust our Diana to outdo everybody! Remember when she was setting her cap at Charles Wroughton, and everybody thought a girl from her background couldn't marry an earl? Now she's shown everyone, and married two of them.'

'I don't think the earldom figures very much this time around,' Beattie said. 'I think she just loves him.'

'I hope so,' said Edward. At the top of the stairs he paused a fraction of a second before turning left. 'I still want to go the other way. Silly, isn't it?'

'Do you like it here?' Beattie asked.

'It's a good house. It will be fine once you've put your stamp on it. Do you like it?'

'I shall, once I've got the servants trained.'

'I thought that was Mrs Branson's job. Isn't that what a housekeeper's for?'

'Yes, but I have to train *her*. We all have our different ways.'

'Poor Beattie, have I made your life more difficult, dragging you back to London?'

'Oh, very difficult! Lady Northcote, with a fine house and dozens of servants and invitations coming by every post! Don't you know it's every woman's nightmare?'

They went into the bedroom. Thank God, he thought, the system had worked sufficiently for a fire to be lit: it was a cold and clammy December day.

'But is it *your* dream?' he asked, turning to face her.

'I'm not sure it's very safe to dream any more,' she said. 'If the war taught us anything . . .'

'If it taught us anything, it ought to be that life is precious and not to be wasted. I want you to be happy, Beattie. It's all I've ever wanted. I hoped that moving here might give us a fresh start – that we could put the past behind us and start again.'

It was never that easy, Beattie thought. They were what the past had made them. But as a human being with self-determination, you could decide to close the box and lock it, and put it away, and don fresh clothes to confront the new day. She looked at his familiar face, lean and almost handsome, a firm face, a kind face, the face of a man who made decisions and took responsibility and cared for others. How wonderful it was that the person he most wanted to care for was her.

'I *am* happy,' she told him, and was rewarded by his smile. He stepped close and took her in his arms, and she shivered with pleasure at the warm strength of his body, and the known, male smell of his skin.

'I love you so much,' he said.

'I love you too,' she said. 'Thank you for taking me back.'

'Oh, Beattie,' he protested.

She hurried on. 'Talking of fresh starts and new beginnings . . .'

'Yes, darling?' When she didn't go on, he held her back from him so that he could look at her, examining her face anxiously. 'Is something the matter?'

'No, quite the opposite. Something very surprising has happened – somewhat earth-shattering, in fact, but, I think, rather wonderful as well. Yes, definitely that. Haven't you guessed?'

'Guessed what?' he said, bewildered.

'I wasn't sure at first, but now I am. I suspect it was that day in August, when we went to the theatre. Or rather, the night afterwards, in the hotel.'

'The hotel?' Still he looked puzzled.

She felt tears close underneath the surface; and laughter too; and the force of life, which was relentless, which would not be denied. So much had been lost, there had been so much pain, and a price paid in blood. But here they were: life pulled you back, you had to go on living; and wasn't she lucky, compared with so many, that she didn't have to face it alone? She had *him*. She put out a hand, and he took it, and she held on to it tight – tight.

'You still haven't guessed?' she said, looking up at him with great tenderness. 'I'm going to have another baby.'